NEW YORK TIM

# ANNE HILLERMAN

# THE TALE TELLER

≪≪≪ A LEAPHORN, CHEE & MANUELITO NOVEL ≫≫≫

DON'T MISS THE
OTHER NOVELS IN THE
## LEAPHORN, CHEE & MANUELITO
SERIES BY *NEW YORK TIMES*
BESTSELLING AUTHOR
# ANNE HILLERMAN

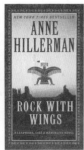

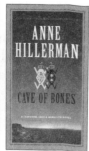

"A must-read for anyone who loved the great
Tony Hillerman novels, now carried on by his
amazingly talented daughter, a superb writer herself."
**—DOUGLAS PRESTON,**
#1 *New York Times* bestselling author
on *Spider Woman's Daughter*

## Praise for Anne Hillerman
## and *The Tale Teller*

"*The Tale Teller* is more than just a police procedural set in the Southwest, it's a reading experience not to be missed. Anne Hillerman has reached a new level of storytelling in this one, and she deserves recognition as one of the finest mystery authors currently working in the genre."      —*New York Journal of Books*

"For all Hillerman fans, it is a joyous experience to be able to once again enter the beloved world of Joe Leaphorn, Jim Chee, and Bernie Manuelito in the authentic voice of Anne Hillerman."      —*Midwest Book Review*

"Hillerman's writing becomes stronger with every new installment in the series, deepening the development of each character. Fans will be intrigued by the intertwining stories that keep them guessing. The picturesque Southwest, as well as the history of the Navajo, come through on each page."      —*Library Journal*

"A natural hit with Hillerman's many fans; [*The Tale Teller*] is also a good choice for readers who are interested in fiction touching on today's social issues."      —*Booklist*

### Cave of Bones

"*Cave of Bones* is simply a pleasure to read . . . Hillerman's best novel yet."
—*Comic Book Bin*

"This fictional universe now belongs firmly in the hands of Anne Hillerman."
—*New York Journal of Books*

"Anne's voice is exceptional, the tool of a natural storyteller."
—*NewsOK*

### Song of the Lion

"The latest from Hillerman continues world-building in a tale that will reward long-term readers."
—*Kirkus Reviews*

"Hillerman seamlessly blends tribal lore and custom into a well-directed plot, continuing in the spirit of her late father, Tony, by keeping his characters (like Chee) in the mix, but still establishing Manuelito as the main player in what has become a fine legacy series."
—*Booklist*

"Fans of Leaphorn, Chee, and Manuelito, characters created by the author's father, Tony Hillerman, will savor this multilayered story

of suspense, with its background of contemporary environmental vs. development issues."
—*Library Journal*

"Though seasoned mystery readers may guess the perpetrator before the tense denouement, the book offers insights on the strength of family ties and the possibilities of redemption after a history of pain."     —*Publishers Weekly*

### Rock with Wings

"Hillerman uses the southwestern setting as effectively as her late father did while skillfully combining Native American lore with present-day social issues."     —*Publishers Weekly*

"With a background of tribal law and custom, Anne Hillerman ties up multiple subplots in concise prose, evoking the beauty of the desert and building suspense to a perilous climax. Tony would be proud."     —*Booklist*

### Spider Woman's Daughter

"*Spider Woman's Daughter* is a must-read for anyone who loved the great Tony Hillerman novels, now carried on by his amazingly talented daughter, a superb writer herself."
—Douglas Preston,
#1 *New York Times* bestselling author

should be a long, enjoyable, successful series. Her depiction of the Navajo Nation is spot-on. I loved this book."

—Joann Mapson, author of
*Solomon's Oak* and *Finding Casey*

"You will love this novel! Not only are old friends Joe Leaphorn and Jim Chee back, we get to know the delightful, intrepid and thoroughly modern Navajo police officer, Bernadette Manuelito . . . Anne Hillerman comes naturally to writing mysteries, and *Spider Woman's Daughter* is nothing less than a smashing debut."

—Margaret Coel, author of *Killing Custer*

"A daughter takes on her famous father's legacy in resuming a series focused on Navajo culture . . . maintaining the integrity . . . throughout."                    —*Kirkus Reviews*

"Pot hunters, archaeologists, controversy over the museum display of tribal objects, and insurance fraud culminate in a heart-stopping, action-packed conclusion as Bernadette and Jim risk their lives to bring a would-be assassin to justice. . . . Fans of Southwestern mysteries will cheer this return of Leaphorn and Chee."

—*Library Journal* (starred review)

"Hillerman fans, rejoice! Joe Leaphorn and Jim Chee have returned, thanks to Tony's daughter Anne. She captures the feel of her father's books, the wonderful understanding of a place and a people that made his so popular, and she has an ear for his unique voice. It's a remarkable accomplishment."

—Charles Todd

"So seamless is the writing transition from father to daughter, it is easy to forget that one is reading Anne, not Tony. That said, Anne brings a welcome female perspective to the table, fleshing out several of the female supporting characters but never forgetting the importance of the two main players who define the series. Nicely done on every level."

—BookPage

"Difficult to put down . . . If you love mysteries, this book is for you."    —Examiner.com

# THE TALE TELLER

## Also by Anne Hillerman

# ANNE HILLERMAN

# THE TALE TELLER

⫷⫷⫷ A LEAPHORN, CHEE & MANUELITO NOVEL ⋙⋙⋙

HARPER

*An Imprint of HarperCollinsPublishers*

THE TALE TELLER. Copyright © 2019 by Anne Hillerman. All rights reserved. Printed in the United States of America. No part of this book may be used or reproduced in any manner whatsoever without written permission except in the case of brief quotations embodied in critical articles and reviews. For information, address HarperCollins Publishers, 195 Broadway, New York, NY 10007.

First Harper premium printing: February 2020
First Harper hardcover printing: April 2019

Print Edition ISBN: 978-0-06-239196-4
Digital Edition ISBN: 978-0-06-239197-1

Cover design by Jarrod Taylor
Cover Photograph © Jamie Grill/Getty Images (land); Jim Gallop/Getty Images (clouds)
Author photograph © Kitty Leaken

Harper and HarperCollins are registered trademarks of Harper-Collins Publishers in the United States of America and other countries.

20 21 22 23 24   QGM   10 9 8 7 6 5 4 3 2 1

For Don

# THE TALE TELLER

1

For the past twenty minutes, Joe Leaphorn, former Navajo police lieutenant turned private investigator when the job suited him, had focused on not losing his temper. He should have stayed retired. Maybe bought a camping trailer and traveled around, taken up bridge, given golf another chance.

And it was all Louisa's fault.

"Just drive over there and see her today," his housemate had prodded him again during breakfast. "You're going to the library anyway. If you don't want to help Daisy, at least you can listen and refer her somewhere else. You still know everybody in law enforcement. From what she's told me, this case might be interesting."

Over the years, he'd learned that Louisa was as tenacious as a badger. It simplified his life to go along with her ideas when they were reasonable, which they usually were. So when he went to the tribal library to return the borrowed books, he made sure he brought his little notebook in case whatever Mrs. Daisy Pinto wanted to talk to him about actually led to a case worth investigating. As of now, he had spent half an hour with her standing in the large lobby between the museum and the library. For most of that time, Mrs. Pinto had been dealing with the public and hadn't made the opportunity to discuss his potential assignment.

"Here." She gave him a sealed envelope. "The museum complex is shorthanded today, so I need to work the information counter until the summer intern gets here. I summarized what I'd like you to do in the letter, and I want to talk to you about it, too. Stay here and we'll chat."

It was a busy afternoon for information seekers, and Mrs. Pinto gave them top priority. The questions were varied:

"Can you tell me how to get an appointment with Miss Navajo?"

"Ma'am, do you know who I should talk to about carrying this T-shirt I designed in the gift shop?"

"Pardon me, but can I get a job here?"

And, more than once, "Excuse me, but where is the restroom?"

Mrs. Pinto represented the Navajo Nation with respect and courtesy to these people who didn't seem to realize they were intruding on the start of a business meeting. Leaphorn's irritation rose as the string of distractions continued. Each interruption made him grouchier.

While she was explaining to a family of sunburned tourists how to get to Tsegi Canyon and the sandstone cliff-dwelling villages of Betatakin, Keet Seel, and Inscription House, he sat down, opened the envelope, and saw that it contained a long, singled-spaced typed letter. He put on his glasses and glanced at it, then stored the thing in his sport coat pocket. Time to go home. As soon as he had ten seconds of her attention, he would tell Mrs. Pinto that if he decided he wanted to help, she needed to schedule a meeting at a time when she could focus on him.

After the tourists headed off, Mrs. Pinto shifted her attention back to Leaphorn before he had a chance to complain. "Louisa mentioned that you do some work as a private investigator. I want to hire you to help me on a case that's rather sensitive. The museum received some unsolicited anonymous donations. My assistant, Tiffany Benally, had been working on this, but she's been ill and the clock is ticking. I spelled out the basics in the letter. I'm hoping you—"

A young man wearing a gimme cap backwards came through the big doors, heading straight for Mrs. Pinto, sweat glistening on his deep brown skin. "We need help outside." Leaphorn smelled the adrenaline and fear. "There's a lady who fainted or something. She's by the skate park. I hope she's not dead."

"We have a guard who is an EMT. I'll get him." Mrs. Pinto rushed off.

The young man hurried back outside, and Leaphorn followed through the door into the July heat. A few youngsters standing in a circle around the body parted for them.

The Navajo woman was young by Leaphorn's standards, thirty-something. He leaned over her supine body. Her eyes were closed, but he could see her chest rise and fall underneath her striped blouse. Her russet skin shone with sweat, her mouth slack. She was thin. She didn't smell of beer, and he didn't see any bleeding or obvious physical damage. He spoke to her. "Ma'am? Ma'am? Help is coming." Her eyelids fluttered but stayed closed. A blue cord, a lanyard like those people use for ID cards, hung loosely against her neck. The end, where there might be identification, had slipped beneath her body.

Leaphorn straightened up and growled at the teens who were closest in the language he spoke best, Diné Bizaad. "Give this woman some privacy." They might not have understood the Navajo words, but they got the message and backed away.

A muscular Navajo in a security uniform raced toward them with a satchel, then squatted down next to the woman. He put his hand on her forehead and spoke. "It might be heat stroke. I've called an ambulance. Do you know how long she's been unconscious?"

"Not long. This just happened."

Leaphorn heard the rhythm of someone running, and Mrs. Pinto rushed toward the woman. "Oh no," she gasped. "It's my Tiffany. Oh, honey. My goodness. What happened?"

The woman's eyes opened, but she couldn't seem to focus. It took her several seconds to respond. "I don't know what happened. I just felt so weak and my head hurts." She gasped for breath.

Mrs. Pinto turned to Leaphorn. "We'll talk later."

The EMT positioned his body to give the woman some shade and ordered a skateboarder to go into the gift shop and bring back as many cold water bottles as he could carry. "Tell 'em it's an emergency."

Leaphorn walked toward his truck, noticing the flashing lights of the ambulance in the distance. A young man in a gray T-shirt, a person he'd spotted in the crowd when he came out to check on the unconscious Tiffany, was watching the excitement from the parking lot, a few yards away from Leaphorn's pickup. The man nodded to him. "What happened to that woman?"

"I'm not sure. She lost consciousness, but when I left she opened her eyes and said a few words." Leaphorn spoke in Navajo.

The man shook his head. "Sorry, sir, I can't understand you."

Leaphorn shrugged and switched to English. "Fainted."

He climbed into his truck, started the vehicle, and heard a grinding sound. It happened every once in a while, reminding him that when he could afford it, he should have it checked. Whatever it was, it was probably expensive to fix.

Before heading home, he drove down the road to the Department of Public Safety office even though few people he knew worked there now, on the chance that one of his buddies would be in. The receptionist, a young woman with black-framed glasses and a serious expression, told him that Sam Nakai and Brodrick Manygoats were both out of the office and offered to give them a message. She wore a name tag that said "Jessica Taylor."

"Just tell them Leaphorn stopped by to give them grief." He spoke in Navajo.

The woman offered him a smile. "I will. Sir, I've heard of you. You're famous around here. I'm honored to meet you."

Leaphorn felt a twinge of pride and embarrassment. "That was a long time ago."

"People remember you, Hosteen. If I can ever help you with anything, just let me know. It would be my pleasure, sir."

"You've been here awhile, haven't you, Jessica?"

"Yes, sir. Two years. I love this job. My uncle was a policeman in Arizona. Now that we have our own Navajo academy, I'm thinking of becoming an officer myself someday."

"Was your uncle with the Highway Patrol?"

"No, sir. He worked for the BIA. He served . . ." Her phone rang. She looked flustered.

"Go ahead. We'll talk more next time."

As he left the building, he wondered about himself. Until a few years ago, his dealings with most civilians tended to be strictly business. Was he becoming one of those garrulous old-timers whom people dreaded encountering?

He walked out to the parking lot, noticing the breeze that had come up against his skin. He found a piece of paper stuck beneath his windshield wiper, probably an advertisement of some kind. He lifted the wiper blade to free the paper so he could dispose of it. If it was an ad, it was clever: just a simple white sheet folded in half with the message on the inside.

It wasn't an ad.

*Lieutenant,*
      *Mrs. Pinto is not who she seems. Be careful around her.*
      *From a friend*

He read it again. He didn't like the idea that someone was watching him, following him, and that the unknown observer obviously wanted to scare him. He put the paper in his coat pocket, next to Mrs. Pinto's letter, with a sense of unease.

He drove home, parked by the back door as usual, and entered through the kitchen. Giddi came from wherever the cat had been sleeping to investigate the intrusion. Louisa considered the cat—she called it Kitty—to be her pet, but now that it was just the two of them, he spoke to it in Navajo.

"It's been an interesting morning so far, cat. A meeting that never happened. A woman unconscious. An unknown person warning me about a bureaucrat."

The cat pranced away, tail in the air.

He realized that he had turned off his cell phone for the conversation with Mrs. Pinto. Even though he was well enough to drive again, Louisa worried if he was out longer than she'd expected.

He turned it on to call her and discovered two messages—neither from her. The first was Mrs. Pinto informing him that the information person had called in sick. She'd have to mind the desk until the replacement showed up, she said, but he should come anyway. He erased it, wishing he had listened sooner and saved himself a frustrating morning.

The second was from Jake, a therapist he had been working with to improve his spoken English. He fast-forwarded to the end and deleted it.

He sat at the kitchen table and re-opened the envelope from Mrs. Pinto. It contained three pieces of white paper: a typed letter and two copies of a contract. He read the letter first.

*Dear Joe Leaphorn,*

    *Thank you for considering this case. As the director of the Navajo Nation Museum, I have two problems I would like your help in solving. The museum recently received an anonymous box with some donations. The reason I am requesting your assistance is that the most valuable item on the list that came with the donations either was not included or has disappeared. Because of the sensitive nature of this problem, I prefer not to tell you any more until you have agreed to offer your assistance as a consultant investigator.*

    *If you will help, I have copies of the paperwork we received with the donation shipment. Before we contacted you, my assistant worked to track down the sender without success.*

*If you agree to work with me, my assignments for you are:*

1. *Find out if the missing item was in fact included in the shipment.*
2. *If it was not included, we would very much like to obtain it, which involves making contact with this secret donor.*
3. *My assistant has also called to my attention that the donor's inventory listed a bracelet, necklace, and earring set. Only the necklace and earrings seem to have been included. If you could track down the bracelet, your help will be appreciated, but it is not as important as the first missing piece.*

The letter went on to detail Leaphorn's reimbursement for time and expenses and the fact that Mrs. Pinto needed the matter resolved before she started her retirement next month. He was thankful that the brain injury had not affected his comprehension of English.

Leaphorn put the letter down, glanced at the enclosed contract, and stood. He had left about a cup of coffee in the pot from that morning. He lifted his mug off the drain rack, poured in the cold liquid, and placed it in the microwave. Louisa said reheated coffee smelled like burning leaves. He didn't mind it, and he had learned long ago not to waste anything.

He pondered Mrs. Pinto's request as he waited for the coffee to warm. What could the missing item be? Perhaps something associated with a ceremony, he thought, something that the collector shouldn't have had in the first place. The fact that the items arrived anonymously also raised the question of their legitimacy. Had they been removed illegally from Indian land? Perhaps they were all stolen merchandise.

He hadn't heard the cat return to the kitchen, but he noticed it looking up at him now, joining him to wait for the ding that indicated the little oven had done its work.

Mrs. Pinto, he thought, had some shrewdness to her. She'd given him just enough information to prompt him to call and set up an appointment to learn more. How had the box been shipped? Why was the gift a secret?

The microwave beeped, and he carried the warm cup to the table. He took a sip of coffee, put on his glasses, and read the letter again. He thought about the questions Mrs. Pinto raised and came up with three plausible possibilities: the missing items, as she stated, were never included; the items were stolen en route to the museum; or the items were removed from the shipment after it arrived.

He jotted a note to ask her if she herself had opened the box. And if Mrs. Pinto hadn't opened it, who had?

If the anonymous package had come through the mail, he had a friend who was a postal inspector who might be of help. He made another note. Leaphorn smiled to himself. Mrs. Pinto's tactic had worked. The case seemed interesting enough to warrant his time.

When he left the police department and decided to do a little freelance investigation for private clients, Leaphorn had told himself that he wouldn't accept cases that didn't challenge him or that required dealing with difficult people. He'd dealt with enough misfits as a cop. From what he'd seen, Mrs. Pinto was smart, organized, and demanding, but he remembered her concern for the young woman in the parking lot. He would talk to her again, this time in a focused setting, and if he thought they could work together, he'd take the case.

He heard Louisa's car pull up and rose to open the kitchen door for her. She put two bags of groceries on the counter. "Hi. How did your meeting go?"

"Too much inaruption." *Interruption*, he silently scolded himself.

Louisa began unloading the bags. She opened the refrigerator and put a carton of orange juice on the shelf. "Are you going to help her?"

"Maybe. Tinkin bout it." *Thinking about it.* Ever since he'd suffered that gunshot to the head, Leaphorn had struggled with spoken English.

Louisa finished with the groceries and stood looking over his shoulder at the letter. He patted the seat next to him and she settled in. Giddi climbed up on the chair next to Louisa. The cat looked smug, he thought, as if it belonged there, too.

"Curious, isn't it? I hope you can find that missing piece, whatever it is." Louisa smiled. "Why do you think she's so secretive? It's not like you're a blabbermouth."

"Bearest." It was the first thing that came to his

mind, but there was truth in it. Fear of embarrassment provided powerful motivation. Calling the donor to ask if the missing item had been included wouldn't be easy, which, he figured, was the reason she was asking him to do the job.

Louisa stood, and he felt her cool hand as she rested it lightly on his shoulder. "If you decide you want to do this, I'd be glad to make some calls where you'd need English. I am still in your debt for all the time you spent traipsing through the Four Corners with me when I was doing my research."

"Tanks." But he felt his insides tighten. If the world spoke Diné Bizaad, his words could fly. And she didn't owe him anything. If there was a debt here, it was his for her hours of arranging his medical appointments, putting up with his frustration, driving him to speech therapy, and all the rest of it, including running the household by herself as his health returned. He wouldn't have healed as fast as he had without her.

Lately, she was getting more mail than usual from Northern Arizona University, the institution that had supported her research. Louisa had put her profession on hold for too long. He encouraged her to stop babying him and get back to work.

He heard her footsteps as she disappeared down the hall. The phone rang. Louisa ignored it. It rang again, so he answered, expecting a woman's voice, one of her friends. Either that or a sales call.

But it wasn't one of Louisa's friends; it was Sergeant Jim Chee. They dispensed with the pleasantries quickly, and Leaphorn waited for Chee to ask him for a favor. The man surprised him.

"Sir, someone named Mona Willeto phoned here for you a couple of days ago and I forgot to mention it. I told her to try the Window Rock office. She said she wanted to talk to you about her brother in prison. I wouldn't bother you with this, but she sounded different than most of these calls."

"What do you mean?"

"It's hard to say exactly. Calmer, I guess. Nicer. You know, like she wasn't going to start yelling about how he never should have been arrested or imprisoned, what a good boy he was."

Leaphorn considered asking for the number and decided against it. "If it's important, she'll call Window Rock like you asked and they'll refer her to me. Sometimes if you look the other way, these things disappear. Remember that, Sergeant."

"OK, sir."

After Chee ended the call, the Lieutenant sighed. What was it about Chee that brought out the overbearing uncle in him? Why did the man still get on his nerves? He'd known him as a rookie, an enthusiastic and somewhat impulsive young man for whom doing the right thing sometimes meant bending the rules. Chee had a deep commitment to making life safer for the Diné. Although Leaphorn still considered the man a work in progress, he was pleased with the officer Chee had become.

When Leaphorn called the museum to speak with Mrs. Pinto to set up the meeting, he learned she was out of the office at a finance hearing for the rest of the day. And, since it was Friday, she wouldn't be back until Monday.

"Do you want to leave a message for her?" The receptionist sounded young and bored.

"Ask her to call Joe Leaphorn. She has the number. Do you know what happened to the woman who collapsed outside?"

"You mean Tiffany? I haven't heard anything about her. Mrs. Pinto gave her the rest of the day off."

2

July at the Shiprock flea market meant hot, even when you came early. Bernie watched Mama stroll from vendor to vendor, examining the merchandise as carefully as if she were actually going to buy something. Two years ago here, Mama had bought the big pot she used for stew after the old one cracked. That was her most recent purchase, but that didn't mean she couldn't look. Mama loved this Saturday ritual.

Bernie had volunteered to make dessert that evening if Chee cooked dinner. She had found what she needed half an hour ago: sweet local peaches, the largest perhaps the size of a tennis ball. They were ripe, soft, and ready to put into a piecrust once she cut out the bird pecks. But Mama enjoyed chatting with the sellers, hearing about their families. Bernie noted with happiness that Mama felt so much stronger and also with a tinge of frustration. She held the fruit in a recycled plastic bag from Bashas' and felt the sweat on her face as the Saturday morning grew warmer. She day-dreamed about being someplace cool, like the shady bottom of Canyon de Chelly.

"Daughter. Daughter!" Mama stood next to a man with his gray hair in braids and a red bandana around his forehead. "This is Mr. Natachi. He used to help me find the right sheep for the colors when I was weaving. His sister is our neighbor."

Bernie moved closer to the pair. The old man smiled at her. "I met you when you were a girl."

"Oh, yes. I remember." He had been Mama's neighbor, too, until about ten years ago when he moved away to live with a daughter. "It makes me happy to see you again, sir. They say you live in Chinle now. I was just thinking about Canyon de Chelly."

"My granddaughter works for senior services there. I help her when I can. She says an old man is a good thing to keep around until I start giving her too much advice." He chuckled. "Now her boyfriend has left her, so she and I drove down here for a while." He grew more serious. "Your mother tells me you are a police officer."

"Yes."

"Well then, you see this bolo?" He raised his hand to his throat and touched the turquoise stone set in silver on the braided black leather cord finished with sterling tips. "Someone came into my house last month and made off with it." Mr. Natachi filled in the details, unfolding the story of how his bolo tie disappeared with the unhurried pace of a person watching the morning turn to afternoon. "This is a good day. I found my tie just now at a booth over there, the one with the man in the straw hat."

Bernie knew that wasn't the end of the story. She felt a line of sweat move down her neck and between her shoulder blades.

"I told the man it was mine, that my uncle made it for me forty years ago. I told him someone took it from my bedroom. He wanted to argue, but I explained it would have the jeweler's mark, a *Y* with a line at the bottom. I showed him the mark on the back, and then I asked him why he stole it. He said he didn't steal it. He said he bought it from a man outside the Walmart in Gallup and that he didn't know it was stolen." Mr. Natachi paused. "I asked him who was that man? What did he look like?" When Mr. Natachi shrugged his shoulders, his braids moved. "The guy in the hat didn't want to talk to me anymore. He told me to take my bolo. I think he was ashamed."

"Where is the booth that had it?"

"Down the next row in the middle, over by the lady selling sage and medicine."

"What did the man look like?" Bernie knew "man in a straw hat" would not work as a defining description for a player in an operation fencing stolen property.

"Oh, he's young, about your age. Not too fat. About as tall as me. The man had a round face." Mr. Natachi rubbed his chin. "Like a guy from Zuni or Hopi or somewhere like that."

She placed the seller's height around six feet, age as early thirties. Possibly a Pueblo Indian. "What was he wearing besides the hat?"

"Jeans, a red T-shirt with cigarettes in the front pocket, sneakers." Mr. Natachi tapped the middle finger on his left hand. "A big ring here. It looked like Sleeping Beauty turquoise."

Bernie knew that flea markets could be places where people came to sell stolen property. She'd seen reports of a rash of break-ins in the Chinle area. If a thief wanted to dispose of hot items, moving away from the neighborhood where they had been stolen made sense. "I want to talk to this man."

"He was over that way." Mr. Natachi pointed with his lips. "Next to the woman with the sage smudge sticks."

"I'll take you," Mama said. "I know right where that is."

Mr. Natachi shook his head. "That man is gone. I scared him away. He's probably in Farmington by now. Or just set up along the road somewhere." He put his hand up to his neck. "I am happy to have it."

"Please wait here, Mama. I'll be right back." Bernie trotted off in the direction Mr. Natachi indicated and found the herb lady and, next to her, an empty vending space. She talked to the woman and to the vendors on either side, and they confirmed that their flea market neighbor had packed up quickly. One said she thought his name was Eric; the other vendor referred to him as Steven.

Bernie did a quick cruise of the market and saw no one who matched Straw Hat Man's description. When she returned, Mr. Natachi was talking about his daughter and her husband, who were driving around the US in a truck with a camper shell. When his story was done, Mama turned to her. "You want to make a pie from those peaches. We should go before it gets too hot to turn on the oven."

Mr. Natachi said good-bye. "I hope you police find the man who had my bolo and the man who sold it to him. I think he told the truth about that."

Mama and Bernie stopped at a lemonade booth and took cups of it to the car. Mama seemed immune to the heat; Bernie wished, not for the first time, that the air-conditioning worked in her old Toyota. Usually when she opened the windows in New Mexico's Four Corners country, the flow of air provided relief from the heat, especially in the morning. But not today. The summer rains were slow in coming this year, and the clouds that made afternoon shade had not yet arrived.

Bernie drove Mama home to Toadlena. Her sister had turned on both fans and placed them strategically so that it was noticeably cooler in the house than outside. Darleen was barefoot, in shorts and a tank top, and had piled her long black hair in a makeshift bun on the top of her head. Bernie took the fruit to the kitchen while Mama told Darleen of their adventure. She gently emptied the peaches into a dishpan in the sink. Juice from the squashed fruit on the bottom filled the room with the sweet smell of summer. She washed them, then found a well-used cookie sheet in the cabinet and moved them there to dry and sort.

Her sister came in to watch. "How was the flea market?"

"Hot. Mama knew half the people she saw shopping."

"And you knew the rest. Did anything interesting happen?"

"Yeah." She told Darleen about Mr. Natachi and the bolo.

"I thought he must be here. I saw the auntie drive by yesterday with an older gentleman next to her and someone who looked a lot like Ryana in the back seat. I'll have to go down and say hello. I haven't seen that girl for years." Darleen smiled. "You think she's still pretty, or did she get fat?"

"I think she'd be gorgeous fat or thin. Just like you, Sister."

Darleen laughed. "Right. And especially in this outfit."

Bernie began to select the peaches she'd use for the pie, putting them back in the bag. She talked as she worked.

"I wish you had come with us. There was a man selling photographs. It made me think that you could sell your drawings there. And you could do portraits, too."

"Did you actually see anyone buy a photo?" She didn't wait for Bernie's response. "Who wants photos when everyone who has a phone can take their own?"

"I just mentioned it because I know you need to make some money. Don't be negative."

"I could sit there in the heat all day watching people walk by looking for cheap socks and T-shirts. I'd rather sit here." Darleen filled a glass with cold water. "You want some?"

Bernie shook her head. "Do we have a Coke?"

"You drank the last one a couple days ago. Those things aren't good for you. Too sweet." Her little sister looked at the peaches and grabbed one. "But that doesn't apply to peaches, of course. All natural."

"I've left some here for you and Mama. I'm making a pie. Speaking of sweet, my husband is cooking dinner. I volunteered for dessert."

"How is the Cheeseburger?"

"Fine. He's off work today."

Now that Mama didn't require her walker, she moved so quietly her daughters didn't realize she was there. She went to the refrigerator, took out a jug of sun tea, filled two glasses, added several spoonfuls of sugar to one, and handed it to Bernie. "No Cokes, but you try this. You still look hot." She took the other one. "I'm going to rest a minute before I go next door. Mrs. Darkwater wants me to help her sort through some clothes for her son."

Bernie took the cool glass and joined Darleen on the couch. "Mama seems good today."

Darleen agreed. "Ever since the doctor took her off that medicine, she feels fine. Even her memory has improved. She still moves slowly, but she's so much stronger. If I had a job, I could go to work and not even worry about her. Now that she's better, she doesn't need me much except to drive and lift the heavy stuff. And to have someone to boss around."

"What's new with your job hunt?" Darleen had been looking for paid work all summer, or so she said.

"Nothing. It stinks."

"I can let you know if I hear of anything."

Darleen hesitated. "Sure, but nothing to do with cops."

"Why not?"

"You and the Cheeseburger have that covered. It's probably too late to get a job anyway if I'm going to quit to go back to school. But how can I go to school if I don't have any money?"

Bernie had already talked to her sister about scholarships, grants, special programs to help students like Darleen. None of her suggestions or advice resonated enough to get her sister moving. Darleen excelled in procrastination. "You could offer to give people rides, pick up groceries for them, things like that. Try my idea about selling some of your drawings at the flea market. Or doing quick portraits, you know, caricatures."

"I don't know how to get a booth and I couldn't afford it anyway."

"I'm sure Mama has ties to someone who would let you share a space. Or you could explore that ride idea."

"Right. The rez Uber. I can see it now." Darleen lowered the pitch of her voice. "'Good afternoon, customer. I'm your driver, but you have to roll down the window to open the passenger door. And leave it down because there's no air-conditioning. Or I'll get out and you can scoot in under the steering wheel. If you want to put something in the trunk, just let me know so I can take off the wire that's holding it shut.'"

Bernie laughed. "OK. My bad."

The phone rang, and Darleen rose to answer. "Hello." Then, "No, this is her daughter." Then, "No, the other one." And, "Yes, sir. Thank you. I'll get her. Just a minute."

Darleen put the phone on the counter and strode down the hall to Mama's room. "It's for you."

The phone hung on the kitchen wall. Bernie made a note to ask Mama, again, about getting the kind of phones that worked on batteries, where she could have several, including an extension in the bedroom instead of this museum piece with a long cord.

"Hello." Mama listened; then she said, "Oh, she's here now. Come over." Then, after some silence, Bernie heard Mama give the person on the phone her and Chee's home number and end the call.

"Nice peaches, daughter. Are they sweet?"

Bernie nodded. "I heard you saying my phone number. Anything I should know?"

"Oh, that was Mr. Natachi. He said his granddaughter, Ryana, needs to talk to you. Remember her?"

"Yes."

"I told them to come on over now, but he said she'll call you later. I remembered something after I gave that man your phone number. This is your day off from being a policewoman. I will call back and tell him not to let her bother you today."

"It's OK."

"No. You work too hard. Unlike your sister."

Bernie hated it when Mama compared them. "I barely remember Ryana. She hung out with Darleen. Why does she want to talk to me?"

"About the bolo. That's all I know."

Mama saw Darleen relaxing on the couch. "Daughter, you should do something, not sit like a lazy woman. You can get rid of those sticker bushes by the front door."

Darleen turned off the TV. "It's too hot now, Mama. I'd die out there, not that anyone would miss me."

Bernie waited for Mama to say something, but her mother turned her attention back to the fruit. Mama picked out a soft peach and took a bite. Bernie saw her smile. "I'll take some to Mrs. Darkwater."

After Mama left for the Darkwater house, Bernie spoke to Darleen. "I'm heading out."

"Catch you later. After I do the gardening." Darleen did not sound happy.

"Good luck finding a job."

Silence.

"Keep your chin up, Sister. You know Mama and I would miss you every day if you weren't here."

"Whatever."

"No. I mean it. Mama says what she thinks and then she moves on. You realize—"

Darleen interrupted. "I know. Don't lecture me. I have a plan for making some money. I'll buy you a Coke if it works out."

Bernie had parked in the shade with the windows open, and the car was cooler than she had expected. She thought about Darleen as she drove away. She should have asked if she had any new drawings and if she'd heard from CS, her some-times boyfriend, or from any of her friends. She worried about her sister's blue mood and knew that depression could be a trigger for someone to resume drinking, and drinking made depression worse, which led to more drinking.

She focused on the drive. She and her husband had promised each other they would relax today, just the two of them. He'd offered to make his fa-mous pork chops on the grill. It would be nice to be together without an agenda.

She expected to find him home when she got there, but she didn't see his truck. When she opened the door to their trailer, she noticed the note he'd left for her on the kitchen table.

*Hi. Largo called me in. Home by 5, I hope.*

The news darkened her mood momentarily, like a cloud drifting past the sun. She put the peaches on the counter and called the station with a description of the man attempting to sell stolen property. Then she reconsidered the plan for the afternoon. It was rare that she had time to her-self, and her brain flooded with undone tasks and then, unavoidably, circled back to Chee. Wilson Sam, the rookie, usually got the Saturday assign-ments. Whatever had called her husband to work on his day off, she hoped it was interesting. Maybe even connected to Mr. Natachi and his bolo. The thought inspired her to call Chee, and she heard his cell phone ringing in the charger in the bed-room.

She washed her hands and got out the butter, flour, salt, and a mixing bowl and combined the ingredients to form the ball of dough that would ultimately become a piecrust. She covered the bowl and put the dough in the refrigerator to chill for an hour. She took the book she was reading outside to the deck. Nearby cottonwoods shaded a corner, and she moved her chair there. It was warm, but cooler than inside.

She noticed the bag of charcoal and envisioned the meaty pork chops to go with the pie. And, of course, Chee would make a salad and she would eat some rather than hurt his feelings. She leaned back in her chair, listening to the liquid music of the San Juan as it flowed between the cottonwood trees. Life was good.

She had just finished a chapter when the phone jarred her. Reluctantly, she went inside. The Lieutenant, Captain Largo, and Mama were the most frequent users of that line.

"Hello?"

"Ah, hello. Is this Bernie, uhm, I mean Officer Manuelito?"

"Yes."

"I'm Mr. Natachi's granddaughter, Ryana. We've met at my auntie's place, but you probably don't remember me. Anyway, my shicheii said that he mentioned something about his bolo being stolen, and, well, I wanted to say that it's nothing for the police to worry about. He's an old man and he just forgets where he puts things. He was wearing that bolo when he left the house this morning. I'm sorry if he caused you any trouble."

The young woman sounded nervous, Bernie thought. Was it because she was uncomfortable talking to a police officer? Or just not a good liar? "I enjoyed chatting with your grandfather. I've dealt with elders who have had some memory problems. Except for his gray hair, your grandfather doesn't remind me of those folks in the slightest."

Ryana sounded more assertive now. "You don't need to get involved. He just forgets where he puts things. I'm telling you not to worry about what he said. OK?"

"No. The fact that your grandfather's burglary was in Chinle and he identified a man with his stolen item here in Shiprock raises a bunch of questions."

The woman's voice grew softer. "We don't want the police involved. My shicheii doesn't remember some things so well now. Please don't embarrass him."

"Can he come to the phone?"

"Oh no. He's . . . he's sleeping. I have to go."

Ryana ended the call. Bernie made a mental note to mention the situation to Chee. He had been consulting with the substation in Chinle about recent unsolved burglaries in which none of the merchandise had been recovered. Officer Bigman was going to Chinle to follow up on that.

She rolled out the crust, placed it in a pie pan, chopped, sweetened, and added the fruit, gently topping it with the second crust. While her hands worked, her brain went back to the bolo and Ryana's unexpected call. She had no reason to suspect that Mr. Natachi was lying; why would Ryana?

Bernie put the pie in the oven to bake and was sipping her first Coke of the day when Chee drove up and climbed out of the police car.

"Hey there. You're back early. How was—"

She stopped talking as soon as she saw him more closely. His face was scraped and his uniform dirty. He limped up the steps to the deck and spoke before she could ask. "I'm fine. It's a long story. I'm going to clean up and then I need to get back to work."

"And I should see the other guy?"

When he didn't respond to her quip, she put her book down and followed him inside, worry shadowing her like a bad dream.

He was in the bathroom and she heard the shower running.

"Tell me what happened."

"A combination of terrible luck and worse judgment. I should have known better."

"So . . ."

"Wait till I'm done here and I'll give you the long version."

He looked better after he had washed the sand out of his hair and the blood from his face and hands. He smelled good, too, when he joined her on the deck.

"Well, it wasn't the finest moment of my career. But I take back what I told you before. There was some good luck involved. I'm lucky I'm not dead. We'd had complaints about a guy selling rotten hay and then not giving people their money back. So I sent the rookie out there. He grew up working on a ranch and knows more about hay than I do. He talked to the guy and at the time the man admitted it and offered to give the customer who complained a good bale. Problem solved, right?"

Bernie waited for the punch line.

"Not exactly. When the rookie had the seller call the jilted buyer, the buyer said he would come right over. He showed up, but he didn't just want the hay, he wanted the seller to pay the vet bill for his horse who got sick from it." Chee stopped. "Don't give me that look, sweetheart. I'm getting there.

"The man who sold the bad hay said no deal, and the buyer swung at him. The rookie stepped in between them and took one in the face. He called for backup and that was me."

"So you got in the middle of a fistfight? How did you—"

Chee interrupted. "I smell something burning."

She rushed into the kitchen, grabbed a dish towel, and removed the pie. The edges of the crust were the color of dark chocolate, and the juice that had bubbled out was smoking at the bottom of the oven. She turned off the heat.

"I'm glad your nose is so sharp."

"Too bad we can't say the same for the rookie now. His nose got flattened. The guy swung hard. By the time I got there, Sam was sitting up with a paper towel to stop the bleeding. The men were both apologetic. Then the guy who got the bad hay asked us to climb up on the truck to make sure that the replacement bale wasn't moldy, and the other guy agreed. The rookie was out of it, so I jumped up there. The hay was OK as far as I could tell, but the baler had picked up a snake and sliced it in two, and the back half with the rattles was moving in the truck bed. It startled me, and I lost my balance and fell out the back of the truck, you know, the open gate. Nothing seriously damaged but my pride."

"How's the rookie?"

"He's hurting. And our plan for a lazy weekend took a hit. I told Largo I'd finish the shift so Sam could take his busted nose home. I've got to get back to work." Chee paused. "The rookie is having trouble breathing, and it looks like someone will have to fill in for him tomorrow, too."

"If Largo asks, I'll work. That's only fair since you're taking the rest of his shift today."

"Let Bigman handle it."

"He and his wife have to go to birthing class."

"Really?"

"Yes, the baby's due any time now."

Chee ran a hand through his short-cropped hair. "I didn't even know they were expecting."

"You haven't seen Mrs. Bigman for a while, have you? I might need to work tomorrow anyway." She mentioned the incident of the bolo tie and the call from the granddaughter. "I need to file a report. Since Mr. Natachi is from Chinle, I wonder if this could be tied to the burglary ring you've been checking into."

"You've got a knack for being where the action is, even on your day off."

"Well, yeah. That's how I met you, remember?"

"You were the best new recruit I ever worked with."

Bernie smiled. "That's not what you told me when you arrived in that big truck after my unit got stuck in the mud."

He grinned at her. "I was playing hard to get. I'm glad it worked."

After Chee left, she typed her conversation with Mr. Natachi about the bolo and her follow-up effort, with special attention to his identification of the man who was trying to sell the tie. She would be happy to find the vendor and figure out why he had stolen property for sale.

She enjoyed her job, the variety that came with each day on patrol. She liked driving, being in the field instead of the office, dealing with people one-on-one. She appreciated the fact that most days, she could look back at her shift and see somewhere that she'd made a difference in someone's life.

She glanced at the loom Chee had built for her. She'd taken pleasure in weaving as a beginner, years ago. She treasured the family legacy, the memory of her grandmother at the loom, and the skill and joy Mama brought to the art.

Someday, she thought. But not today.

Bernie was glad that Mama and she had gone to the flea market early. She had time for a run on her favorite trail along the river, her regular weekend afternoon routine. Running earlier would have been cooler, but she liked the midday break, the opportunity to shake off whatever she'd dealt with earlier and get reinvigorated for the evening. She changed into her shorts and tank top and put on her running shoes and the nylon pouch that held her phone and ID. She grabbed a water bottle and a hat and jogged off, finding her stride within a few minutes.

She wouldn't have noticed the body if it hadn't been for the dog.

3

The name of the postal inspector that had eluded Leaphorn popped into his head when he awoke, early as usual, on Saturday. Jim Bean, that was it, and recalling it made him smile. His memory was a little slower than at his prime, but still working. It was a good way to start the day.

He rose, greeted by that familiar, wonderful scent that told him Louisa had started the coffee. He dressed quickly and headed into his office to get the address book, where he knew he had Bean's information. He found an office number in San Diego and realized that his dealings with Bean dated back to the day when not everyone and his grandchild had a cell phone. He jotted it down along with some other notes and headed to the kitchen.

After the first sip of coffee, he asked Louisa for the favor.

"Sure, Joe. But we may just get an answering machine. It is Saturday, you know."

"Try."

She called, and he watched her punch in another number, probably Bean's extension. He heard her explain that she was calling on behalf of Joe Leaphorn. She left a message with their home number and his cell. He could tell by the unbroken cadence of her voice that she spoke to a machine. As he listened to her speak, he thought of something else.

"One mo?"

"Of course. But let's eat first. The oatmeal is ready."

Oatmeal was Louisa's go-to breakfast. He made the best of it, sometimes imagining he was chomping on bacon or fried Spam. He'd complained once, and she had explained the value of whole grains as an antidote to the evils of a modern lifestyle, and then suggested that if he didn't want oatmeal he could visit the restaurant of his choice and enjoy the heart attack special. He thought he might come to enjoy oatmeal, and he had evolved enough to find it tolerable. And he'd learned not to whine about a housemate who fixed a hot breakfast for him.

As they were finishing, he heard the chime of the doorbell, probably someone wanting to convert them politically or spiritually, he thought. Louisa, both gracious and curious, rose to check on it. He recognized the second woman's voice, finished the last bite in his bowl, and headed into the living room.

If her very presence in his house wasn't enough

of a clue, he knew as soon as he saw Mrs. Pinto's face as she stood there, shoulders slumped, that something was wrong.

"Lieutenant, I'm sorry to intrude on your morning, but I didn't want to talk about this over the phone."

Louisa said, "If this is business, perhaps I should—"

"No, no. Please stay here. You need to know what happened, too." She swallowed. "Tiffany died last night."

"Tiffany?" Louisa's voice asked the question.

Mrs. Pinto pressed her hands together. "My assistant. She's the woman who collapsed outside when the Lieutenant came to see me yesterday. The one who fell near the skate park."

He was glad Mrs. Pinto stayed with English for Louisa's benefit. He had no trouble understanding.

"Please sit down." Louisa motioned toward the couch. "I'll bring you some water. Or would you rather have coffee?"

Mrs. Pinto moved to the sofa and waved off the offerings. "Louisa, stay here and listen."

Leaphorn sat across from Mrs. Pinto with Louisa next to him. Louisa said what he was thinking: "Did she die from the fall?"

"I'm not sure what happened. I'll tell you all I know." Mrs. Pinto exhaled. "I went to see Tiffany at her house last night."

Leaphorn wanted Mrs. Pinto to tell the story at her own pace so she could better focus on the details, but Louisa rushed in with her questions.

"She was home? They didn't admit her to the hospital after that fall?"

"She told the ambulance people she felt better . . . that the heat made her weak, and that she'd been sick. I heard the ambulance man advise her to rest, keep cool, drink plenty of water, and to get someone to drive her to the hospital if she had a bad headache, felt nauseous, confused, dizzy, a whole list of things. They wanted to take her to get checked out, but she refused to go. I stayed with her until the medics left, and I made her go home for the rest of the day."

Mrs. Pinto paced three steps toward the kitchen, then came back and sat on the sofa across from them. "I should have persuaded her to go in the ambulance. She'd been getting sicker for about two weeks. She had grown so weak she asked me to reduce her hours to half-time until she felt better, and I did. That's why the project I talked to you about is so far behind. Her older sister hit a rough spot and moved in, so I knew that if something happened, Collette could help. I could kick myself for not making her go to the hospital."

"I know you did all you could." Louisa leaned toward her friend.

"Tiffany called me about eleven last night. I could tell she'd been crying. She said she got sick because she had been disrespectful of the past." Mrs. Pinto looked down at the table. "I asked her what that meant, disrespectful of the past, and she said she couldn't talk about it, but that she was having trouble catching her breath. She said she was going to ask her father to arrange a healing ceremony. She thanked me for helping her yesterday and hung up." Tears filled Mrs. Pinto's eyes.

"I didn't like any of it, so I dressed and drove over there. When I got to the house, I thought Tiffany was dead, but she was still breathing. She looked terrible, pale, really sick. Her little pills were there, lined up in a box close to her bed. I called the ambulance, and then her sister Collette showed up, but it was too late to help her." Mrs. Pinto shook her head once. "Tiffany was my friend as well as my assistant. I let her down."

Louisa reached for a box of tissues on the lamp table, took one, and passed them to Mrs. Pinto. The woman took one and wiped her eyes. Louisa said, "Were you with her when she died?"

"No, no. Not exactly. Collette told me to go out with a flashlight so the ambulance could find the place more easily. I was anxious and I thought the fresh air would calm me down and I could tell that Collette wanted time alone with her sister to say good-bye. She passed while I was outside."

Louisa shook her head. "I'm going to bring us all some tea."

The cat, which had been lurking in the doorway, paraded past them as though it had been anticipating a pause in the conversation to make an entrance. It followed Louisa into the kitchen.

Leaphorn waited for Mrs. Pinto's emotions to settle, then spoke to her in Navajo. "What did Tiffany mean when she said she had been disrespectful of the past?"

"I asked her. She didn't answer." Mrs. Pinto

clasped her hands. "If she had trouble with the job, she should have told me. When the museum receives anything that could be sacred, dangerous, connected with the dead, or contaminated, it goes to a separate place to be prayed over. The medicine men handle it because we don't want to take any of those risks. That's how we dealt with the box I told you about."

"Did Tiffany say anything else that seemed unusual?"

Mrs. Pinto seemed to have been waiting for the question. "She told me she needed to talk to a hand trembler to get a diagnosis of what was really wrong with her, that the medicine her white doctor had given her that used to help wasn't helping. She told me she knew her illness was linked to all the sadness that came in that box, even though the doctor said it was stress that had compounded her breathing problem."

Leaphorn was a skeptic when it came to hand tremblers, those who sit with a troubled person and arrive at a diagnosis of what taboo they broke so the proper traditional healing ceremony can be requested. "Sadness? Why would she say that?"

"I didn't ask her." The teakettle whistled, and she waited until the sound stopped. "You probably think I'm superstitious for even mentioning this. I don't believe in chindiis, in ghosts, in supernatural evil. I'm not on the Jesus road or the peyote trail either. But something is not right here. I counted on her to help us get that donation issue resolved."

"What medical issues did Tiffany have?"

Mrs. Pinto pressed her lips together, then exhaled. "After I hired her, she told me that she had a rare genetic respiratory disease, but not to worry, she had talked to a specialist and it was under control. She was well when the box arrived last month, but after that she seemed to get sicker and sicker, leaving early or skipping work altogether. If I wasn't so close to retiring, I would have found an intern or a volunteer to help, but I didn't have time to train someone new. The department will be reorganized when I leave. *If* I can leave as planned now, with this complication."

They listened to Louisa puttering in the kitchen for a moment.

"Joe, we didn't get off on the right foot yesterday. I regret that. I sincerely hope you will agree to work with me."

Leaphorn nodded. "I'd like to see the items and the list that came with them. I need to know what is missing besides the bracelet and why it has to be a secret."

"And then you'll sign the contract?" Mrs. Pinto gave him the hint of a smile. "Come to my office this afternoon. I'll be there from two until six or even later."

Louisa entered with a tray loaded with iced tea, honey, napkins, and some cookies.

Mrs. Pinto switched to English. "It will be nice to be inside with the coolness. It's already hot, and too early. I've been blaming the heat for making us irritable. I'll be glad when the rains come. They are later than usual this year."

Louisa put the tray on the table. "I always liked teaching summer sessions because of the air-conditioning. The heat gets to everyone, makes us impatient."

She handed the visitor a glass of tea.

"Thank you." Mrs. Pinto took the glass, but she looked at Leaphorn when she said it.

Around three p.m. Leaphorn arrived at the museum. Unlike his earlier visit, this time the place was quiet. As they had arranged, he followed the signs to her office. The door stood open. Mrs. Pinto motioned him in when he rapped on the frame and then turned back to her computer. "I will be done here in a minute, and then I will show you the donations. Have a seat, Lieutenant."

She had arranged her paperwork on her desk in several stacks in plastic trays, the pages lined up with the edges straight. A manila folder with "Joe Leaphorn" printed in block letters sat in the center. On the wall Leaphorn saw a painting by Ernest Franklin, a picture of a hogan in the snow with Church Rock in the background.

She shut down her computer and rose. "Thank you for coming." She took the folder with his name on it with her as she headed to the hallway. He followed toward the back of the building, past a silent parade of closed doors. Although she was decades younger than he, she was shorter and many pounds heavier. She waddled down the hall, and he matched her pace easily, even without his cane.

Finally, Mrs. Pinto unlocked the last door on

the left. "Here it is." She flicked on the light and crossed her arms over her ample belly.

Leaphorn walked toward the long table in the center of the windowless room. Someone had arranged the items all by category. The jewelry caught his eye—rings, bracelets, old ketohs (or bow guards), necklaces, earrings, and brooches. Most of it looked to be Navajo or Navajo imitation, and many of the pieces included blue stones in various hues. Turquoise, he thought, the gift that tradition said came from the sky itself, and the talisman that helped ensure the fertility of a shepherd's flock. The three small pots looked as though they had been made by Pueblo Indians. Next to them sat two simple, classic brown Navajo ceramics. The piñon-sap coating made their smooth surfaces shine. He saw a small folk art wagon, a little male and a female character on the driver's bench, pulled by a draft horse. A nice assortment, he thought.

Two folding chairs waited at the end of the table. Mrs. Pinto placed the folder with his name in front of one of them on the table. "When you are done looking, I thought you might like to examine the paperwork that came in the donation."

He stepped toward her. "Who opened the box?"

"First the medicine people, and then it came to Tiffany to unpack. She handled many valuable shipments and there was never a problem before."

"Tell me what's missing."

Mrs. Pinto sat down and rubbed her hands over her face.

He waited.

"It's a dress, a biil, that the collector says Asdzáá Tlogi made sometime around 1864."

"I'm sorry. I don't recognize—"

"Asdzáá Tlogi." She said it louder this time. "Juanita. The wife of Chief Manuelito."

Leaphorn sat down. "Hwéeldi. It came from there."

"Yes, from that period in history where not much survived."

No one who knew the Lieutenant would describe him as overly emotional, but Leaphorn felt his chest grow tighter. The warrior Manuelito, with Juanita at his side, was among those leaders who brought the People back to Dinetah, their homeland, after the Long Walk of 1864 and years of suffering at the Bosque Redondo prison camp. Along with others, he signed the treaty that officially gave the Navajo people the right, in the eyes of the US government, to live on a portion of the sacred land the Holy People had assigned them. Over the ensuing years, the size of the Navajo Nation had grown as tribal officials managed to gain titles to other land that had always been theirs. Without Manuelito and the others' ability to make peace, the story might have ended differently. And Juanita stood by the leader's side.

Mrs. Pinto interrupted his contemplation. "If the gift is what the collector states, then it needs to be here. I don't mean just the museum. It needs to be in Navajo land."

He opened the folder she'd offered. The yellow

notebook paper, the kind that comes on legal pads, had cursive handwriting, all of it with a black pen. He glanced at the date—four weeks ago. The salutation read, "To Whom It May Concern."

*After owning and enjoying these items for many years, I have decided they deserve a larger viewership and a new home, so I am donating them to the Navajo Nation. My gift comes with no restrictions, but I urge the museum to treasure my treasures.*

On the next page, on the same notebook paper, he saw a numbered list with handwritten descriptions of the items, 1 to 15. Some of the descriptions involved several sentences, others just a word or two. The small script drifted down the page at an ever-increasing slope. The list had a randomness to it, with a man's ring listed between two wedding baskets.

The list continued onto a second page. Leaphorn skimmed to the final notation:

35. Traditional Navajo Biil, woven circa 1860, attributed to Asdzáá Tlogi, Canyon de Chelly area. May have been worn on the Long Walk.

Leaphorn studied the items on the table again. "I don't see the baskets or the saddle blanket."

"That's right. We removed them because they might be contaminated by preservatives or infested with insects. We stored them elsewhere until we know what we are dealing with. Anything with feathers, leather, or other organic material gets that treatment. It's common museum practice today. I'll show them to you when we finish here if you wish."

"What did Tiffany say when you asked her about the missing dress and the bracelet?"

"She swore she never saw the biil, and that no woven dress of any sort was included in this shipment. There were bracelets, and we didn't know which was missing until we matched what we got with the descriptions on the donor's inventory sheet. None of the items had numbers."

"The silver bracelet, anything else about that I should know?"

"It was part of a set." Mrs. Pinto tapped the list. "The earrings and necklace that went with it arrived."

"I am wondering how implicitly you trust your assistant. Had there been any prior issues with valuable items?"

Leaphorn noticed the exhaustion on the woman's face. "No. I know she was loyal to me. I have never had reason to question her." Mrs. Pinto tapped the folder again. "Any more questions before you say yes and start helping me?"

"Why did you come to me instead of alerting the police? If the dress was stolen, this should be their job."

Mrs. Pinto looked at him over the rim of her glasses. "I didn't call the police because I don't know for sure if a crime was committed. I don't know if the dress came in the box. And if it did, I don't know for sure that it was Juanita's. I need more proof than a handwritten note to confirm that it was Juanita's. We museum people like to have what we call provenance, a paper trail that explains how the person who owns an object acquired it, as well as when and from whom."

Leaphorn nodded. He knew Navajo law enforcement was understaffed and focused on crimes that hurt people first, not the possibility of a missing museum donation. If he had been in her position, he would have hired a PI, too.

Mrs. Pinto continued. "Secondly, I know you worked with that museum in Santa Fe, so you have some experience with this. And you live right here in Window Rock and I like working with people I can meet face-to-face.

"Finally, after Louisa told me about you doing investigations, I remembered that when you were with the police department, you found a poor woman who had been locked in one of those bunkers out by Fort Wingate. You didn't give up and I admired you for that. This case is totally different, but it might take some persistence. I hope you can resolve it in a day or two, but if not, you'll need to figure it out in the next two weeks."

Mrs. Pinto folded her hands. "And there's one more thing. When you drove away yesterday, I heard a grinding sound. That led me to assume that, besides appealing to your curiosity and your sense of honor as a Navajo when it came to an important piece of our heritage, you might need a part for that truck of yours. Could be expensive."

Leaphorn smiled. "That's a good explanation." The woman might be demanding, but she was smart. He appreciated the way her brain worked.

He stood and walked slowly to the end of the table and back again, doing a brief survey of the material. "This is a nice collection. Some lovely and interesting things here."

"I agree, of course. But the star of the show is the piece that we can't find." She stood. "Before you ask, we searched for the return address on the box in our donor file. Nothing. Then I had my assistant do a reverse address check on the computer— you know, those programs that fill in the name of who lives where. That address is bogus. I put Tiffany's work in the folder for you."

"How was the box shipped?"

"The old standby. US mail."

Leaphorn signed two copies of the letter of agreement. Mrs. Pinto put one in his folder and showed him a smaller brown envelope. "Tiffany took some photos of what you see here as well as the baskets and saddle blanket." She closed the folder and handed it to him. "How long before you will know something?"

He recognized the urgency. "I will check in with you midweek."

"Or sooner. My retirement clock is ticking."

The sun had heated his truck's door handle almost to the point of pain. Leaphorn climbed in. The steering wheel was hot to the touch. He turned the key, noticing the grinding again.

Louisa, as he had come to expect, greeted him with a question.

"So, what do you think of Daisy's proposal? Will you try to help her?"

He nodded yes.

"I'm glad."

He put the folder and the brown envelope on the kitchen table and motioned her to join him. He removed the photos and thumbed through them; then he examined the list. Whoever sent the box had assembled the items with care and, as the letter implied, seemed to have personally collected them over a number of years.

He handed the list to Louisa.

She made little humming sounds as she reviewed it. "Look at this." She tapped her index finger on a line in the inventory and read: "'Earrings, necklace, and sterling silver storyteller bracelet set with bears, trees, et cetera.' Is there more information on these?"

He pushed the pictures to her and watched as she quickly sorted out the bracelet photos. She rose and returned with the magnifier they kept in the kitchen drawer and used it to examine two pictures more closely.

"It's not here. The storyteller bracelet is not in the photos."

Leaphorn looked at the number again, 30, and nodded. "Rye. Missin." He meant "right," but he could tell that she understood.

"I think this could be the same jeweler who made a bracelet I bought years ago when I first came to the Southwest. A gentleman named Peshlakai. I'll get mine; maybe it has that mark the inventory describes, and that could help track it."

"Go head."

"You're humoring me, Joe, but you never know."

She left him to search for her bracelet, planting the seed of an idea. If Louisa clearly remembered where and when she'd purchased her jewelry, artists might remember, too, or might have kept records of their customers. He filed the thought away.

Louisa returned before Giddi had an opportunity to jump onto her chair. She had a silver bracelet and a grin on her face. She showed him the artist's stamp. "It looks like a *P*. Peshlakai. And this one is a storyteller, the same as the donor describes. What do you think? It must be the same artist."

He looked at the description again and then at Louisa's bracelet and its images of a hogan, a woman weaving, and sheep grazing. He studied the small *P* inside the band. She could be right.

She slipped the bracelet onto her wrist. "You know, I spent a lot for this way back then. I remember I almost missed my car payment because of it. I imagine this person's work is worth even more now. Maybe that's why it's missing."

He thought about that. A stolen bracelet would be easy to sell. An old textile would have a smaller market—and anyone who knew its story would also understand that it should never have been for sale. An odd combination.

He refocused on his idea of contacting the artists, first the jeweler whose work was missing and then, perhaps, the others. The people who had made the major pieces, he speculated, would be more likely to remember who bought them. The photos would help. He wondered how many of the artists still lived.

Leaphorn picked out a photograph of a basket, a complicated design that looked modern. He handed the picture to Louisa.

"It's an interesting piece." She looked at the typed list. "If this is number 12, the basket maker is listed as Holiday."

He handed her a pencil. "Mark?"

She nodded and put a check mark on the list.

He thumbed through the pictures and selected a few more for a pile he mentally labeled as "unique and valuable." The task didn't take long.

Leaphorn stood, noticing that his back objected. Louisa rose, too. "This is fascinating, Joe. I'd like to help. Maybe I could call some of those Pueblo artists whose work you pulled and ask them who owns it now. I figure they'll speak English. I'll leave the Navajos to you."

He nodded. She kept encouraging him to resume his work with his speech therapist, but he found it frustrating. In circumstances where he really needed to speak English, he asked someone like Louisa to help. If he had to communicate complicated information, he used his laptop and typed in English. Slow and not spontaneous, but it did the job.

"Oh, while you were at the museum, the phone rang. It was Jim Bean. He asked me to tell you that he's coming through Window Rock tomorrow and would like to see you. He gave me his cell number." Louisa paused. "He invited me, too, but I'd feel like a third wheel. You guys will want to talk about the old times."

"Wade a mint." Leaphorn took his phone out of his pocket and found the right screen. Then he nodded.

She gave him Bean's number and he added it to his contacts, then sent Bean a text.

His old associate's response was almost instant.

CU tomorrow 10 @ Navajo Inn.

After years of resisting technology, Leaphorn now realized it was a useful research tool. He didn't see the need to learn Twitter, Instagram, and the many other applications young people couldn't live without. But for quick, simple communication and research, the internet served a fine purpose.

He went to his office. Giddi padded in to check on him, and he gave the cat a few pats before it calmly strolled away.

He typed in "Juanita and Manuelito Navajo" and got 73,000 results before he could take the next breath. He scanned the list and quickly found one that had Juanita's name first. He clicked on it to find a picture of her in a biil, with a necklace and high moccasin boots, a belt of large silver concho discs at her waist. She looked peaceful and strong.

He clicked on several other pages and at the end of half an hour had learned little except that doing research like this himself would take time. The library at Northern Arizona University had a fine collection of articles and photos relating to Navajo history and especially old weavings. He called up the library website and typed in his request. He knew it was Saturday, but someone could be working at the reference desk. If not, they'd see his question first thing Monday.

4

The first time Bernie ran past the spot on the trail that afternoon, she noticed the dog. It sniffed at the ground, totally uninterested in her. Good, she thought. She'd been chased by, growled at, and threatened with sharp dog teeth enough already to last a lifetime. She ran until she came to the place where the fallen cottonwood tree blocked the trail. She stopped, sipped some water, felt the good fatigue in her muscles. Time to turn back.

The dog was still there, sitting now. She slowed from a jog to a walk, her basic distrust of canines struggling with her intuition as a police officer. She stopped in front of the animal, a brown-and-black mixed breed of some sort, about forty pounds. It wore a green collar. The dog trotted off toward the river, then came back. Slowly, as though it wanted to trust her.

"Easy, fella. I'm not going to hurt you, and you aren't going to hurt me." She spoke calmly, as she had been trained, even though her heart was beating like a hummingbird's. She followed it, curious as to what the animal found so intriguing. The grasses and snakeweed grew thick here along the river, but the red athletic shoe stood out. Her eyes followed the shoe to a black pant leg. The man who wore them lay facedown. The dog paced around the body and whined.

Her first thought was a heart attack.

"Hey, sir, are you OK?"

If the awkward posture hadn't already yelled crime scene, the man's hands secured behind his back with white plastic ties confirmed her suspicions. She squatted close to feel for a pulse, pressing her fingers firmly against the gray skin of his neck. Nothing. He had holes in his ears for earrings but wore no jewelry. Bernie stood and pulled her phone from the nylon pouch, hoping to find cell service. Not here. If she could change one thing about being a police officer, it would be to end encounters with the dead and the evil chindiis they left behind, but she knew it came with the job.

She retraced her steps, following the path she'd taken as she approached the body, this time focusing on anything else out of the ordinary that could be a clue to what had happened here. When she reached the trail, she looked at her phone again and walked until she finally saw a single bar. She dialed the substation. Sandra answered.

"I found a male body off the river trail, about halfway in. I'll wait for backup."

"Yikes."

"That's what I thought." A man on a mountain bike pedaled by, focused on the trail. She made a

mental note of his appearance. "I need you to call
the Feds, too. This guy is a homicide."

"You heard that the rookie had to go home?"
Sandra didn't wait for confirmation. "Backup could
take a while. Hang in there." Bernie typed the description of the bike person into her phone. Un-
likely that he had any connection with anything, but
the trail was now a crime scene. She kept the phone
handy and returned to the spot on the trail closest
to the body. The dog waited there. She glanced at its
collar for an ID tag, but it didn't have one, just the
simple strap fastened around its neck.

She walked back toward the body, moving carefully and taking pictures of anything that seemed
relevant. She looked for a dropped cigarette butt,
a discarded water bottle, a footprint where the
vegetation wasn't so thick, a thread snagged on
the weeds, any clue that could have been left by
whoever was responsible for the dead man. She
saw places where someone might have stepped
close to the body but no sign that it had been
dragged in from the trail. Nothing seemed out of
the ordinary—except for the corpse in the red
shoes and torn black pants and the dog. She found
no signs of struggle and no blood other than what
looked like a cut on one of the victim's hands. The
dog paced and panted, walking to the body and
then circling back toward her.

Bernie returned to the trail, looking for more
clues as she waited for backup to arrive. She con-
centrated now on keeping anyone else whom the
dog made curious from disturbing the scene.

A middle-aged man wearing sunglasses approached. He slowed from jogging to walking when she moved to the center of the trail. He was breathing hard.

"Sir, I'm a Navajo police officer, and this trail is closed. You need to go back to the parking lot."

"You don't look like a police person." He took off his hat and glasses, wiped his face with the sleeve of his T-shirt. "You're kidding. Are you serious?"

Bernie pulled out her ID as the man spoke and held it for him to see.

"Whoa. What happened?" He used the hat as a fan. "Why close the trail unless someone died out here of heatstroke or something?" The man glanced toward the river, but Bernie knew he could not see the body from where he stood.

"What's your name, sir?"

"Fred Martinez."

"Did you see anything unusual out here today?"

"No."

"Have you seen this dog before, Mr. Martinez?"

"Nope. I thought it was yours. Do you need any help, with anyone . . . or anything?"

"No, sir. Please go back to the parking lot."

Martinez jogged away. The conversation with him foreshadowed the rest of the people she encountered on the trail.

Bernie knew that when backup arrived she'd still be here, either as the officer who would close the trail or as the one to keep an eye on the body and bar access to the crime scene from the river. She expected the backup person to be Chee, but

she didn't know where he might be in the sprawling district their substation covered, what call he
was currently handling, or how long it would take
him to arrive.

After she had done as much as she could to record
the crime scene exactly as she'd found it, she sat on
a tree stump that offered a view of anyone on the
trail and of the weeds that concealed the victim.
She turned back a bicycle rider, two teen girls ready
for a run, and some other disappointed walkers and
joggers. She collected their names and contact information. She also spoke to half a dozen exercis-
ers returning to the parking lot, people who had
passed the place on the trail where a detour led to
the body. Even though each of them said they had
seen nothing unusual, she typed in their information and suggested that someone might want to
interview them in detail.

When no one intruded, she watched the dog
pace as she considered the crime, wondering if it
would sniff at something else and lead her to a
clue, but it didn't. She heard it barking and noticed
how it worked to keep a few persistent crows away
from the place the body lay. Too bad it couldn't
tell her what had happened to the man in the torn
black pants.

Bernie had finished her water by the time Officer Harold Bigman arrived. His exhaustion showed
itself in the way he walked, his arms swinging
limply and his head down.

"Hey, Bernie. What have you got?"

"Over there in the weeds." She pointed with her
chin. "A male, maybe forty-something, hands bound

behind his back. Down the slope a few yards. You can't see the body from here."

He glanced toward the place and turned back to her. "I'll take your word for it."

She wasn't surprised that he didn't want to hike over to look at the dead man. Dealing with the dead could bring trouble with their chindiis, and even less traditional Navajos had heard enough stories of the evil associated with these spirits to try to limit contact. And homicide investigations on the reservation fell to the FBI.

"I didn't notice your car."

"No, I ran from the house."

"When did you get a dog?" She saw Bigman's gaze shift toward the weeds where the dog stood panting. "He looks hot."

"It's not mine. I saw it here, and that's why I left the trail to investigate. It was acting suspicious, pacing into the weeds and then back to the trail. It has that green collar but no tags."

"Hmmm. Questionable dog with no ID. It's actually a male, by the way. Do you think he's a suspect?" Bigman grinned, then turned serious. "It's good you came by before some civilian stumbled across the body and freaked out."

"Yeah, and we're lucky that this trail doesn't have another entrance. People start at the parking lot like you did. We need to shut it down in case there's any evidence left along the route."

"If you do that, I'll stay here with the body and the mutt until the Feds send us home." Bigman gave her the keys to his unit. "There's some cold water in the trunk. You look like you could use it."

"Thanks. There's an advantage to the heat. It keeps down the foot traffic."

"You have a way of looking on the bright side, Sister."

But as he spoke, she saw a woman in black shorts jogging toward them. "I'll stop that one and then wait at the trailhead. If you see anyone headed back to the parking lot, be sure to get their contact info and find out what they saw."

Bernie told the woman the trail was closed because of an incident the police were investigating. The jogger, a Navajo in her twenties, looked startled and turned around without argument. Bernie followed the woman to the trailhead, encountering no one else. She found the water in an insulated cooler along with a rope in Bigman's car that would help secure the dog.

In the next half hour, she turned away two gray-haired ladies and a young male jogger.

Then came a person who wanted to argue with her. He was a bilagáana with disturbingly blue eyes and a deep tan. He ignored her when she called to him. She saw his earbuds and moved to block his path, noticing that his skin glistened with sweat. "Sorry, sir, this trail is closed for now. A police incident."

He removed his headphones. "What did you say?"

She repeated the message. "No one can use the trail right now."

"Oh, come on, missy. Why should I believe you are a cop?"

"I'm Officer Bernadette Manuelito." She stood a bit straighter and pulled out her identification.

He studied it. "OK. I can tell by looking that you're a runner. I'm training for the ultra-marathon at Canyon de Chelly, and this trail has those sandy places where you have to work harder. I've already run it once and I need my second lap. I won't bother anything. What's the harm?"

"You train here often?"

"Every day." He grinned at her. "You know how it is when you're anticipating an event. You don't want to break your rhythm."

"Have you seen anything unusual?"

"Like what?"

"Oh, something different. An altercation? A stranger hanging out near here?" Bernie waited. She could tell from the change in his expression that he had thought of something.

"I don't know anything, but what if I did?"

"It looks like a serious crime may have been committed. If you have any information that would help us, you should share it. You know who I am. You are?"

The man took a step back. "I'm Ed Summersly. I encounter the same runners out here a lot. It's not like we're a club or anything. I spotted a rez dog here a while ago. I thought it was odd because it was just hanging out over there where the trail curves a little, maybe a mile before the cotton-woods. It wasn't with anybody as far as I could tell."

"Did you stop?"

"No. I'm not a dog person."

She asked for his phone number and the spelling of his name, and he reluctantly complied. She put them in her phone.

"Since I've been a good guy, can I run?"

"Sure. Go ahead but not here. Not today."

Summersly gave her a dark look, shook his head, and jogged back to his car.

A few minutes later, her phone buzzed, and it was Chee. She filled him in. "I'm waiting at the trailhead by the parking lot, keeping people away until the Feds get here. Bigman is with the body."

"Did you get your run in before all this?"

"Yeah. Highlight of the day. How are you?"

"My knee hurts from that dumb fall. I got some ice for it. Things are slow out here. A car break-in at the casino, that's the big news so far."

"Be safe."

"You, too. Is there any shade?"

"A little."

A car with a pair of bicycles on the roof pulled into the lot, parking next to a black Honda, and she ended Chee's call to intercept the would-be cyclists.

A few clouds had scooted over the sun, and the afternoon, while not cool, had not grown any warmer by the time the gray sedan pulled up. Bernie recognized the car and felt her anxiety rise. She hadn't expected to see FBI Agent Sage Johnson on duty on a summer weekend.

The first time they had worked together involved a hostage situation in which Johnson got the name of a crucial person in the scenario wrong. That and other mistakes led to the injury of a key witness. The FBI woman had suggested coffee for what Bernie interpreted as a fence-mending session, but they never got around to it.

The agent lowered the window. Jazz and cool air flowed out.

"Manuelito." Johnson wore a white blouse. Her dark ball cap said "FBI." "What's up?"

Bernie explained what she'd found. "Officer Bigman arrived about ninety minutes ago. He's with the body. I came up here to close the trail."

"Do you know this place?"

"I do. It's a five-mile loop that starts and ends here. I run here often."

"A hot day for running, isn't it?"

Bernie didn't respond.

"Tell me what's waiting for me up there."

Bernie explained. "When I realized what I'd come across, I was careful to retrace my steps. I have photos and information on the people who came by after I found the body."

"You don't need to defend yourself. It's good for the investigation that you discovered the victim rather than some kid on a bike. Everything I hear about you is exemplary. You being here is lucky."

The compliment made Bernie uneasy. "You know, I've had better luck. Next time, I'd like to find a winning lottery ticket, not a dead guy."

Johnson climbed out of the sedan and locked it. "I'm going to the site. Stay here to keep the trail closed until Agent Berke and the ERT arrive."

Bernie knew ERT was the Evidence Response Team. "Will do."

Two more vehicles, a white coupe with a smashed front end and a relatively new dark blue SUV, pulled up to the parking area. Johnson studied them, then turned her attention back to Bernie.

"How far is the body?"

"Maybe fifteen minutes." Bernie picked up the rope and a water bottle and handed them to Johnson. "You or Bigman might want these for the dog."

"I'll be in touch for a follow-up interview, probably tomorrow. I'd like to get this investigation moving."

The sight of a white woman in jeans walking up a closed trail made it harder for Bernie to persuade the newcomer Navajo runners climbing out of their vehicles that the area was, indeed, off-limits, but she did it. FBI agents from the ERT arrived within half an hour, and one took her place as trail and parking lot monitor.

Bernie grabbed another bottle of water from Bigman's unit and left his keys with the FBI parking lot man. Picturing the red shoes and the torn black pants, Bernie started the jog back to their trailer.

Questions swirled as she ran. Who was the man? Why was he dead? Why was he there? Where had he been killed? Had the dog followed him?

She was halfway home when Chee's truck pulled up next to her. "Hey, beautiful. Want a ride?"

"I don't know. Are you trustworthy?"

"I may have ulterior motives, but I brought you a Coke." He reached across the seat and opened the passenger door.

The truck's air-conditioning felt great, almost too cool on her sweating arms. He handed her the cold can, and she rubbed it on the back of her hot neck before opening it and taking a sip.

"You just earned about a million husband points. Are you done working for today?"

"Well, they say even crime takes a holiday. So, yeah, for the moment."

"Who says that about crime?" Bernie put on her seat belt.

"Give me a minute." Chee chuckled. "I think it's the title of an old movie about a cop who sets up an elaborate scam to catch a crook."

"I never heard of it."

"That's because you're so young and cute."

For the first time in hours, she began to relax. "Me?"

"You're cute even when you're hot and stinky. But if you'd like a shower, I'll get dinner going while you're in there. And then you can tell me more about what happened if you want to."

As she felt the water against her skin, she flashed back to the trail and the body. Something bothered her about the crime scene, and it was more than being near the corpse.

Why make the effort to dump a body off a popular trail where it was likely to be discovered? Had the killer left the body as some sort of message? Who was the victim and how did he die?

She pulled back the thoughts and shampooed her hair. She turned off the water and grabbed for a towel. The FBI was in charge of homicides. She had plenty on her plate, but she'd talk to Largo and Johnson about helping with the case. There were plenty of Navajos who might recall more than they'd told her, and she had their names.

She walked out to the deck where Chee was cleaning the grill. He smiled when he saw her. "Your mother called while you were in the shower. I told her I'd let you know."

"What did she say?"

"She told me that you look too thin and to make sure you eat. She told me not to let you work so hard. She said she wants to talk to you about your sister. That covers it."

"I'll call her later. Let's take it easy for a while."

Chee chuckled. "I know you. You want to make some notes about that crime scene."

"Johnson said she needs to interview me again, probably tomorrow and—" The ringing of the house phone interrupted her. "And I bet that's Mama."

"I bet you're right."

Bernie looked at the caller ID before she answered. "Lieutenant! How good to hear from you."

"Hello, Bernie. I hope you're enjoying this beautiful day." Joe Leaphorn's voice sounded strong, and she loved the natural rhythm of his Navajo.

"Chee plans pork chops on the grill, and I made a pie to go with them. Come join us tonight." As she said it, she cringed at a vision of the sweet blackened mess.

"I can't. Speaking of Chee, is he free to come to the phone?"

"Yes, sir. Just a moment."

Chee's side of the conversation was brief, a string of "Yes, sirs," one "I'm really not comfortable with that," and then, "I'll think about it."

He said good-bye and put the phone on the table. She waited to hear what he'd share.

"Largo asked the Lieutenant if he'd mentor Wilson Sam."

"Why?"

"After the hay-sale argument, the captain is seriously annoyed with the rookie. He wants to help Sam before he screws up again and gets fired or killed."

"I meant why the Lieutenant. Sure, he's smart and well respected, but he isn't an active member of the department. He'll have to figure out what's going on with the rookie. Someone like you already knows the story."

"Largo thinks highly of the Lieutenant, plus, he has experience as a mentor, and now that he's retired he might have time to do it."

"So, why the phone call?"

"He heard about Sam's injury, and he wanted to check the story with me."

She could tell from the way Chee ended the sentence that there was more to come.

"Leaphorn's reluctant because he's at the beginning of a new PI case, but he owes Largo a favor. He asked if I'd give him a hand. I said I'd consider it, but I feel uncomfortable, like a snitch or something."

"I understand. But we'll be even more slammed if the rookie gets fired. If you can help, that would be great."

"The Lieutenant offered to meet with the rookie for an initial interview and then talk to Largo about his assessment. That might get me off the hook."

Chee began dinner preparations, and she continued to work on her chronology of discovering the body. Compiling the notes heightened her recall. She revisualized what she'd seen as she approached the path, searching not only for the extraordinary but for something slightly askew that might have relevance in the murder. She wrote down everything she remembered, no matter how minor and boring.

She'd nearly finished when she felt Chee's eyes on her.

She looked up, and he spoke. "Is something bothering you, sweetheart?"

"Why?"

"You're scowling."

She closed the notebook. "I can't get the sight of that body out of my mind."

"Dealing with the dead is part of the job, but it's not something I ever get used to either. And it's good that we don't. It keeps us human."

"I have more questions than answers."

"I know you. They are good questions."

As soon as he said it, she remembered Johnson's compliment and mentioned it to Chee. "I think she was just making nice with me."

"My philosophy is that when someone gives me a pat on the back, I accept it. It balances those times someone said something mean."

She smiled. "I better wrap up these notes." As

she wrote the final observations, she felt the tension drain away, as though putting what she'd seen on paper allowed her to leave it behind. At least for tonight.

They finished dinner, and because Chee had cooked, Bernie was cleaning up before she served what she could salvage from the charred pie. Baking and crime solving clearly didn't mix.

Chee enjoyed the evening's quiet. The rosy afterglow of sunset and the shift in temperature from hot to pleasantly warm added to his sense of well-being. He listened as crickets chirped their songs of longing, and then he heard something out of tune, a car turning onto his road. Officer Bigman, wearing khakis and a plaid short-sleeved shirt, climbed out of the white SUV. He hugged a round green watermelon to his chest. Chee respected Bigman as a fellow officer and liked him, too, but it was unusual for Bernie's clan brother to come for a visit.

Chee called to him. "Hey there. You taking your watermelon out for a ride?"

"Something like that."

"Well, bring it on over."

Bigman walked up the steps to the deck and placed the melon at the center of the table. It rolled to position itself onto a flat spot with a quiet thud.

Chee used a knuckle to thump it. "Sounds ripe. Early for watermelon, too."

Bigman chuckled. "And as I see it, it's never too early for ch'ééhjiyáán. I can eat watermelon at six a.m. or at midnight. Breakfast, lunch, and suppertime."

"Speaking of supper, we've got some salad and a pork chop if you're hungry."

"I ate at home with the mother-to-be. She can't have much at one sitting anymore, so she's snacking all the time. So am I." He patted his belly.

Bernie joined them. "At least have dessert with us. I made a pie."

"Is there coffee to go with that invitation?"

"Sure." But she hesitated a moment too long.

Bigman shook his head. "Don't go to any trouble."

Chee chimed in. "But I'd have some, too, if you make it."

"Sure, but try not to say anything exciting until I get back." Bernie went inside.

Chee motioned Bigman to a seat. "I haven't seen your wife for a while. I didn't realize you were about to become a dad."

Bigman focused on the watermelon. When he spoke, his voice was soft. "To tell you the truth, I don't know if I'm cut out to be a father. Melody tells me not to worry, but I mean, it's scary, bro. Scarier than facing a drunk with a broken bottle and a bad attitude. What do I know about being a dad?"

"Man, you'll do just fine. You know how to solve problems. Think of it that way."

"I'm not sure. I haven't been around many babies. They're little and vulnerable. How can you figure out what they want?"

"Well, if you get stuck, you can always ask

Bernie's mom. She has advice on everything. Or watch a video on the internet. That always works, right?"

Bigman laughed. "You ever think about having a kid?"

"I do. Being a dad would be great. You have a chance to help a new person learn all about the world." Chee thumped the melon again. "Relax. It will all work out."

Bigman stretched his legs under the table. "I guess you heard what happened when Bernie went for a jog. It was an exciting Saturday for the Shiprock substation."

"She told me you were the backup."

"Yeah, until the Feds came."

One of the things Chee liked about his Navajo friends was that they knew how to be quiet. They listened to Bernie run the water and to some birds along the river. A few moments later, the familiar aroma of coffee drifted through the kitchen window. Chee heard the click of the cabinet opening and pictured Bernie moving the cups to the counter.

She rejoined them with napkins, sugar, and the three cups of coffee on a tray. She set that all on the table. "I'll get the pie."

"Sit with us first. I want your ideas on something, Sister." Bigman helped himself to coffee. "I was telling him about our adventures along the trail. Did you hear what happened after you left?"

"Did the dog confess?"

"Not yet. I know you think it was up to something."

"Usually they are, even Chihuahuas. So what happened?"

Bigman grew serious. "Well, Agent Johnson walked up there to take a look at what you found, all confident and everything. I told her the scene was as secure as possible and motioned toward the red shoes. She went to the body through the weeds. I noticed that she took the same path you did. She squatted down by the guy's face, and I heard her swearing. Then she straightened up all of a sudden and put her hands on her chest. She said, 'Michael, Michael. You stupid jerk. I told you to be careful.' Then she started swearing again and walked away from the body, toward the river."

Bernie moved a cup of coffee toward Chee. "Wow. What else did she say?"

"Nothing. When she came back, I said, 'So you recognize him?' and she just turned toward the trail for a while and then asked me questions about what I'd seen. I wonder if the man was a former agent or a guy she investigated, or maybe an informant or something."

"Maybe even an old boyfriend." Bernie took a cup of coffee for herself. "I'll see what she'll tell me when we do our interview."

Chee noticed Bigman fidgeting. Talking about the dead, even obliquely, wasn't recommended for fathers-to-be. Time to change the subject. He gave the melon another final thump. "Sounds about perfect. Since you brought this lovely thing, I believe we should enjoy it."

"Absolutely. This is your house. You do the honors."

Bernie heard her cell phone buzz from where it was charging in the kitchen. She remembered that she had not called Mama.

"I've got to catch my phone, so I'll bring plates and a knife. I'll be right back."

The call was Agent Johnson. She went right to business. "I've got some questions about the people you encountered on the trail. Can you meet me at the office tomorrow?"

"You're working late."

"Yeah. I don't like the way that dead guy showed up here. Nine a.m. OK for you?"

"Yes." As if I have a choice here, Bernie thought. "I have some questions for you, too."

"I'll tell Largo about the meeting." Johnson ended the call.

She brought out the knife, plates, and more napkins. Chee sliced off the end of the watermelon and then a thick round that he cut into thirds. He put a wedge on each plate. Bigman picked up the melon and took a bite. "A good one."

Chee tried his. "This is the taste of summer. I'm glad you brought it."

Bernie's was untouched, and he noticed the look on her face, one side of her mouth a bit higher than the other. "That was Johnson, wasn't it?"

"Yeah. We're meeting tomorrow. I'm glad. It will be nice to share what I saw, even though it doesn't seem like much. If she knows the dead guy, that should make the case easier to solve. I want to talk to her about staying involved in the investigation."

They ate for a few minutes, and then Chee reached for her hand under the table and gave it a squeeze. "See that guy sitting there, the man who brought the watermelon, a cop who confronts gang-bangers high on meth or a maniac with a knife on a regular basis?"

"I do."

"Well, he needs some reassurance as he prepares to face his own little bundle of joy."

Bigman cleared his throat. "The situation is totally different. I got training to become a cop, but what do I know about diaper rash, bottles, putting a Little Someone in a car seat? I've never been around a tiny new person. It makes me nervous, I admit it, to think this little soul will be dependent on me and his mom."

Bernie said, "You'll learn. Our parents did."

"I hope so. I feel more comfortable at a traffic stop than in charge of a newborn."

"You'll be a fine father. Don't worry." She took a bite of the watermelon, juicy, delicious, and the color of a brilliant sunset. "Did you get this at the flea market?"

"No. My neighbor's boy grew it at his grandmother's place."

"They had a few at the flea. Hey, do you remember Mr. Natachi?"

Bigman nodded. "He's the gentleman who lived near your mother, right? I think he was kind of sweet on her."

"That's the one. I ran into him this morning at the market. He's living in Chinle now with his granddaughter, Ryana. They came to visit his sister, and he found his stolen bolo tie here in somebody's booth."

"That was fortunate."

Chee wiped his mouth with a napkin. "Not so much for the guy who had it for sale. Bernie got a description of him."

Bernie said, "He left after he returned the old man's bolo. A few hours later, Ryana called and implied that her grandfather didn't remember things very well and that the bolo hadn't been stolen. Mr. Natachi seemed sharp to me."

Bigman pursed his lips. "That sure gets my attention. It makes me think someone in the family took it. Maybe a relative on drugs, something like that. Something to follow up."

He finished his melon and put the rind down on the plate. "Sergeant, I, ah . . . this is awkward. I need to ask you a favor. I know I'm supposed to go to Chinle tomorrow to work with Lieutenant Black there on those stolen-property cases. But Melody believes that the baby will decide it wants to get born while I'm out, you know. Or while I'm driving where there's no cell service for her to call me."

They watched Bigman collecting his thoughts.

"You and Largo get along great. I was wondering if you could ask him if he'd send the rookie to Chinle? The experience would do him good."

Chee said, "Did you hear what happened to him?"

"Don't tell me." Bigman smiled. "He tried to bust that tough gal from Newcomb who always has the weed in the back of her car."

"No, no." Chee exhaled. "He placed himself in the middle of an argument about some rotten hay and got a broken nose and a puffy eye for his troubles."

"How bad is he?"

"He has to breathe through his mouth. His eye has swollen into a tiny slit." Chee narrowed his own in sympathy.

"That explains why I got the call to back up Bernie even though I was out in the middle of nowhere."

"I was glad to see you. When is the baby due?"

Bigman made a tent with his fingers. "Any day. Next week? Tomorrow? The official arrival date is ten days from now, but Melody doesn't think she'll last that long. It's my fault she's anxious. I told her I'd attend the classes with her about labor and delivery and all that, but I got called in to work those nights."

Bernie wrinkled her forehead. "Every week?"

"Actually, I volunteered for duty so I could miss the classes. I didn't want to be there for that female stuff. Now, this is the last week, and Melody told me there's a film about the whole birth process tomorrow night and then intensive coaching for both of us the next three nights. She said she really needs me to go with her. She never said that before. Then she started to cry." Bigman turned his hands palms up. "I'd rather go to Chinle, but I might get stuck working where I couldn't get back in time for the movie or the last three classes. You know that a case can get dicey, even one that seems simple like this burglary stuff."

They knew. Drug use and burglaries went together like weft and warp, and they'd heard rumors of mafia types hanging around Chinle. Bernie and Chee had both been on more than one call where something that should have been simple grew complicated and violent, and took a long time to resolve.

Bernie wiped the watermelon juice off her hands with a napkin. "I'll go to Chinle for you. Chee can get Largo to OK that."

"No, I'll handle the Chinle burglary stuff." Chee saw Bernie frown. "You have to stay here to deal with Johnson and the body, and to figure out if the Shiprock guy selling Mr. Natachi's bolo has ties to Chinle and the rest of the crimes there. I've worked well with the Chinle commander before, so that ought to make things go a little smoother. It's all up to the captain, of course, but I think he'll agree."

"Thanks." Bigman sighed. "I appreciate whatever you can do for me, man. Melody is really on my case about this darn movie. I hope the rookie gets back to full steam soon."

"We all do. He'll need to pull his weight so you can be with the new mom and help with that little one when it gets here. Your wife will need a break and some extra attention, too."

Bernie nudged him with her elbow. "Sergeant Chee, how did you get so smart about family dynamics?"

"Oh, it's another of my superpowers."

Country music that sounded like Loretta Lynn on a bad day intruded on the night. Bigman looked startled, then pulled his phone from his pocket. "It's my wife. Do you mind?"

"Go ahead." They listened to him say "Yes" and "Of course" and "It's all set" and then "Don't worry, I'm leaving now."

He turned to them both. "She has bad leg cramps. I've got to go. Thanks for talking to Largo about this, Sergeant."

"That movie might come in handy when you're on patrol and a baby is about to get born. Think of it that way."

Bernie smiled. "I get any calls involving pregnant women, I'm referring them to you. You'll be the department's specialist."

Bigman winced. He gazed at the watermelon. "I want you guys to keep that, but could I take a piece home for the missus?"

"Sure." Chee cut a big slice.

"Bring it in the kitchen, and we'll put it in a bag." Bernie walked inside, and Bigman followed. "You want some pie, too?"

When she removed the tea towel covering it, the fragrance of fresh peaches, cinnamon, and sugar competed with the char of burned crust. The smell reminded her of how the mystery of the bolo had absorbed her. Now the murder had added to the problems to solve. She could hardly wait to talk to Johnson tomorrow.

"You keep the pie. I forgot that Melody is supposed to watch her sugar."

"Let us know about the baby."

After she walked him to the door, she cut a piece of pie for Chee and one for herself, using a fork to break off the burned parts. She took dessert back to the deck. They watched the stars begin to show themselves in the dark distance.

"I'm looking forward to working the local connection in the burglaries. I want to find the man who tried to sell that bolo."

"Mr. Natachi was fortunate that you came along when you did." Chee put his arm around her. "I've never seen Bigman like that. He's so uptight, you'd think this was the world's first kid. Do you picture me that way when I'm about to become a dad? All nervous and worried?"

"No, you'd just call on another of your superpowers. I know I'm not ready for parenthood yet. Are you?"

He kissed her in answer. Then he reached for the pie.

5

The Navajo Inn was about half filled, the customers a mix of area families, bilagáana and Diné, along with summer tourists, all enjoying the bounty of the breakfast buffet. Leaphorn spotted Jim Bean at a table by the windows.

"Yá'át'ééh." Bean stood to greet him and flashed his ready smile. Leaphorn noticed that his friend had thickened around the middle and had a glint of gray at his temples.

Leaphorn sat across from him, and the waitress brought coffee. He put the brown envelope from the museum director on the table between them.

"I read about what happened to you a few years ago, Lieutenant. You look pretty darn healthy for a guy who almost died."

Driving to the restaurant that Sunday morning had stirred Joe Leaphorn's memory of the attack that put him in the hospital. He never again parked in the spot where the shooter had ambushed him. He gave Bean a look intended to say he did not want to talk about the incident.

"I got your note that speaking English gives you a bit of trouble. Don't worry about it. Just say it and I'll figure it out."

"Ya still workin?"

"I'm planning to retire next year. I want to write a book about postal inspectors." He held up his large hand, palm toward the Lieutenant. "Now, I know you're thinking that nobody much cares, but you'd be wrong."

Leaphorn raised his eyebrows.

"Don't give me that look. The Postal Inspection Service is the oldest federal law enforcement agency, even older than the Declaration of Independence. We go back to 1772, when Ben Franklin became the first person appointed as what they called a postal surveyor. His job was to make sure the mail stayed safe and got to where it was going. The Continental Congress named him postmaster, and when George Washington became president, he kept Franklin on the job. We were the first federal law enforcement agency to use the title of Special Agent for our officers, and we kept it until 1880, when Congress decided we had to call ourselves inspectors."

Leaphorn sipped his coffee, and Bean changed the subject. "So, from what Louisa said, you have a case you think an old postal inspector might help with."

"Rye. Read dis." He'd typed up a note explaining the anonymous gift that he needed to trace, the phony return address, and the fact that a potentially valuable item was missing. He gave it to his friend.

Bean read and nodded. "You need to find out if the piece was actually in the box before you can claim it was stolen. That means tracking down the shipper, who obviously doesn't want to be found."

"Thas wha I tink." Leaphorn cringed at his broken English. His professors at Arizona State University would be horrified.

Although he had dutifully eaten his oatmeal that morning, the aroma of sausage and bacon from the buffet table gnawed away his resistance. He looked toward the line of people, and back at Bean.

"Joe, I just saw the waiter put down a full tray of potatoes." Bean pushed his chair away from the table. "Let's go."

Leaphorn took a bit of everything except the oatmeal in the big cauldron. He noticed that Bean loaded his plate with fruit but added a sampling of the other choices. He enjoyed his friend's passion for life—he went for the gusto. As Leaphorn served himself some bacon, he heard a voice.

"Save me a little of that."

Across from the bowl with the melon and strawberries, he saw a woman he privately referred to as Dahsáni, or Porcupine. The Diné honored the animal as one of the People's protectors. Tribal Councilor Elsbeth Walker deserved the name, not only because of her prickly attitude but also for her strong commitment to whatever cause she took up on behalf of her constituents. An unsmiling teenage girl and a young man in a wheelchair followed her in line.

"Councilor Walker, good morning. This is Jim Bean, a friend from my days as a lieutenant."

The councilor nodded to Bean across the buffet table. "Elsbeth Walker. Nice to meet you." She spoke to him in English. "These are my children, Annie and Dylan."

Mrs. Walker said, "Mr. Bean, what brings you to Window Rock?"

"Catching up with a friend, this old man here."

"Are you in law enforcement?"

"Yes, ma'am. I'm a postal inspector."

"I happened to be in Washington at a meeting a few years ago when those letters with anthrax caused such a panic. Was that one of your cases?"

Bean stabbed a pair of plump link sausages and moved them to his plate. "Well, yes, ma'am. The FBI did quite a bit of the work with us on that."

Annie looked bored and embarrassed. Her brother seemed interested in him and Bean. Because of Dylan's age and the wheelchair, Leaphorn wondered if his disability came from military service in one of the recent conflicts. The Navajo Nation had a high percentage of veterans, disabled and otherwise.

Walker looked at Leaphorn and switched to Navajo. "You were going to call me for coffee."

"No, you said you'd call me."

Walker smiled. "I did say that. I'll do it." She acknowledged Bean with a nod of her head. "Nice to meet you."

Back at the table, Bean finished his eggs and started on the pancakes. "How are you doing as a retiree, Joe? Finding things to keep you busy?"

"Ya." Leaphorn wanted to say he enjoyed the variety of private investigation work and the opportunity to look into cases he would not have handled on the police force, but the idea was too complicated for his spoken English.

"How's that guy who worked with you doing? I forget his name, but the fellow who wanted to be a medicine man on his days off."

Leaphorn knew he meant Jim Chee.

"Kay. Merry."

"Married? Well, they say there's someone for everyone. I tried some of that online dating stuff." Bean picked up a piece of crisp bacon with his fingers. "I met some stinkers, and then I struck gold."

If Bean expected him to share details of his private life, he'd have to wait a long time. Leaphorn tried the fried potatoes mixed with onions and green peppers. He could see Louisa frowning at him as he added salt. Delicious.

"Yes, sir. Finally, I met a keeper. Smart, beautiful, kind, and sweet. Her name is Wanda. I'll introduce you next time you come to Phoenix."

Leaphorn nodded. "Ya workin some inerstin cases?" *Working*, he thought. *Interesting.*

"Lately, it's been employment fraud. You know, make money at home, pyramid schemes, mystery-shopper scams. These crooks are amazingly clever, and most of the people ripped off are too ashamed to complain, so the scams keep on rollin'." Bean paused. "You remember the anthrax attack, the one that lady referred to, when some creep sent poison through the mail?"

"Ya."

"We worked that case by tracking down who would have had access to the poison. You might try working backwards on the mystery-gift problem, you know, puzzling out the origin of the missing piece or some of the rarer items that actually arrived. Moving from that angle to track the shipper."

Leaphorn nodded.

"You already thought of that, didn't you?"

Leaphorn smiled.

The men ate in silence for a while; then Bean looked again at the paper Leaphorn had given him. "That gunshot didn't hurt the part of your brain in charge of planning, did it?" He folded the sheet. "I ought to know something in a few days, if luck is with me. I'll be in touch."

"Tanks." Leaphorn reached for the bill, but Bean put his hand out to stop him.

"This is on me, or rather, on the government. I have an expense account for this trip, and I need to keep my network strong."

They walked out of the restaurant together into the warm Arizona afternoon. Summer clouds were building, but Leaphorn knew from experience that they would not bring moisture, except perhaps a brief, light sprinkle. The monsoons that briefly drenched the Arizona desert had yet to arrive.

"I'll work on your problem tomorrow. If you think of some details that might help, here's my email." Bean handed him a card. "That's the best way to contact me. I can be hard to reach on the phone."

Leaphorn recognized the lie. Bean's consideration for his disability touched him.

Back home, he found Louisa at the dining room table with a large picture book.

"How was your meeting?"

"Fye." He thought of the easiest way to explain what Bean would do. "Wade a mint." Leaphorn went to his office for his computer, then moved Giddi from the chair the cat had claimed and sat next to Louisa. He opened his laptop, typed out a summary, and turned the screen toward her. They had done this before.

Louisa read the note. "Did he think he could help you?"

Leaphorn shrugged. "Maybe." Then he typed a rehash of Bean's advice about tracking the outstanding pieces as clues to the collector donor.

"That's the same idea you had. That's what I've been working on. Look at this." She turned to a page in the book she had marked with a Post-it. "Do you see the similarities between the description Daisy Pinto gave you of the bracelet and this?"

"Course."

"Indeed. They are from the same artist. This one received best of show at one of the first Heard Museum Indian Markets, so besides its workmanship, the artist's acclaim adds to the value. I didn't realize I had such good taste." She tapped the photo. "And so did whoever wanted to give it to the museum. And so did the thief. If there was a thief."

Leaphorn looked at the photo and the caption, which included the name of Robert Peshlakai, a Navajo silversmith from Fort Defiance, Arizona. He hadn't heard of the artist, but that wasn't a bad thing. It meant that the man probably hadn't caused serious trouble.

Louisa closed the book. "I'm going to do a little internet search for Mr. Peshlakai."

"Guh."

Louisa pulled out her cell phone and typed in something, studied it, typed in something else, read whatever came up on the screen, and frowned. She put her phone down. "There are a lot of Peshlakais in the jewelry world, but Robert Peshlakai isn't much of a marketer. No website. No Facebook. The only place I could find that carries his work is the Hubbell Trading Post."

Leaphorn remembered the phone number and called. When someone answered, he spoke in Navajo.

"Hold on, sir. I'll get someone to help you."

Leaphorn identified himself to the next speaker.

"Yá'át'ééh. I'm Gene Willie, trading post manager. You're that detective lieutenant from Tséghá-hoodzání, right?"

"Retired lieutenant but still in Window Rock." He thought about the best way to approach the topic. "I'm doing some work as an investigator now for a client who has a question about something she thinks the jeweler Robert Peshlakai may have made."

"Can you hold on?"

"Sure." Leaphorn heard a muted conversation and realized that Willie was dealing with a customer.

Willie returned after a few moments.

"Well, Lieutenant, things may be going your

way. If you'd like, you can meet Mr. Peshlakai. He told us last month he would be coming in today to pick up a check."

"When do you expect him?"

Willie chuckled. "Hard to say. He usually gets here just before closing time, or maybe just after."

"And when is that?"

"We're on summer hours, so six p.m., more or less."

"I'm interested in talking to him, so if he gets there before I do, could you ask him to wait?"

"I'll ask him. But he's a feisty one. I can't promise he'll stay. Is he in trouble?"

"Not as far as I'm concerned. My friend, who will be with me, has a beautiful bracelet she bought at your trading post a while back. She thinks Mr. Peshlakai made it, but I'm not sure. I'd like him to take a look." He was glad Louisa didn't speak enough Navajo to understand that he questioned the authenticity of her precious bracelet.

"That's interesting. Artists don't like someone stealing their designs."

Right, Leaphorn thought, and the suspicion of plagiarism gave Peshlakai another reason to meet a couple of strangers. "I have some photos of baskets and pots I could use help identifying. Would you be willing to take a look?"

"Why not, as long as I have time."

He told Louisa his idea and invited her to join him on the trip. Neither of them had been to the historic trading post for years. They planned to arrive about five p.m. to look around and to be there when the jeweler arrived. Unlike many places he'd visited on the Navajo Nation in his line of work, the Hubbell post was an easy drive on paved roads and only about half an hour away. Louisa wore the bracelet, and he took some of the photographs Mrs. Pinto had given him.

Louisa had done the chauffeuring for months. Thankfully, those days were gone. He made a much better driver than passenger.

He noticed Louisa looking at her bracelet. "I wonder how old Mr. Peshlakai is. I must have purchased this twenty years ago, and it doesn't look like something made by a beginner. When I bought it, I remember that there were matching earrings and a pendant for sale, too, but I couldn't afford the whole set. I loved the bracelet the most. I looked at the set a long time and finally decided it was better to have groceries for the month than more jewelry."

"Smar." Leaphorn noticed the sedan that pulled onto AZ 265 West, and slowed to give the driver space. "Food is guh."

She laughed. "That's what I figured."

They passed the Window Rock flea market, busy as usual, and crossed Black Creek Wash and then the junction for St. Michael's school and mission. Then came the clinic, a gas station, a family restaurant where Leaphorn met with potential suspects and witnesses in his days on the force, and an assortment of other businesses.

The road started as four lanes with piñon and juniper trees on both sides. It narrowed to two lanes as it climbed to 7,000 feet. The route dropped into sage and sheep country. Crows soared against the vivid blue summer sky.

When they came to the junction for Kinlichee, Louisa had a question: "What does that word mean?"

Leaphorn pronounced the Navajo name for the settlement, Kin Dah Lichi'i. "Red hows in da distance. Pueblo ruins." The truck scooted over Fish Wash with coal-rich Black Mesa framing the horizon to the west. Leaphorn turned left just before they crossed Ganado Wash, glad that the Hubbell Trading Post National Historic Site entrance marker stood large. The junction would otherwise be easy to miss.

They bounced along the washboards and over handmade speed bumps for a quick half mile. He smelled the green alfalfa in the field across from the sandstone building that housed the visitor center and bookstore. The road ended directly in the dirt parking lot. He recalled that the historic Hubbell home and outbuildings lay beyond.

Leaphorn assessed the other vehicles before he parked, a little game he played. Could he figure out which cars and trucks belonged to whoever was inside? He assumed the two white vans were part of a school or church field trip. Among the other vehicles, he saw a truck from the 1990s or maybe 2000 with Arizona plates. It looked well used and well loved. He tied it to the trader who worked here, and the other vehicles to visitors. He didn't see anything that looked appropriate for an aged silversmith.

Louisa took off her seat belt. "I love this place. So rich with history. Several of my students wrote papers about it. Do you know the story?"

He nodded. The Hubbell Trading Post, the oldest trading post operating on the Navajo Nation, dated to just after the treaty the US government made with the Navajos after the Long Walk. The buildings were just a little younger, Leaphorn thought, than Juanita's dress. Don Lorenzo Hubbell had the business sense and social skills to create an establishment that functioned for decades, beginning in 1878. He did business with the Navajos who returned home after four years of hellish captivity, encouraging them to create silver jewelry, baskets, and rugs to exchange for flour, coffee, canned goods, and other items not easily found on the remote reservation. Besides being a store, the post had served as a home to the Hubbell family and a haven for visitors, among them Theodore Roosevelt. After Don Lorenzo's death, family members operated the establishment until 1967. Then the 160-acre homestead, buildings, and trading post were sold to the National Park Service.

Louisa opened the passenger door. "I haven't been here in ages. I hope Mr. Peshlakai has arrived. I'm eager to show him my bracelet."

Leaphorn wanted to spend a few minutes looking at the old post. He planned to talk to the trader about the other possibly valuable items in the photographs, check in with the jeweler when he arrived, and go home.

The Arizona heat baked them as they headed to the entrance. Stepping into the front room was like walking into the past, although the goods on the shelves included disposable diapers and batteries.

The Western National Parks Association main-tained the trading post much as it had looked when the Hubbell family operated it.

"It's just like I remember." Louisa smiled. "I bet the jewelry is still in the next room."

Leaphorn watched her head directly to the counter that held bracelets. He stayed in the main room, waiting to catch the eye of the trader who was dealing with a young Navajo woman buying a yellow container of engine oil. In the old days, this post and most of the others throughout the reserva-tion had traders who were non-Navajo. Leaphorn was pleased to see Diné on both sides of the trans-action now.

The woman paid, and the man came from be-hind the counter and greeted Leaphorn. "Yá'át'ééh. You must be the one I talked to on the phone."

"Yá'át'ééh. Joe Leaphorn."

"Gene Willie." He introduced himself formally with his clans, the Navajo way.

Leaphorn, who usually didn't follow this formal-ity, reciprocated. "This old store looks better than ever."

"It's a labor of love. The visitors like it, and the locals are happy to have a quick place to pick up some aspirin and another market for their weaving."

"My friend Louisa is in the other room. Let me introduce you. And then I brought the photos I mentioned. I could use your help to solve a mystery."

"Sure, but first I have to give an introductory talk to the students, high schoolers from Indiana. You're welcome to listen in."

"Thank you." Leaphorn would have preferred

to get the business done, but he assumed Louisa would enjoy it.

She looked up from the jewelry case when he and Willie entered the room. Leaphorn did the honors.

"Is Mr. Peshlakai here?"

"Not yet."

"I'm excited to have a chance to meet him. What an opportunity to make a personal connection with an artist who made something that I love." She extended her left arm toward Willie. "This is one of my favorite things." She slipped off the bracelet and passed it to him. "You'll see the jeweler's mark inside."

Willie set it on his right palm and moved his arm up and down, judging its heft. Then he moved it closer to his face, looked at the mark, and handed it back to her. "It's beautiful, and I think you are correct. It could be one of his early pieces. His new work is lighter, maybe because silver is more expensive. You'll have to ask him."

Leaphorn noticed the dozen or so young people in shorts and T-shirts gathered in the adjoining room, most of them fiddling with their phones. Willie excused himself. "Time to talk to the kids. Come on."

They followed him and took a seat on the folded rugs. Like the rest of the post, the room displayed relics from the old trading days, including antique guns, traps, saddles, and animal heads.

Willie spoke with ease, using a rug with the classic storm pattern as a template for his talk. He explained that each rug told a complicated story and that only the weaver herself could provide the complete explanation. Leaphorn thought of the missing dress. What tales could it relate of struggle and survival, of the strong woman who wove it with her own hands and wore the dress with pride?

Willie mentioned spirit lines, a technique weavers use to keep their creative gift from being trapped within the rug's borders. He discussed how the term *chief blanket* confused history because the Navajo had no chiefs.

He draped a blanket over his shoulders. "Worn this way, the blanket says that I am in the market for a wife." The students chuckled appropriately.

Leaphorn looked for Peshlakai. He'd assumed that the man would have arrived by now. As a cop, Leaphorn figured, he had wasted at least a full year of his life waiting for people who came late or not at all. As an investigator, he had tried to change that pattern. He didn't like finding himself in the same situation again.

When Willie finished, the students asked a few questions and filed out to tour the old Hubbell home. Willie and Louisa resumed their conversation about jewelry, and Leaphorn listened with half an ear until impatience got the better of him. He rose from his comfortable seat on the pile of rugs, noticing the stiffness in his knees, and spoke to Willie in Navajo. "Can you take a quick look at the pictures I mentioned?"

Willie moved his hand toward the other room. "Sure thing. Put the photos on top of the jewelry display case in there, spread them out. Peshlakai knows most of the silversmiths around here and all over Navajo. You can talk to him about any jewelry."

"You think he's still coming?" Louisa glanced at her watch. "It's almost closing time."

"I do." Willie grinned. "But before we block your view with photos, is there something in the case I can show you, ma'am?"

Leaphorn winced. Louisa had already looked at the jewelry. Wasn't that enough?

"Are any of these Robert Peshlakai's pieces?"

Willie tapped the case. "See that brooch in the center with the greenish stone? That's the only one I have left. He brought it in earlier this summer." The trader walked behind the counter, opened the case, and reached in for the box with the pin. "The man did amazing work, didn't he?"

Leaphorn heard a vehicle approach the building.

Louisa took the brooch and placed it in the palm of her hand. "It's gorgeous. Look at the detail. He's quite an artist."

Leaphorn said, "You said *did* amazing work. Is he retired?"

They heard the front door open. "Anyone workin' here?" The male voice calling from the front of the store had an accent. West Texas maybe, Leaphorn thought. Not Peshlakai.

"I'll be right there, sir."

Louisa gave Willie the pin, and he returned it to the locked case. They followed the trader into the big room.

A potbellied man in khaki shorts stood at the counter with two little girls, one on each side. They wore matching T-shirts that said "Regent Family Reunion, Sedona, Arizona."

While Willie sold the man cold drinks, Louisa examined the books and boxes of herbal tea. "Joe, did you hear what Willie said about the origin of Ganado red? That's not quite the same as the story I know. Interesting, isn't it, how these legends develop and change over time?" Leaphorn watched the tourist take forever to pay and leave. Louisa paused her lecture when Willie came over to them and switched topics. "How long before you close?"

"Another fifteen minutes. If it were my call, we'd do this the traditional way, and I'd wait until Peshlakai got here. But since the store is part of a national system, we follow the rules."

The time was nearly up when a vehicle that needed a muffler pulled onto the road. Leaphorn followed the noise to the front of the store and, through the screen door, saw the truck park. A short, round Navajo man climbed out on the passenger side. His thick gray hair swung against his shoulders as he walked to the door.

"Hey there. I made it."

"Yá'át'ééh." Willie introduced Louisa. Leaphorn switched to Navajo and did the traditional introduction with his clans. Peshlakai reciprocated. They were not related.

"I think I've heard of you. You used to work out of Window Rock and you were a cop or something?"

"That's correct." Leaphorn was accustomed to encounters like this. Usually the person then referred to a relative he had arrested.

But Peshlakai surprised him. "My son married into your late wife's clan. I never had the privilege of meeting her, but I heard that she was a fine woman. And they speak well of you, too."

Leaphorn nodded. Emma had been the love of his life. He thought of her less often now, but always with a pang of revisited grief and a longing for her sweet, calm presence.

Willie turned to Peshlakai and spoke in English. "This lady here wants to show you something."

Louisa removed the bracelet. Without a word, she handed it to the artist.

He looked puzzled for a moment. Then he grinned. "I made this after I got out of the army. I gave it to my wife, but, well, we sold it here at this very store." He ran his index finger inside the band. "You've worn this many times. I guess you like it."

"It's my favorite. Was it one of the first you created?"

"Sort of. I started making jewelry in high school, whenever I had a little money for silver and my uncle had the time to teach me. Silver didn't cost as much back then, but back then I didn't have any money. Same as now." Peshlakai chuckled.

He returned the bracelet to her, and Louisa slid it on her wrist as she spoke. "I was admiring your pin in the display case. It's lovely, modern. A bit simpler but more sophisticated than this and in the same spirit."

"Thanks. Ahéhee'. I don't see so good now, so I try to make it easier on myself."

Willie focused on Louisa. "That bracelet of yours

is a classic, museum quality, and I'm not just saying that because the artist is in the room. People hold on to them."

Peshlakai grinned. "If you ever get tired of your old bracelet, I'll take it off your hands."

Leaphorn wondered what his lady friend would say, and she surprised him by saying nothing.

Peshlakai turned to Leaphorn. "So, now that you're retired, are you thinking of becoming a silversmith and giving me some competition? Is that what you wanna talk about?"

"No." Leaphorn looked at Louisa. "I hah trouble wid English."

Louisa said, "I'm going to look at those lovely rugs again while you two talk."

Peshlakai watched her walk away. "Nice lady. Good taste in jewelry. So what lies can I tell you?"

"I do some consulting for the department. They pay me to help with cold cases. When I have the time and interest, I take on some private clients."

"I know about that from TV. You do missing-person stuff?"

"Well, a few years back a woman hired me to search for her daughter, a girl in her twenties who was working out here in Navajo and disappeared. I tracked her down." It turned out the daughter was dead, but he didn't tell Peshlakai that. "The person I'm working for now also asked me to find something that's missing. She received a box that had gifts and a list of information on them. She asked me to see what I could learn about a bracelet that wasn't included in the package. The description mentioned what sounds like your jeweler's stamp. She'd like to track it down, and that's why I came to talk to you."

"Why not just ask the guy who sent it?" Peshlakai laughed. "I guess I could be an investigator."

"She would have asked, but the box arrived anonymously."

"He's probably her old boyfriend. Maybe even the ex-husband."

Leaphorn realized he hadn't asked Mrs. Pinto about any personal relationships with collectors or friends that might have generated the gift. But the package was addressed to the museum, not to her. "It wasn't that kind of a present. Nothing romantic about it."

"Oh." Peshlakai drew his lips together in a thin line. "Did the things come from someone who died?"

"Not as far as I know. The bracelet was part of a set that included earrings and a necklace. She gave me a photo of those. If you'd be willing to look, I'll show you."

Leaphorn shifted his weight. His back complained about too much standing, and both knees joined the chorus. He waited for the man to agree to or reject his request, or ask a question.

Peshlakai exhaled. "I want to make sure that nothing I made got involved with the dark side, you know? Murder, suicide, or something like that. Could you tell from the picture?"

Leaphorn considered the question. "The photos show the earrings and the necklace and the table they sat on. Nothing more."

"Do you figure this lady's friend who sent the box was involved in a heist or something?"

"I don't think so."

"OK. Let me see."

Leaphorn put the envelope on the jewelry case and pulled out the stack of photos. He had arranged the pictures of jewelry together with the earrings identified as Peshlakai's work on the top. Next came the necklace.

The jeweler held the first picture close to his eyes. "Do you have another photo of these?"

"No."

"Well, they might be part of a group I did way back when. Or maybe not." Peshlakai picked up the necklace picture and examined it. "I can't tell because I can't see details on it well enough. Sorry, man. I like these. Even if they aren't mine, they're good work."

"Let's assume they are yours." Leaphorn took a step closer to the jeweler. "Would you have made a bracelet to go with them?"

"Sure, I could have. Back in those days, someone convinced me that ladies liked things that went together. I used to say, 'If you buy the bracelet, I'll give you a deal on the earrings.' Or I'd put it the other way if someone wanted to buy just the earrings."

"Did you keep track of who bought your jewelry?"

"Sort of. Just the expensive stuff, or things on consignment to galleries and such." He handed the photos back to Leaphorn. "I used to tell the men who came with their wives, 'You know you'll probably do something to get her riled up. Better to have a nice gift on hand so you don't end up at Walmart in the middle of the night.'"

Peshlakai motioned toward the photo. "I made earrings like that to go with the bracelets a long time ago. They sold pretty well."

Leaphorn saw Louisa heading toward them. He hoped she wouldn't interrupt the interview. She did. "So, are you two about done?"

Peshlakai switched to English. "Talking about this brings back memories from those days when I could see real good."

Louisa pointed to the glasses that hung around her neck. "I have to wear these now for anything up close. Crossword puzzles, reading a book, instructions on a prescription bottle."

"You're lucky. My eyes have the kind of problem that can't be fixed with glasses. They named it macular degeneration. My wife used to say I was a degenerate, back in the days when beer was my buddy, so I guess it fits." He chuckled. "She tells me I shouldn't be driving, so she does most of it. It makes me feel bad, but there's not much I can do."

Leaphorn understood the situation. In a remote, rural world where public transportation was hard to come by, separating a man from his wheels condemned him to begging for rides or living in isolation.

Louisa took a step toward the door. "Let's talk outside. Mr. Willie has to close up. It's already past six." She glanced at the door and then back at them. Neither man moved. Louisa frowned. "When Joe was hurt, I did the driving. It made him nervous when I was behind the wheel. He's a terrible passenger. Right?"

Leaphorn winced.

Peshlakai winked at him.

"Did Joe show you the pictures?"

"Yes. I looked at the earrings and the necklace. They're real nice. I hope I made them."

"My friend Daisy told Joe they should have been in a box with other items, some interesting things, actually, that came without a return address. Can you imagine that?"

Leaphorn scowled at her, but Louisa kept talking.

"If you're heading back to Fort Defiance now, we're on your way. I can call Daisy. You and your wife could stop at our house and then we could—"

Leaphorn put a hand on her arm, and she grew quiet. He felt her body tense. The woman gave him a dark look. He removed his hand and switched back to Navajo. Louisa went outside.

"Daisy is the woman who hired me. She's a friend of Louisa."

"If Daisy, that woman you're working for, could let me see the real earrings and the necklace, instead of looking at the picture, I would know for sure if I made them. I'd love to hold these again."

"That might be possible. How can I reach you?"

"No problem." He slipped a slim black phone from his pants pocket. "My wife got this for me so she can keep tabs." He gave Leaphorn his number. "I'll put yours in here, too, so I can call you when I need to talk to a gray-haired investigator."

Leaphorn hesitated, then watched the man input his cell number. Peshlakai's screen had type several times larger than that on Leaphorn's phone.

Willie came up to them with some papers in hand. "Did this guy tell you some of his best stuff is in museum collections, places like that? Once he got famous, I didn't think we'd see him again. But here he is." He handed Peshlakai a check and a form to sign.

The men moved to the porch. Peshlakai made his good-byes and climbed into the blue truck. He knew the trader was ready to go home, too, but he had a final request. "Can you quickly look at those photos I mentioned?"

Willie motioned to the wooden bench on the porch. "Sit."

Leaphorn extracted the pictures. Willie perched next to him and motioned to Louisa, who was coming back from the now-closed bookstore, to join them.

"No thanks. I need to walk a little." Leaphorn heard the edge to her voice.

He explained to Willie that his client wanted to thank whoever had sent the items in the pictures. "Some of these things look old and interesting. I wonder if any of these pieces might have come from here." He hoped he'd said enough to capture the man's interest.

Willie glanced at each picture and set a few aside. He handed the larger pile to Leaphorn. "These are nothing special, as far as I can tell. Some of them might be from known artists, or have some value because they are old, but if I were you, I wouldn't waste time on them." Willie picked up the smaller pile. "These are worth following up."

From the smaller pile, he gave Leaphorn two photos of baskets, describing them as finely crafted and exceptionally well designed. "They look like the

work of the Black and Holiday families or their relatives, fine Utah basket makers."

Willie offered insights on a large brown pot with
a handle that looked like braided clay and a stone
carving of a bear, giving Leaphorn the names of
the possible creators and their prize-winning legacies. He handed the pictures back. "Did these all
come from the same collection?"

"I don't know, but they arrived in the same box.
Were any of them sold here?"

"Unfortunately, no—at least not while I've been
in charge. I would remember them."

The trader picked up the photo of the saddle
blanket. "This is wonderful. You don't see this style
much. It's worth following up."

Leaphorn used the comment to move the conversation forward. "Speaking of weaving, have you
heard that a dress Juanita made may still survive
somewhere?"

Willie leaned back against the wall. "One of her
biils is in the collection of a museum in California. She wore it in the photograph of the two of
them, Juanita and Chief Manuelito, the famous
portrait. Remember? The biil came to the Window Rock museum for a visit a few years ago. It
ought to come home to Navajoland."

"I agree." Leaphorn recalled the photo of Manuelito in his tall black hat and Juanita at his side,
one shoulder bare in a classic woven dress. It had
become an iconic image of strength and persever-
ance in the face of oppression. "Do you know of
any other Juanita dresses from that period or earlier?"

Willie sat a bit straighter. "Hwéeldi. It used to be that people didn't talk about it, and some still don't. Without the strength of those relatives, the Navajo Nation would not be here. We rose from starvation, we rose from the ashes. If there is another dress, I'd love to have one here to show people. Or better, I guess, to keep it at the museum. They get more Navajos there."

Unless it was a heartless joke, whoever mailed the box thought so, too.

Willie stood. "I hope I helped you. Don't forget to come back in August for our auction. It's mostly rugs, but we've always got some good-looking jewelry your friend might like. The money benefits our scholarship fund."

Leaphorn saw Louisa approaching, as though she'd been waiting for them to finish. "I'll tell her about it. She's our social director."

Things had been different with Emma. Their social life had revolved around her extended and extensive family, with a secondary smaller orbit of obligation that came with his job. Emma's jewelry had been gifts from her relatives—except for her wedding ring.

Louisa was quiet on the drive back to Window Rock. He enjoyed the peacefulness and used it to puzzle out the next step in his investigation. First, he'd follow up with Jim Bean. If Bean's leads didn't pan out, or if the inspector came up empty-handed, he'd talk to Mrs. Pinto about showing Peshlakai the earrings and necklace to see if he could identify them. Then he'd work to find the buyer. And he'd explore the suggestion that the box might be a gift from someone who knew Mrs. Pinto. He sensed that Peshlakai hadn't told him everything.

He glanced over to Louisa to ask her about making some calls for him tomorrow and what ideas she had for dinner. That's when he noticed that his passenger was crying.

6

Bernie awoke when the sky turned pale gold, a few minutes before sunrise. She greeted the gift of a new day with song and white cornmeal, made coffee, but didn't go for a run. She reviewed her notes about the body and the people she'd encountered on the trail, adding details that had come to her overnight. Then she made a sandwich to take along for the shift she expected to work after the FBI interview. She ate half of the leftover pork chop for breakfast along with a slice of watermelon.

She knocked on the bathroom door and said good-bye to Chee. "I'll call you when I'm done in Farmington and let you know how it went."

She heard his voice over the water in the shower. "Great. We'll talk later."

"How's your leg?"

"Good as new. I'm spending some time with Cowboy today."

"Tell him hello for me."

Cowboy Dashee, Chee's longtime friend, worked with the Hopi Tribal Police.

When she checked in at the substation, Largo was already there. He motioned her into his office.

"I guess Chee told you about the rookie."

"Yes, sir. The argument over the hay. And his bad eye."

"I'll need everybody to work some overtime until he's here again."

"Of course." She'd expected the request.

Largo shifted gears. "Agent Johnson called me to confirm your interview at her office in Farmington."

"That's right."

"I think our FBI agent is mellowing. How did you do with her yesterday?"

"Fine, I guess." Bernie leaned back in the chair. "She tried to chat for a second about the weather."

Largo smiled. "I don't know if you were in the right place at the right time or the wrong place at the wrong time to find that body."

"Me neither. Both, I guess. Have they identified the victim?"

"Not that they've told us."

"Sir, as long as I have the interview, I'll work the rest of the day. I'd like to stay involved in the murder investigation. I want to talk to Johnson about letting me follow up with the Navajos who might have seen something important. I'd have a better rapport with them."

"That makes sense to me, but with the rookie out, you've got a lot of other stuff on your plate. Don't forget about that Chinle bolo that turned up at the flea market."

"I won't."

The thirty-mile drive took her past rural northwestern New Mexico homesteads, the turnoffs for two Navajo casinos, convenience store parking lots, roadside vendors with baskets of tomatoes and green beans, and plenty of car lots. The hogback, the road's most interesting geologic feature, sat a few miles west of Farmington's sprawl. She took US 64 across the bridge over the La Plata River and it became Main Street. Traffic was light, typical for a Sunday morning.

She parked and walked to the front door. Agent Johnson had been waiting and let her in. "Thanks for coming, Bernie. How about some coffee?"

"Sure."

She followed Johnson to an employee lounge, considerably larger and better equipped than theirs at Shiprock. The room had an upscale coffee machine and a full-sized refrigerator. Bernie selected Sumatra because it had the same letters as *smart*, plus some extras for good measure.

Johnson refilled a plastic water bottle.

"I was surprised to see you at the scene yesterday, Bernie. How have you been?"

"Busy and hot. I'll be glad when the rains come and cool things off." It was always hot in the Four Corners in July. She should have said something else, but being with Johnson made her nervous and awkward. "How about you? Have you had a good summer so far?" Bernie thought about calling the agent by her first name but couldn't do it.

"Yeah, it's fine. Busy and busier with the new body."

"Did you identify the dead guy?"

Johnson moved toward the door as though she hadn't heard the question. "Bring your coffee, and let's get started."

Bernie followed the agent down an empty hallway to her cubicle. She put her coffee mug on the desktop, using a coaster with the FBI seal that matched the one on her cup. FBI—Fidelity, Bravery, and Integrity. Johnson sat and motioned her to a chair across the desk. The agent pulled out a notepad and pen.

"Thank you again for being here today. I'd like you to start at the beginning. You mentioned that you'd come to the trail for a run. Begin there, and tell me as much as you remember."

Bernie took her notes from her backpack.

"What's that?"

"Oh, I jotted down some things I thought might be relevant to the investigation. I want to be as thorough as possible."

Johnson listened as Bernie started with her arrival at the trail, mentioning the cars she saw in the dirt lot, describing them as best she could. She recalled a sweaty middle-aged Navajo man, close to six feet tall, in jeans and a sleeveless shirt who stood slightly hunched with his hands on his knees at the trailhead. A woman with a blond ponytail had been unlocking a car, a small unleashed dog sniffing the dirt around the front tire. She noticed Johnson open her notebook and write something.

"Did you get the names?"

"No. That was before I knew about the body."

"Please continue."

Bernie mentioned that she had seen no other people until after she passed the dog, about ten minutes into the run. She detailed the initial dog encounter and continued chronologically.

Johnson made the occasional notation but did not interrupt.

Bernie described how the dog eventually led her to the red shoe and the black pant leg. "From the position of the body, I thought someone had fallen, maybe tripped and ended up in the bushes, knocked out by the fall. I called to the person, and when there was no response, I moved closer. That's when I saw the plastic ties and the blood on his hand, and I assumed whoever it was was dead."

Bernie sipped her coffee. The memory made it bitter.

"Did you check for a pulse?"

"Yes. No pulse."

Johnson nodded once. "Go on."

Bernie straightened in her chair. She chronicled the people she saw while she waited with the body. She referred to her notes a few times to make sure she had the details correct.

"I noticed that there weren't any drag marks. I didn't find sign of a struggle along the path. I examined the plants at the edge of the trail and took pictures. They weren't trampled, and the dead person's shoes and pants didn't seem dusty. I didn't spot anything that could have been a weapon and, except for the smear on his right palm, no obvious blood." She mentioned that she had done a quick survey, looking for additional evidence as she walked back to the body after calling it in.

Johnson put her pen down. "Would you like a break? We can start again when you're ready."

Bernie shook her head and gave the woman credit. The agent had learned a few things—or perhaps recalled what she'd learned at the academy—compared to the last time Bernie had worked with her.

"All right then, tell me what you did next."

"I went back to the edge of the trail to wait for my backup, Officer Bigman. Before he arrived, three people I'd already seen on the trail came by, returning to the parking area." She mentioned that she had their names and contact information. "The dog continued walking up to me and then back to the body. Again and again. When Officer Bigman showed up, I told him the deceased's location. He stayed there, and I went to the trailhead to wait for you and your crew and to bar anyone else from access." She mentioned her encounters with a couple of ladies in their fifties and a teenage boy.

"Then a man argued with me. Hold on. I want to make sure I get his name right." Bernie glanced at her notebook. "Ed Summersly." She gave the agent his description. "He told me he ran the trail every day and had already run it once before I saw him. He hesitated when I asked if he'd seen anything unusual and then mentioned the dog. He was the only person who asked to see my ID. After he left, I turned back a few more people. Then you and your crew drove up. That's it."

"Do you have Summersly's contact information?"

"Yes. I made a list for you of everyone I talked to."

"Thanks." Johnson turned back to her notebook and jotted something down.

Bernie waited until she was done. "I have some questions for you."

"Before that, I want you to go through the chain of events for me again. Add any new details that come to mind about the first people you saw, the ones you encountered *before* you found the body. Take as long as you need." Johnson paused. "You did very well with your report."

Bernie repeated the story. This time, it took a bit longer. She remembered a few more details: a fancy watch Summersly wore and a missing finger on the sweaty Navajo's left hand. When she finished, her throat was dry and her coffee had grown cool.

Johnson looked up. "Would you like more coffee?"

"No, but water would be good."

The agent left the room and quickly returned with a cold bottle.

Bernie unscrewed the cap and took a sip. "What do you know about the man I found out there?"

"The deceased was a male, possibly in his forties, about six feet tall, a hundred and eighty pounds, slim build. He had no identification. The cause of death looked like a stab wound to the chest. We don't know yet how long he had been dead or how long the body lay there by the trail before you found it."

"Officer Bigman mentioned that you seemed to know the victim. Did you?"

Johnson didn't react to the statement. "Anything else?"

"What happened to the dog?"

"Bigman took custody of it. More questions?"

"Just the obvious. Who did it? And why?"

"Those are our questions, too." But from the way she said it, Bernie suspected Agent Johnson already had an idea of the answers.

It was late morning when they finished. The agent thanked her for her time and said she might have some additional questions. Bernie called the station, and Sandra told her she was on duty until five p.m. and conveyed Largo's assignments for the rest of the day. "He said you're working for the rookie."

"No, I'm working for the Navajo people."

"You're feisty today."

"I guess I miss having today off."

As Bernie drove back toward Shiprock, she ate her sandwich in the car and finished the bottle of the FBI's cold water.

She called Chee, hoping he'd have phone service. He picked up her call on the second ring.

"Hey, beautiful." He said something else, but his voice drifted into a dead zone and then she heard ". . . interview?"

"I'm finished with the FBI, at least for now, but I'm on duty until five. So far things are slow. Where are you?"

"Ute Mountain Rodeo. Cowboy's nephew is in the team roping . . ."

She could barely understand him. She knew the event arena sat about an hour north of Shiprock near Cortez, Colorado. "We've got a weak signal. You're fading in and out."

He said something else she couldn't decipher, but his laugh came through clearly. Then he said, "Have you talked to the Lieutenant?"

"No. Should I?"

"He called this morning about coming to the station . . ." His voice turned to garble and then ". . . the rookie can't drive with one eye." The reception was getting worse. ". . . so hot out here even the rocks are sweating . . ."

"Tell Dashee 'Hey' for me. I can't understand you, so I'm signing off."

"What? I'm losing . . . sweetheart."

She drove out to investigate a person walking unsteadily on the highway. As she cruised along, she called Mama on speaker. It took a while for her mother to answer.

"So, are you and Cheeseburger coming to see me today?"

"I'm working, but I might stop by later."

"I thought this was your day off."

"It was. Now I'm on until five or so, but you know how that can go."

"You work too hard. I worry about you. When will you ever have time to weave?"

They'd had that conversation many times before. Bernie didn't want to go there.

"Mama, did Sister talk to you about helping find a little space in a booth at the flea to sell drawings?"

"No. Come to the house today. We can talk to her about getting a job and . . ."

As Mama talked, Bernie noticed a convertible ahead of her driving on the shoulder. As she approached, it came to a stop. She glanced at the California license plate and then saw a camera sticking out the window. Visitors taking photos. Nothing she had to worry about.

Mama's story continued to include an unexpected conversation with an old neighbor.

"It was good to have time to talk to Mr. Natachi. His granddaughter brought him over and he stayed until just now."

"Were they going back to Chinle today?"

"His granddaughter has to work, so if they stay, they will drive back early." Mama made a clicking sound. "I told her they should leave now so she can sleep in her own bed before tomorrow. She doesn't listen. She reminds me of your sister."

Bernie flashed her lights at a car that passed in the opposite direction considerably above the speed limit. She watched as it failed to brake and swerved across the centerline. "I've got to go check on a bad driver, Mama. We'll talk later."

She disconnected before her mother could protest and headed after the vehicle. As it turned out, issuing that ticket for speeding and distracted driving was the big event of her shift. The man walking in the road had strolled away by the time she reached the place he'd been spotted.

She drove northwest toward the Carrizo Mountains to check on a missing elder, but the man returned unharmed while she was there and wondered why a police car had parked outside his house. His wife and daughter told her about a neighbor who, they said, was neglecting his horses. Bernie drove over to check and discovered that the father had been in the hospital. The son worked during the week but was there now and had arranged for his adult daughter to stay at the house and care for the livestock. Problem solved without her help. Something to celebrate.

She had finished her shift, except for the paperwork, called the station, and then drove to Mama's house. What was going on with Darleen now that they needed to discuss?

Mama, absorbed in a television show, greeted her with a nod. "Sit here with me. I like this program. It's funny." The show featured home videos of cats falling into fish tanks and riding robotic vacuums, kids attempting daredevil stunts on bikes and the like. The fans were still on, and the house, while not exactly cool, was cooler than Bernie's car.

Mama commented on the program and the ads with equal enthusiasm. When a pitch for new cars came around a second time, she pushed the mute button. "You can bring me a cookie, daughter. Have one, too."

Bernie found the cookies on the counter. She brought two to Mama and one for herself along with napkins. They looked homemade.

"That's right. The neighbor lady brought them when she asked your sister if she would go over there and watch the baby."

"Is Mrs. Darkwater sick?" Bernie knew the neighbor doted on this grandchild.

"She's fine. She and her son went to a movie in

Farmington, and then for groceries. They would be home too late for the little guy."

Bernie had seen the grandson. A cute kid. "Why didn't the boy just come over here?"

Mama shrugged. "That's what I said, but his dad has his own ideas. He doesn't want the boy watching TV."

Mama turned on the sound so they could listen to a commercial for perfume that featured only music and a very thin blond woman. Bernie thought about another blonde, Agent Johnson, and how Johnson had ignored her question about knowing the dead man. Few things made Bernie more curious than being denied information. Johnson hadn't refused her request to help with the investigation, and Bernie planned to reinterview her witnesses, especially the folks who were on the trail when she had arrived.

Mama ate the first cookie and hit the mute button.

"When you start weaving again, you have to do it every day. Your hands can lose their place, lose the rhythm. Weaving keeps your mind from flitting around like, like . . ." Mama paused. "Like those little k'aalógii. You have to sit still. Then your hands and your brain can work together."

"I'm like one of those butterflies now, moving from spot to spot. I enjoy being busy."

Mama frowned. "Don't let the loom sit alone too long." She shifted on the couch and changed topics. "Now, we have to talk about something else. Your sister. That girl disappoints me. She's not looking for a job. She found an idea on the computer about making money at home. She had to pay for something, a kit that tells how it works. It sounds bad to me, to have to pay to have a job. But you know how your sister is. You explain this to her."

Mama fiddled with the remote, turning up the sound for a spot about cruise ships. When she said she was ready for bed, Bernie told her good night and went next door to Mrs. Darkwater's house. The dog started to bark as she approached, and Darleen came to the door. She shooed the animal away with a wave of her hand and smiled at Bernie. "Hey, you! Come on in. I want to show you something."

They sat at the table, and Bernie noticed her sister's sketchbook.

"What are you drawing?"

Darleen smiled. "It's the little guy who is in bed. I did it this afternoon to give to his dad and Mrs. Darkwater when they get back. What do you think?"

Darleen usually didn't show anyone her work until she had revised it many times. The picture was Spider-Man with a child's physique and a sweet little Navajo face.

"It's wonderful. Really good, Sister." She passed the pad back. "Why Spider-Man?"

"The kid loves Spider-Man. I don't have the chin quite right, but it mostly looks like him." She put the pad down. "Hey, do you want some water? It's warm in here."

"It's cooler here than at Mama's. Do you think Mrs. Darkwater would mind if I took a Coke?"

"She doesn't have any. Just tea, water, and juice boxes for the young one. It's cooler because Mrs. Darkwater keeps the curtains closed during the day. Our mother likes to let the sun in even when it's a thousand degrees outside."

They went to the kitchen. Darleen removed a water pitcher from the refrigerator, poured a glass for herself, and gave one to her sister. Bernie set it down on the table.

"Mama told me that you bought a kit or something so you can make money at home. That could be legit, but you know there are a bunch of scams out there."

Darleen stiffened. "Mama didn't tell you the good parts. I'll save money on gas because I don't have to drive to work every day. And clothes and eating out like you do at an office."

You could bring a lunch like I do, Bernie thought, but she didn't interrupt.

"I only had to pay for the supply kit, and when it comes, I'm in business."

"What will you be doing exactly?"

"Easy-peasy. Stuffing envelopes."

"It sounds fishy. What else do you know about it?"

Darleen frowned. "Why are you and Mama always so negative? You never believe I can do anything."

"I'm not negative. I just want to make sure you don't get ripped off, and right now it sounds like you're paying to work."

"Back off. Give me a break, and treat me like an adult."

Bernie took a sip of the cold water. "It's nothing personal. Scams are everywhere."

"Stop being a cop for a minute, won't you?" Darleen picked up a pencil and went back to the drawing.

Bernie finished her water. "You know, that portrait of the boy as Spider-Man gave me an idea. You could do quick sketches of kids and sell them. You know, maybe instead of school portraits?"

Darleen focused on her sketch for a while and then put down her pencil. "How was that pie?"

"I let the crust get too brown, but the fruit part was great."

"Mama and I ate the peaches you left. They were delicious. Did she go to bed already?"

"Yes. I need to go, too. Can you keep an eye on the dog for me?"

"Oh, he won't . . ."

Bernie frowned.

"Sure. I'll grab him so he doesn't follow you to the car."

"I'm serious about that scam. You be careful, OK?"

"You worry too much, Sister. You're getting more like our mother every day."

Bernie let the comment go. She walked to her unit and looked up at the golden afterglow of the high desert sunset. It reminded her of days when life was simpler, when she was a child and spent the summer mostly outside with the sheep, and the long, warm summer stretched into forever.

She took a few deep breaths and felt the calm

course through her. Then she started the unit and headed toward home. She phoned Chee to tell him she was on her way.

Ship Rock, Tsé Bit'a'í, the Rock with Wings, rose majestically from the desert floor. The stars had just begun to sparkle over the craggy volcanic monolith that played a role in the People's sacred history. She lived surrounded by beauty, one of those rare, fortunate people who had a job she loved in a part of the world she treasured. Sure, it was challenging, dangerous, sometimes discouraging work. But she wouldn't trade places with anyone.

She pulled into the substation to drop off the unit and pick up her Toyota. Before she killed the engine, the radio came on. She turned around and called Chee again. "I just got a call about a man at the hospital, threatening staff with a pocket-knife. He's someone I've dealt with before, and he's probably off his medications. I'll be home as soon as I can."

"Be safe. I'll save you some dinner."

She added to her list of gratitude the love of a good man.

7

When Joe Leaphorn woke up Monday morning, even before he climbed out of bed, his brain began to organize the problem at hand. Actually, two problems. His major focus went to the Navajo Nation's gift and the complications that had developed with Peshlakai's hesitation to confirm that he had created the bracelet now missing.

But first, he had to consider the more immediate issue awaiting him as soon as he walked down the hall for his first cup of coffee. What had offended Louisa?

He accepted that he'd never been good at dealing with women when it came to the danger-fraught world of emotions. When he had women as clients, as coworkers, as crime victims or suspects, the guidelines for expected behavior from both parties were relatively clear. But with his housemate and good friend, the rules shifted or made themselves up as they went along. He admired

Louisa—a logical, practical woman. Her devotion after his brain injury had surprised him. He'd encouraged her to return to her research, and now that she had finally followed his advice and done so, he saw more sparkle in her eyes. He thought about what to say over breakfast and came up only with the standard male response to a disgruntled female.

He dressed and went to the kitchen, where everything seemed normal. He poured himself a cup of coffee and noticed the predictable oatmeal on the stove. He sat across from Louisa at the table, and she said the words he both expected and dreaded.

"We need to talk, Joe."

"Sorry bout yesaday." He took a sip of his coffee.

"I thought you wanted my help with this museum problem, and when I tried to help, well, you clearly didn't want it."

He remembered, now, what had set her off. "Wade a mint." He rose and went to the office for his laptop. He came back, sat down, typed out the few sentences he'd conjured up, and handed her the computer.

I realize I never talked to you about the rules I have for separating my private life from my profession. I understand why you were confused. With Mrs. Pinto dropping in to tell us about her assistant's death, it stands to reason that you'd assume it was acceptable to invite Peshlakai here. Mrs. Pinto is your friend, and she'd been in our home before. Peshlakai is an unknown and so is his family. I try to

never do anything to increase the risk of exposure.
If I'm meeting an informant, it's always in a public
place.

Louisa handed the computer back to him, then
rose and went to the stove and began to serve the
oatmeal. "I get it. That doesn't give you the right
to be rude to me."

Rude? Had he been rude? He remembered putting his hand on her arm to get her attention, but
he didn't raise his voice, didn't actually tell her to
be quiet, to stop interrupting his interview, to quit
acting like she was the investigator.

"I am sorry." He said it again, pleased that it
sounded like good English. He hoped the issue was
settled.

She brought the oatmeal back to the table and
set the bowls down. "It's not just that. You resented
my presence yesterday, despite the fact that my
bracelet had offered a possible clue and I was the
one who suggested we find Mr. Peshlakai." Her
voice grew louder. "I saw you bristle when I mentioned showing the photos to Mr. Willie and again
when I reminded you that it was getting late. You
were happy when I walked away, weren't you?"

He knew by her tone of voice that she had more
to say. He ate a spoonful of oatmeal.

"I'm confused. You ask me to help you, and then
you get angry at me when I try. Do you understand what I'm saying?"

He nodded. He didn't recall feeling angry. He'd
call it irritated.

"If you don't require my help with this case,

with any of your work . . . well, that's fine. You're the detective. I'm the professor and I need to get on with my own life. I don't want another day like yesterday, OK?" Unshed tears welled in her eyes.

"Kay." He didn't like seeing her cry. He saw no harm in agreeing with her. In his experience, problems like this either went away or boomeranged back, and if they came back, sometimes he better understood the reason for the conflict.

They ate without talking, long enough that he thought the situation had resolved itself. But Louisa had more to say.

"I'm going to Flagstaff for a department meeting as a consultant."

He remembered. The session was tomorrow, and she'd asked if he wanted to go along for the three-hour drive, maybe stop in Holbrook on the way to see some friends. They could visit the Lowell Observatory before coming back. He'd told her he'd think about it.

She ate the rest of her oatmeal and then spoke again. "I've decided that I'm driving over this morning so I can catch up with some of my colleagues, get a sense of what's going on, do a little shopping. And I think we could use a break from each other after yesterday."

She took her bowl to the sink. "I'm packed, and I'm leaving now. I'll be back when I've done what I can at the university and when I've figured out how I feel about staying here."

She gave him a half smile. "I like you, Joe, but I won't stand for being put down."

"Dent mean to." He'd already said sorry.

After she drove away, he poured himself the last of the coffee and turned off the pot. He should have asked her to make sure that right front tire on her car had enough air. It looked low when she came home with the groceries. He rinsed his bowl and her cup and put them in the drain rack. He noticed that Louisa had forgotten to feed Giddi, and he gave the cat some kibble. He wondered if she had taken her phone charger. She tended to leave it in a socket by the toaster. He checked and, sure enough, there it was.

He grabbed the computer and went to his office to work on Mrs. Pinto's case. He opened his little brown notebook and reviewed the facts and questions that had caught his attention during his meetings at the museum, the conversation in his living room, and yesterday's session with Bean at the Navajo Inn. He added what he'd learned at the trading post with Willie and Peshlakai. He made himself a fresh "to follow up" list. The process clarified his thinking, and he began to develop a plan to settle the case.

His cell phone rang around nine. He thought it might be Louisa, but the number came up as Robert Peshlakai. He answered.

After some pleasantries, Peshlakai said, "I've been thinking about that photo of the earrings. It was like seeing a relative you had forgotten about, but then you think, maybe it's just someone who looks like him. If I could see those things up close, I'd know for sure. I have to drive into Gallup today, and I could stop by and see them. If they are mine, I could tell you and the lady a story, too."

Leaphorn considered it. "Do you recall who bought them?"

"I don't know about that, but I remember who I asked to sell them for me. I mean, if they really are the ones I made."

That was enough for Leaphorn. "Let's meet in the parking lot of the museum complex at ten. Does that work?"

"Yes."

"I'll call back if there is a problem. Otherwise, I'll see you at the museum. You know where that is?"

"Sure, it's the biggest thing around for miles."

It probably was too early to find Mrs. Pinto at work, so he went back to his computer to check his email and saw a message from Bean.

Joe, great to see you looking so healthy. Keep it up. Did I tell you to hold on to that box? Make sure your client doesn't recycle it or something. Keep it safe in case we need to check for fingerprints. If you can, take a look at the postmark and let me know where the donation was mailed. I'm dead in the water until I know about that postmark. JB

Leaphorn called Mrs. Pinto, and his luck held. She would be in the office at ten. He would introduce her to the jeweler, and she would show Peshlakai the earrings and necklace in hopes that he could identify them.

He was considering another cup of coffee when the phone rang.

Captain Largo's voice boomed over the line. After some chitchat, Largo said, "Hey, Lieutenant, remember that rookie I mentioned to you?"

"I do. Chee gave me some background on him."

"Well, he's off work for a few days until the swelling around his eye goes down and he can breathe. If you can make it up here while he's on leave, this would be a good opportunity for you two to get together."

"How about late this afternoon?" Leaphorn suggested a time.

"I'll tell Sam to meet you at the station. I'll call you back if there's any problem."

"Have you mentioned this mentoring idea to him?"

"Not yet."

"Tell him that I heard about his work at the Shiprock car bombing."

"You want me to say his work, huh? Not his screwups." Largo chuckled. "Good idea."

"How's the guy's Navajo?"

"Marginal. Improving since he's worked here. He understands more than he lets on. He's reticent about speaking, but he has to when he talks to the old-timers."

"I can relate to that with my troubles with English." And, Leaphorn realized, Sam certainly would view a gray-haired retired lieutenant as an old-timer.

"If you don't want to drive home after your meeting, stay with me. We can swap a few lies. At least let me buy you dinner."

"Thanks. Let's see how it goes." The trip was only ninety minutes, and he'd driven many times

that distance in his days on the force without anyone offering him a meal and a bed. Age made a
difference, he thought again, and Largo's offer
reflected both friendship and the long, kind Diné
tradition of respect for elders.

Leaphorn arrived at the museum a few minutes
early and Mrs. Pinto met him in the lobby. They
passed a tall, gray-haired gentleman in polished
boots and dark jeans pacing in the hall outside her
office.

Mrs. Pinto spoke gruffly to him. "You'll have
to wait until someone comes to unlock the door.
Go on back there." The man frowned and moved
away from her down the hall like a person in a hurry.

She entered her office and invited Leaphorn
to sit.

"Who was that?"

"The father of my Tiffany. He came to collect
the personal items from her desk."

"You sounded angry with him."

She turned off her computer monitor and swiv-
eled to face him. "I am. He's been spreading terrible
rumors about me. But that's not why you're here.
Tell me about this Peshlakai and how you think he
can help."

"He made the bracelet I suspect is missing. I
know you're more interested in the dress, but I think
this could lead us to it." Leaphorn told her about
the trip to the Hubbell Trading Post yesterday. "I
don't think this will take long. Either he will recognize the earrings and the necklace or he won't."

"I hope he can explain how his bracelet, if it is

his bracelet, is connected to the disappearance of Juanita's dress."

On the way out, Leaphorn spoke to the man in the hall. "I'm sorry about your daughter."

The man studied the floor. "She was my beloved, my blessing. My beautiful, perfect girl. Be careful. You know what I mean?"

"No, I don't."

The man hesitated and glanced toward the open door of Mrs. Pinto's office. His voice fell to a whisper. "What happened is that woman's fault. Adilgashii."

Suddenly, the air-conditioned hallway seemed too cool. *Adilgashii*. Leaphorn knew the word. Witchcraft. A dark explanation for unexplainable evil.

Leaphorn waited for Peshlakai in the July warmth outside the building. As he stood there, he recalled Tiffany's emergency and noticed that a promise of summer rain hung in the dusty air. He watched the clouds begin to build.

Robert Peshlakai was dressed in new jeans, pressed with a crease in front, a short-sleeved shirt with pearl buttons, and a dove-gray hat with a silver band. He had a blue plastic case in his hand. "Yá'át'ééh, Columbo."

"Yá'át'ééh. You look like you're going to a wedding or a Round Dance."

"I am hoping to see some old friends again."

Leaphorn glanced at the truck and the short woman behind the steering wheel. "Your wife is welcome to come in."

"I said that, too. She's going to call her mother while I'm inside, and she likes the privacy."

Mrs. Pinto had wrangled up a third chair for her office and invited them both to sit.

As he made the introductions, Leaphorn realized he didn't know Mrs. Pinto's clans, so he used her name and her title at the museum and told Peshlakai that she was a friend of his housemate, Louisa.

"Oh, yes, the woman with such good taste in jewelry."

Mrs. Pinto said, "I appreciate you helping Joe with this. It's quite a mystery."

"This investigator told me you got a gift, and you want to know who sent it. If the earrings and the necklace are mine, I might recognize them. I brought some notes and records." He set his blue case on the desk. "The old man showed me the picture of them, but I had trouble making out the jeweler's mark."

Mrs. Pinto opened her desk drawer, took out the earrings and the necklace, and put them on the desktop across from him. "Take a look."

The jeweler had it right, Leaphorn thought; the photograph did not do them justice. The earrings were beautiful, gracefully crafted bear-paw designs, well balanced to dangle from the ear delicately, calling attention to the face and the curve of the neck. The necklace was simple—a silver bear with an intriguing turquoise eye on a sturdy-looking silver chain.

Peshlakai reached for the necklace and held it in his right hand. He ran his finger over the shape of the bear and its blue eye. He moved it closer to his face, examined the silverwork and the stone, and then looked at the back. He gave the earrings the same close attention.

After some long minutes, he sat them down again on the desktop. Leaphorn waited for Peshlakai to collect his thoughts.

His client was less patient. "Is this your work?"

Peshlakai rubbed his thumb along the bear paw. "I made these a long time ago to go with a storyteller bracelet that had a family of bears walking in the woods. I always put my jeweler's mark here." Peshlakai leaned toward her and extended an earring. "Right here where the post is."

He opened his blue case and pulled out a magnifying glass and used it to examine the back of the earring.

Leaphorn watched. Mrs. Pinto somehow managed to remain silent.

Peshlakai put down the magnifier. He smiled. "It is my mark."

Leaphorn felt a wave of relief as part of the puzzle fell in place. "Yesterday, you indicated that you had given these and the bracelet that went with them to someone. Did you keep a record of who it was?"

Peshlakai tapped his forehead. "All stored in here, but some of the boxes are a little dusty. For the last few years, my wife has helped me. She keeps sales on the computer. She thinks I might be forgetting things."

He reached in the bag and this time pulled out an old-fashioned three-ring binder. "This is my old inventory list. I ought to have the information in here. Well, we'll see."

Leaphorn noticed that the book had brief sections of script and small photos.

Peshlakai turned the pages, moving toward the back of the notebook. "Here." He tapped a sheet with several small color photos. "I can't see my photos too good now, but I know that's right." He moved the book toward Leaphorn. "Tell me what this says."

"'Four sets of earrings, necklaces, and bracelets, storyteller designs. Fat Boy. Indian Market.'" Leaphorn read the date and studied the picture. "Yes, this is the three-piece set."

Peshlakai closed the book. His demeanor changed as quick as summer lightning.

Mrs. Pinto leaned toward him. "Something wrong?"

Peshlakai sat up a bit straighter. "These all disappeared a long time ago. I can't help you after all."

Leaphorn took a breath. "What do you mean disappeared?"

"I mean, I don't know what happened to them." Peshlakai brushed an imaginary speck of something from the front of his shirt. "This guy I knew from high school, Fat Boy, was traveling around to arts and crafts fairs. Selling stuff he made, wood carvings of animals and things like that, and some things for me and some of his other friends. He took what I had on the list I showed you. He drove to Santa Fe the weekend of that big Indian Market. That was the last I saw of it and of him."

Leaphorn patted his shirt pocket and felt his little notebook and a pen. "I'd like to talk to Fat Boy on the chance he might remember something. Any idea how I can reach him?"

Peshlakai sighed. "It's too late, man. After he picked up my stuff, Fat Boy was on the Devil's Highway and he got in a bad wreck. A drunk wrong-way driver near Tohatchi rammed him head-on. They say my friend and the dude driving the truck that hit him died at the scene. That was a long time ago."

The Devil's Highway got that name for two reasons. The feds designated it as US 666 and many people lost their lives in accidents there, just like Peshlakai's friend. After years of badgering, the powers that be changed the numbers to US 491.

Mrs. Pinto said, "Your jewelry was valuable. I'm surprised you'd just let it go." The judgment in her voice filled the room.

"It wasn't like that. I hadn't heard what had happened, so I kept calling Fat Boy when the market was over. I knew the guy, and I trusted him. I figured that he'd give me my jewelry, or the money for it, next time I saw him." Peshlakai shrugged. "Time went by, and I was getting irritated with him. In September, I ran into his brother at the fair here, the big one."

"And?" Mrs. Pinto's voice was level, but Leaphorn noticed her foot tapping under the table.

"I asked about Fat Boy, and the man told me about the accident. I found out he was dead, killed in a car wreck." Peshlakai exhaled. "I felt bad about that. Then our baby was born and I got some jewelry commissions, and, well, I guess I just moved on. I had not thought about that friend for a long time. I'm sorry he died so young."

The room fell silent. Peshlakai stood. "I can't tell you anything else. I need to get on to Gallup."

Leaphorn stood, too. "Thanks for helping with this. If you can give me Fat Boy's legal name, you know, the name that he would have had on his driver's license, I can check on what happened to the jewelry that might have been in the car."

Peshlakai hesitated. "I never called him anything but Fat Boy."

"Do you remember what year it was when this happened?"

Peshlakai told him, then added, "It was mid-August. I remember going outside the night he left for the market and seeing a spectacular meteor shower."

"Do you know if your friend was taking any weavings to the market?"

"I don't know. He always had enough stuff to make the trip worthwhile." Peshlakai paused. "The way he could do it was that he had a friend who gave him space in front of his store."

Peshlakai picked up the earrings again, studying them, holding them gently in the palm of his hand. "I made these and the bracelet for Lisa—she was my girlfriend then. I told her I would give them to her if she would marry me. She told me I should sell the set because we would need the money with a baby coming. She said I could make something for her later, when we could afford it." He put the jewelry back on the desktop. "She married me anyway, you know. And I never made another bracelet quite like that one."

With that, Peshlakai picked up his blue case and said his good-byes.

After he left, Mrs. Pinto motioned to Leaphorn to sit down again. "I can't see any connection between the bracelet and the textile, except that they are on the list together. I hope you haven't wasted a lot of time running down a dead end."

He swallowed his annoyance. "If you want me to stop, just let me know."

"No. Louisa told me you're the best, and I believe her. I like things I can understand, and this has grown more complicated and confused, not less." She leaned toward him slightly. "I'm overwhelmed here without Tiffany. I counted on her to help me wrap up the loose ends before my retirement. Have you heard what caused her death?"

Leaphorn realized it was time to put in a call to his buddies at Navajo Police. "Those reports take a while."

"What are you doing next to find the dress?"

"I'll follow up on the accident and see what happened to the vehicle. Maybe Fat Boy dealt with textiles, too. Maybe someone in his family claimed the car and then sold the items to a collector."

Mrs. Pinto cleared her throat. "Too many maybes for me. Good luck, Joe. Remember the deadline. I don't want to leave this mess for whoever comes to replace me."

"I'd like to have the box the donations came in. The postal inspector asked me to save it in case he needs it. He wants a photo of the postmark, and he said he might need to check it for finger-prints."

"It's in Tiffany's office."

Unlike Mrs. Pinto's office, Tiffany's was nearly empty. Some new pens and a pad of paper sat near her computer. He looked for the box, even bend-ing over to check under her desk. What rule of nature was it, he wondered, that said some prob-lems grew more convoluted as time went on?

He went back to Mrs. Pinto.

"What do you mean it's not there anymore?" She took her glasses off, examined them, and put them back on. "Oh, I'm sorry. I know what hap-pened. Tiffany's father needed something to put her things in, and I told him to take it. I wanted him out of here. It's just a box."

"What's his name?"

"Something Benally. Tiffany never mentioned his first name."

"Do you know how I can get in touch with him?"

He noticed a touch of impatience in her voice. "Call Erin in HR. No, talk to Daryl, his Navajo is better. Say I'm authorizing him to release Tif-fany's emergency contact information to you. She listed her father for that." Silence, and then, "Will you have something for me on the dress by the end of the week?"

"I'll wrap this up as soon as possible. That's all I can promise." If he hadn't known better, her in-sistence on quick resolution of a complicated case would have made him suspect Mrs. Pinto herself. But if she had taken the items, she certainly would have destroyed the inventory list. Instead, she had shown it to him and begun the investigation.

She gave him the hint of a smile. "Tell Louisa hello for me."

He stopped at the HR office to talk to Daryl, who was out.

Leaphorn thought about calling Louisa from the truck on his way home to tell her about the forgotten charger and to update her on the case, but reconsidered. She'd probably still be driving, and while he appreciated cell phones, he didn't like the idea of her chatting while she was on the road, even hands free. To make matters worse, she kept her cell phone in her purse and had to rummage around to find it. He'd call later.

Back home, he put a cup of water in the microwave for instant coffee and decided to ask Jessica Taylor, his new friend in the Window Rock office, if she could do him a quick favor. He needed to read the report on the accident that killed Peshlakai's salesman Fat Boy twenty years ago. He could have contacted the New Mexico Department of Transportation himself by email, but a phone call would be quicker and the young woman had seemed eager to help. Her contacts at NMDOT would be current, too.

"The accident was on US 666 near Tohatchi, and both drivers died." He gave her the year of the crash. "It was in August, around the time of the big Santa Fe Indian Market, and that's always on the same weekend, near the end of the month. And there was a meteor shower around that time."

"Sir, I'm sure I can find the date of the market

that year. The reports are available digitally, so I don't think this will take too long."

"Great. I'd appreciate seeing what you find as soon as possible."

"I'll work on it right now." He heard the enthusiasm in her voice. "If I can't find what you want, I have a buddy there. I'll tell him one of our consultants is looking into a case that might be connected to the accident."

"That's perfect. Let me know as soon as you've got something." He said it again to reinforce the urgency.

"I sure will, sir. Happy to help."

When the phone rang, he hoped it was Jessica, but the caller ID said "NAU." He picked it up expecting to hear Louisa.

"Hello. May I please speak to Mr. Joe Leaphorn?"

"Leaphorn."

"I'm calling from the reference desk at the NAU library." The woman gave him her name. "This concerns your inquiry about Juanita . . . Umm, I don't know how to pronounce the Navajo words."

"Asdzáá Tlogi."

"Oh, I see. I'm researching our archives and will email you the sources and information. But I thought you might also want to talk to a curator of textiles who specializes in early Navajo weaving. Would you like her contact information?"

"Peas."

She gave him the woman's name and phone number, and he jotted them down.

"Email?"

"Oh, of course." The librarian told him the address, which consisted of the curator's first initial, last name, a number, and the university suffix.

"Tanks."

"I should let you know that I haven't found anything much so far. Only reference to one dress, the one in the portrait. I'm sure you know about this."

"Ya. Nudder one out there?"

"I'll let you know what I find."

He typed up a quick note to the textile expert explaining he was a private investigator attempting to track down a possible museum donation. Did she know of any existing weavings by Juanita, also known as Asdzáá Tlogi? If so, where were they now? He requested photographs if she had any. He cc'd it to Mrs. Pinto.

When Louisa came back, he would ask her to help with the university research. That ought to make her feel better.

He called the HR department at the museum, asked for Daryl, got put on hold and then disconnected. He thought again about Tiffany's father. In the old days, families buried their own dead. The arrival of mortuaries changed that. Leaphorn used his laptop to research Navajo tribal funeral packages and, after just two calls, found the funeral home that had been contacted about Tiffany Benally's remains. He was in luck; a Navajo speaker was on staff and came to the phone.

"I'd like to send her family my condolences. Can you give me an address for her father, please?"

"Just send it here and we'll forward it. That's

our policy, I mean, not to share personal information."

Leaphorn thanked the woman and asked if her day was busy. It wasn't. He learned that she had come to be on the office staff of a mortuary because of both her Christian faith and a non-Navajo boyfriend whom she had met at church whose family was in the business. She liked her job because it gave her a chance to help people.

"How did you know Tiffany, sir?"

"I met her through her job at the museum."

"She really loved that work. She liked putting together the education programs, you know, the ones that encouraged people to stay in touch with the culture. Things like the importance of animals and their stories. And the shoe games during the winter."

"How did you know her, Miss . . . ?"

"Oh, call me Sue. We went to high school together. Her father really kept an eye on her and her older sisters. He drove them to school from Big Rocks to Gallup because he wasn't sure what might happen to them on the bus. We can't help him with any funeral plans yet because there might be an autopsy, but he's fighting that. He's more traditional, you know?"

"An autopsy. That's interesting." He knew that the Office of the Medical Investigator investigates any death occurring in the State of New Mexico that is sudden, violent, untimely, or unexpected, or cases where a person is found dead and the cause of death is unknown.

"I only met Mr. Benally once. A tall man with gray hair. I can't recall his first name."

"It's Lee. You were probably thinking LeRoy, right?"

"Lee Benally. That's it. I'd really like to drive out there and talk to him. If you could remind me how to get to his place, that would be great."

"I'm sorry. I can't because of our policies, but I'm here until five. If you mail your note to me, I'll give it to Mr. Benally and ask him to call you. You don't want to drive all the way out to Big Rocks and find that he's not there."

He thanked the woman and hung up, then did a search for a phone number for Lee Benally of Big Rocks and came up empty. He had a bit of time before he needed to go to Shiprock to meet with Largo's problem child. He would drive there, find the house, and, assuming someone was home, retrieve the box and find out why the man disliked Mrs. Pinto.

Before he left home, he filled Giddi's dish with cat food and topped off the water bowl. He went into the bedroom and put a change of clothes and toiletries into an overnight bag. He didn't plan on sleeping away from home, but he knew the unexpected always waited around the corner.

8

Chee made good on his promise to Officer Bigman.

The captain was at his computer, as expected, with the usual stacks of paper on his desk. Chee summarized his thoughts on the Chinle crime spree and the possible Shiprock connection.

"I think the recovery of that bolo was a breakthrough. I want to interview the old gentleman about the burglary, and the granddaughter is worth talking to, too. I know the team leader there, Lieutenant Black. It will be easier for me to handle that side of the investigation than it would be for Bigman."

Captain Largo spread his hands on the desktop. "Talk to Black before you do anything. He's been looking into the link between gangs, burglaries, and drug traffic out there."

"I called him this morning. He said he welcomes

all the help he can get. Bernie wants to follow up on the flea market angle because she talked to Mr. Natachi."

"Fine. We'll keep Bigman busy closer to home." Largo shifted in his chair. "Did you and the Lieutenant discuss the rookie?"

"Yes, sir."

"That kid was lucky he didn't get beat up any worse." Largo frowned. "Between us, I'm surprised Bernie hasn't taken a swing at him. But that's not her style, is it?" He didn't wait for Chee's answer. "Has she talked to the Lieutenant about her issues with him?"

"You'll have to ask her, sir, but I don't imagine so. She tends to handle things herself."

Largo looked at the pile of folders on his desk. "You doing anything else I should know about, Chee?"

"No, sir."

"OK then, get to work."

Chee considered his approach before he called the number he had for Mr. Natachi's granddaughter. He dialed from his cell phone instead of the office. When the mechanical voice came on, he left a message. "Hi, I'm Jim, Bernie Manuelito's husband. I've got a question for you. Can you please give me a call?"

He followed up with a text, did some paperwork, and called her again an hour later, this time not leaving a message. Then he phoned Bernie out on patrol.

"Hi. Where are you?"

"On the way to deal with a possible case of child abuse." Largo had asked her to come in early to cover for the rookie again. Chee heard the under-tone of dread beneath her usual cheerfulness. He couldn't blame her. He hated those calls, too.

"I'm going to Chinle to follow up on the bur-glaries. Do you know where Mr. Natachi lives? And do you have a phone number for him? All I have is the granddaughter's."

"I can't help you, but I know Mama can."

So he called Bernie's mother. Mr. Natachi, she told him, did not have a phone. She didn't know the address, but he lived outside of Chinle toward Canyon de Chelly, past the last turnoff and be-yond the Spider Rock overlook. His house sat off a dirt road, across from a couple of cattle guards. She described the view of the mountains. "He says it's not close to anything, and that's why he likes it. He lives in a small home his daughter brought in behind the main house where Ryana and the boy-friend are, or maybe it's just her now. I'm not too sure about that boyfriend."

"Ahéhee'." Chee figured he could find it from her description.

"How was that pie my daughter made?"

"Good."

"Did she burn the crust?"

Chee thought about how to answer. "The peaches were perfect."

Mama laughed. "That one tries to do too many things at once. You tell her to come and see me, and I will show her how to take it out of the oven in time."

After he hung up, he remembered that he should have asked about Darleen. Next time.

Chee enjoyed driving, especially when it involved interesting places on the Navajo Nation, and even more when Bernie sat next to him. The trip to Chinle took about two hours. He got there in time to catch Black before he left on a call. They went to the break room to talk.

"Have some coffee if you want." Black handed him an empty mug inscribed with the word "Wildcats." "I made it, so it's at least half decent."

Chee poured a cup and took a seat.

Black joined him. "So some of our stolen jewelry is finally turning up?"

"It was just one piece, but it makes me wonder if other stuff stolen from here is winding up in our backyard. I want to get your off-the-record take on the situation."

Black explained that the burglaries had his team baffled. "The stolen merchandise hasn't been recovered. The problem started with a few reports in April and has been steadily on the increase. Whoever is doing this seems to know their targets. Until you called, I hadn't heard of any merchandise showing up in Shiprock. I appreciate whatever help you can offer with this."

Chee sipped the coffee. "The link to the flea market was a lucky break. If my wife, Bernie, hadn't been there—she's an officer, too—and picked up on it, we wouldn't have had the lead. The old man showed her where the booth was, but by then, the guy was gone. Bernie got a decent description of the flea market seller and she's following up on that."

"He got spooked and folded his tent. They sell from tents?" Black laughed. "Who's the guy who got his bolo back?"

"A Mr. Natachi. You know him?"

"Herman Natachi?" Black pushed his glasses up to the bridge of his nose. "He's the old gentleman who came by the station a couple of weeks ago to report some missing jewelry. I remember how polite he was. He couldn't say for sure when his bolo had disappeared. He had an invitation to a relative's graduation from college in Tsaile last month, and that's when he realized the bolo he wanted to wear was gone."

Chee considered what Black had said. "Sometimes elderlies forget things."

"You're right, but from the rest of the conversation and the way he described the missing bolo, his memory seemed fine."

"Did he lose more than the bolo?"

"No. He had a ring in the dresser next to his bed, and he mentioned a ketoh. They were still there. You don't see those old pieces so much anymore." Chee knew a ketoh was a wrist guard, like an oversized bracelet, from the days when hunters used a bow. "And he had a fancy rodeo buckle on display and no one took it."

Black stood. "Let me find the paperwork to be sure I'm remembering this right."

The lieutenant returned a few minutes later with a folder. "This is all in the computer somewhere, but I wanted to show you exactly what he wrote. The handwriting says something, too."

Chee leaned toward the open folder. He had dealt with enough challenged elders to recognize the way problems showed themselves in shaky or illegible handwriting. Mr. Natachi's penmanship was graceful and solid.

Black chuckled. "Some of the younger officers coming in now would have trouble reading this."

"Really?"

"Yeah. They aren't teaching cursive writing much anymore. My daughter just prints and types. But she's learning to speak Navajo in class and that's important. You can't expect the schools to do everything."

Chee closed the file. "You know Ryana, his granddaughter, called us and said the old man made all this up."

"She called you?"

"She called Bernie, actually, and denied that he was a burglary victim."

Lieutenant Black closed the folder. "That's the Ryana who lives out that way toward the canyon, maybe with a boyfriend. She's Navajo but with a Mexican-sounding name. Flores, Fresquez, something like that. That must be who you mean, right?"

Chee nodded. "Did she come with Mr. Natachi when he made his complaint?"

"No." Black paused. "I remember her because years ago some boyfriend was beating on her and a neighbor called about it. Of course, when the officer got there she didn't want to talk and said she got that split lip from walking into a door. The boyfriend was nowhere to be found. Later, I heard he was married and went back to his wife."

Black brought the conversation back to the burglaries. "We don't have any leads. They target jewelry and electronics in the break-ins, stuff that's easy to sell for drugs. They're careful. No one sees anything, and they don't leave fingerprints or other clues we've been able to work with."

"Anyone ever interrupted them?"

"Not yet. Not that I know of."

"And none of the goods have turned up?"

"Not until now. We have surveillance at the flea markets in the area and at those roadside sales that pop up around here. No luck." Black closed the folder and stood. "Say hello to Mr. Natachi for me."

Chee recited the directions Bernie's mother had given him.

"Sounds about right. It can be hard to tell what's a road and what's not out there. The main house, Ryana's place, is along a little wash. You're lucky it hasn't rained. It gets slick because of the caliche. Watch out for loose horses. Good luck."

Chee started the green-and-white SUV and headed from Chinle out toward Canyon de Chelly. Tséyi', the place deep in the rocks, made his heart sing. Sacred country, a refuge, a quiet oasis even with van and jeep tours taking visitors into the canyon to see the pueblo ruins. He viewed this landscape as a living reservoir of the spirit tied to stories of the People's emergence into the glittering world as they transitioned to five-fingered creatures. No matter how many times he saw the canyon's buttes, spires, and mesas, they never failed to move him to a state of peace.

In contrast, he thought of those who had lived here during the time of General James H. Carleton, Kit Carson, and their soldiers and pictured the terrible scene as homes and crops burned and fruit trees were destroyed. He felt the sorrow of terrorized families forced to abandon the very heart of Dinetah and to make the Long Walk.

The canyon stirred many emotions. The songs he had learned in his quest to become a hataali rose in his memory. He drove into the parking area, opened the door to the morning's heat, and walked the trail to the end of the Spider Rock overlook. Magnificent. He said a prayer of gratitude and added a request to Spider Woman for protection for himself, for Bernie, for all their fellow officers, for every good person they shared the world with.

He stood in the sun, happy to be alive.

Back in the SUV, his thoughts turned to the case and the interview ahead with increased clarity. It troubled him to think that someone, most likely Navajo since this was Navajoland, would steal from an old man, especially in the vicinity of such an important landscape of the spirit.

He attended to Mama's directions and made a right turn off the pavement just past the mile marker she mentioned. He headed south over a succession of hard-packed dirt roads that didn't deserve the name. With only a few wrong turns, he found a house with a smaller home behind it. A tan sedan and a battered orange and white truck from the 1980s were parked alongside the main building. As he dodged the ruts and craters in what could have been a driveway, he noticed the dry gray tumbleweeds, shredded plastic bags, and yellowed newspapers that had collected around the pickup.

There were no vehicles near the smaller house, but that didn't surprise him since Mr. Natachi probably wasn't driving anymore. Also missing were the dogs that alerted rural residents to arriving visitors. The late morning was quiet; he could barely hear the traffic on the canyon overlook road.

Chee sat in his unit for a few minutes for the sake of courtesy, and when Mr. Natachi didn't appear, he climbed out of the SUV. As he walked toward the house, he noticed a tire track in the sand. From years of habit he bent down to look more closely, finding a spot where the tread was nearly smooth.

He knocked on the front door. He waited and then spoke loudly enough to be understood over the radio inside. "Mr. Natachi, it's Jim Chee from Shiprock. Your friend Bernie's husband."

Chee rapped again. He spoke louder this time. "Hello, sir. Are you in there?" When no answer came, he tried the knob. The door opened.

The room's warm air smelled faintly of fried onions. The radio had switched from country music to a weather report: continued hot and dry. He moved through the doorway, stopped, and called again more forcefully. "Mr. Natachi, it's Jim Chee. I'd like to talk to you."

Noise from the radio was the only response.

The housekeeping here reminded him of his own home in the pre-Bernie days, when he survived without her propensity for having everything in its proper place. It had a casual man-living-alone look to it. Not exactly messy but hovering on the line. A coffee cup with a bit of dark liquid at the bottom sat next to a jar of peanut butter and an open box of saltine crackers. On top of a pile of papers, Chee saw an advertising circular for hearing aids with the name Herman Natachi on the label, quick reassurance that he had come to the right place.

Chee stepped toward the back of the house, where he assumed he'd find the bedroom. Based on his experience, he prepared for the worst but hoped to see an empty bed.

"Mr. Natachi. Mr. Natachi?"

The room was empty, the bed made. No sign of a disturbance, just a pair of brown-framed reading glasses and a leather-bound book on the table next to the bed. Chee felt the stiffness flow out of his neck and shoulders. On a shelf across from the bed he noticed a beautiful belt buckle, a prize for roping someone had won at a rodeo ten years ago. If he was like most people, Mr. Natachi kept his jewelry in the bedroom, and sure enough, on top of the nightstand Chee saw the bolo tie with the silver tips Bernie had described.

In the old days, some people used the pawn system for safeguarding valuables. Chee remembered his relatives going to the pawnshop to rescue their favorite turquoise necklaces and silver belt buckles for special events, then re-pawning them. In his grandparents' days, people had nothing much in their homes to steal and the rare pilfering was handled among the clans, not by the police.

Chee wrote a note on his business card, asking for a call, and wedged it between the screen and the front door. He might have guessed wrong about Mr. Natachi and driving. Or maybe the old gentleman had a buddy who picked him up—that would explain the fresh tire track. He ruled out a trip on a horse; neither this house nor the one nearby had a corral.

He decided to check the nearby house to talk to Ryana before he headed to Chinle. She might know where her grandfather was. Maybe Mr. Natachi himself had stopped in for coffee and Chee could interview them both.

He opened the door to his SUV and realized the July morning had heated the interior to pizza-baking temperature. He relocked it. The walk would do him good.

The sun, glaring from a cloudless sky, had begun its daily job of baking the already desiccated landscape. He remembered the times he'd been in Washington, DC, in the summer, where trees blocked the sky, a monotony of green dominated the color scheme, and the thick air left a sticky residue on your skin. In his opinion, brown held more interest. A person could see the bones of the earth out here. He felt at home.

Like Mr. Natachi's place, the larger house also seemed deserted. A shade covered the front window. A plastic bowl half full of water sat on the porch, but, again, no dog barked. He rang the doorbell, waited, then knocked. He studied the door frame, where a large spot of what looked like blood stood out, red against the white paint, at about shoulder height.

He rapped again, louder and more persistently. "Ryana? Everything OK in there?"

Then he heard a voice behind the door. "Grandfather?"

"No, it's Jim Chee."

"Who?"

"Mrs. Manuelito's son-in-law. I'd like to talk to you."

"Who?"

"Open the door so we can hear each other better."

"I can't talk now. I've got to go to work, my ride is on her way."

"I see blood out here. Are you hurt?"

"Blood?" The space on the other side of the door drew quiet.

"Where do you work?" Chee felt sweat accumulating in the places where his hatband touched his skin.

"At the senior center."

"I saw a car out there. Why do you need a ride?"

"Oh, that's my boyfriend's. He's not here right now or he'd drive me."

"I'll give you a lift. We can talk in the car. My unit has air-conditioning."

"Oh, what the hey."

The door opened.

He'd seen a lot of surprises in his days as a cop,

and this was another. Ryana was almost as tall as he was, something around six feet, with jet-black hair that fell to her shoulders in a neat, blunt curtain. She had sparklingly clear dark eyes and, as far as he could tell, perfect skin. She wore jeans that hugged her long legs and a shirt with a green-and-black print design, cut low enough to allow room for a silver-and-coral necklace to rest against the burnished skin of her chest. She met the textbook definition of beautiful.

"Come on in."

He followed her, admiring a hanging lamp made of antlers over the dining table. He smelled the residue of coffee and toast from her small kitchen. She walked ahead of him into the living room.

"Sit. I just need my shoes and a minute to call Elsie. I hope she hasn't left already to pick me up."

"I have to talk to Mr. Natachi, too. Do you know where he is?"

"No. He and I usually have coffee before I go to work. I guess he made other plans and didn't tell me. I heard a car drive up to his house this morning." Chee recognized worry in her voice. "What did you say about blood?"

"I'll show you."

"OK."

Ryana disappeared down the hall and closed the door. He hadn't seen any bandages or noticed wounds on her hands or arms. The shade drawn over the window that faced the road gave the morning light the color of Canyon de Chelly's sandstone. He listened to the unexpected crunch of tires on the dirt road. Then he heard the gunshots.

9

The closeness of the gunshots propelled Chee to his feet. He moved his hand toward his gun as he raced for the door.

"What was that?" Ryana came from the bedroom, a shoe in her hand.

"Stay here. I'll be right back."

He ran outside in time to see a black car pulling away from the house. He watched a person slowly rise to hands and knees in the cloud of dust the car left in its wake. The man crawled for a moment and then collapsed, rolling onto his back. Chee saw the red stain on his denim shirt. He sprinted toward the person, keeping an eye on the retreating car.

Behind him, he listened to Ryana's racing footsteps and the wail of her scream. He knelt next to the victim. He knew that the gunshot could have nicked an artery, injured the heart or the lungs. If the spine was involved, moving the man could cause more damage. He also realized it would take time, too much time, for an ambulance to find the house.

Ryana grew quiet and squatted next to him. "They got him. They hurt my shicheii. Oh my God. This is on me."

The old man's lips parted at the sound of her voice and he moaned. Ryana began speaking to Mr. Natachi in Navajo.

Chee trusted his instincts and made the decision. "We'll have to get him to the hospital." He ran to his unit and moved his first aid kit and a blanket from the trunk to the front seat.

As he drove toward them, he rolled down the windows to allow the sunbaked air to escape. He parked as close as he could to the injured man, grabbed the blanket, gloves, tape, and a package of sterile dressing from the first aid kit.

"He's still alive." When Ryana looked up, he saw the blood on her shirt. "What's that sound?"

"I think it's air flowing into his chest from the bullet hole." He noticed her focus on the pinkish foam seeping through the man's shirt.

Ryana looked at him. "Tell me what to do. I've had a bunch of first aid classes as part of my job at the senior center."

He put on one pair of gloves and quickly moved the fragments of cloth from Mr. Natachi's shirt away from the edges of the hole. He handed the second pair of gloves to Ryana. "I'm placing the plastic from the dressing over that hole to keep the air from rushing in. I want you to tape it here along the edges. Not too tight."

"There's so much blood." He heard her fear.

"Don't think about that. Put on the gloves and do this, and tell your shicheii that you need him to live."

The improvised bandage worked with the wound well enough that Chee felt comfortable moving the old gentleman into his unit.

"Help me get him onto the blanket, then we can lift him."

Ryana was strong and knew how to follow instructions. Using the blanket as a sling, together they placed him on the back seat. She squeezed into the car near her grandfather's head.

Chee closed the back door and slid behind the steering wheel. "You know how to find the entrance to the ER." He phrased it as a statement so she would respond in kind.

"Yes. Can you get back to the pavement?"

"Sure." His sense of direction and orientation had always been good, and his years in law enforcement had strengthened that quality. He remembered seeing signs for the hospital and was positive he could find it himself on the first try. But he wanted to keep the young woman involved so she wouldn't panic and create an additional problem. He used his cell phone to advise the Chinle station of the situation. He described the black sedan with dark tinted windows and the white license plate he saw leaving the house and the direction in which it was headed. If he had been a little quicker, he knew, he might have captured the plate number.

They had reached the asphalt by the time that call was done. He turned toward Chinle.

"How's he doing?"

"His eyes are closed, but he gave my hand a squeeze." He heard the catch in her voice. "Do you think—"

"He'll be OK." Chee infused his voice with so much confidence even he believed it. "You said this was on you, Ryana. What did you mean?"

"I just . . . Oh, slow down. We're coming to an intersection. Turn left."

He put on the brakes, thankful that the truck with the trailer behind him wasn't following too closely. "Tell me where to go a little sooner, won't you?"

"Sorry. This is a shortcut."

"Why did you say this was on you?"

"No one would want to harm my grandfather. I thought I'd fixed everything but—" She stopped to stifle a sob. "He doesn't look so good. Do you really think he'll make it?"

The radio came on before he could respond.

"Sergeant Chee, I have notified the hospital that you are on the way. When you arrive, a crew will be in front with a gurney. Is there a family member or someone we can contact to provide the hospital with the necessary information?"

"Hold on." He turned to Ryana. "Can you stay at the ER with your grandfather and talk to the people there?"

"Yeah."

"What's your last name?"

"Florez."

Chee went back on the radio and gave the dispatcher the name. He had turned on his emergency light bar as soon as he had left Ryana's house. "There's more traffic, so I'm turning on the siren. I don't want to take a chance on anyone hitting us as we drive through Chinle." He reached for the switch, then pulled back.

"Tell me who did this."

He heard another sob.

"Tell me so I can catch the son of a gun and make him pay for hurting an old man."

"I . . . I . . . I'm not sure."

"Tell me anyway."

She choked out the name. "Yazzie. Arthur Green Yazzie."

Chee called the dispatcher with the information, then turned on the siren and made his way through Chinle with record speed. He parked at the ER entrance, and followed the hospital crew, the old man, and Ryana to an exam intake room. The Chinle IHS staff was quick, professional, and appropriately noncommittal about Mr. Natachi except to say he would need emergency surgery and possibly a blood transfusion. Ryana moved away from her grandfather, giving the staff room to work, and Chee stood next to her. "I need more information about the shooter. What else do you know?"

"Nothing."

"You said someone drove to his house this morning. Did you see the car?"

"No, I just heard the noise. I was in the bathroom."

"I, or someone, will go back to your house to search for the shell casings and whatever else we can find to figure out who did this."

"Do what you need to do. I can't think about that now. Didn't you hear what the doctor said about blood? It's not good to have a stranger's blood in your veins. I have to see if I can be a blood donor. Or if he'll survive without it."

Chee understood. Many traditional Diné believed that blood from a blood bank carried unseen dangers. Some who had received emergency transfusions reported nightmares, fatigue, visits from chindiis, and even taking on the personality of the donor. To have blood that had flowed in a non-Navajo or a person who was now deceased could bring danger, and even blood from another Navajo might cause problems. A relative made the best donor, and the closer the kinship, the better.

He shoved those thoughts aside. "Ryana, the hospital has traditional healers who can help with this. Tell me who Arthur Green Yazzie is and why he would shoot your grandfather."

She stared at the floor.

"You have to help so no one else gets hurt. Including you."

When she looked up, he saw the shiny tear streaks on her face. "I need to be with my shicheii." She moved away, toward her grandfather's bed.

Chee raised his voice. "You said this was on you. You need to help fix things."

Ryana started to sob. A nurse who had been watching them took a step closer and gave him a stern look. "Mr. Natachi is going to surgery in a few minutes. They need time alone. You can wait in the hall."

Arthur Green Yazzie. The name drummed in his head, reverberating like a soundtrack in a B movie. He went to his police unit, radioed the station, and talked to Black.

He relayed the story of the shooting in detail, providing a better description of the car, including a roundish dent in the rear bumper.

"You said earlier a white license plate. Arizona?"

"I just got a glimpse, but no. I think California."

He added Ryana's reaction and the name she'd given up.

"How's the victim?"

"Still alive. They're taking him to surgery. Have you heard of this Yazzie guy?"

"Green Yazzie was the go-to guy for bad news out here for a long time. It followed him like a stench. But he never got violent. I haven't thought about him for a while. If he's back in the area, he's been a good boy."

Chee remembered Ryana's reticence to give him the name. "It happened pretty quick and the car had tinted windows. I didn't get a look at who was in the vehicle, but my gut tells me at least two people. The driver and the shooter."

"Somebody needs to see if Ryana has more to say." Black paused. "You want to work this case."

It was a statement, not a question, but Chee responded anyway. "You bet. Can you get a search warrant for Ryana's place and Mr. Natachi's home?

The tracks I saw might match those of the shooter's vehicle, and I noticed blood on the door frame of her house."

"Will do. I'll talk to Largo, tell him what's up and that I'd like you to take charge of this."

Attempted murder—or homicide, if Mr. Natachi died—took precedence over nabbing speeders, dealing with drunks, and even shutting down meth labs. Largo understood how what looked like a minor incident could evolve into something bigger. And, of course, the FBI also could be involved.

"I'll call now." Black sighed. "I like that old man, and if he has a chance to survive, it's because of you."

After that, Chee thought about the best way to make the phone call he'd been dreading and arrived at no conclusion. He dialed the number before he could talk himself out of it.

Leaphorn answered on the third ring. "Yá'át'ééh. Make it quick, Chee. I'm on my way out."

"So, I was at a house outside of Chinle, working a burglary case. The man I went to interview got shot while I was there. His granddaughter ID'd the shooter as Arthur Green Yazzie." From his years of working with the Lieutenant, Chee knew better than to add his speculation and opinions.

"Arthur Green Yazzie?"

"Yes, sir."

"She's wrong. He's still incarcerated. Besides, he was an addict with a history of burglaries and even some robberies but no violence. The case I worked that sent him to prison was a few years ago. He got a long sentence." Leaphorn told him where the man was serving time. "Are you the investigator on the shooting?"

"Yes, sir."

"Call Mona Willeto—she's Yazzie's sister, remember? The call you told me about a few days ago. Let her know I asked you to find out what she has to say. Tell her I'm slammed on the case I'm working now. Use your judgment to decide if she knows anything about what happened in Chinle. Got it?"

Chee thought Leaphorn had ended the call, but then the Lieutenant was back. "And if you decide it is important, don't wait three days to give me the message."

Chee called Mona Willeto and left his cell number as well as that of the Shiprock substation for follow-up on her voicemail.

He returned to the room where he had left Ryana, Mr. Natachi, and the nurses. It was empty. At the desk, he found the nurse who had been with them and asked about the old man.

"He's in surgery, then he'll be in recovery. He won't be able to see anyone for quite a while. I'd estimate four or five hours from now at the soonest."

"Do you know what happened to the young woman who was with him?"

"After you left, she answered some health questions about him and waited until he went to surgery and the doctors determined that he didn't need a blood donation right now. I haven't seen her since. She was eager to get out of here." The nurse pushed a strand of hair back in place. "A lot of people aren't comfortable in hospitals."

"I was making some phone calls in my car, facing the building's exit. I never saw her leave."

"She didn't want to talk to you, did she? I know you have a job to do, but you badgered that poor girl. Couldn't you see she was heartbroken?"

Chee thought of several responses, none appropriate.

He called Ryana's cell phone but wasn't surprised when she didn't answer. From his unit he radioed Black with an update, including Leaphorn's statement that Yazzie should still be in prison. "I'm going back to Mr. Natachi's house. I want to take another look at the place where he was attacked." In the rush to get the injured man to the hospital, he could have missed something.

"OK. We're working on a search warrant."

On this second trip along the rim of Canyon de Chelly, Chee encountered more traffic. The Navajo families who sold souvenirs to visitors had set up at the scenic overlooks with the canyon's buttes, ruins, and natural sandstone architecture as their backdrop. The rebuke from Leaphorn still burned. He'd made a mistake in not giving the Lieutenant the message right away, but Leaphorn hadn't wanted to talk to the woman anyway. The Lieutenant was acting grumpier than usual.

He thought about Mr. Natachi's situation. Why, near one of the most sacred places in the world, would a man be abducted, returned to his home, and then shot? Why had Ryana accepted responsibility for the incident? He couldn't put the pieces together, but he sensed that the beautiful young woman was deeply involved.

The officer dispatched to limit access to the site of the shooting sat in his unit at the junction of the main road and the rutted drive that led to Ryana's house. Chee introduced himself, and the man, Ralph Slim, did the same. "The lieutenant told me to expect you. No one has been by since I arrived. He wants me to wait until the search team got here and we get a warrant. Was the incident by the main road?"

"No, closer to the house. Is there a back way in?"

Officer Slim grinned. "You know there is. Everybody has a back way and an alternate to that and then the way you can walk up, come on horseback, or with a four-wheeler. I haven't heard any vehicles since I arrived except those on this road."

"When did you get here?"

"A while ago. If I'd known you were coming, I would have ordered lunch."

"I hope I won't be here that long."

Slim turned down the music on the radio. "Yeah, me, too. Black expected to hear from the judge within the hour."

Chee parked next to the patrol car. He stood in the shade to make a call. When Ryana had not answered after the sixth ring, he heard the beep of an incoming call and picked it up.

Bernie's voice was tinged with concern. "I just heard from Sandra that you're investigating a shooting out there. What happened?"

He filled her in. "The man who got hurt is that friend of your mother, Mr. Natachi."

"Wow. It was bold to shoot the old man in broad daylight with you there."

"Whoever did it might not have noticed my unit, and I was inside when it happened. I wasn't able to see the shooter or the license plate number."

"So, does this mean you were in the wrong place at the right time? Kind of like me and the body yesterday." The brightness in her voice lightened his mood. "You're lucky you could ID the car. And Mr. Natachi probably wouldn't have survived long without you."

"I hope he will be able to say who did this to him." Chee felt sympathy for the victim well up and transform into anger. He changed the subject. "What's happening out your way?"

Bernie's voice had energy in it. "I'm chasing the flea market guy who fenced the stolen bolo. I'll let you know how it goes."

"Anything else?"

"Nothing exciting. I spent a while serving papers and arrested a dude for public intoxication. Now I'm on my way to a collision that involved a cow."

"People should never let their cows drive."

She groaned.

Chee told her about his conversation with Leaphorn and the newly accused Green Yazzie. "If Green Yazzie's sister calls for me at the station, can you talk to her?" He gave her a little background.

"No problem."

He saw a Navajo Police car approach. "Thanks. Gotta go."

"You be safe out there."

The two crime scene investigators were officers he'd worked with before, solid professionals.
They gave him a copy of the warrant to read while
they took out their gear. Chee explained what he
had seen.

While the officers knocked on the door of Ryana's house and then entered to leave a copy of
the warrant and begin their search, Chee walked
slowly down the dirt driveway. He ambled toward
the main house, eyes on the ground, looking for
tracks, bullet casings, anything to help the investigation. He stopped near the spot where Mr.
Natachi had emerged from the car before being
shot. The hard-packed soil had sandy pockets that
helped preserve the tracks. He saw a few shuffling impressions from Mr. Natachi, his own boot
prints, other shoes that were probably Ryana's,
and, to his delight, tire tracks that matched those
he had seen outside Mr. Natachi's house.

He took photos of all of it, careful not to dis-
turb the impressions. Then Chee used his cell
phone again to take a picture of the tire track in
front of the old man's house. The afternoon was
calm, not even a whisper of a breeze. For now, the
still air and dryness preserved the evidence.

He searched for shell casings and eventually
found one among some rocks, the brass glinting
in the sun. He took a picture of it. He found two
more, accounting for every shot he remembered.

He told the investigation team about the casings and the tracks and his photos. They would
retrieve and preserve the evidence. Time to go.

Chee drove back to the Chinle station, updated Lieutenant Black, and then called the prison. After several transfers and long minutes on hold, he learned that, as Leaphorn had said, Arthur Green Yazzie remained incarcerated.

He passed the information on to Black.

"So, either Ryana lied, or the man who shot her grandfather looked enough like Yazzie to confuse her. Too bad we can't pin this on Yazzie. It would have been great to wrap up this shooting." Black twisted his wedding ring. "You mentioned that you wanted to take a look at the other recent burglaries. Mark Adakai from dispatch pulled the files for you. I don't think you'll find much that will be helpful, but he will set you up on a computer back there."

In the next room, Chee noticed that one of the tables had three kinds of cookies, some chocolate-dipped strawberries, a dish of nuts, and a plate with cheese and crackers in several shapes and flavors. "Looks like someone's having a party."

"Had a party. Mark's nephew graduated from Miyamura High School down in Gallup over the weekend. He helped with food for the celebration, and he brought us the leftovers. There's water and sodas in the cooler."

Chee helped himself to an oatmeal cookie, a strawberry, and a napkin. "I've been thinking about Mr. Natachi's burglary. Why do you think it's connected to the other cases?"

"Good question. First, the timing. He came in to report it during the recent rash of burglaries, and even though he couldn't say for sure when the

bolo disappeared, it made sense that he was another victim of the crime spree. The reports all
mentioned the usual items—jewelry, guns, electronics, cash if it was lying around—and, again, the
bolo fit the pattern."

Black rested his hip against the edge of the desk.
"All the homes were isolated, no neighbors to hear
anything. None of the victims reported any vandalism. Not like what we see sometimes when a
place is disturbed, destroyed really, from anger
or meanness. These dudes are neat; no couches
slashed, no kitchen drawers dumped out, none of
that."

"How many incidents?"

"Nine in the past three weeks. And no fingerprints at the scenes."

Chee paused at the number, exceptionally high
for an area of about 5,500 residents.

"How do the burglars gain entry?"

Black shifted position. "You know how it is with
some of these elderlies. They grew up in a safer
world. A lot of them leave their doors unlocked
or windows open. In a couple of cases a lock was
jimmied."

"Did Ryana's place get hit when her grandfather's
jewelry was stolen?"

"If it did, she didn't report it. Come on, I'll show
you the reports and you can tell me if you get any
bright ideas."

In a back room, a few uniformed officers sat at
computer monitors. Chee's entrance drew some
nods of recognition. Black motioned him to an
empty desk, and a young man came over to them.

"Hey, Sergeant Chee. I'm Mark Adakai. I'll set you up here."

Black smiled. "You're in good hands with Mark. Have a seat."

Chee adjusted the chair to suit his height.

Adakai rolled up the empty chair next to Chee's and brought the computer to life. He clicked on an icon, and the burglary information appeared as a vertical list of files. He showed Chee how to access the reports and pictures of the stolen items. "This should be what you need, Sergeant."

"Thanks."

"I'm working at the desk over by the window, so come and get me if I can help." Adakai started to leave, then hesitated. "I heard about Mr. Natachi getting shot. Do you know how he's doing?"

"He's at the hospital now. Is the gentleman a friend of yours?"

"I remember him from when I was a kid and he'd visit our school to see his granddaughter, Ryana. The teacher might get him to teach us a little Navajo, tell a story, you know? I met him again when he came in to file the burglary report. He still knew my name."

"Well, Mr. Natachi got his bolo back."

"No kidding?" Adakai's eyes widened. "How did that happen?"

Chee told the story.

"Did the police find the guy who was trying to sell it?"

"We're working on it. What do you know about the gentleman's granddaughter?"

"Let's see." Adakai picked up a pencil from the desktop and rolled it between his thumb and fore-finger. "Ryana grew up here, but her family orig-inally was from the Toadlena area. Her mom and dad both worked for the tribe. She went to Phoe-nix after she graduated from high school." He stopped. "You wanna hear stuff like that?"

"Whatever you've got. Her aunt lives near my wife's mother's place. I'm curious about her."

"So, when her parents retired, they bought an RV. They're traveling, seeing the country for a year or two. Cool, huh? Ryana came back to take care of their house and to be with her grandfather.

"Evidently Ryana hit a rough spot in Phoenix. Drugs, booze, whatever." Adakai paused. "I'm just telling you what I've heard, OK?"

"Sure thing."

"When she came back, she looked up some of her old friends here and someone helped her get that job at the senior center. That must have been about twelve months ago." Adakai tapped the pencil's eraser against the desk. "Have you met her?"

"Yes. I talked to her this morning when I went out to interview her grandfather about the rob-bery. She's certainly a beautiful woman. What did she do in Phoenix?"

Adakai hesitated. "She claims that she did some movie work."

"She's pretty enough to be an actress. Are you two friends?"

"Acquaintances. When she got back here, I asked

her out a couple of times, but she decided I wasn't her type."

Chee waited, but Adakai didn't offer any stories.

"Ryana says her grandfather's burglary never happened and claims he's getting forgetful. But the old man seemed sharp to my wife, and she's familiar with old folks. And then Ryana blamed a man who is in prison for shooting him. I'm having a hard time figuring out what's up with her. What do you think? Is she telling tales?"

Adakai rolled the pencil down to his palm and then back to his fingertips.

Chee said, "This is just between us."

"Well, even in high school, Ryana went for the bad boys, left us nice guys in the dust. Right after graduation, she got serious with an older dude who moved here from Nevada. His wife showed up, kicked Ryana out, and made a big stink. Everyone in town knew about it. Mr. Nevada went home, and that's when Ryana moved to Phoenix.

"When she came back, like I said, I tried to befriend her, ask her out to dinner, but she had that attitude. I hear she's with some weird white dude now. They say he got busted in Fresno, but there was some problem with the evidence. All this is just rumor anyway." A phone rang in the other room and Adakai looked toward the noise. "That's about it. I gotta catch that call."

"What's the boyfriend's name?"

"Something like Micky, Nicky, Ricky."

"Thanks. And thanks for bringing those cookies."

Chee filed the information away and turned

back to the computer. He wasn't optimistic. From his training, he knew that burglars hit more than 2.5 million homes each year in the United States, and police solved fewer than 15 percent of the cases. He opened an electronic report. A handful of the Chinle victims had included copies of the receipts for their televisions or computers, paperwork that would make it easier for police to return the items if they were ever found. Some of the reports had pictures of the stolen jewelry, usually with someone wearing it. The most recent burglary had occurred six days ago. Chee studied the picture of an elderly woman wearing a squash blossom necklace, an outstanding combination of silver, turquoise, and good design, easy to identify if it turned up at a flea market or online. He glanced at some of the scans of victims' handwritten descriptions of the items, most of them in Navajo in the wobbly penmanship that sometimes comes with age. It saddened him that a person would steal these irreplaceable family treasures, most likely to feed an addiction.

When he thought he had a grasp on what had been stolen, he called Largo and updated him on the way a case about a bolo tie had morphed into attempted murder. He expected to find Largo annoyed with the way Black had poached him from his Shiprock duties; the information was a peace offering.

"Yeah, I know. Black filled me in when he asked if you could work with him to follow up." He heard Largo sigh. "Why is it that whenever you go out on a simple case, it turns complicated?"

"I don't know, sir." Chee hoped it was a rhetorical question. "Lieutenant Leaphorn used to ask me the same thing."

"Speaking of Leaphorn, the rookie can breathe through his nose again and see with both eyes. I told him about Leaphorn coming to meet with him this afternoon, and he thinks it's a reward or something."

Chee understood the rookie's assumption. Personal attention from the legendary Lieutenant came with bragging rights.

Later that afternoon, Chee called the hospital and learned that Mr. Natachi had survived the operation and was in the surgical recovery area. He left some notes, thanked Adakai for his help, and drove back to the hospital, hoping to catch Ryana.

Mr. Natachi had been moved to a regular patient room. He seemed to be sleeping. Ryana sat in a chair by her grandfather's side, holding his hand. She looked up when Chee entered.

"I got your calls, but I couldn't talk. I had to get things settled at work and find a substitute so I could be with him." She gave Mr. Natachi's hand a squeeze and released it.

"How is he?"

"They say the bullet shattered some ribs. He's stable for now and not in pain. But who knows what might happen."

"Have you spoken with him?"

She nodded. "A little. He opened his eyes a few times, but he hasn't talked back."

Chee walked to the bed and leaned in toward Mr. Natachi. "Hello, sir. Can you hear me?"

The old man nodded, his chin barely moving. Chee noticed that the oxygen tube had pulled free of one nostril and gently replaced it.

"I'm a policeman." He switched to Navajo and introduced himself formally, adding that he was the son-in-law of Bernie's mama. "I want to find out why this bad thing happened to you."

The old man opened his eyes and motioned to Ryana to come closer. He spoke softly in Navajo. "This is nothing. Promise you will keep that one safe." He moved his lips to indicate his grand-daughter.

"Yes, I promise. Sir, who hurt you?"

Instead of an answer, Mr. Natachi closed his eyes.

Chee turned to Ryana. "Did you understand what we said?"

She nodded and wiped her nose with a tissue.

"I promised to protect you. The only way I can is if you give me the truth about what happened."

She looked at the floor. "I told you all I could."

"Your grandfather would have died if the man in the car had aimed better and if we hadn't brought him here. Don't you care?"

A silent tear escaped and made a glistening line down her cheek.

"Ryana, you know who shot him. This happened because of something you did or didn't do, or something you saw. I will try to protect you, but I need your help."

He took a breath. Exhaled. He could see that she was listening.

"If you love your grandfather, you'll tell me why he got shot so I can find the person who did it. And don't lie again about Arthur Green Yazzie. I called the prison."

"My poor shicheii. I never wanted any of this." He heard anger in her voice as well as grief. "Leave me alone. Go back to Shiprock."

"I can't. You heard your grandfather."

Ryana took the old man's hand again. "All right then. If you want to help, give me two thousand dollars."

Chee took a breath. "Why? What do you need all that money for?"

One of the machines connected to Mr. Natachi began to beep, and at the same time the chime of an old-fashioned doorbell filled the room. Ryana glanced at the phone in her lap and shut off the doorbell with a quick swipe of a finger.

She stood. "It takes the nurses a while to get here. I'll let them know about the beeping. Will you stay with him while I do that and go to the restroom?"

The machine kept beeping.

"Two thousand, huh?"

"Sit here, closer to him, while I'm gone. Hold his hand."

She leaned over the old man, whispered into his ear, and kissed his cheek before she left.

Chee took the vacant chair. "Sir, who did this to you?"

Mr. Natachi said nothing.

"The attack on you, was it meant to scare her?"

Mr. Natachi's eyes stayed closed, but his chin moved subtly toward his chest and back up again. He looked gray and tired, but Chee pressed on. He repeated a version of the who-did-it question, this time in Navajo.

The machine's noise had increased to the point where, Chee deduced, someone in the parking lot could probably hear it. He spoke louder to be heard over the commotion. "Your granddaughter is involved in something that worries you. Something not part of the way the Holy People told us to follow. Something dangerous. I need to understand what this is to protect her."

Just when he concluded that the old man had gone to sleep despite the racket, Mr. Natachi opened his eyes.

"Yes." He spoke with a vigor that surprised Chee. "Dangerous and evil."

Having Ryana out of the room made it easier to say what came next.

"Your granddaughter asked me for a lot of money. If she had it, would that make her safe?"

Mr. Natachi didn't hesitate this time. He moved his head right to left and left to right twice and whispered, "No" and then, in Navajo, "Ndaga'."

A nurse came in, and the old man shifted his attention to her. She was a bilagáana but greeted them both with "Yá'át'ééh." She walked to the machine and stopped the noise with the push of several buttons and then spoke to the patient. "I'm going to check your vital signs, and George will be in to x-ray your chest. He can do it right here in the room. Do you understand?"

Mr. Natachi nodded.

She focused on Chee. "I'm Lucinda. I'll be his nurse for the rest of the day and again tomorrow. Are you his son?"

"Sort of." He read the question in her eyes. "I'm responsible for Ryana, his granddaughter."

"What a beautiful young woman. I saw her with him when I started my shift." She noticed that the ID badge on her strap had flipped backwards and turned it.

Chee saw her name and photograph. "How is he doing?"

"Better than the doctors expected. The next twelve hours are crucial. By the way, Ryana's blood type matches his, and she agreed to be a donor if necessary. He's doing OK for now without a transfusion."

Chee said, "I know he'll be happier if he doesn't need blood from anyone. Can I check in with you for an update on his condition?"

"Of course. My hospital cell number is on the information board." She pointed to it. "Or just call the nurses' station and they'll connect us. It's nice that Mr. Natachi has family here. Having someone who cares helps people recover."

Chee nodded. That was one of the many reasons Navajo traditional healing ceremonies worked. The realization that dozens of friends and relatives would come to support you, bringing food, firewood, and their songs and prayers gave powerful energy to the patient.

After the nurse left, Chee asked again about the shooting, but Mr. Natachi either was asleep or pretending to be. He waited with the old man until the X-ray technician arrived and he knew without question that Ryana wasn't coming back. He wondered what she had whispered to her shicheii.

On his way to the car, Chee dialed her phone, then texted: Call me asap about your grandfather. He viewed his promise to Mr. Natachi with regret. But he'd given his word to an elder, and so it was.

Back at the Chinle station, Adakai showed him the information he'd compiled as requested on Ryana's time in Phoenix. The file included her Arizona driver's license, a car registration for a BMW, and one paid speeding ticket. No references to any involvement with Arthur Green Yazzie or other criminal activity. It looked as though Yazzie's intersection with the law had all been in Lieutenant Leaphorn's era and mostly on Leaphorn's part of the vast Navajo Nation.

He saw Adakai at his workstation by the window and waved the man over to him.

"Thanks for the file on Ryana. I'm curious about something. You said she did some acting for the movies in Phoenix. I wonder if she had a screen name, you know, like Marilyn Monroe was really Norma Jean something."

Adakai rubbed his left hand with his right, stroking a tasteful, small star tattoo. "I gave you everything I found. Maybe Ryana made up the movie story to look more important, more accomplished than she is. She's stuck on herself. I think

I said that already. I wouldn't put it past her to lie. You already mentioned that she lied about the bolo." Adakai took a breath. "Did you have any luck on the burglaries?"

"No, nothing yet. I'm working on that unless somebody else gets shot while I'm here."

The old man looked peaceful when Chee returned to the hospital. Ryana was not in the room with him. Chee knew that, when his time at the hospital was done, Mr. Natachi would also ask for the type of healing that involved songs, herbs, and sandpaintings in a ceremony to return him to hozho, to a state of peace, balance, and harmony.

Nurse Lucinda told him, without being asked, that the X-rays showed that Mr. Natachi's lungs were clear. "And, so far at least, there's no sign of infection. Considering what he's been through, that's quite something." She readjusted the IV. "When Ryana came to check on him, she asked me to tell you not to be mad about Walter. That she just mentioned him because she'd seen something about him on television."

"Could you run that by me again?"

Lucinda reached into her uniform pocket. "I knew I'd have trouble remembering the name." She pulled out a yellow slip of paper and read from it. "Arthur Green Yazzie. Sorry about that. You want this?"

"No. I know who it is. When did Ryana leave?"

"About half an hour ago. Before she left, she donated some blood. She told me she had a lot to take care of, and she might not be back for a while. She specifically asked me to tell you not to worry about her. Wasn't that sweet?"

No, Chee thought, it wasn't sweet. It meant she didn't want him on her trail.

10

Before heading to Shiprock to meet with Wilson Sam, Joe Leaphorn had driven to the Big Rocks area, and with a few well-worded questions, neighbors helped him to track down the modest home of Lee Benally. A boy, around twelve or thirteen, came to the door and said his grandfather wasn't home. Leaphorn introduced himself and showed the young man his Apache County deputy card. The boy, who said his name was Andrews, suddenly looked interested. Leaphorn asked if he spoke Navajo. "I don't, but I understand some of it because my grandfather talks to me that way."

Leaphorn explained his errand as concisely as possible.

The boy smiled. "He brought some of my shimayazhi's things here from her office in a box. I think that could be what you're talking about." Shimayazhi, or Little Mother, was the Navajo version of maternal aunt but, as the translation implied, spoke to a closer connection.

"Would it be all right if I came in to take a look?"

The young man opened the door. "He put the box on the kitchen table." He showed Leaphorn the way and then returned to the couch and whatever form of electronic diversion had occupied him before the interruption.

Leaphorn carefully unloaded the contents—a traveling coffee mug, a small ceramic jar that held paper clips, a stuffed bear, a box of Navajo tea, some colorful pictures that looked as though a child had made them, a pink bag for makeup with "Tiffany" in glittering sequins on the side, and other things a young woman would have at the office to make her day more comfortable and remind her of life outside work. Leaphorn picked up the box, careful not to add his fingerprints to the label or the tape that had sealed it.

He spoke to Andrews. "I moved your aunt's things to the tabletop. Everything is there. I'm leaving with only the box itself. Take a look."

The boy glanced up from his game at the empty brown carton, then went back to his screen.

"Please tell your grandfather to call me if he has any questions. I left a card with my phone number on the table."

"OK."

"I see that she had your picture there on her desk."

The boy looked up again. "I made the frame for her, too, with dogs dancing all around. She really liked it. She liked it so much that she asked me what I wanted back, and then she told me she would get me a dog someday. I don't care if it's a big one or not." The boy paused. "Why did she have to die?"

Leaphorn shook his head.

"It's scary. The medicine was supposed to make her better. Do you believe in witches?"

"No." Leaphorn didn't know what else to say. He noticed the boy holding a cell phone up to the television. "What are you doing there?"

Andrews grinned. "I'm trying to learn accents, you know? So I record them from shows like this and then I play them back and practice." He gave Leaphorn an imitation of what might have been French. "I'm good at recording stuff. My teacher has me record when someone comes in to talk to our class. She didn't even know you can use a phone for that and then transfer the sound to another file on the computer."

"How are you doing on Navajo?"

"It's hard. But there are websites and those two movies, you know about them?"

"I do. *Star Wars* and the one about the fish. What was that called?"

For the first time, the boy responded in Navajo. "*Nemo Hádéést'íį́. Finding Nemo.* But I liked *Star Wars* better." He gave Leaphorn a shy smile.

The brown cardboard container now sat next to him, heading to Shiprock in the seat Louisa often occupied. He photographed the postmark as Bean requested and sent it to him. The inspector texted him back: The photo is usable but don't quit your day job. He knew Bean would let him know when he had news. Even if the news was bad.

Leaphorn had not taken his truck north on US 491 for a long time. It had been even longer since he had been alone in the vehicle for more than a quick trip. He appreciated driving again along with walking without help and, best of all, the ability to say what was on his mind as long as he did it in his native language. He regretted the complications that limited his English. Still, for a man who could well be dead, he told himself, he had nothing to complain about.

The road carried more traffic than he recalled. Or maybe the lack of Louisa chatting about the scenery, the events of her day, national politics, and plans for tomorrow allowed him to better focus on the highway. He headed toward the flat-topped Chuska Mountains, drove past Tohatchi, crossed Naschitti Wash, and headed north toward Sheep Springs.

He turned his brain to the strange case of Mrs. Pinto's missing textile and the unexpected death of her assistant. He heard the voice of Tiffany's father warning him about Mrs. Pinto, hinting at witchcraft, and recalled the note he suspected the man had left on his windshield. He added the story of Robert Peshlakai's long-lost jewelry and the discovery of two of those pieces in the mystery box.

The utility van with Texas plates in front of him flashed its brake lights, and Leaphorn slowed, calling his full attention back to the road. He passed Newcomb, famous for its role in the development of Two Grey Hills weavings and named for trader Arthur Newcomb. Renowned hataali

Hastiin Klah had lived near here years ago. His own mother had lived in the area, too, dying just a few years after she buried his umbilical cord beneath a resident piñon tree. He'd received a scholarship to study cultural anthropology at Arizona State. He'd loved his course work and planned to get a master's degree and become a teacher and perhaps a consultant. But money for teaching assistants was tight the year he graduated. While considering his budget, he received a letter from the tribal councilor who represented the chapter where he had grown up, mentioning that the Navajo Nation police were looking for recruits. He decided that some practical experience would improve his chances of getting into grad school and that the police job would help him pay for his degree.

His father wasn't surprised when he told him he was planning to return to Navajoland. "You had to go back to your mother's home. That's why she buried your birth cord, to tie you to the land."

He passed the entrance test without difficulty and discovered that real-life law enforcement held more challenge than the world of academia. He enjoyed working on the Navajo Nation, not being the only Indian in the room. He became a better detective with each successive case.

He'd lost his appetite for the work after Emma died. He retired at the top of his career, turning down more than one request to be considered as Navajo Nation chief of police.

His thoughts turned to Arthur Green Yazzie and Yazzie's sister. He remembered the man. Maybe whatever crisis or daydream inspired the woman to seek him out had passed. Perhaps Yazzie was up for parole and his sister wanted to thank him for the work that sent the man to prison and tell him how incarceration had made her brother a better person. The family planned to welcome her brother back into their strong, supportive arms.

Leaphorn smiled at the fantasy. In his long career, relatives of a felon had never contacted him after a person had been in prison as long as Green Yazzie. Usually, the convict also had victimized and betrayed his parents, sisters, brothers, cousins, and the rest of his clan, leaving them wary and brokenhearted. While they wished the freed man well, they kept their distance.

The road stirred memories of other cases Leaphorn had handled in which the victim, the victim's family, and sometimes even the alleged perpetrator of the crime talked about witchcraft as the reason for the evil that transpired. He passed Bennett Peak to the west and then Ford Butte. Despite their American names, the monoliths came with Navajo stories of witches and skinwalkers, tales of evil meetings for initiations and other supernatural doings.

Ship Rock rose on the northern horizon as he passed Barber Peak—hardly a peak at all but a relic of the ancient volcanic eruptions that had formed these rocky outcroppings. He watched as Table Mesa, actually three close, flat-topped plateaus, came closer into view.

He pulled off the highway at a convenience store outside Shiprock. Besides needing fuel, he wanted to talk to the manager. Largo had mentioned that Wilson Sam, his potential mentee, had responded to a robbery here.

Leaphorn climbed out of the truck and looked for a squeegee to clean the bugs off his windshield. The buckets of washer fluid were half full but held no tools. He went inside to ask for the equipment and pay for the gasoline in cash. Louisa teased him about this, but old habits die hard. He had lived for years on a cash-only basis. Knowing how much money was in his wallet kept him from overspending. He considered a credit card a tool for emergencies.

The teen girl at the cash register took his money and turned on the gas pump. "The squeegees have been disappearing out there. It's like they want a vacation, kinda like the rest of us who work here. Especially after the robbery." She reached under the counter and pulled out a pole with a sponge and scraper on the end. "Can you bring it back, please?"

He nodded. "Is da manjer aroun?"

"Mrs. Roland is in the back."

"Speak Navajo?"

"Some."

He switched. "I'm a consultant with the Shiprock police following up on that robbery. I'd like to talk to her about that when I'm done outside." Leaphorn gave the girl his card.

From the look on her face, she understood at least some of what Leaphorn said, and the card made it official. "I'll tell her."

He filled the gas tank and washed his windshield, using a paper towel to remove the streaks. Then he moved the truck to one of the parking places in front of the store and took the squeegee back inside. Mrs. Roland, a middle-aged Navajo in a white polo shirt with the company logo on the pocket, greeted him at the counter. "Let's go into the back office."

The "office" was a repurposed storage closet. She moved a cooler from a folding chair and offered Leaphorn the seat. She perched on a nearby box. Her Navajo was good. "Are you working undercover?"

"I'm a private investigator now and a consultant with the Navajo Police."

"I'm glad you stopped by. Did they find the hold-up guy?"

"Not yet. The investigation is ongoing." That sounded better, he thought, than the "nothing new" response Largo had given him. "I wanted to talk to you for some follow-up."

"Sure. Whatever." Mrs. Roland ran her hand through her short-cut gray hair. "You want a soda or bag of chips? On the house."

"No, thank you. I have a few questions about the officer who responded to the call. I understand that you were the one who spoke with him."

"Yeah, it was me all right. The night person didn't show up, so I had to cover that shift. It was a busy evening, too. Not that I'm complaining. I'm glad I was here. I'm a marine, served in Iraq. Some of my team here are high schoolers. It takes more than a punk like that to shake me up, but I'm grateful the kids didn't have to deal with him or with that young cop."

She told him a man wearing sunglasses, jeans, boots, a ball cap, and a hoodie entered the store alone about eleven p.m. "I was suspicious right away. He went over to the cold drink case and stood there until the lady I was making change for left. Then he came over to the cash register with his hand in his sweatshirt pocket like he was pointing a gun at me. He said he had one and told me to give him the money."

Mrs. Roland exhaled. "I gave him the cash. I shoulda taken him down, but I didn't wanna risk getting shot over a hundred bucks. He ran out, and I could see him get into a silver SUV parked right in front. I didn't get the license number, but it was one of those turquoise New Mexico plates. I called the police."

"Tell me about the response."

"Well, the officer got here pretty quick. He was a young guy, very formal. I hadn't seen him before. When I had the other robberies, one time a lady cop came. Short, smart, friendly. I was hoping she'd be the one they sent out here. The other time it was a nice guy, kinda chubby. I remember him joking about how he had to live up to his name, Bigman. I think this one was Wilson Sam something, or something Wilson. I've got his card."

Leaphorn knew the questions the rookie had asked about the robbery and Mrs. Roland's responses would be covered in his report. "What did you think of Sam?"

"He seemed . . . I'm not sure how to put it." Mrs. Roland readjusted herself to rest her back against the wall. "It was like he was too busy or too important or something to listen to me. He had a bunch of questions, took photos, asked about surveillance footage. I told him it would be hard to ID the guy from that because of what he had on and where he stood, but the officer didn't believe me. He acted like I was dumb. He called me *honey*." Mrs. Roland studied the ceiling a moment. "That man had a know-it-all, I'm-tougher-than-you attitude. He would have made some of the team nervous, and that's not what you want when a robbery already has them on edge."

"Can you give me an example of that?"

She rubbed her chin. "So, I thought he might want to talk to the woman I mentioned, the customer right before the robbery. She left the store with her cigarettes and was smoking outside. She could have seen the guy, maybe without the glasses and the hoodie, or noticed what he was driving. Something like that. When I tried to tell Sam, he snapped at me to stick to the facts, that he didn't want to hear about a girl who needed a nicotine fix. I saw that attitude in a few young bucks who came to Iraq. They thought it covered up their jitters about being in a bad situation. It got to be a habit, trying to act like you know what's up when you really don't."

She sat a bit straighter. "You've been around the block a few times, Joe. You've seen it. Men who act like jerks."

"It makes me ashamed. I appreciate you telling

me this about Sam. You have good instincts, a good memory, a good attitude. Did you ever consider joining the police force?"

"I looked into it when I got outta the service. But I was married back then, and my husband was glad to finally have me home and not worry about me. Then he got Parkinson's." Roland moved off her perch. "Sure you don't want a bottle of water or something for the road?"

"Water would be great. I appreciate you taking time to talk to me. You have my card in case you think of something else."

She nodded.

He noticed the heat as soon as he opened the doors to the asphalt in front of the store.

He had left his phone in the charger in his truck and glanced at it now. He'd missed a call from Bernie. He listened to her message, but she must have had bad coverage because he couldn't understand it. He called her and got voicemail. "It's Leaphorn. I'll be at Shiprock for a meeting. Call me or come by the station."

Leaphorn parked at the station, and Largo greeted him like the old friend he was. They shared a few stories and got down to business. Largo told him the rookie had not arrived.

"That's fine. I stopped at the gas station where he'd responded to the robbery." Leaphorn summarized Roland's comments. "I'd like to see how he wrote it up before we talk."

"I thought you might. You'll find some other information here, too." Largo handed him a folder. "I appreciate you doing this, Lieutenant. I'd like to keep the rookie on the force because he has a lot of potential. And I'd like to keep him alive. The incident where somebody broke his nose could have been worse."

Largo led Leaphorn into an empty office. "Take a minute to look at that stuff. I'll let you know when Sam gets here. You can talk in the interview room."

Officer Wilson Sam arrived on time. Leaphorn's first impression confirmed what he'd heard. The young man wore the uniform well and looked physically fit, lean and muscular. They walked together down the hall to the interview room. Leaphorn motioned Sam to the empty chair where the interviewer usually sat. He spoke in Navajo. "Sit there. We'll chat a little."

He noted the young man's lack of surprise at being offered the power seat. Leaphorn introduced himself with a brief overview of his career and mentioned that he and Largo had worked together and that he had mentored Sergeant Jim Chee.

"Well, you know who I am." Sam leaned back. "The captain said you wanted to talk to me about an incident I responded to, that bomb in the high school parking lot. Is that right?"

"Yes. Let's start with that."

"Did he tell you I was one of the first responders?" The rookie crossed his forearms and rested them on the table.

"I heard you got to the scene shortly after the car blew up, and that you found the man who died. Tell me about it."

Sam began at the beginning of the assignment. Leaphorn noted that in his rendition of the story the rookie gave himself a larger role than the written reports had allotted him. He spoke concisely and had good recall of the details.

"What did you think of the other law enforcement people who were at the incident?"

"I know why you're asking. The captain didn't like the way I took charge and wants Manuelito to have most of the credit. He doesn't appreciate the fact that I can think for myself. So is that why you're really here? Tell me the truth."

Leaphorn had anticipated the question. "As I mentioned, Largo and I go back to the days before cell phones. The incident with your nose told him that you have some things to learn. He believes you could become a fine officer, so he asked me to consider working with you to sharpen your skills. Because of your injury, he figured this would be a good time for us to get acquainted."

Sam put his hand to his face. "You know this thing? It wasn't my fault. I was doing my job, and next thing I knew . . . baaam. I'm on the ground, bleeding like crazy."

"So when you see a fight . . ." Leaphorn left the sentence unfinished.

The rookie smiled for the first time. "They stopped once I got hit. The surprise factor. But, yeah, I don't wanna stop a fight this way again. You want the details?"

"Not right now. I'd like to talk about something else." Leaphorn opened the folder Largo had given him and extracted the rookie's report on the gas station robbery. "On my way here, I stopped at the station on 491. I spoke with the manager before I read your report. I have questions about some discrepancies."

The rookie uncrossed his arms. "That's the way things go, isn't it? The witness can't remember or gets it wrong. I write up what she says. Time goes by, and her story changes, right? Women are the worst. They like to hear themselves jabber away, and it takes them too long to get to the point."

"In my experience, there are ways to help people recall details or discuss incidents they have witnessed that might be embarrassing. Many veteran officers use these—you could call them tricks of the trade—to build rapport and learn more about a crime." He paused, giving Sam an opportunity to pursue the topic.

"I can't see that rapport would have made any difference with that old woman. She got testy. Change of life or something. I needed to cover the basics and move on." He gave Leaphorn a condescending look. "Time moves faster these days, quicker than when you worked as a cop."

Leaphorn removed two pieces of paper from his folder. "This is your report." He tapped it. "The next page details my observations from my interview with Mrs. Roland earlier today. We discussed the incident and your visit. Would you like to take a look?"

Sam sighed. "I'm sick of being second-guessed, called a screwup. Is that really why you're here?"

Leaphorn put the pages back in the folder. "I'll say it more clearly. The captain asked if I'd be willing to mentor you, and I told him I needed to meet you first."

"Mentor? Like when kids get in trouble and someone is assigned to them, some grown-up who is supposed to help them go straight."

Leaphorn said nothing.

"I don't need that kind of attention. Thanks anyway. Do you mind giving me that paper with your observations?"

Leaphorn handed him the sheet of paper, wondering if the rookie really cared or if he mistakenly thought he could prevent Largo from seeing the comments.

"Anything else, Lieutenant?"

"Yes." Despite his irritation, Leaphorn kept his voice calm. "Son, lose the attitude. It could get you killed. And one more thing. An honorable man treats women with respect. Now get out of here."

After Sam left, Leaphorn tried Bernie's phone again. This time she answered and they spent a minute on small talk.

"Sir, I was looking forward to seeing you today, but I'm dealing with a stolen-vehicle issue out by Rattlesnake. I don't know when I'll be done."

"OK then. Next trip. Say hello to Chee for me."

"I will. He's in Chinle." Bernie explained briefly.

"What happened with that body you found over the weekend?"

"The Feds are on it. Agent Johnson's not saying much. I've been reinterviewing the Navajos I saw out there, but no one has been helpful. There's one man I haven't been able to find yet, but I hope to wrap that up today. We could use a break in the case." Then Bernie laughed. "My best witness is the dog and he's not talking."

He waited for her to ask about Louisa and end the call, but Bernie surprised him. "What are you working on, Lieutenant? Chee said you're really busy these days."

"Oh, it's complicated."

"Your cases usually are, and I think that's why you take them. You're making me curious."

"I'll tell you over that pie you promised me."

After that, he walked to the captain's office. Largo looked up when Leaphorn knocked on the door frame.

"Come in. I've got some stuff to finish here, then we can have dinner and swap lies about the old days." He motioned Leaphorn to a chair. "What do you think about working with the rookie?"

Leaphorn stayed standing in the doorway. "I'm not the right person, and the officer doesn't think he needs any help.

"You might ask Chee to handle it. He knows the man." Leaphorn glanced at the clock on the wall behind Largo's desk. "Let's do dinner next time. I'm working a case with a deadline, and I need to get back to Window Rock and think about it."

"Sure. Since you're headed that way, can you do me one more favor?"

"What is it?"

"It involves a stop at animal control in Fort Defiance. Bigman brought in an abandoned dog found at a crime scene, and our Shiprock shelter is full.

Sandra could drive it down there in the morning, but since you're going south, would you mind?"

"No problem."

"I'll call to make sure someone is around to receive it."

The call was successful.

Largo loaded the kennel into the bed of Leaphorn's truck. "Dinner next time then, my friend. Thanks for coming. Watch out for the crazies."

Normally, Leaphorn would have phoned Louisa to tell her about his day and let her know that he was on the way home. He could have reached her in Flagstaff, of course, but she had told him she wanted time alone. She'd call when she was ready, he decided. He remembered the phone charger she'd left at the house. Maybe she couldn't call. No, she would use the phone at her old office to ask him to bring the charger and then, well, they could talk.

He drove a different route home, NM 134 past Sheep Springs and then over Narbona Pass at 8,721 feet. The highway took advantage of the natural break between the Tunitcha Mountains to the north and the Chuskas to the south. In the fading light, he saw thick clusters of Gambel oak and slender white aspen trunks with their quaking, roundish leaves. The steep climb to the summit drew runners and cyclists training for competitive events, including a popular race up this same road. The panoramic view of Navajoland stretching to the east was their reward, and now his. He pulled off the highway to enjoy the vista. His disgruntlement at Wilson Sam was gone.

Leaphorn lowered the window. The cool air smelled of ponderosa pine and spruce, and he absorbed the calm. When he drove back onto the highway, he noticed motion with his peripheral vision, and then a large black bear stepped out of the trees and onto the road. Leaphorn lifted his foot off the gas and steered into the other lane, glad there was no oncoming traffic and willing the animal to run back toward the trees and not in front of his truck. It bounded away from him with strong, lumbering beauty. Leaphorn exhaled.

He cruised past the junction for Crystal, famous for its weavers, noticing small herds of cattle grazing on the native grass, seemingly unconcerned about sharing the territory with a large predator. The road continued its descent, heading southwest toward the Arizona border. The golds, pinks, and crimsons of the sunset gave the landscape a deceptive softness. Some considered dusk a time to relax; he found the present moment perfect for rehashing the problem of Mrs. Pinto's missing textile and bracelet.

What had he overlooked? Could someone want Mrs. Pinto to think the shipment contained a precious remnant of the past if it didn't? His thoughts returned to Tiffany's sudden death. Mrs. Pinto had said the young woman was worried about not respecting the dead. If she was a thief, she had reason to be concerned. Could she have taken her own life?

As he approached Fort Defiance, his cell phone rang. He answered on the speakerphone, thinking it was Louisa, but he recognized Jessica's voice.

"Young lady, you're working late."

"No, sir. Well, yes, I have the late shift. I wanted you to know that I found that report on the old accident you wanted."

"Great work."

"It's not me, really. They are organized at the New Mexico Department of Transportation. They located what you needed right away using the date for the Indian Market and the fact that two people died on 666."

"When can I take a look?"

"I could email it."

Leaphorn hated reading long documents on the computer. He waited for her to move to the next option.

"Or, tell you what, I'll print a copy. If I'm gone, I will leave it on my desk with your name."

"I'd appreciate that. I'll come by for it tonight."

"Sir, can I ask you a question?"

"Go ahead."

"Why did you want this?"

Appropriate, he thought, and respectfully timed. "Part of the case you are helping me with involves some items that may have been in one of the cars in that accident."

"Cool. A clue from an old case, like something on TV. That rocks. I'll leave the report here for you tonight."

"Thank you. And I'm hoping you can do me another favor." He asked her to check on Tiffany Benally, to see if she had a record.

"Glad to help. When would you like this?"

"In about an hour if you can."

"I'll do my best."

He arrived in the town of Fort Defiance, rang the bell at the animal shelter, and stood by the kennel in the back of his truck while he waited for a staff member. Leaphorn noticed that the dog was sitting calmly. It looked at him with clear, trusting eyes. He had a stash of jerky in the glove box, and he pulled it out and offered a piece to the animal. It took the treat gently from his hand and swallowed without chewing.

The attendant, a young man with braces on his teeth, lifted the dog and the cage out of the truck for him. He spoke in English. "Is this the animal from the Shiprock police station?"

Leaphorn nodded. "What happens to it now? This dog was found with a dead person. I think it could use some extra attention."

The attendant looked puzzled. "Sorry. I don't speak Navajo."

Leaphorn tried English. "Wha happen to da dog?"

"I don't know what happened to it. The guys up there in Shiprock know its story, so you should ask them. It's probably a stray causing trouble."

"Get dopted?"

"What?"

"Da dog get a home?"

The man shrugged. "Who knows, man? We've got a lot of dogs here. We'll keep it until we know that the investigators don't need it. Then, if no one wants it, we'll put it down."

Leaphorn recalled Largo saying that the dog stayed with the body, even though it was hot, even though it could have gone to the river to cool off and get a drink. Good luck to you, dog, he thought. You were a loyal friend and you deserve a second chance.

He turned on the radio to KTNN and heard Pine Tree Clan Singers, and then an ad for the Native Broadcast Enterprise Scholarship, and then a sales pitch for Cowboy Bob and one-stop shopping for Chevrolets. The half-moon was up when he pulled into the Window Rock police station. Jessica was on the phone, but she had a large envelope and a sweet smile for him. He put the envelope on the passenger seat with the cardboard box, drove home, and started a pot of coffee.

While the coffee brewed, he sat at the table and, with a sense of excitement, took a look at the information.

The report, compiled by New Mexico State Police officers and archived by the New Mexico Department of Transportation, was thorough, too thorough almost—filled with information that didn't matter to his case. He flipped through the pages, learning the makes of the vehicles involved, the estimated time of the accident, and the fact that both drivers were deceased when the first responders arrived. At the scene, the investigating officer found four empty beer cans on the floor of the cab of the truck driven by Rick Fernandez. The report noted that Alvin Begaye and a passenger, a woman named Rita Begaye, were in the sedan with Alvin driving. Rita's address and phone number were included, and the information matched Alvin's. Given the woman's age and the surnames,

Leaphorn assumed she was Alvin's wife, sister, or cousin. Rita had gone to the hospital.

The report made no mention of what had happened to the vehicles, but Leaphorn assumed they had been towed to the nearest impound lot. Before he went to the trouble of tracking that down, he'd use the old phone number and address to search for Rita Begaye. If he was fortunate enough to find her, he would see what she could tell him about the jewelry that might have been in the car the day of the accident.

It was too late to call her now. For the second time since taking the case, he felt like he was making progress. He wished Louisa had been there to share his delight at the breakthrough.

Jessica had included a note that Tiffany Benally had no criminal history.

Leaphorn headed toward his bedroom. Giddi followed.

"What are you doing here?" The cat's green eyes studied him, and then she jumped on his bed. Giddi usually slept with Louisa. He let her stay.

11

As always, Jim Chee's voice over the phone made Bernie smile.

Her day, she told him, had been routine and frustrating. Her efforts to track down the heavy-set Navajo man she had observed before she realized her jogging path was also a crime scene had been futile. Now she faced paperwork, and then she was off to see her mother. "Did I tell you Sister is considering one of those work-from-home offers?"

"No. Did you try to talk her out of it?"

"Of course, but you know how hardheaded she can be." Bernie laughed. "What's new in Chinle?"

"I heard a rumor that Ryana used to work in the movies. I found proof that she had a fancy car in Phoenix, so maybe she used to be famous. But when I searched, nothing. And Mark, the tech expert here, couldn't find any information on that either. I guess it's another lie."

"Did you ask her?"

"I haven't had a chance."

"Darleen might know. They spent time to-gether over the weekend. I'll see what Sister has to say."

"Thanks, sweetheart."

"Will you be home tonight?"

"You bet." She heard his tone brighten. "I can't wait to see you. Any news on the Bigman baby?"

"No. Sandra would have told me and everyone in the Shiprock chapter."

After Chee hung up, Bernie recalled her first encounter with Ryana, back when Mr. Natachi and the girl came every weekend to visit at the house down the road. Ryana radiated happiness. She and Darleen played together. Later, when both girls were sneaking up on adolescence, they would race on the high school track. Ryana, with her longer legs, usually won. Then Ryana's parents moved to start work in Chinle, the girls got involved with other friends, and they lost touch except when the family came back to see Mama's neighbor Auntie Dolly.

Bernie called Darleen. Her sister sounded un-usually perky for such a hot afternoon.

"Guess what? My envelopes just got here. I can start to work."

"Sister, before you do, I could use your help with something, too. An investigation."

"Whoa. Really? What is it?"

Bernie explained.

Darleen started talking as soon as Bernie stopped.

"That is so, so cool. Ryana didn't mention making movies. Maybe we could rent one or stream it on the computer."

"Chee has been calling her, but she isn't answering. Is there any way to find out what movies she made without asking her directly?"

"Yeah. I'll check it out and call you back?"

"I'm going to visit Mama tonight. We can talk then."

"Sure thing. Hey, I'll show you the supplies for my job then, too."

"I wish . . ." Bernie stopped. The deed, however foolish and ill-advised, was done. "I wish you good luck in finding out about Ryana's life in the movies."

"Maybe she was just a voice-over, you know, like in the Navajo *Nemo* or something. I'll check on it right now, Sister. You know what else?"

"What?"

"This is the first time you've asked me to help with a case."

Bernie had been at the substation about an hour when Sandra buzzed her.

"No baby yet. Darleen is on the phone. She sounds excited. Is everything OK with your mom?"

"I think so. I'll let you know. Put her through."

Darleen sounded breathless. "You won't believe what I found, what kind of movies Ryana was making."

"Tell me." From the tone of her sister's voice, Bernie guessed they weren't preschool music videos.

"Naked movies of the triple-X kind. Gross. Is this stuff against the law or anything?"

"No. Ryana is an adult and as long as she did it without being coerced and the movies don't show anyone getting killed or—"

"Don't even go there."

"I hope you're not too upset."

"This stuff is embarrassing, you know?" She heard Darleen exhale. "I can't believe it."

"Was there more than one movie?"

"I found three, then I decided to call you. I couldn't look at any more. I called because I know you wouldn't want to talk about this with Mama around."

"How did you discover the movies?"

"It was tricky. I couldn't find anything under Ryana's name, and I was running out of ideas, and then I remembered how people in entertainment change their names, like that woman involved in the porno business who sued the president. I thought of how you can put up a photo of someone on a social network site, and the computer tells you who it is. I had a photo of Ryana from the weekend. I wasn't sure how to do it, so I asked CS."

CS, perhaps Bernie's least favorite of Darleen's male friends, was a would-be video artist. "Is CS there?"

"No, he's in Santa Fe. He'll never finish editing his movie. He helped me over the phone. A bunch of photos of Ryana came up with a different name, and when I searched that, her movie name, I found, well, what I found."

"What's Ryana's movie name?"

"It's Roxanne Dee." Darleen spelled it. "I guess the Dee stands for Diné."

Or delicious, Bernie thought, or devious. She asked Darleen to send her links to the videos. She wasn't sure how or if Ryana's movie career fit into Mr. Natachi's stolen bolo. As she was thinking about that, Sandra buzzed her.

"Is everything good at home?"

"Yes."

"Largo wants you to check out a place near Toadlena where a young woman Chee needs to interview may have gone." Sandra gave her Ryana's name, her cell number, and Mama's neighbor's address.

12

Sometimes Joe Leaphorn got lucky, and this was one of those times. He called the old number for Rita Begaye and found it still in service. He listened to the phone ring, and as he considered what sort of message would best prompt a call back, a person answered.

"Yá'át'ééh." Leaphorn asked for Rita Begaye, fully expecting to learn that no one by that name lived there.

Instead, the young voice on the other end said, "Big Rita or Little Rita?"

Leaphorn considered the question. "Big."

"She's not here."

"OK. Lil."

"Hold on."

Leaphorn heard a television in the background. He'd begun to wonder if the child who answered the phone had forgotten about him when a woman's voice interrupted his musings.

"Yá'át'ééh."

Leaphorn asked if she spoke Navajo, and when she said she did, he introduced himself as a retired police detective working to help a woman in Window Rock solve a mystery. "I found the name Rita Begaye on the report of an old accident along with this phone number. You are not in any trouble. That Rita was a passenger in a car that was involved in a fatal accident. Was that you, ma'am?"

"Yes. What is this mystery?"

Leaphorn shared the same version of Mrs. Pinto's assignment he had distilled for Peshlakai. He mentioned that the anonymous gift included the necklace, earrings, and the missing bracelet. He told her Peshlakai had created the set and believed it had disappeared after the accident. "That's what I want to talk to you about."

It only took her a moment to respond. "Peshlakai? I don't remember much about that jewelry." He heard uncertainty in her answer. "It was ages ago."

"Maybe if I ask you some questions, memories might come back. It won't take long. It's important."

"Go ahead then."

"First, just to confirm, were you in the car that was wrecked?"

"Yes."

He waited, but she didn't volunteer anything more. He decided to move slowly.

"Would you tell me about that trip?"

He heard her sigh. "The one who died was my husband. We were just married, and I had never been to Santa Fe or to a big art show like that one, the famous Indian Market. I don't like talking about it. Why are you stirring this up?"

Leaphorn explained his assignment again, this time adding a bit about the missing textile and his speculation that tracking the bracelet would help him find the dress. "I read the accident report on the crash, but it left out a lot of things. Mr. Peshlakai told me that the last time he saw that bracelet, he consigned it to your husband for the sale. I'm wondering how it got packed in a box that came to the museum."

"You think the dress in that box belonged to Juanita?"

"That's what the donor wrote. We need to make sure. If it's true, it would be a treasure for our nation. I think the missing bracelet could lead me to the person behind the gift."

"OK then, here's what I remember."

She started with the car wreck. It was late at night after a busy day. US 666 was two lanes and dangerous because of speeding, animals, drunks, and more. They had been driving for hours, and had just passed Tohatchi when she saw headlights approaching and moments later realized the oncoming truck was headed right for them. "I think the man was drunk. My husband moved to the far side of the road and then to the shoulder. The other guy just kept coming at us. It happened fast. You know how loud those trains in Gallup are? The sound was louder, worse. It gives me nightmares still."

He heard her take a deep breath.

"After that, my brain went fuzzy. I remember a woman talking to me in an ambulance. I had to stay five days in the hospital. They told me my husband died right away. The one who did this to us died there, too, on the highway. We were only married two months before the accident." Leaphorn heard the rumble of old grief in her voice. "I hate that road. I don't care that they changed the name. Two little months, and then he was gone forever. My arm and my ribs were broken, and my heart was broken, too.

"When they said I could leave the hospital, I called my sister to help. She told me I needed to get my suitcase, you know, my clothes and all that. There was some trouble because I didn't want to see the car. He had died in there, you know? My sister found somebody to help with that part, I mean, getting my things out and my husband's things, too."

Rita told him how she'd stayed with her sister, unable to work or care for herself.

"The money my husband made from the show went fast, but it helped me get by until I could work again. He liked to carve animals. I have a few of them still. That's what he took to market. Those things and the jewelry for Bullfrog."

"Bullfrog?"

"Yeah. That's what he called Peshlakai."

He heard the suggestion of a smile in her voice for the first time. "Bullfrog had beautiful silver work. I loved those bracelets, especially the one with a family of bears. My husband said he would trade for one for me, but they all sold out in Santa Fe. That was a good weekend until it turned into sadness."

Both he and Bullfrog Peshlakai had made a mistaken assumption, Leaphorn realized. "Let me be sure I've got this right. You and your husband had already been to Santa Fe. The accident happened when you were coming back, is that right?"

"Yes. We were there the day before the official market opened and all day on Saturday. We didn't stay Sunday because, like I said, he had almost sold out, and we were tired, ready to get home. We packed up a few eagles and a little bear and some jewelry and left before it got dark Saturday night. I wanted to get on the road because I had to work Monday. I lost that job because of the accident."

"Did your husband keep records for his business, any notes on what he sold?"

"When he finished a piece, he made a little sketch of it and he would write the asking price, a space for the sale price, and the time it took to make it. When it sold, he put down who the buyers were so if he ever got in a gallery or had a show, he could send an invitation, an email or something like that. I don't know how he got so smart."

"Did he include the people who bought Bullfrog's jewelry on the list?"

"I don't remember. I know he kept that money separate and . . . Hold on." Leaphorn heard a muffled voice in the background, and then Rita was back. "I have to go. We have to leave for the doctor's."

"One more question: Do you still have the paperwork from that show?"

When Rita spoke again, her voice was different, softer. "I saved it. I don't know why, exactly. We had so much fun on that trip, and then it was all over forever. I miss him."

Leaphorn knew what it was like to miss someone, how the numbness of shock fades into profound, bone-deep loneliness. "If I could take a look at those records, it might help the lady who hired me get some peace of mind."

"I work in the evenings, but if you come by tomorrow, or I could meet you somewhere, I can show you what I have."

"That would be great." Before he hung up, he remembered something. "Do you remember anyone ever calling your husband Fat Boy?"

For the first time in the conversation, she laughed. "All his friends called him that because he was so skinny."

Leaphorn contacted Mrs. Pinto. Over the years, he'd learned that even if he couldn't give them much news, clients wanted updates. But she didn't give him time to get in a word.

"I'm glad you got my message."

"I didn't get it." He noticed the flashing light on his message machine for the first time. "What did you want to talk about?"

"Come down to my office. I'd rather show you in person." He heard the panic in her tone. "I wouldn't ask if I didn't think it was important."

She hadn't asked, but he didn't say that. "I can leave in ten minutes."

The atmosphere at the tribal museum and library seemed quieter—and not just because there was no tour group in the building. Leaphorn noticed it right away, a somberness that seemed to penetrate the walls. He told the young man at the information desk he was there to see Mrs. Pinto and headed to her office.

She rose when he entered. "Thanks for coming. I don't know how to handle this."

"What happened?"

"Take a look."

They walked together into the rapidly warming day. She led him to an empty parking spot that captured a bit of shade. An orange cone blocked vehicles from using it.

"I always park here, under this tree. This morning, I found that thing in the middle of my usual spot. I'm not superstitious, but this isn't good."

"The cone?"

"No," she snapped at him. "I had them put it there. They moved the dead thing over that way." She pointed with a jut of her chin.

On the ground just beyond the cone, he saw an old rag. No, he realized, it was the body of a cottontail rabbit. In the old days, a person suspected of witchcraft might receive such a warning. The next time the dead thing could be the witch. Even those who didn't believe would be upset to find a dead rabbit purposely left in their parking spot.

Mrs. Pinto turned her back on the scene. Leaphorn nudged the rabbit out of view with his boot.

It wouldn't be long, he knew, before some other animal would welcome the free meal.

As they walked back to the building, he asked, "Why do you think this happened?"

"Ignorance, suspicion, jealousy." She opened her eyes a bit wider. "Because I'm successful, people think there's something evil going on with me. I'm surprised you haven't heard the rumors. The progression of Tiffany's illness stirred things up. That poor girl kept going to the doctor. She was lucky that her sister helped with the appointments and that she worked in a pharmacy so she could pick up the medicine. Tiffany hated it that no one could figure out why she kept getting worse." She frowned. "Her father thinks witchcraft caused her problems and that I had something to do with it because I asked a lot of Tiffany."

"From what you told me, the girl liked you and her job. She enjoyed working hard."

"True, but the sicker she got, the more Mr. Benally resented me. When I spoke to Tiffany about it, she told me not to worry. She thought with her sister helping, her dad would back off a little." Mrs. Pinto shook her head. "And I thought I could ignore his craziness. But I'm disgusted by this dead cottontail business. What should I do?"

He had handled similar questions as a cop, too. "If something like that happened to me, I'd ask myself who might have a grudge against me. If I came up with someone, I'd seek out that person and try to get things resolved."

She sighed. "Come inside, cool off a minute, and give me an update on your progress."

Leaphorn felt his cell phone vibrate and chose to ignore it, as was his habit when he was with a client. But he thought about Louisa, and then the information Bean had promised. By the time he pulled the phone from his pocket, he was too late to catch the inspector's call. "I'll be right there. I'll meet you in your office."

"OK, but don't be long. I have a meeting in fifteen minutes." Mrs. Pinto continued her march toward the building.

Leaphorn listened to Bean's message. "Joe, sorry I missed you. I've got a good lead on who sent that box, but I'm in the field until six. Call me after that. Six my time. I never know what time it is for you guys in the summer in Arizona. What's with that daylight saving mess, anyway?"

Leaphorn smiled at the message. The state of Arizona didn't observe daylight saving time, but the Navajo Nation—even communities within Arizona—did. That meant that in the summer, it was an hour earlier in Ganado or Window Rock than it was in Flagstaff, Phoenix, and the rest of non-Navajo Arizona, including the Hopi villages and tribes of the Grand Canyon. Navajo tribal government kept all of the Navajo Nation in sync with the Mountain Time Zone while Arizona went its own way.

He walked inside to give Mrs. Pinto the good news about Jim Bean's message and Rita Begaye's sales records, two ways to help track the mysterious shipment.

Mrs. Pinto shook her head.

"Considering what little you've found so far, I guess it's worth checking out, but Rita Begaye's notes about old jewelry sales don't seem like much of a lead. The post office might turn into something. I'm profoundly disappointed that this is taking you so long."

As he rose to leave, Leaphorn flashed on several tart responses, but he let her comment hang between them like forgotten laundry. He understood why the doctor treating Tiffany attributed her symptoms to stress. He had dealt with difficult clients, each a challenge in his or her own way. Still, he would be relieved when he closed the book on this assignment. And he'd screen Louisa's friends more closely before saying yes to them again.

"Sir?"

The voice interrupted his thoughts as he walked to his truck.

A man in a Navajo Emergency Medical Services uniform approached. "I was one of the guys who helped the lady who collapsed out here a few days ago. I saw you helping at the scene. You're a retired cop, right?"

"Lieutenant Joe Leaphorn. You speak Navajo."

The man nodded and introduced himself. "I was on ambulance duty the evening she passed away."

Leaphorn waited.

"I wish we had taken her to the hospital that afternoon. She might still be alive if she'd listened to us."

"I've been in those situations. You can't force someone to do what you know is best." Leaphorn paused. "What happened the night she died?"

The ambulance man shook his head. "All I know

is that she was dead when I saw her that night. The older lady who worked with her was outside with a flashlight so we could find the house and said she was still breathing when she left her. The woman who died was alone when we got there. Then another woman showed up—I don't know if she was elsewhere in the house or had just arrived."

The young man studied his black Nikes for a moment. "We couldn't bring Tiffany back. It was too late."

Leaphorn heard his phone buzz as he was driving home and glanced at it. Jim Chee. He let the call go to message. He called the police station and spoke to the chief about Tiffany's death and his concerns. The man, a Window Rock officer who had worked with Leaphorn years ago, confirmed that an autopsy had been ordered because the death was "unattended" and "suspicious."

Leaphorn fixed a late lunch for himself and fed Giddi, who seemed hungry but turned up her little black nose at the cat food. He gave Louisa's plants some water because he thought they looked a bit droopy. He felt rather droopy himself. He usually took a nap after lunch, but he remembered the call from Chee he'd let go to voicemail.

He left a message for Chee with Sandra at the Shiprock station, then asked, "Is Bernie around?"

"No, sir. You could probably get her on her cell. She's working on that robbery case and tracking down witnesses for Agent Johnson. Want me to give her a message?"

"No need. I'll catch her later."

He would call Louisa that evening after he talked to Bean, he decided. They'd have more to discuss, and she might offer some good insights into the case. The woman was smart, and besides that, he missed her. Maybe even more than the cat did.

Leaphorn called promptly at six, and Bean answered on the second ring.

"I thought you were calling an hour from now. Six o'clock."

"Six here."

"Well, whatever. This is a good time to talk." Bean paused. "Listen, I'll try to spell things out so you don't have to ask too many questions."

"Kay."

"So, Joe, your luck holds. I tracked the box to the Winslow, Arizona, post office. I found out who was working that day. Six people. The first three I talked to didn't recall anything. A couple of them barely remembered coming to work that day." He chuckled. "But with the fourth person, I think we hit the jackpot."

Leaphorn was pleased to hear Bean say "we."

"This guy is one of our veteran employees, Arnold Sakiestewa. He recalled a woman struggling with a big box when he was headed out to his car for lunch. He helped her haul it in. Here's the best part. You still listening?"

"Ya."

"He commented on the box being heavy, and she said, yes, it has a lifetime of memories inside. Cool, huh?"

"Ya. Aoo'."

"Anyway, I asked Sakiestewa if he knew the woman and he said . . ." Bean paused with his natural storyteller's drama. "He said she comes in three or four times a week to check her box for mail. With a little finagling, I got her name. Mary Nestor. I emailed you the address and phone number we have on file for her, and Arnold's info, too, in case you want to talk to him directly or have Louisa do it. I hope this helps."

Leaphorn felt the old, sweet pleasure of moving forward in a case. His spirits lifted. "Tanks ahéhee'."

"My pleasure. Tell Louisa hello for me."

"Beckfst on me nest time."

"It's a deal. Take care."

After Bean hung up, Leaphorn smiled. He debated whether to retreat into his office and immediately check his email, but he made the call to Flagstaff he'd been putting off. He dialed Louisa on the kitchen phone before he could talk himself out of it, wishing his English were better or her Navajo stronger. The problems they'd had communicating, he thought, led to all sorts of irritations. And if he was annoyed with her, he figured it was probably mutual.

"Yá'át'ééh."

"Yá'át'ééh yourself. It's nice to hear your voice. How are you?"

"Kay." It was nice to hear hers, too.

"Are you making progress on Mrs. Pinto's case?"

"Tink so. Bean gay me da name of a suspec." He hated the ignorant way he sounded.

"That's wonderful."

"How ya doin?"

"Oh, I'm fine. Tired. The more exposure I have to campus politics now, the more I'm glad to be a lowly consultant. But I realize how much I miss the interaction with faculty, as quirky as they are, and the energy and optimism of college students. It's great to be back here, at least in that respect."

He waited for her to say something else, something like she'd be glad to get home.

"They've invited me to work with some honors classes in the fall. I'm not sure I want to, but I'm flattered to be asked. I told them I'd like to hear what the proposal is. They set up a meeting tomorrow for that."

"Den home?"

"Ah, Joe, I don't know. I still have to do some thinking."

"Giddi misses you. Slept wid me." He thought of saying, *I miss you, too*, but she must have known that already.

"Give her a pat for me."

"Kay." He heard noise in the background and then Louisa again.

"I've got to go. Julie and I—you remember her—are catching a movie. Be sure to feed the cat and make sure there's water. And speaking of that, could you check the houseplants? If they start to droop, you know what to do."

"Kay."

She said good-bye and was gone.

13

Leaphorn went to his office and found the inspector's email. As promised, Bean provided Mary
Nestor's Winslow address and a phone number.
He wished he had checked before he called Louisa
so he could have asked her to help translate a tele-
phone conversation tomorrow. But, he realized,
there was no way to do it while his housemate stayed
in Flagstaff.

Who could substitute? He considered Jessica
from the Window Rock station. He needed to call
her tomorrow anyway to thank her for the Begaye
accident report and tell her how helpful it was.

Then, as was his longtime habit before he went
to bed, he made notes on the progress of the case
and added "Call Jessica to help with Nestor interview" to his to-do list. It joined "Consider how to
approach Mary Nestor re anonymity" and "Confirm meeting with Rita Begaye."

He set up coffee for the morning, as he had

done in the pre-Louisa days, and settled in to watch the ten o'clock news. He was marveling at how the weatherman mentioned the severity of the drought and, in the next segment, referred to the coming clear, sunny days as "nice weather" when the cell phone rang. Chee's voice reminded him that he'd ignored the sergeant's call earlier and not even listened to the message he'd left.

"Sir, am I calling too late?"

"Almost. What can I do for you?"

"Largo told me that you decided not to work with the rookie." Chee stopped there.

"That's right."

"He wants me to do it."

"You know that guy. You've already spent time with him. You can hit the ground running."

"You're right about knowing him." Chee cleared his throat. "I think that could be a problem. I don't have an open mind."

Leaphorn took the cell phone into the bedroom. "Sergeant, do you think Sam has what it takes to become a good officer?"

"I'm not sure. He's energetic, he's smart enough, and he works hard. But frankly, he's too cocky and he doesn't listen to good advice. I may have been that way, too. It seems to come with being young."

You had your faults, Leaphorn thought, but arrogance wasn't one of them. And in his mind, Chee was still young. "Largo obviously believes he has potential or he wouldn't have asked you to spend time with the man. If I were you, I'd find out why he wanted to be a cop in the first place. Ask what he sees himself doing a year from now, then five years from now. That might give you some clues as to how to bring him along."

Leaphorn could almost hear Chee thinking. "There's something else on your mind, Sergeant. Go ahead."

"Largo may not have seen this side of the rookie, but I know about it because of Bernie. I suggested that she bring it up with the captain, but, well, you know her. She wants to handle it herself."

"You're referring to his attitude about women, correct?"

"Yes." He heard the surprise in Chee's voice. "I don't know how to get him to change because he doesn't see it as a problem."

Leaphorn heard his cell phone chime with a text message and ignored it. "The new FBI special agent out there is a woman, right?"

"Yes, sir. Sage Johnson."

"See if she has a minute to talk to you about this. She could have some insights into how to deal with a misogynist."

"I'll give it a shot. How's your case coming, sir?"

"I got some good information today. It's not there yet, but success is in the wind. And, Chee?"

"Yes, sir?"

"I came down too hard on you for that Green Yazzie situation. Thanks for telling me about the call."

"Let me know if I can help you with anything else. Say hi to Louisa."

After that, Leaphorn checked the text. It was from Councilor Walker. Like the woman herself, it got to the point.

Yr working w Pinto @ NN museum. Let's talk. See you in a.m. at Nav. Inn?

Interesting, he thought. Walker kept her ear to the ground. He'd always admired her, especially when he and she were on the same side of an issue. He texted OK and a time. She sent back a thumbs-up.

Leaphorn read a bit in bed and then turned off the light and stared at the ceiling. The house seemed empty and too quiet without Louisa. He felt Giddi as she jumped onto his bed. Instead of curling up near his feet as she had last night, she snuggled against his hip. He appreciated her soft warmth, and she remained with him until he stirred with the morning light.

Before he left for breakfast, he sent Louisa an update on the case. He knew she'd be interested in the Rita Begaye development. Or at least he hoped she would be.

He thought about his meeting with Walker. He looked forward to learning what she had to say about Tiffany, Mrs. Pinto, and the situation at the museum.

He drove to the Navajo Inn early and ordered the morning special, a pork chop with toast, potatoes, and two eggs. He envisioned his housemate sitting across from him with her bowl of oatmeal. On second thought, he asked for just one egg.

He had enjoyed the egg, finished most of the pork chop, and was spreading grape jelly on his toast when Councilor Walker approached the table. She sat down before he could greet her.

"I know I'm late. Finish your breakfast while I check in at the office." She said it as a statement, not a suggestion.

By the time the server came around with coffee, Walker had done what she needed to do electronically and Leaphorn had eaten two of the four toast triangles. The waitress filled the empty cup in front of Walker and topped off his.

"I'm glad you could meet me this morning." Walker stirred sugar into her coffee. "You look good, Joe. Are you recovered from what happened?"

He knew she meant the brain injury. "Mostly. My biggest problem is remembering my English and getting the words out."

"You're lucky you had your Diné Bizaad to fall back on. How is your . . ." Her forehead wrinkled. "The lady who you live with."

"She's well. She's in Flag doing something at the university. She enjoys the chance to reconnect with those friends and the academic life. They've asked her to teach in the fall." He sipped his coffee. It was good, hot and just strong enough.

He had said enough about Louisa. "How are your children, Councilor?"

"Fine. Well, not exactly, but they're OK. As well as can be expected."

She straightened in her chair. "I understand the director at the museum hired you to do some work for her. Tell me about it. How's that going?"

"If that were true, I couldn't talk about it without her permission."

To his surprise, Walker laughed. "I knew you would say that. I know it's true. I'm glad she was smart enough to find you. Everyone in the building has been upset since the young woman who was her assistant died. I hope she has you checking into that. What caused her death?"

He sipped his coffee. "They say she was sick."

"I've heard she was witched." Walker let the words hang over the breakfast table for a moment. "But I don't believe in that. Tiffany always treated me respectfully, answered my questions as best she could when I called about council business and her boss wasn't handy. I liked her. But recently, I sensed that something bothered her, some weight on her shoulders. I asked her what was the matter, but she wouldn't talk about it. Or couldn't. Did she confide in you?"

He shook his head. "I never had the opportunity to know her. The only time I spent with her was in the parking lot after she collapsed and we called an ambulance."

"When was that?"

"The afternoon before she died."

Walker pressed her lips into a straight line for a moment. "Her father is taking her death very hard. He feels bad that she died alone."

"I heard that her sister lived there at the time." Leaphorn searched his memory. Collette. "And Mrs. Pinto was outside, watching for the ambulance."

"Well, they say that Collette told her father she

had gone out to get some groceries. She came back to find Mrs. Pinto there and Tiffany dead. I've been acquainted with their father for years. He thinks Mrs. Pinto caused his daughter's death by, well . . . you know how some people think. Have you met him?"

"Yes."

"And?"

"And what?"

When she smiled, the wrinkles around her eyes added texture to her face. "And, Joe Leaphorn, tell me why that young woman died and why the museum director hired you and what is going on over there that she wants to cover up. You make a difficult conversation even more difficult. And I am not even forcing you to speak English."

He smiled back and lowered his voice. "I've heard the talk of witchcraft. Rumors like that have always bothered me, as they bother you. As I said earlier, I can't talk about why my client hired me except that it concerns a gift to the museum. I would never involve myself with any kind of cover-up."

"I didn't mean to imply that. I admire your integrity, and that's why I wanted to talk to you." Walker spread her fingers on the table in front of her. "Tiffany wasn't in the best of health, but she felt well enough to go to work the day she died. I don't believe in witchcraft, but my intuition tells me something strange and bad happened to her, and it could be related to her job."

"Do you have a plan?"

"I know some of Tiffany's friends. I'll see what I can learn about this—if she had any enemies, if she was doing anything dangerous, anything that would have hinted that someone wanted her dead." She finished her coffee. "I'm due at a meeting. I'll see you here Friday at nine. You'll know more by then, and that gives me time to find out what I can."

She started to lay some dollar bills on the table, but Leaphorn shook his head. "I'll get this."

"Next time, it's on me."

He nodded. "I know better than to argue with you."

"When is your housemate coming back?"

"I'm not sure."

He noticed a sparkle in her dark eyes. "I'll see you Friday."

## 14

Before Bernie contacted the man in charge of booking vendor space at the Shiprock flea market, she did some checking. Her sources confirmed that the operator worked hard to keep out the bad element and was quick to remove anyone selling anything illegal or suspicious. Then she phoned him to ask about the vendor who had Mr. Natachi's bolo.

"Oh, that must have been Eric Stevens. He's a longtime seller with us. He comes once, maybe twice a month."

"Have you heard any complaints about him selling stolen merchandise?"

"Nope. He wouldn't be there if I had. If I get a hint that anyone is using their booth to fence stuff, I shut them down. Tell me why you're asking about him."

Bernie explained.

"I'd believe him if he said that he didn't know it was stolen. Stevens is a stand-up guy."

"How can I reach Mr. Stevens?"

Bernie called the number, caught up with her paperwork, and called again. On the third try, someone answered.

"Hello. May I speak to Eric Stevens?"

"What are you selling?"

She identified herself and explained the reason for her call.

"I should have known better than to buy that bolo. You ever heard them say if a deal seems too good to be true, it probably is?"

"I have."

"That string tie had some beautiful workmanship, top quality. Hey, you know I gave it back to the old gentleman, right? No questions asked."

"He told me that's what you did." Bernie remembered the happy tears in Mr. Natachi's eyes. "When I walked over to talk to you about it, your space was empty. You'd packed and left. Why did you take off? The market still had plenty of customers. Did you have something to hide?"

"No, nothing like that. I just didn't want to get balled up with having to tell my story to a cop and then explain to the manager why a cop was talking to me. That scares away buyers."

"Where did you get Mr. Natachi's bolo tie?"

"I bought it from a man in Gallup who told me it was his uncle's. He said his uncle asked him to sell it because he needed the money for groceries."

"Where was this?"

"In front of the Walmart. When the dude came up to me and said I could have it for three hundred bucks, well . . . I looked at the bolo, and sure enough, it had that great classic look. I thought the story could be true and that I was helping the family. I guess I shoulda known better."

"Can you describe the man selling it?"

"Navajo, in his twenties or early thirties. A little plump but strong-looking, like a bulldogger or something. He was kinda dressed up, jeans and a new button shirt, boots." Stevens paused. "He acted normal, you know, not high or anything. His story made sense except for something that happened later."

"What's that?"

"After I gave him the money, I went inside the store, and I saw him in the grocery department. I thought he'd be buying flour, potatoes, eggs, meat, you know. But he was in the bakery department picking up a big ol' cake. Anyway, I puzzled about that."

"When did you realize the bolo was stolen?"

"Not until the old gentleman came by my booth. Trust me, I wouldn't have bought it if I'd known. It was more expensive than the items I handle out there, but the tourists are around so I thought it was worth a chance. I figured if it didn't move at the market, I could sell it online. It was worth at least double what I paid. At least five hundred dollars."

"You said he wanted three hundred for it."

"He did, that's right. I talked him down." Stevens stopped. "It was worth what he asked, especially because of his story, but I'm used to negotiating with people."

Bernie tossed out a few more questions about

the person who sold the bolo. Stevens estimated the man's height at around five-foot-seven and his weight at 190. He hadn't noticed any scars or a wedding ring, but he mentioned that the man had just had a haircut. He hadn't seen what vehicle the man was driving.

"When are you back at the flea again?"

"This weekend. I just got a bunch of cool sunglasses. Five bucks. Come and see me."

"I might."

"For you, four fifty."

She typed up her notes, disappointed that, except for the bolo seller's description, the interview seemed to lead nowhere. She was heading off when Sandra buzzed her.

"Remember that woman who was trying to reach Leaphorn?"

"Mona something?"

"She wants to talk to Chee, but . . ."

"I'll take it."

Arthur Green Yazzie's sister got right to the point. "What's with you people? I don't know why this is so complicated. All I need is to talk to Lieutenant Joe Leaphorn. What's so hard about that?"

"The Lieutenant asked my husband and me to see if we could help you because he's involved with a big case. May I give him a message or do anything for you?"

"He's on a case? He was old when I seen him in court with my brother." The voice on the phone was tinged with frustration. "He's been old since before I was even born. Someone should tell that dude he is old enough to retire already. I bet he's been working longer than I've been alive."

Bernie smiled. "He did retire from the police department, but he still assists with complicated cases, and he does some freelance work as an investigator and consultant. That's why he's hard to reach."

"I bet he's like my aunt and he doesn't enjoy talking on the phone much either."

"I'd be glad to help you if I can."

"No, that won't work. It's personal." Mona Willeto gave Bernie her number. "Just ask him to call me as soon as he can."

"How is your brother? I heard—"

But Willeto had already hung up.

Bernie was on the way to a call about a stolen vehicle when Largo contacted her on the radio. "After you're done with that, Agent Johnson wants to talk to you. She said it wasn't urgent."

As it turned out, the stolen truck wasn't urgent either. It hadn't actually been stolen, just "borrowed" by a clan brother who forgot to tell the owner, drove it until it ran out of gas, and then abandoned it along the road and hitchhiked home. By the time Bernie arrived, the alleged thief had already confessed, arranged a ride to pick it up, and scrounged up money for gas to drive the vehicle back to the owner. Problem solved. She suspected that the family following through on a threat to call the police had motivated the confession and resolution.

When she had cell service, she called Agent Johnson. Cordova, Johnson's predecessor, always had a quip, a joke, or at least a how-ya-doin' for her. She knew Johnson would get right to the point. "Hi. It's Bernie. I heard you wanted to talk."

"I have some follow-up questions for you about the body you found."

"I'm driving but go ahead."

"I'd like to talk face-to-face. Where are you now?"

Bernie told her. "I don't have my notes on what I saw out there. I can be back at the substation in about half an hour, pick up my notes, and meet you somewhere. I know Largo sees this as a priority."

Johnson surprised her. "It sounds like you've already done a lot of driving today and I haven't been out of the office. Let's talk about this on your turf. I'll let Largo know."

"That will work. Do you know who the victim was?"

"Yes. See you in a bit."

Bernie steered over the familiar roads and into the outskirts of Shiprock, noticing that the clouds had started building up earlier in the day and towered to look more like those that could bring rain. Their shade kept the heat in check. She thought about stumbling upon the dead person and the rest of the scene, sifting through her memories to see what she might have missed. She pictured the sweaty man she'd encountered before she found the body. Perhaps Johnson's team had found him.

Chee used the computer at the Chinle station to try to learn more about Ryana. He discovered that the senior center had honored her as employee of the month back in January. The announcement in the newsletter, along with her smiling photo, noted that she had been on staff for a year. He remembered Ryana's comment that Elsie would give her a ride to work and noticed that Elsie Bitsóí, food services assistant director for the senior meal program, had presented the award.

Then Chee called the hospital and talked to nurse Lucinda. "You won't believe it, but Mr. Natachi is down in X-ray. The portable machine wasn't working right the first time. They fiddled with it for an hour."

"How is he?"

"No worse."

"Has Ryana been by?"

"I haven't seen her."

He drove to the senior center and made his way to the multipurpose room. A few women were clearing the tables and directed him to Elsie. The room smelled of pinto beans and corn bread, and reverberated with the sounds of organized old age: the lucky letter-number combinations of bingo and a television on too loud in counterpoint to the clatter of dishes in the industrial kitchen.

Elsie Bitsóí greeted him like a friend. She looked to be forty-something, give or take five years. Chee noticed her strong hands and the blunt unvarnished nails of a woman who worked hard at the kind of job that sent a person home tired. Her white blouse had darker semicircles at the armpits.

"I've been worried about the girl and her grandfather. I knew something was wrong when she called me to tell me not to pick her up today. She said she needed some time off. She just called again and she said her grandfather had been shot. What's going on?"

Chee leveled with her.

"No! That poor old man. He would never harm anyone." She shook her head before Chee could cobble together a response. "What a shame."

"Do you know where Ryana is now?"

"No. I told her to go ahead, take today off, do what she had to. That girl is a good worker. She never complains about overtime—she even requests it. When her boyfriend left, she asked me for a ride until she figured out what to do. I didn't mind. Like I said, Ryana works hard."

"Did she ever talk to you about being in the movies?"

Elsie gave him a wink. "I'm too old and fat to be a movie star."

"I mean, did Ryana ever talk about her work in the movies, you know, the films she made while she was living in Phoenix?"

"That girl was in the movies?"

"That's what I heard."

Elsie laughed. "She never talked about that, but she's so pretty, she could be a movie star. I'll have to ask her."

"I heard that Ryana had a BMW. What happened to it?"

"She sold that car. They drove her boyfriend's car, a little sedan. She told me he had one of those computer jobs you can do from home, from anywhere, you know what I mean? He came here out of California. She told me Nicky knew a lot about security, you know, about how to keep someone from stealing your identity, stuff like that."

Chee nodded. It was easy to get information from a woman who liked to talk.

"Ryana said he wanted to offer a safety program here, you know, talk to the elderlies. Most of these old ones don't have computers, but after she said he would talk about other things, too—good lighting, grab bars, rugs that don't slip, stuff like that. I said OK. Nicky did a good job."

"What other tips did he have?"

"Oh, he said, 'I bet I can tell you where you keep your jewelry.' And he asked people to raise their hands if he got it right. His first guess was in a box on your dresser. Most people raised their hands. Then on a shelf in the closet. Then in the top drawer in the bathroom. Then under the bed. Only three people hadn't raised their hands, and two of them said they didn't have any expensive jewelry. The other lady said it was none of his business."

"That's interesting." Smart woman, Chee thought. "What was that lady's name?"

"Mrs. Youngman."

Her name was not on any of the reports he had just read.

Elsie talked on. "His program was interesting. I'd show it to you if I could. We always ask to video those presentations, but Nicky said no, no video. I don't know why. He's handsome for a white man. Shiny black hair, tall, kinda slim. He wore two gold earrings."

"What did Mr. Natachi think about Nicky?"

Elsie frowned. "You should ask him that."

"So, he didn't like him?"

"I think one trouble was that Nicky's older than her. He might be forty-five."

As she spoke, Chee began to construct a scenario that made sense of the burglaries and Mr. Nata-chi's shooting. "Do you know Nicky's last name?"

"No. You could ask Ryana, but he's old news. He left her."

"What happened?"

"Well, sometime last week he just went away, no argument or nothin'. At least, that's her story. He took his computers out of the house but left his car. That was strange, but I told her it was his going-away present because he felt guilty. I think he has another girlfriend who came by for him, and that's why he's avoiding Ryana. He's too chicken to even say good-bye." Elsie sighed. "I gotta get back to work. When you see Ryana, let her know I'm thinking of her. Want a cold drink to take with you?"

"No, thank you. I appreciate your time."

"Tell Mr. Natachi to get better. Tell him I'll give him an extra cookie when he comes in for lunch."


Chee answered Bernie's call from the comfort of the senior center lobby, enjoying the air-conditioning.

"Hey, where are you?" She sounded good. "At the movies?"

"You're right, sweetheart. It's *Blazing Saddles*."

"So the heat's gotten to you."

"I'm at the senior center at Chinle learning more about Ryana." He explained, "The film is down the hall."

"Speaking of movies, what did you think about Darleen's information?"

"What do you mean?"

"The pornography."

"What? What is Darleen up to now?"

"No, not Darleen. Ryana," Bernie explained. "Darleen sent you the link. I'm heading back to the office. Agent Johnson wants another interview about the body, but we're doing it here. Speaking of interviews, I tracked down the guy who tried to sell Mr. Natachi his own bolo."

"You solved the case, and now you tell me?"

"I wish, but no. The guy who had the bolo at the flea told me the same man-at-Walmart story he told Mr. Natachi."

"Did the guy who sold the bolo look like a handsome six-foot, forty-something white guy with gold earrings?"

"Nope. A shortish, younger, kinda chubby Navajo in a new shirt. I'll send you the full description in case you run into him out there." She laughed when she said it.

When Bernie got back to the substation, Sandra was full of news.

"Bigman says the missus is cleaning everything in the house. When my sister started her cleaning binge, the baby came two days later." Sandra looked at her manicured nails. "And the rookie is back on duty tomorrow. His eye still looks terrible, swollen, black and blue. I told him he should wear a patch like a pirate. I'm glad he's better. It makes things easier for the rest of you guys."

"Did he say anything about the meeting with the Lieutenant?" Bernie knew that Sandra knew everything that happened at the substation.

"He said, 'Some old guy came up from Window Rock to tell me how to be a policeman.' As if he didn't know who the Lieutenant was. He should have been honored, but he just doesn't get it. I cleaned up the interview room for them so you and Agent Johnson should use it."

"Have you met her?"

Sandra nodded. "When she first got the position, she stopped by to introduce herself to the captain, and I happened to be here. We said hello. That's about it. After she left, the rookie made some snarky comment and Largo shot him a look to shut him down."

Bernie found her notes from the running trail and gave them a quick review before Sandra buzzed to let her know that Johnson had arrived. Right on time, too.

Bernie led the way to the interview room. "Would you like coffee, a soda, some water?"

"A soda would be good. Something with sugar and caffeine."

Bernie smiled. That was always her choice, too. "We've got Coke and Mountain Dew."

"Mountain Dew."

When she returned with the canned sodas, Agent Johnson had taken a seat and placed a folder on the desk. Bernie sat across from her and handed Johnson her drink.

Johnson lifted the pull tab and took a long sip. "Thank you for meeting with me today. I needed to follow up on a few of your observations based on what the crime scene investigators found. I am especially interested in the people you encountered when you first entered the trail, before you saw the body."

Bernie opened her notebook and found the information. "I saw a woman with a blond ponytail and a small dog climbing into a car, a jeep or something. Then there was a sweaty, heavyset Navajo man, close to six feet tall. Maybe fifty-five, around there anyway. He wore jeans and a sleeveless T-shirt, white. He was standing slightly hunched with his hands on his knees at the trailhead. His index finger on his right hand was missing. I saw a man I later interviewed, Ed Summersly."

"Back up to the sweaty guy. Did you notice that man's shoes?"

Bernie thought about it. "They were dirty, covered with dust as though he had been walking on a sand road." She paused. "Or had climbed up the sandy bank to the trail from the river."

"Did you see where he went after you left?"

"He was still standing there when I started on my run. I assumed the man had been catching his breath or vomiting."

Johnson had been making notes, and she looked up. "Did you check on him?"

"No." Bernie read an implication in the question. "Are you a runner, Agent Johnson?"

"No."

"On a hot day, if a person has done some serious exertion, it's not unusual to get nauseated. I figured that's what happened. Is this man important?"

"Would you recognize him if you saw him again?"

"Yes." She smiled at Johnson. "I've been looking for him, but so far no luck. If I keep answering your questions, will you answer mine?"

Johnson smiled back. "We think the man you saw may be tied to the body, may have brought it up from the river. That might be why he was sweaty and vomiting."

And, Bernie deduced, he also may have been the murderer or the killer's accomplice.

"Did you see anyone else with sandy shoes?"

Bernie considered the scene again. "No." The purpose of abandoning the dog with the body grew clearer. "So the dog was extra insurance so someone would eventually find the dead guy."

Bernie remembered Bigman's comment. "I heard that the victim might have a personal link to you."

"You brought this up before. Why?"

"I understand that you called the victim by name. That seems to point to dumping the body in a place that would command the attention of the agent in charge."

Johnson pressed her lips together to form a pale, bloodless line. Bernie could see her thinking. "When you first found the body, did you do any investigation down toward the river?"

Bernie had already spoken to this. "No."

"Did you hear any boats or see any boaters?"

"I didn't. What happened to the dog?"

"It's in custody. Officer Bigman took charge of it, took it home the first night, and it's now in detention in Fort Defiance."

Bernie pictured Mrs. Bigman's reaction. A visiting dog is probably not what you dream of with a baby arriving around the next corner. Maybe Bigman smoothed it over by offering her some watermelon.

Johnson said, "I talked him into it. It was late, we all were tired, and I needed to make sure the animal was safe until we determined why it was there."

"Did the dog have a microchip?"

"It was chipless."

"So, who was the dead guy?"

"You ask a lot of questions, officer."

"I want to know about the crime, the victim, and why he was killed. He's the first dead person I ever found on a jogging trail." She hadn't meant it to be funny, but Johnson chuckled.

"You've given me another reason to stick to swimming." Johnson looked at the Mountain Dew can. "The agency will release the victim's name tomorrow. But he wasn't Navajo and he didn't live close by. You found a guy from Kansas who got involved with some bad juju on the West Coast. The Bureau persuaded him to give up his gang associates in exchange for a new start. Michael could have stayed in our protection program, but he missed his old life." Johnson sipped the soda. "Let's wrap this up."

They went over Bernie's answers, and she recalled that the suspicious man had some sort of tattoo, or maybe it was a thin band, on his wrist. Other than that, she couldn't think of more to add.

Johnson thanked her. "I want to mention something else. Sergeant Chee asked me to meet with him about an officer named Wilson Sam. Is he the man who worked with us when that young girl was taken hostage, or pretended to be a hostage?"

"That's right."

"I told Chee I'd call him on this. I've been putting it off. Can you give me his cell number?" Bernie thought she saw a touch of worry on Johnson's face.

She told the agent the number and Johnson put it in her phone. She looked at the empty soda can, then picked it up, crushed it, and tossed it in the wastebasket. A perfect throw.

Bernie watched. "Nice."

Johnson smiled. "That was an easy shot. I was on the team in high school and played for fun after that. How about you? You play basketball?"

"Our Lady Chieftains got to the regionals before we went home. I wasn't exactly indispensable on the court in high school, but I had my moments."

"How are the college teams out here in desert country?"

"The Lobos can be good, but you have to go to Albuquerque. Watching the high school ball is fun." Bernie thought about saying they ought to go to a game together when the season started up again. But she didn't.

After the agent left, Bernie drove out to a call

about shoplifting at the old Toadlena Trading Post and, after she took the report, decided to swing by Ryana's aunt's place to see if the young woman was there. Her cell phone buzzed.

"Hey there." Chee sounded tired. "I need your help. And don't worry, Largo has already approved it."

"Darn, I was hoping it was something personal. You know, like getting a bag of charcoal so you could grill some of your burgers for dinner. Or even more personal than that."

"Sorry, sweetheart. This is police work. But I'll make it up to you."

"What can I do?"

"Two things. Ryana's ignoring my calls and I need to talk to her about the shooting. I think she might have gone back to her aunt's house."

"Largo mentioned that, too. I'm headed over that way."

"Secondly, can you send me the information that Darleen found?"

Bernie knew both her sister and cell service in Mama's area were unreliable. "Sure, but not until I get a better signal. Do you think it ties in to the burglaries?"

"Maybe. Ryana asked me for two thousand dollars. I think she's being blackmailed. That might give her a motive to steal."

"Are you sure she wasn't joking about the money?"

"The more I learn about this, the less sure I am of anything."

Bernie had to drive by Mama's house to reach the auntie's place, so she stopped there first. Her mother was in the kitchen, washing some radishes, another of those vegetables Bernie never ate unless Mama made her.

"Daughter, I'm glad to see you." Mama dried her hands as she spoke. "Stay for dinner. Look at these. Beautiful, aren't they?"

"I can't stay, Mama. I have to go down the street to look for Ryana. But I need to tell you something first."

"What?"

Bernie hesitated. "Mr. Natachi got shot at his house in Chinle. He's in the hospital. The police are looking for the ones who did it."

Mama didn't speak for a while. Then she said, "Ryana came back here. I waved at her, but she didn't wave back. She was driving fast."

Bernie put herself in the mind of the young woman. Her grandfather is abducted and shot. She tells a law officer it's her fault. She flees, even though she's clearly devoted to the old man. It added up to big trouble.

Mama watched her think. "Your sister walked over to talk to her. Her auntie isn't home yet."

"I'm going down there. I'll stop by later."

Mama frowned. "If the granddaughter is afraid of something, I don't want your sister to get involved. Tell that girl I need her to help me right now. And you be careful."

Bernie could have walked, but not knowing what to expect, she took the police unit.

The front door stood open, and Bernie saw the girls sitting at the dining table. She walked right in. "Hi there, you two." Ryana looked pale, nervous.

Darleen smiled as she spoke. "Hi. What are you doing here?"

"Sister, Mama needs you to help with supper. She sounded serious about it, so you should go now."

Darleen, who liked to argue, didn't. "Take care, Ryana. See you later."

"Thanks for coming by." Ryana rested her chin in her hands. "I really needed someone to talk to."

Bernie sat next to the young woman in a spot where she could see out the window. Ryana had dark circles under her eyes and wore no makeup. She seemed exhausted.

"I heard about your grandfather. I'm sorry that happened."

Ryana stared straight ahead.

"The officer who talked to you, Sergeant Chee, asked me to find you. He wanted me to make sure you were safe."

Bernie noticed Ryana's silent tears.

"Whatever it is you're afraid of, Chee and I can help. But we have to know where to start."

Ryana glanced at Bernie's uniform. "I wanted to kill myself, you know, when I came back to Chinle. There was nothing there for me except my grandfather. But then I got that job working with the elderlies and that really helped. And I met Nicky, and he made me feel better. He didn't ask about my past, he accepted me as I am now. But lately . . . everything started going bad again."

"What happened?"

"Nicky left. Just took his computers and the dog and poof." She raised both arms like a conductor. "And this morning, my grandfather almost died.

It was my fault. I'm doing the best I can, but I can't undo the past."

Bernie wasn't sure what that meant. "You can't change the past. But if you could, what would you change? I mean besides your grandfather getting shot."

"That's easy. When I got that letter, asking me for money and threatening to tell my grandfather about the movies, I would have talked to my shicheii. Told him everything."

"What letter?"

The sound of a car on the road distracted them. A new large white SUV pulled into the driveway. A man in a suit strutted to the door, another man behind him. They were either FBI, Bernie thought, or former military. In any case, they brought bad news for Ryana. She was glad she wore her uniform and had her weapon.

She turned to Ryana. "Do you know these guys?"

"No."

Bernie rose to meet them. She relaxed a little when she recognized one of the men as Berke, the FBI agent who had been with the ERT where she'd found the body.

The men showed her their credentials; then Berke stepped toward the young woman. "Are you Ryana Florez?"

"Yeah."

"Is that tan sedan yours?"

"No."

"Then why is it here?" Berke seemed to notice Bernie for the first time. "And why are you here, Manuelito?"

"This is my neighborhood."

"I thought you lived near the trail where you found that body."

"I do. That's my neighborhood, too."

Berke made a sound between a laugh and a grunt. "So it's just coincidence that you found Ryana?"

"My mother noticed her drive up and I came by to say hi. And you guys, why are you curious about the car?"

Ryana's voice had a touch of whine. "Did Nicky file a stolen car complaint or something? Is that why you're here? I just borrowed the car. No big deal."

Bernie knew it would take more than a boyfriend's call about a missing vehicle to bring federal agents to a quiet little house on the reservation. "Why don't you two sit down." Bernie pointed to the empty chairs at the table. "It might be easier to ask your questions."

Berke sat, and the act made him less intimidating. The other man stayed by the front door.

Ryana picked at a cuticle. She looked guilty of something, even if it was only being young and scared. "Can Bernie stay?"

Berke turned away from the young woman and gave Bernie an I-dare-you look.

Bernie leaned toward him. "I'll stay."

"Just a few little questions." He turned to Ryana. "Why are you driving the sedan parked outside here?"

"I don't have a car, so Nicky lets me drive his."

"Where is he?"

"I don't know."

"You don't know?"

"I don't know." Ryana looked at Bernie. "When I got home from work a few days ago, he was gone."

Berke seemed to know that the two of them lived together; he didn't ask about that. "When was that exactly?"

"Thursday."

"Why would he take off without his car?"

Ryana exhaled. "I think he has a girlfriend who picked him up."

"Why do you suppose that?"

Ryana gave the classic examples: phone conversations purposely moved out of her hearing, computers closed, and text messages hidden when she approached. "He wouldn't talk about any of this when I brought it up. He seemed distant, distracted. He wasn't affectionate."

"Did you two have an argument?"

"No. He clammed up. Since he wouldn't explain what was going on, I assumed there was another girl. Now I've been wondering if Nicky had money troubles or maybe got diagnosed with a bad disease. Whatever it was, he wouldn't tell me. Then he was gone."

"Other than this mystery woman, did you notice any new friends?"

Bernie caught the sarcasm in Berke's question.

Ryana shook her head. "No new friends. Nicky kept to himself. Worked at home on his computers."

"Was he involved with drugs?"

"No. No drinking either, at least not around me."

Berke made a note. "Do you know where he went?"

"No. He hasn't even called me. I can't decide if he's a jerk or if I should be worried about him."

"Tell me again why you have the car out there."

"I borrowed it to drive here to talk to my auntie. I needed some space to think. She's always a good one when I'm worried."

Bernie would have asked, *Think about what? Worried about what?* but Berke took a different tack.

The agent gave Ryana a cold smile. "You do seem worried, maybe a little nervous? I think it's because of whatever is out there in that car."

Ryana's chin quivered and she blinked away the tears. She looked at Bernie.

"Agent Berke, someone gravely injured this woman's grandfather recently and she helped get him to the hospital, where he's fighting for his life." Bernie stopped to let her words sink in. "Even without her boyfriend disappearing, Ryana's reaction is understandable."

Berke looked surprised. "I'm sorry about your grandfather. Did the shooting have any connection to your boyfriend's car?"

Ryana stared at the floor.

"I'd like you to unlock it and open the trunk for us." Berke motioned to his partner, who left the house and returned a few minutes later with a legal-sized brown envelope.

"I don't think Nicky would want anyone poking around—"

Agent Berke cut her off. "Miss, your life will be easier if you cooperate with us. After you sign this consent-to-search form, we'll take a quick look and let you go on with your day, talking to your auntie in peace. It's not your car, right? Why worry?"

Berke's partner gave him the envelope, and he

took out an official-looking piece of paper and a pen. Ryana looked at Bernie, and Bernie nodded. The Feds wanted to make sure they had all the i's dotted and the t's crossed. Ryana signed, gave the form to Berke, then reached for her handbag.

Berke said, "Give the purse to Officer Manuelito, and she'll get the keys to me."

Bernie knew that the agent wanted to ensure that Ryana didn't pull out a gun. Ryana looked puzzled but did as requested. "They're in that little front pouch."

Bernie handed Berke the keys. He juggled them slightly in his hand. "Stay in here with Manuelito and my partner."

Ryana had parked in front of the house, and they watched from the window as the trunk lid sprang up a few inches. Berke nudged it open with his elbow. He looked in, then straightened up and made a call on his cell phone.

"What's happening out there?" Ryana's voice was barely more than a whisper. "I don't like this."

"Ryana, shouldn't your aunt be home soon?"

"She told me she was stopping at the grocery after work. I hope these guys are gone before she gets here."

Bernie watched as Berke leaned into the trunk. "Wait here." She went outside before Berke's partner could stop her. In the trunk, she saw computers of various sizes, cameras, and boxes. Berke had gloves on and held a large plastic bag that contained a silver-and-turquoise concho belt. She noticed other Indian jewelry sorted and bagged, along with mailing boxes and sealing tape. The trunk looked like a portable shop.

He turned to Bernie. "Why are you involving yourself in all this?"

"That man who got shot is a good friend of my mother. Ryana is almost like my niece."

"You Navajos take family connections to the limit, don't you?" Before she could take offense, he added, "You're lucky to be part of something like that, Manuelito. But that young woman in there is gonna need more than luck and relatives. She's gonna need a good lawyer."

15

Leaphorn stopped by the police station on his way home from breakfast with Councilor Walker to ask Jessica if she could help with the call to Mary Nestor, the woman who had shipped the box. A thirty-something man he didn't know sat at her desk.

"Jessica's off for a few days. Anything I can do?"

"Do you know when she'll be back?" he asked in Navajo, and saw the man switch gears.

From the answer, Leaphorn knew he'd understood the question, but the man spoke in English. "In a week, unless she gets bored out there in Las Vegas."

"Is Officer Manygoats around?"

This time, the man's response came in a mix of Navajo and English. "He just left, but he'll be back shortly. He was griping about all the reports he has to write."

Leaphorn took out his little book and wrote Manygoats a note. He handed it to the young man.

"I'll be sure he gets this."

As he walked out, Leaphorn decided to ask Louisa to make the call. He could type out the questions and email them to her along with the lady's name and phone number. Louisa had good skills as an interviewer—she was a trained listener who had compiled dozens of oral histories. But as he started his truck, noticing the grinding sound again, he recalled that whatever he'd done to anger Louisa concerned the Peshlakai interview. Should he let her cool off a bit longer before asking a favor?

Why was it, he wondered, that situations that seemed simple on the surface grew more complex and convoluted as he searched for an answer? Not only his relationship with Louisa, he thought, but the case itself.

Giddi met him at the door, meowing loudly. He assumed that she'd finished her food or lapped up the water in her bowl, but no, she had what she needed. He had done his duty as cat wrangler, and she, of course, ignored both offerings and kept up the racket.

The message light on the landline was blinking, and he checked it after he put water for instant coffee in the microwave. It was a male voice. "Lieutenant Leaphorn, this is Jake. Hope you're doing well. I've been missing you at our speech therapy sessions. You can schedule more appointments by giving me a call. I look forward to hearing from you, sir." He deleted the reminder, grabbed his coffee mug, went to his office, and typed notes from his morning meeting with Councilor Walker.

Reviewing the conversation brought him back

to Tiffany, the missing dress, and her unexpected death. In the old days, museums treated textiles with strong pesticides to preserve them. When these materials came home, repatriated to tribal museums or perhaps to families of the original owners, they sometimes brought sickness from the poison used to keep them safe. But the Navajo Nation Museum was a modern facility. Mrs. Pinto and her staff isolated items that might have been treated with toxic chemicals until they could be tested and cleaned. If Tiffany had stolen the textile before it was checked, could pesticides have made her sick, or worsened the illness she suffered from already?

The interlocked questions all revolved around the box. He now knew the name of the sender, Mary Nestor, and how to contact her. The link between Peshlakai, Fat Boy, and the reemergence of the long-lost jewelry added a new avenue to explore. If Rita Begaye had the name of the person who had purchased the bracelet from her dead husband, and if that person was Mary Nestor or a Mr. Nestor, the case moved closer to solution. Mary Nestor held the key.

He pictured meeting Mary, envisioning a frail elderly white woman. In the fantasy he heard her say, *Oh my goodness, I guess I forgot to mail those things.* She would hobble into the back room of a tiny house cluttered with a lifetime of collecting. Out she would come with the precious dress and the bracelet as a bonus. He'd present them to Mrs. Pinto, and she'd retire happy knowing that her dead assistant had nothing to do with the items' disappearance. Louisa would thank him for helping her friend. And he'd get a check to fix his truck.

Two immediate problems shattered his scenario. First, Mary Nestor wanted her gift to be anonymous. She could deny any association with the gifts and hang up on him. Or reject the call in the first place. Second, if she agreed to see him, how would he talk to her? He could be forceful, persuasive, and even charming in Navajo. But his spoken English crippled him.

He noticed the empty hummingbird feeders on the porch. Louisa put something in them from a mason jar in the refrigerator, a recipe she cooked up in the microwave. He found the jar and used what was left as a refill. He left the empty jar on the counter so she'd realize she needed to make more.

He sipped the coffee, lukewarm now, and pondered the obvious, logical solution to the Mary Nestor problem. Winslow was about an hour's drive from Flagstaff. Time to talk to Louisa about the case and see if she was still angry with him. If she could persuade Mary Nestor to meet him, they could drive to Winslow together.

He composed the note to Louisa in his head and was on his way back to the office to email her when the cell phone rang.

"Hey, Lieutenant, it's Manygoats. I got your message. The autopsy report's not ready, but I was able to get a little information from an inside source. Tiffany's body showed no signs of trauma, no bruising, bleeding, anything like that. But it looks like she might have been smothered."

"Smothered? You sure?"

"I'm not sure of much these days, but that's what the guy said. He told me the skin around her nose and mouth was white, and they found fibers in her nose, like maybe someone pressed a pillow over her face."

"How long for the toxicology results?"

"I'll ask."

"When you do, mention that Tiffany worked at a museum and may have been unintentionally exposed to pesticides or other chemicals. And that she was taking medication. Did you learn anything else?"

The officer's tone changed. "My source said that the examiner, a specialist named John Trestrail, called this an interesting case because of Tiffany's rare lung disease. Evidently, most people treated for it with the drug she was taking get better. They will add that drug to the tox screen. Maybe an overdose or something. It's all up for grabs at this point."

Leaphorn went back to pondering what to say to Louisa when his cell phone chimed with a text. A message from Rita Begaye. Two little words: Found it.

He sent back, See you this afternoon.

He emailed Louisa an update on the case and the news that he was coming to Flagstaff and wanted to talk to her and that he hoped she would help him make a call on the Pinto case. Then he added, Quiet here without you.

Rita Begaye lived in Oak Springs, Arizona, a settlement on the way to Flagstaff if one took Indian

Route 12 south toward I-40. He enjoyed the drive into the high country of ponderosa pines and rock cliffs, and he found her place with a minimum of difficulty.

A woman was sitting outside, evidently waiting for him. She looked older than she'd sounded on the phone, like a person who had squeezed more than her share of living into the allotted years. When she smiled, he saw a glint of mischief in her eyes.

"Welcome. It's cooler out here than in the house." She motioned to a chair with a flowery print pad. "Can I offer you some water?"

"Thanks."

She returned to the porch carrying a tray with napkins, two big green plastic cups, and a plate of round cookies covered with powdered sugar. She set it on the table and then handed him the water. "Help yourself to a treat. I baked them last night. I was too excited to sleep."

He saw a spiral notebook on the bench beside her and she noticed him noticing.

"After the accident, I put my husband's carvings and that notebook away. I don't know how much help this will be, but I was glad it turned up. I marked the pages he wrote while we were in Santa Fe." She picked up a cookie and set it gently on a napkin. "It's interesting to see his handwriting again. Sure stirs up memories."

Leaphorn took a cookie out of politeness and discovered it was good. He took another when she passed the tray to him.

She reached for the notebook and removed a paper clip she had used to mark a place. She extended it toward him. "This is what he wrote about our trip. You can see the date at the top. The writing in black is for his own work."

Alvin "Fat Boy" Begaye had been an excellent record keeper, an exception to the dual stereotypes that artists can't manage money and that Indians are poor businesspeople. In clear penmanship, Begaye had described the item, its price, and when it sold. More often than not, he captured the name and even the address of the buyer. He left a space for comments. By several of his carvings he'd written "discount" and by one name "wanted red but took blue." Leaphorn showed the note to Rita.

"I remember that. The man liked the horse but wanted one with a red saddle blanket. My husband told him blue was more authentic, talked him into it. He told me that next time he'd make some red and black ones, you know, like a rug design. But there was no next time." She glanced away, out toward the road. "This August it will be twenty years since he died. It feels like yesterday, and it feels like a lifetime ago."

Leaphorn let the memory sit. He handed the pad back to her, hiding his disappointment. "I don't see any of the consignment items. Did he note those?"

She turned the page. "Here. 'BF' stands for Bull-frog."

The same neat handwriting compiled Peshlakai's consignments in a shorter list, just ten items. Leaphorn found a bracelet with necklace and earrings. The buyer was Lloyd Rafferty, with an address in Gallup, New Mexico. He jotted down the information, feeling the thread of a solution to the missing textile slip from his grasp. He handed the list back to Rita.

She sat it down. "I hope it helps."

"Me, too. Thank you for going to the trouble."

"You know, I'm glad I did it. It gave me some peace."

Leaphorn considered how to ask his last question, or if he needed to ask it at all. Experience had taught him to forge ahead.

"I noticed that, when I mentioned Robert Peshlakai, you seemed to know him."

Rita leaned toward him. "I do. He's married to my sister, Lisa, but he and I dated before I met my husband. He's a good man. I don't want to stir up any jealousy."

When he left her, Leaphorn drove south until he hit Interstate 40 near Lupton. He merged into traffic and headed west toward Flagstaff. His disappointment that a person named Rafferty, and not Nestor, had purchased the bracelet began to fade. He stopped to get gasoline and to stretch his legs in Holbrook and to send Louisa a text with his progress and ETA. He pumped the fuel and went inside for coffee to go. When he came back, his phone was buzzing in the charger.

It was Louisa. "I got the text and checked that name for you. No Rafferty at the Gallup address you gave me and none in that town at all. Shall I expand the search?"

"No tanks."

"Let's meet at my old office. You remember where that is?"

Of course he did. He made an affirmative grunt.

"I can call Mary Nestor from there. Then we can talk. If all goes well, we can treat each other to dinner. Be safe out there, and I will see you soon."

"Dinner on me." He had a clear idea of what the talk would be about: his shortcomings. He didn't like the sound of "if all goes well."

The last time he had driven to Flagstaff had been several years ago, on a trip that concerned another old weaving, what they called a Tale Teller rug, a textile that also dated back to around the time of Hwéeldi. That case, pursued as a favor for the wife of a friend, stirred uncomfortable memories. All Navajo weavings could be described as Tale Tellers. Each uniquely reflected its creator and the time of its creation.

With Nestor's link to the bracelet in question, Leaphorn considered the other loose ends that could help him meet Mrs. Pinto's deadline. He'd pass Rafferty's name on to Peshlakai. Perhaps Rafferty had become a patron and the jeweler knew how to reach him. He thought about Councilor Walker and their plan for breakfast and her connections to people who knew people who knew Tiffany. He had the feeling that the pieces were almost in place, but he couldn't decipher the puzzle.

He appreciated the part of the drive where the interstate entered the cool ponderosa forest outside of Flagstaff, the tall pines a factor of altitude and increased moisture—although this year, the mountain country of Arizona lacked the normal precipitation. He watched the San Francisco Peaks rise in the distance and recalled the stories his relatives had told of how the Holy People created the mountains and their intervention to make the world safer for the five-fingered ones. He smiled, remembering his uncle's words: "*I wish they had done a better job of it, then you wouldn't need to be a policeman.*"

Clouds shrouded the top of Mount Humphreys. If he didn't know this country so well, Leaphorn would have assumed the possibility, finally, of rain on the parched land. A gift that the Hopi would tie to their prayers to the katsinas who dwelled there.

He took the exit for Northern Arizona University and made his way to the building where Louisa had worked. He saw her car in the lot and then found a welcome spot of shade for the truck. He noticed that the hallways had been repainted and the carpet replaced since he had last been in Louisa's territory. The door to her office, or what had been her office when she taught here, stood open. He saw her organizing some books, moving them from a box to a shelf. He knocked.

"Come on in. I'm almost done."

A wooden bench with cushions upholstered in shades of gray and orange sat against the wall. She motioned him there and sat next to him. "How was your trip?"

"Fye. You look guh." Louisa seemed reenergized, he thought.

"Thank you. It's been nice reconnecting with my colleagues. I'm looking forward to finishing my research and finally putting my book together."

Leaphorn nodded. He'd encouraged her to return to the project, a compilation of comparative contemporary spiritual beliefs of Southwestern tribes. Part of his motivation was to divert her searing intensity away from him and into the larger world.

"I'm sorry the Pinto case has brought so much frustration. Maybe this phone call will make the difference. Shall we do it?"

"Sure. Peas."

She walked to the desk. "I looked at the questions you wrote. I'd like to suggest some changes, but I don't want to impinge on your territory."

"Go aheh."

"What if I started by saying that she must be surprised to get this call and then reassuring her that we will not reveal her identity?" Louisa went on. Her changes both simplified and softened the inquiries.

He nodded his approval, glad they could agree and do this in person so gestures could fill in for spoken English.

"There's a phone in the next room, on that desk the interns use. Bring it in here to listen to what Mary Nestor has to say."

He nodded, found the phone, and came back to her office.

She dialed the number. A man answered.

"May I speak to Mary Nestor?"

"Hold on. She just got home."

A few minutes later, a woman came on the line. Her voice and intonation told Leaphorn she had probably grown up in Dinetah and was younger than he'd expected. He jotted down a note and handed the message to Louisa as she was introducing herself and the reason for the call.

When Louisa finished those remarks she said, "Excuse me, ma'am. Do you speak Navajo?"

"Aoo'. Yes, but I'm a little rusty. Why do you ask?"

"I am handing this call to my Navajo friend Joe Leaphorn. He and I are working together on this project, and he is curious about something."

Rather than starting with the task at hand, Leaphorn introduced himself the traditional way, telling her the clans he came from.

Mary did the same in halting Navajo, then switched to English. "Sorry my Navajo is so rough. I mostly use it with my dad, and I haven't been spending much time there."

"Your Navajo sounds fine. Better than my English these days."

"So, together, we're bilingually challenged. What's this call about?"

"A box arrived at the Navajo Museum filled with old things. I believe you sent that box."

He heard only silence. Then, in the background, a man's voice: "Mary, Barbara needs you."

When she spoke again, Leaphorn noticed the change in her tone. "I can't tell you anything about that, and I have to go."

Leaphorn spoke quickly, before she hung up. "I really need to talk to you about the box. Only one question, just a minute of your time. Your privacy is safe with me."

"I don't—"

"Help me lift the heart of a worried woman and a father who is missing his daughter very much."

The male voice sounded more insistent. "Mary. Now, please."

"I'm off tomorrow morning. Call me on my cell." She rattled off the number and ended the call.

Louisa sighed. "What do you think?"

"Les go see her tomorrow."

"Where does she live?"

"Winslow. Come wid me."

He could see Louisa thinking about it. He reached for a pad on the desk and wrote: "The box was mailed from the Winslow post office and we can talk to the employee there. Mary's Navajo is marginal, so I'll need your help with English. I would enjoy your company."

"OK. I'm sure Marsha won't mind if you'd like to sleep at the house tonight. She says her couch is comfortable." Marsha was the talkative colleague with whom Louisa stayed when she came to Flagstaff on college business. Leaphorn had met her once, and that was plenty.

He shook his head.

"I nee some quiet to tink."

They made plans to meet on campus in the morning.

Leaphorn found a motel, plugged in his laptop, checked his email, considered tomorrow's interview, had a hot roast beef sandwich at a nearby diner, and called it a day. He awoke refreshed. Louisa was ready when he pulled up in his truck.

She smiled. "Shall we take my car?"

He shook his head. "I drive."

Interstate 40, the quickest way to Winslow, drew an abundance of truck traffic and, in the summer, a bevy of tourists in sticker-covered RVs. Unlike the orange barrels and shoulder repair work he had encountered on his way west, the two eastbound lanes lay clear of construction. They left ponderosa pine country for red rocks, piñon and juniper trees, and then flatter, emptier landscape. As many times as he had driven this route, Leaphorn never tired of it. The vast sky where he'd seen double rainbows and clouds bigger than skyscrapers made whatever problem he puzzled over seem insignificant.

He asked Louisa if she'd ever been to Winslow.

"Maybe pulled off the freeway for gas there. I've heard lovely things about the old hotel La Posada. When I was working full-time and lived in Flag, I should have checked it out. Thanks for asking me to come with you."

Louisa sat quietly. He appreciated not having to work to speak English and used the time to consider the best way to approach Mary. He anticipated Mary wondering how he had found her, and decided he would say he was a detective and leave it at that. He would stress that he and Louisa would keep her identity private. He'd say that the woman who had received her great gift had a question. He'd ask if the special dress had been in the box and move on from there.

He would call Mary when they reached the outskirts of Winslow and persuade her to let them treat her to a soda, a cup of coffee, or lunch in exchange for a brief conversation. Simple and effective, if she would take his call.

He studied the scenery as he planned for the encounter, noticing the ribbon of a long train to the south, a few cumulus clouds beginning to build, joining the high, icy cirrus clouds in the brilliant blue of the summer sky.

Louisa broke the silence.

"Joe, I enjoy helping you, you know that. I find your work as an investigator interesting, and you do it well. I'll assist you with this case—I mean, if you want me to. After that, you'll need to figure out something else."

"Waz wrong?"

She angled toward him. "I don't want helping with your work to get in the way of our friendship. I offered some suggestions when we were at the Hubbell Trading Post, and you found my ideas intrusive. I'm not one to go where I'm not wanted. I need to get back to my own interests. That's better for both of us."

He recalled his irritation when she interrupted his interview and even invited Peshlakai to their home. His reaction came automatically from years of police work, shutting down hysterical parents and girlfriends, talkative drunks, pesky bystanders who butted in to an investigation. It wasn't personal. Now he wanted to say the right thing, and until he knew what that might be, he didn't say anything at all.

"Joe, do you understand?"

He shrugged. "Les talk when I can type."

"We'll do that."

"You help me wid dis one?"

"That's what I said." He heard the edge to her voice.

He saw the exit for a rest area and pulled off the interstate. He found a parking place behind the row of trucks lined up like a neighborhood of small buildings, all facing the highway. He took out his notebook and jotted down some thoughts. He preferred typing because the speed more closely matched the workings of his mind. But this would do. He handed the book to Louisa. She read his note twice and then gave the book back to him.

"That plan looks good, but, as you wrote, we'll have to see how things develop. Sometimes a little chitchat can loosen people up. I noticed that with my oral histories. Breaking the ice, you know, establishing rapport with a stranger, that's the hardest part."

"Rye."

"And Mary will already be suspicious. We can veer from this plan if she isn't forthcoming."

He nodded. He'd step in if he had to.

He called Mary, but she didn't answer. He left a message, then sent her a text with the information that he and his friend Louisa were in Winslow and wanted to meet her. He offered to treat her to lunch, stressed that the meeting wouldn't take long, and underlined their respect for her privacy.

They waited, watching the traffic pass. In less than a minute, his phone chimed. Mary suggested a place to meet, El Falcon on the east end of town, in half an hour.

## 16

Winslow had seen its share of ups and downs. A thriving railroad town, a trade center where Navajo and Hopi met, and a village that wore its Route 66 heritage like a badge of honor now welcomed tourists on their way to or from the Grand Canyon or Albuquerque. Leaphorn gave Louisa a five-cent tour, starting at another Hubbell Trading Post, the traders' center for shipping fleece, rugs, and more to East Coast markets. Then they walked to the Standin' on the Corner Park.

"I haven't thought of that Eagles song for a long time. When was it a hit, sometime in the 1970s?" She sang a few bars. "Those were the days."

They strolled over to look at the mural that showed the girl in a flatbed Ford from the song. A couple of gray-haired tourists were taking a photo next to the life-sized bronze of a young man with a guitar.

At El Falcon, they sat at a table with a view of local traffic and waited for Mary. Leaphorn took a chair facing the door and another mural, a large painting of a town on a beach. When the waitress returned with ice water and plastic-coated menus, he asked about it.

"Oh, the original owners here were Greek and had that commissioned as a reminder of their old home. We're all so used to it we forget it's there."

Like a lot of things, he thought, including the interesting woman who sat across from him. He realized that he had grown so accustomed to Louisa's presence that he'd forgotten to tell her how much he admired her and enjoyed her friendship.

He was preparing to say just that when he saw a Navajo woman arrive alone. Sunlight from the window shimmered on her black hair. He motioned to her, and she walked toward their table. She took a seat at the end of the table, between him and Louisa. They got the introductions and pleased-to-meet-yous out of the way.

"This place gets busy later." Mary picked up her menu. "Let's order, and then we can talk."

"Speaking of that, Joe is more comfortable speaking in Navajo, and I'm fine with it. If it's something I need to hear, he'll speak English."

"Louisa, you don't speak Navajo?"

"I don't. I'm afraid I don't have the ear for it."

Leaphorn said, "From your name, I wasn't expecting you to understand Diné Bizaad very well. I'm glad you do."

"I understand better than I can speak." She said it in English. "It's wonderful to hear Navajo again. And my last name, Nestor? That came from my late husband. He was killed in Afghanistan."

She was younger than most widows, only forty at most.

The waitress told them about the chicken taco and steak salad specials and took their orders. Then Mary leaned across the table toward them. "I'm exploiting your offer to buy me lunch. You two made the trip for nothing. I can't tell you anything about a box of gifts."

"Please don't say that." Louisa's voice had the tone she probably used with her students when they disappointed her. "The lady who received the donations is my friend. She got so excited when she realized what you had sent. Especially because, from what you wrote, one of the pieces has an important link to Fort Sumner."

"Fort Sumner?"

"The Long Walk?"

Mary shrugged.

"Joe should explain."

Leaphorn studied Mary's face for clues that she was faking ignorance. Didn't see any.

"Hwéeldi." He hoped that hearing it in Navajo might jar her memory.

She raised her shoulders to her ears again.

Leaphorn spoke, in some detail, about the forced eviction of the People from their sacred homelands by the US government, their grueling march across much of New Mexico to an internment camp they shared with the Mescalero Apaches. He mentioned the children and elderly who died on the way, the years of illness, hunger, and sadness, and the survivors' joy when they returned to the heart of Dinetah instead of being shipped off to Oklahoma.

The waitress brought their meals. Mary listened, her hands in her lap, her food untouched.

"Every Navajo alive today is an heir to this time of sorrow and to the resurgence that followed. Our grandparents' fortitude when they returned to start over is why we Navajo not only survived but grew strong again."

As he spoke, he realized that if Mary didn't know about Hwéeldi, she could not have described the missing dress. He needed to learn more about her. When he stopped talking, he saw the tears in her eyes.

"I remember learning something about this in school, but I was too young to understand how terrible it was. What an outrage! My shimásani never talked about that, but she, or at least my great-grandparents, must have experienced that terrible time. When I visit my father, I'll ask him if he can share the stories he has heard."

She looked at her untouched sandwich. "You know, my grandmother was always careful about food. She never wasted anything. If my sisters or I dared to complain about what she gave us to eat, she frowned that terrible frown of hers and we ate. Do you think that was because of Hwéeldi?"

Leaphorn took a sip of his coffee. "All our families were touched by Hwéeldi, one way or another. Even those who fled the soldiers and hid suffered. That's why my client, Mrs. Pinto, was happy when she noticed a dress on the inventory list related to the Long Walk. The weaving could be a way to open discussion between the generations, to educate young people who don't understand the way the survivors rebuilt our culture. According to your note, the biil was created by a very powerful and famous woman, one of the leaders who helped us grow into what we are today."

He paused, but she didn't protest or ask a question, so he continued.

"To have an item created by Juanita's own hands, her brain, her heart, in a place where many of our people could appreciate it, would be very important to our Diné history. But the biil never arrived."

Mary pursed her lips and exhaled. She spoke in English now, and rapidly. "You've got this all wrong. All I did was take that box to the post office. I am the one who mailed the box but not the one who gave those things away."

Louisa looked surprised, but Leaphorn recalled his first phone conversation with Mary and the voices in the background. "I appreciate you coming to talk with us. I need to contact the person who made the donation and gave you the box to mail."

She shook her head. "No."

"I can give you my information, and you can ask the person to call me or, if you prefer, to call my client, Mrs. Pinto, now that you understand why this is important."

She shook her head again and squeezed her lips together.

Louisa could help with this, he decided, so he moved to English. "You packed da box?"

"No. I offered to help, but he's very particular about that old stuff. He should have gotten rid of some of it when he closed his gallery, but those things had memories of when he was a young man.

Some go back even before he and Barbara moved to Winslow." She paused. "I can't say anything else. I'd lose my job and, worse, he would know I had betrayed him. He might hate me."

Leaphorn took a bite of his meatloaf, waiting for what Mary would add.

Louisa put down her iced tea glass. "I understand. We don't want to get you into trouble. I haven't been to Winslow before. It seems like an interesting town. Have you lived here long?"

"Since I was seventeen."

"So you didn't grow up here?"

"No, my family is from a little place between Window Rock and Gallup."

"That's beautiful country."

"It is. I miss it, but this is home to me now."

Leaphorn ate a bite of mashed potato, watching as Mary uncrossed her arms and nibbled at her sandwich.

"Winslow must have seemed like a big city to you at first." Louisa smiled that smile he'd seen when she was doing her oral history interviews. "Did your family have relatives or friends here?"

"I didn't move here with my family. They stayed near Window Rock. My sister and I came out together, but she left and it was just me."

"Wow. At seventeen. Was that an adventure for you?"

"It was. I came to help a lady who had volunteered as a VISTA worker at our high school. At the end of my senior year, she and her husband decided to move because he had an opportunity to open a gallery here in Winslow. I had just graduated, so she asked me and my older sister if we could help drive and get her new house in order. I had already been driving for a year and my dad was OK with it."

Louisa said, "I know some fathers who would have objected, even grown angry."

"Angry? He lost his temper once in a while, but only when we had it coming. Dad always told us how much we girls meant to him. He said he would miss me and that I was always welcome to come home, but that he knew I would be fine. The confidence he had in me gave me the courage to say yes. It was hard work, but it was fun, too."

Mary smiled at the memory. "It was hot and exhausting, but I liked it. My sister went home. Then the lady got sick and it turned out to be cancer. I stayed and helped her and filled in at the gallery. By the time Barbara was done with her radiation and the chemo, well, it was like I was part of the family, or at least part of the business. They invited me to remain here and I did."

"Was the gallery nearby?"

"Everything's close here. It was a great location, right downtown. We were always busy during the tourist season, and we shipped a lot of art to buyers who came on those bus tours. I miss it."

"When did the gallery close?"

"He shut down his art business about two years ago. Since then he's been selling things online. I usually take a box or two to the post office each week."

Louisa nodded. "It sounds like they really appreciate what you do for them."

"They're good people. They don't have any kids, so they treat me like family."

Leaphorn cleared his throat. "Can you tell me where the items in the box came from?"

She answered too quickly. "I don't exactly know." She repeated in English.

Leaphorn took another bite of meatloaf. Even though the meal was cold, it was still tasty, and like Mary, he had been trained never to waste food.

"I understand that you're not sure. But what would you guess?"

She answered in English, and he interpreted that as a sign of stress. "Well, since the box went to the Navajo Museum, I'd guess that what he packed could have come from his private collection. It was either that or from the inventory he moved from the gallery to the house after the shop closed."

Louisa shoved her plate to the side. "Mrs. Pinto noticed that also missing from the box was a bracelet. I have one that resembles it. This one." She stretched her arm with Peshlakai's storyteller artistry toward Mary. "Did you see anything like it when you worked in the shop?"

Mary cleared her throat and spoke faster. "We sold a lot of jewelry. The owner and his wife would buy direct from the jewelers or shop at fairs and markets." She looked at the bracelet again. "That's lovely. Wish I could help."

Leaphorn knew she was lying.

The waitress asked about dessert. Leaphorn shook his head. Mary, who hadn't eaten much of her sandwich, requested a piece of chocolate cake and a to-go container. Louisa ordered a dish of ice cream.

"I understand that your employer doesn't want any credit. But what if some present arrived at his door?" Louisa flashed another smile at Mary. "You know, a tin of cookies, a bouquet, something like that? Anonymously, just like what he sent. What do you think?"

Mary shrugged.

Leaphorn could see her relax a bit more.

"You mentioned the lady's cancer. I know some great herbal tinctures and infusions that make a good tea. Maybe something like that? Or a plant, or . . ."

Leaphorn finished his meal as the ladies chatted. He knew Louisa was fishing for details, but they'd moved out of his comfort zone with talk of tea and cookies. He'd rather discuss how to spot a gang member by studying his tattoos.

Louisa opened her purse, took out a piece of paper and a pen, and handed them to Mary. "Mrs. Pinto will need to know where to ship the gift. Could you write the name and number for her?"

Leaphorn cringed, and Mary ignored the ploy. "I have been thinking about what Mr. Leaphorn told me about Hwéeldi and the weaving. It touched my heart. The man who had the gallery mentioned that there were things he owned that he would like to give away when the gallery closed. Maybe he forgot to put the old dress in the box."

Leaphorn said, "So you understand why we would like to talk to him to find out for sure."

"And you understand why I can't tell you any

more than I have. A clever person like either of you can figure out how to find him from the information I've given you."

Mary reached into her pocket and extracted a red wallet. "I have to get to work. The lady gets a massage to help with her pain. She will be ready to leave in twenty minutes, and it takes me fifteen to drive there. Then we stop at the grocery."

Louisa put a hand on Mary's arm. "Put your money away. This is on me. My friend Mrs. Pinto would want that."

Leaphorn watched Mary pick up her box of food, leave the restaurant, and climb into a white Mercedes sedan. When he squinted, he could make out three characters on the car's license plate, enough for Jessica to follow up if necessary. He turned back to Louisa to see her fiddling with her phone, typing. "I can figure this out. An Indian art gallery on Main Street that closed two years ago after twenty years in operation."

"Rye. Rafferty."

She looked at him, puzzled.

"Rafferty bought da bracelet."

"That's good. I'll tease this out."

Leaphorn grabbed the check, took it to the cashier, and came back.

Louisa grinned. "Lloyd and Barbara Rafferty. They own a place off Highway 87. I put the address in my GPS."

"Les go." He stood, keys in hand.

"Hold on. Mary left her sunglasses on the table. Let me grab them." Louisa put the glasses in her purse.

He would have given the glasses to the woman at the front counter for Mary to pick up. But Louisa had a mind of her own, and he was learning when to roll along with it.

He lowered the windows before he turned on the air-conditioning. Louisa climbed in. "I imagine Mr. Rafferty's instinct will be to slam the door on us, assuming he opens it to a couple of strangers in the first place. Talking to an aging lady college professor might make the situation smoother than dealing with a guy who, despite being retired, still looks and acts like a cop."

Leaphorn focused on driving. After the second stop sign, he realized she had a point.

"You take da lead."

"I'll say this harmless-looking college professor needs a favor for a friend, who has a question about Indian art, his area of expertise. We would have gone to the gallery, but we realized it had closed. What do you think?"

He nodded.

"Once we're in, I'll tell him more of the truth, that the questions concern an item Daisy thought she was receiving as a gift, but the gift never arrived. I will say that Mrs. Pinto doesn't know his identity and that we won't tell her but that I'm wondering if he forgot to send it. And I'll introduce you as my friend. How does this sound?"

"Kay." If Louisa could build a bit of rapport with Rafferty, the plan could evolve. If he put the dress in the box, Rafferty would assume it had been stolen. Bad for the museum staff's reputation, unless Rafferty blamed it on the post office or on Mary.

As he expected, they found the home in an older, well-kept part of Winslow where houses sat far apart overlooking the city, with views of the Little Painted Desert and the San Francisco Peaks. The home was perched at the end of a paved driveway. Beauty surrounded those who lived here. Louisa intertwined her fingers. "I'm nervous about this." Then she pushed the round white button to the right of the carved wooden door. They heard a chime and then a voice. "Who is it?"

Louisa gave her name. "I'm a professor from Northern Arizona University in Flagstaff, Mr. Rafferty. I would have contacted you through the gallery, but I see that it's closed. I have a question about a piece in your collection. Or at least something you used to have."

She's already improvising, Leaphorn thought. In his years as a cop, he'd seen too many operations fail when a team member went off on a tangent.

They heard the latch release and felt the wave of air-conditioning as it moved from the cool home toward the warm porch.

A slim man with a head of thick white hair and brilliant blue eyes studied them. Louisa had the lanyard with her NAU ID card around her neck and showed it to him. "NAU? What do you teach?"

"Nothing at the moment, but cultural anthropology is my field. I'm doing research now. I just finished consulting with a summer program. This shouldn't take long. I appreciate your help."

"Who's that gentleman with you?"

"My friend Joe Leaphorn. He offered to drive since I've never been to Winslow."

He turned to Leaphorn. "Yá'át'ééh."

"Yá'át'ééh." Leaphorn asked, in Navajo, if the man spoke Navajo.

"No. I understand a few phrases, like that one we said, but no, sorry. Wish I did."

Louisa took charge again. "I'm here to thank you. My friend Daisy Pinto is the director of the Navajo Museum."

"Never heard of her." Leaphorn noticed Rafferty stiffen.

"She told me she wished she could find who had sent that wonderful box so she could extend her gratitude and find out more about the items."

"That's interesting, but it doesn't concern me, Professor. You both need to leave."

Leaphorn had expected the man to deny his involvement. "We hab questions abow a missin biil."

Rafferty sucked in his breath. "Missing? What do you mean?"

Leaphorn spoke slowly, in Navajo, hoping that Rafferty could understand. "This is about Juanita's dress. The Hwéeldi dress, the great treasure you want the Navajo people to have. It was not in the box."

The old man took a step away from them. "How did you find me?"

Leaphorn switched to English. "Navajo detective."

Rafferty looked at him. "That's you, right?"

"Rye."

When Rafferty smiled, his teeth had a glint of gold. "I thought you had more business here than

a friend and a driver. Let's get this over with before my wife returns."

Rafferty turned from them and headed down the
hall, the heels of his polished dress shoes clicking
against the tile floor marking each purposeful step.
They followed to a large living room decorated
with paintings of the desert and stone sculptures. A
coat-like garment with ornate, Plains Indian–style
beadwork hung under glass on the wall between
two large windows. Rafferty motioned them to the
couch. "What do you mean the dress is missing?"

Louisa answered. "When Mrs. Pinto looked at
the inventory list you sent with the gift, she noticed a reference to a weaving from around the time
of the Long Walk. But when she examined the
contents of the box, that piece was not there."

Leaphorn noted that Louisa didn't speculate or
cast any blame.

"The lady must have overlooked it. I packed it
first. There's some mistake."

Leaphorn shook his head. Louisa spoke. "No,
sir. We wish that were the case."

Rafferty paced to the window and studied the
view, then turned toward them. "That old dress
didn't look like much, but it reflects an important
part of Navajo history. I was amazingly fortunate
to acquire it—that's a story in itself—and I treasured it. But I always felt that it didn't belong to
me, that it belonged to history and especially to
the Navajo Nation. I could have sold it ten times
over to other collectors or museums. It *was* in the
box." He underlined the verb with his tone of voice.

"You know, I used to greet all my students by name after two classes. Now it takes me half a semester. We all get more forgetful as we age." Louisa's tone kept the remark conversational.

"You've noticed I'm what I call seasoned, but I'm not so far gone that I'd neglect to add the very heart of the donation to the shipment." Rafferty stepped toward them. "Come this way. I'll show you something."

They followed through another hallway, this one decorated with paintings of deer and rabbits and Pueblo Indian dancers, art that Leaphorn recognized from reading he had done about Dorothy Dunn. In the early twentieth century, the woman led a fine arts program at the Santa Fe Indian School that taught many Native artists a salable, distinctive style that collectors came to love. Walt Disney invited some of the artists to Hollywood to work in his production studio. They declined.

Rafferty opened a door and flicked on the lights, motioning them in ahead of him.

Leaphorn felt the dry, chilled air of the storage room and recognized the museum-quality sliding drawers and movable shelves. What treasures did they contain? On the top of a repair table, an alabaster carving of an eagle lay on its side. The lower third of one wing had broken, and the piece sat nearby awaiting reattachment.

Rafferty stopped in front of a storage cabinet. "When I was in the business, I spent every summer going to Indian shows and art fairs in New Mexico and Arizona. Barbara and I don't have children to argue over these things, so I'm finding homes for them while I can. I'm donating them anonymously."

He tapped the label on the drawer as he read aloud: "'1860s Navajo textile. Juanita Manuelito.'" The drawer slid out smoothly with his touch. Except for a large brown envelope, it was empty.

"If, as the professor so tactfully suggested, I've grown senile, the piece would be here. Clearly it is not."

Leaphorn looked at the drawer. "You sure iz Juanita's?"

"Well, Detective, I'm sure Juanita wore it because I have a photograph of her wearing it. And because of the times, I'm almost positive she wove it herself." He picked up the envelope, opened the flap, and slipped out a piece of paper, a photocopy of a portrait, a second color photo, and a typed sheet.

"Here she is." The black-and-white reproduction showed a young Juanita, fiercely beautiful, dressed in a biil. Unlike the dress she wore in the famous portrait with her husband, this garment was simpler.

The second photo was a color shot of the dress itself in what looked like a plastic bag.

Leaphorn pulled out his phone and moved his index finger up and down, as though it were on a camera's shutter. "A pitcher?"

Rafferty shrugged. "Go ahead as long as you promise not to tell anyone where you took it."

Leaphorn snapped a few shots.

Louisa said, "Why is the biil in that bag?"

"Textiles are prone to insect infestation. The

same is true with artifacts that have leather, feathers, anything that a moth or a silverfish might consider edible. It was stored with pesticides to keep it safe."

Leaphorn frowned.

"Don't worry, Mr. Detective. I made sure the toxins were removed before I shipped it." Rafferty replaced the papers, closed the drawer, and led them back through the house.

"One mo question. Insurance?"

"Everything in the house is insured. But the box?" Rafferty sighed. "No. Because I sent it anonymously, I couldn't insure it. Everything I have ever mailed through the post office from the gallery always has arrived safely. Every time, for more than ten years." His voice vibrated, and Leaphorn felt the anger. "Everything, I guess, except this precious dress. Was the box damaged when it arrived?"

"No."

"Then, Mr. Detective and Madame Professor, shipping insurance would not have made a difference. You are dealing with a case of theft."

As they followed him toward the front door, Leaphorn thought of how to pose a complicated question with the fewest words. "I nee to axe another kestin bout da gifs."

"Excuse me?" Rafferty frowned. "Was anything else missing?"

"Yes."

Louisa answered before he could find the words. "A bracelet by a Navajo artist named Peshlakai."

"I think your friend has a robber on her staff." Rafferty opened the big front door.

"May we be in touch if the museum has a question about something you've sent?"

He hesitated, then extracted a slim black wallet and handed each of them a white business card. "I trust you to protect my anonymity. Understand?"

"Of course."

Leaphorn nodded slightly and put the card in his pocket.

Rafferty closed the door behind them.

As they drove away, Mary passed them driving the white Mercedes, headed toward the house.

Louisa said, "We've got a lot to talk about on the way to Flagstaff."

## 17

Jim Chee returned to the Chinle station for another look at the burglary reports. If he learned as much as he could today, he could save himself a drive tomorrow and use the phone and computer instead of gasoline and boot leather to continue the investigation.

This time, he noticed more similarities in the crimes. With the exception of Mr. Natachi's case, all the victims reported that the break-ins happened on a weekday while they were away from home. Chee checked a calendar. Each burglary was on Tuesday or Thursday morning. Interesting. Did the criminal have a job that gave him those days off? Perhaps he or she was someone from outside the community who had reason to be in Chinle on those days and added crime to the schedule?

Chee noticed, again, that the reports mentioned no "vandalism." Whoever committed the thefts knew where to look. Some of the places were as obvious as jewelry boxes. Some were more original. One woman, Mrs. Morgan, kept her treasures in a cookie jar on the kitchen counter. Another used a large coffee can in the refrigerator. He wondered if the thief was selling the items to someone who specialized in old Navajo jewelry or exchanging everything taken for drugs. He made a note to follow up with Indian jewelry dealers.

The only case that didn't fit the pattern was Mr. Natachi's. Chee remembered the house and realized that Mr. Natachi's television had not been stolen from its place of honor in the living room. The intruder left the valuable rodeo buckle, also in plain view, untouched.

There was, he thought, no such thing as a victimless crime, and these burglaries disturbed his sense of hozho, of balance.

His cell phone buzzed and he glanced at it. It was Elsie. "I called the hospital to check on Mr. Natachi, but they won't tell me anything. I called Ryana, but she didn't answer. So I called you. How's the old one doing?"

Chee heard the worry in her voice. "He was resting comfortably when I checked and the nurse told me he seems a bit stronger."

"I'm glad. Some of the people here have been asking, you know, the staff and his buddies who come to the senior center. Mrs. Morgan told me to let him know she's praying for him."

"Mrs. Morgan? Was she one of the people who lost something in a burglary?"

"Poor thing. Her great-grandfather made that necklace."

Chee thought about that. "What about other people at the center?"

"My goodness, it has been awful. So many of these elderlies lost things. Do you want to know who they are?"

"Sure." He wasn't surprised when her list matched the reports. "Do you have programs at the center every day?"

"No, we can't afford that. Just twice a week."

"Tuesdays and Thursdays?"

"That's right." Elsie made a clicking sound. "I hope you can get their things back."

"Me, too. So I guess Nicky's program didn't help much?"

"It should have. We brought him in before the burglaries."

Chee was closing his computer when his phone buzzed again. This time it was Bernie. He realized he had worked way past dinner and hadn't called.

But that wasn't what was on her mind.

Bernie left Agent Berke to finish his examination of the trunk and went back in the house. A few moments later, she saw Berke pick up a piece of paper, study it, then put it back in the trunk.

Bernie motioned Ryana over to the couch and spoke softly. "I need to ask you about something before Berke comes back in."

The second agent started toward them.

"Give us a minute."

He frowned, then returned to his post at the door.

Ryana whispered, "What's the question?"

"Someone mentioned to Sergeant Chee that you'd made some movies. My sister worked with a guy who knows a lot about video and he helped her find the work you'd done. And—"

"Don't say anything else." Ryana grasped the arm of the couch so hard her fingernails turned pale. "I know what I did. I was stupid."

"Did Nicky have any connection to that?"

"No." Ryana sucked in her breath. "Are you going to talk about the movies with these guys?"

"Do the movies have any tie-in to what's in the car?"

"How could they? I don't even know what's out there."

Bernie nodded. For once, she knew Ryana was telling the truth.

Berke came through the front door with a look of determination. He and his partner conferred briefly, and then the other man went out to stand by the car.

Berke spoke to Ryana. "Tell me about the items out there."

"A spare tire, a jack, maybe some jumper cables."

"Don't get smart. I found a note addressed to you. Do you know what it said?"

She shook her head. "Like I told you. I never opened the trunk."

Berke twisted his lips into a smirk. "I memorized it for you: 'Ryana, you'll know what to do with this. N.'"

"Know what to do with what? What was in there?" Ryana's voice had a touch of panic. "What aren't you telling me?"

Instead of speaking to the question, the agent gave her a look reserved for idiots or young children. "You have more information about Michael Debois and how and why he died than you're telling us. Playing dumb doesn't work with me."

Bernie sucked in her breath. Michael was the name Bigman had passed on to her, the name he had heard Agent Johnson say when she saw the dead person near the running trail. And the name Johnson had mentioned to her.

Ryana leaned away from the agent. "You're crazy, man. I don't know any Debois."

"You called him Nicky Jones. What do you know about his murder?"

Ryana's mouth fell open. Bernie noticed that she had started to shake.

"Nicky's dead? Nicky! What happened?"

"You tell me."

Bernie heard a low rumble and saw the flashing lights of an approaching tow truck bounce against the windows. "Are you seizing the car?"

"Yeah." Berke glanced out the window. "I called for the truck as soon as I realized what we were dealing with."

"Tell me what happened to Nicky?" Ryana sounded panicky and scared. "Are you sure he's dead?"

Berke gave her a hard look. "We can get into that tomorrow. I'll have more questions for you when we know everything you've got in that trunk."

"I'm not . . ." Ryana stopped talking when Bernie put a hand on her arm.

Bernie frowned at the FBI agent. "Stop it. Don't

be a bully. You're badgering her. She's answered your questions several times. Act like you've got a heart."

"Who are you, Officer Manuelito, to lecture me? I've probably been doing this job since you were in high school."

"Ryana's another victim here. She's trying to co-operate." Bernie felt like punching the jerk. "Whatever credentials you have don't give you the right to be cruel."

"This doesn't concern you, but that attitude of yours concerns me, and I'm going to make it a problem for you." Berke glared at her, then went outside to supervise the tow. He drove off with his partner, following the sedan and the big truck, without another word to Bernie or Ryana.

Ryana stood at the window, watching Nicky's car disappear. Bernie sat on the couch. After a few minutes, Ryana retreated to the bedroom at the back of the house. Bernie kept thinking about what to tell Ryana's aunt, but she had only come up with a handful of ideas when Dolly Natachi drove up in her little Ford. Bernie gave her the information about her brother first, stressing that he was responding to the hospital treatment.

Dolly took that news well. "When I saw that police car out there, I tried to think of what I'd done to get myself in trouble. Then I wondered about my brother and if someone had come with bad news. I'm glad he's holding his own."

"My husband, Sergeant Chee, has seen him, and so has your niece, Ryana."

"Ryana said she wanted to spend the night, and

that she needed to talk to me about something important. I thought she would be here by now."

"She's in the bedroom. I heard her crying."

Dolly shook her head. "This breaks my heart. First my brother and now Ryana's troubles. Too much bad news for one day."

"Did Ryana say what she wanted to talk to you about?"

"Her boyfriend moved out and she didn't know what to do." Dolly sighed. "When that girl came back from Phoenix, we all thought she would settle down. But then she let that guy Nicky move in with her. He was nice enough, but not very forthcoming."

"What was she doing in Phoenix?"

"She said she found a waitressing job and took some acting classes. But that girl bought a fancy car. When she came back to live near her grandfather and went to work at the senior center, she was happy. But then something changed. She sold her car. She started to work lots of overtime. I wondered why she needed all that money because she never went on vacation. Never bought expensive stuff. When she and my brother visited this weekend, I sensed that something made her fearful. Maybe that boyfriend was mean."

Bernie thought about how to put what she needed to say next. "Two FBI agents came here before you arrived, to talk to your niece. They told her the boyfriend, Nicky, had been killed. They took the car Ryana drove out, Nicky's car, because of something suspicious in the trunk. From the tone of their questions, they think the one in the bedroom knows something about the murder and what's in the trunk."

Dolly stared at the ceiling and Bernie gave her time to absorb the information. When she finally spoke, her voice was calm and steady.

"I know that girl. She's made mistakes, but she would never hurt anyone. She told me she took classes so she could help the elderlies where she works if they had a heart attack or something. Those FBIs don't have it right. They should leave her alone."

Bernie called Agent Johnson from the patrol car. It was after hours, but considering what had happened, she figured she might catch the agent in the office.

"Manuelito? What's up?"

"My mother's neighbor's niece, Ryana Florez, was questioned in the murder of someone named Michael Debois, a man also known as Nicky Jones. He's the person I found by the trail, right?"

"I'd heard that word spreads fast in Indian Country, but this beats the record."

"I was with Ryana when Berke showed up this afternoon. She told the truth about not knowing what Nicky had in the trunk. Why did you guys target Ryana?"

"I can't talk to you about this now. Let's just say that girl isn't who she seems."

"I agree with you on that."

She heard Johnson exhale. "Like I said earlier, I'm not talking about Nicky, but I owe you lunch. Call me back on my cell phone, and we'll make a date." Johnson gave her the number.

Bernie dialed right back.

"OK, if I were talking, I might say that Michael became Nicky because of his computer skills on the dark side and some special information he shared with me. When he got bored with being safe, he decided to move to Chinle and resume his old life of online scamming and then ventured into new territory. If I were talking about this, I might say his murder is linked to that string of burglaries in Chinle, an online account that was hacked, and to a certain people who hated him. But I can't talk about this."

"So . . . the sweaty guy was involved?"

"Hired help. Your description of his missing finger came in handy. So, thanks." Bernie heard some muffled conversation in the background, and then Johnson said, "Gotta go."

"Did you know that someone shot Ryana's grandfather?"

"Berke mentioned that. There's always something going on out here in Indian Country, always a subtext. That's what I'm learning about the reservation. It's complicated to figure out who knows who, who is related, who owes somebody a favor. Every answer seems to spawn a flood of fresh questions."

Johnson's insight surprised Bernie. "What are your questions?"

"I am puzzling over why, besides being involved in helping kill her boyfriend, a young woman with no record of violence would conspire to attack her own grandfather."

"Run a search for Roxanne Dee. Then tell me

why Ryana asked my husband for two thousand dollars."

Bernie pointed the unit to Mama's house, wishing she'd walked so she would have had more time to anticipate the questions from her mother and Darleen.

The aroma of chicken soup greeted her as she entered the house. Mama was in the kitchen, a good thing. Darleen looked worried.

"What happened over there? We saw that white car drive off and that little car that Ryana had up on a tow truck."

"I'll tell you about that in a minute." Bernie spoke softly. "I let Mama know about Mr. Natachi getting shot."

"That's why she made soup. All the chopping helps her not be so angry when bad things happen."

Bernie said hello to her mother.

Mama kept her attention on the pot she was stirring. "This is almost ready. I just have to let the spinach melt."

"I'll set the table, Mama, and then I'll serve it. One of your shows is on TV."

Mama washed her hands, saving the water in the plastic tub she always kept in the sink. "Your sister needs to finish making salad and then we can eat."

Darleen came into the kitchen. "I know how you love salads, so this one is special. It has marinated cucumbers." They heard the TV click on and Darleen lowered her voice. "So what happened over there?"

Bernie spoke in a whisper. "Ryana got questioned by the FBI because of what was in the trunk of that car." She didn't wait for Darleen to ask. "A bunch of jewelry, computers. They suspect her of being involved in murder."

Darleen's eyebrows rose with surprise. "It's crazy. Murder? No way. That wasn't even her car. She told me she had to sell her car because of the blackmail."

"You said blackmail?"

"Yeah." Darleen's voice rose. "Can you believe . . ."

Bernie put a finger to her lips.

Darleen whispered, "You remember those movies, right? Well, somebody threatened to show them to her grandfather if she didn't pay him to keep quiet. So she did, but then the guy kept coming back, asking for more money. Finally, she told him she couldn't pay, and she thinks that's when he hurt Mr. Natachi."

"Wow. Do you believe her?"

"Why not?"

Bernie opened the drawer with the silverware as she spoke. "Well, Ryana lied to me about her grandfather's bolo being stolen and about his memory. And then she lied to Chee about who shot him."

"Ryana told me the blackmail guy was really angry when he called her." Darleen opened the refrigerator and pulled out the salad and the container with the cucumbers. She took a tomato from a basket on the counter and washed it. Then, talking the whole time, she reached for a paring knife. "The dude threatened to harm Mr. Natachi if she didn't come up with two thousand dollars. She started to cry when she told me."

"Did she recognize the voice?"

"No. She doesn't know who is doing this. That makes it worse." Darleen poured cucumber pieces into the salad bowl. "I didn't know what to say when Ryana told me." She took the tomato, cut it into wedges and added them. "I was glad when you showed up and I had to get out of there, but I wish I could have helped her."

Mama's voice came from the living room. "Girls. Let's eat. You are too slow in there. Stop talking and get moving."

Bernie barely tasted the soup and ate just enough salad not to be rude. Her mind kept returning to what Darleen had told her.

Mama wanted to talk about Mr. Natachi and shared pleasant memories of him dating back decades. Mama knew her way around a story, and Bernie let the words wash over her with no obligation to respond or react. She left as soon as she could without disrespect. When she said she had to get to work, she told the truth. She needed to share what she'd learned with Chee.

"Blackmailed? That's what I wondered when she asked me for two thousand dollars."

"Sister said Ryana has been paying someone to keep this movie stuff quiet."

"Does she know who?"

"She told Darleen she doesn't."

Chee's tone grew lighter. "I learned a few things today, too. All the burglary victims participated in programs at the senior center. Nicky taught a class there, and besides telling them they should consider grab bars in the bathroom, he talked about ways to safeguard valuables at home."

"Grab bars in an outhouse? Did he know some of the old ones don't have indoor plumbing?"

"Sweetheart, you're getting in the way of my story."

"Go ahead."

"He asked the old folks to tell him where they kept their valuables so he could assess the safety. A few days later, their things disappeared without any obvious disruption, as though the thief knew exactly where to look."

"Interesting."

"Ryana recommended Nicky's program to her boss, and she was there when the victims gave up the hiding places. That links her to other thefts as well as her granddad's. If someone is blackmailing her over the movies, she's got motivation. You said her car had jewelry and computers in the trunk?"

"Not hers. Nicky's." Bernie remembered Ryana's reaction to the letter Agent Berke read. "She honestly didn't know that stolen property was in the car. And Johnson told me that Nicky wasn't really Nicky."

She explained.

"Any word about the Bigmans?" Chee sounded tired.

"Not yet."

"You've had a long day. If you want to stay in Chinle tonight . . ."

"I don't. I want to curl up next to you. I can make some phone calls out of Shiprock tomorrow, and Lieutenant Black and his folks can wrap things up.

We need to verify that some of the stuff in that trunk came from the elderlies at the Chinle center."

As he finally headed home, a chalky half-moon rose over the high desert. He knew stories, of course, about creatures who roamed at night causing trouble. He'd seen enough trouble for one day.

Time to go home.

The lights were on in the trailer when he pulled into the driveway. Even though she'd had a long day, Bernie had waited up. Her smile chased away most of his fatigue. He kissed her, and she responded, then slipped away. "I've been considering the whole messy Ryana business. I have some ideas I want to bounce off Agent Johnson tomorrow, but I'd like to try them out on you."

"Sure, honey, but I could use some food to get my brain in gear."

"Mama sent soup home with me, and we have peaches. You can eat while I talk."

He finished the soup as he listened to Bernie's account of Ryana's situation.

"Did I tell you Mr. Natachi got me to promise to keep Ryana safe?" Chee smiled. "How could I say no to that old man?"

"Good luck with that."

"He knows something is going on with her, but he won't talk about it."

Bernie had been standing as they talked, but now she sat down across from him. "I think there are two scenarios here, and that's what has us confused. I got involved in this because of Mr. Natachi's bolo, and it looked like it was tied to the other burglaries."

"Right. But now I don't think so."

"Me neither. I believe the man with the fresh haircut who first had the bolo is key to this whole mess."

Chee nodded. "Too bad you don't have a better description of him."

"No kidding."

Chee picked up his dishes and started toward the sink. "Have you heard anything from the Lieutenant about his big case?"

"No."

He looked at Bernie, realizing, again, that she was beautiful. "Let's get to bed, sweetheart. We can deal with this tomorrow."

18

Instead of heading back to Flagstaff, Leaphorn drove to La Posada. He parked in front of the old hotel. "Les talk."

Louisa gave him a puzzled look. "Get your laptop. I can read your typing better than your handwriting and it's quicker."

He would have done it anyway and bristled at her bossiness. They walked through the hotel's big front doors, past the gift shop and the lobby, and out to the garden. Except for a woman walking a fuzzy white dog, they were the only people there. They found a bench under the portal and declined a waiter's offer of wine or a soft drink. Leaphorn opened his laptop, and she opened the conversation.

"I could see, back at the restaurant, that the discussion about tea bored you, but I hope you realize I was building rapport with Mary."

"I unnastan. So kay."

"No, this has turned out badly. I'm discouraged."

Leaphorn typed: Rafferty told the truth about packing the dress. That narrows the possibilities.

"Narrows them to what? You think someone at the museum stole it?"

He didn't appreciate her tone, but the question was legitimate.

He resumed typing. That could be, and Tiffany had the access. Or someone at the post office, either here or in Window Rock. Maybe Mary removed it from the shipment. But I—he deleted the "I" and typed "we"—have made progress. We know for sure that Rafferty is the donor and that he put the dress in the box. We know it exists. Now we have to find it.

Louisa looked at the screen. "Mary? You saw how loyal she is to the Raffertys. It was a struggle for us to find out whom she worked for. I don't see her stealing from them. A random postal employee? Think of how many packages they must process in a day. How would someone at the post office even know what was in there? And it would be smarter to take the whole box. No one was expecting it, so no one would know it was gone."

Leaphorn thought. He typed, Good point about the post office. I still have questions about Mary.

"I watched Mary when you said what you did about the Long Walk. She had clearly never heard that story before, and without it, she wouldn't understand that the dress had value. But she knew a lot about the bracelet, didn't she?"

Leaphorn nodded. He typed, If whoever took the items had taken the inventory list, no one would have even known they were missing.

Louisa tented her fingers. "What if whoever did

this wanted to embarrass the museum and Mrs. Pinto?"

"Rye." He typed, Or Tiffany? Any more ideas?

"Not right now." She shook her head.

Leaphorn typed, Let's talk to Bean's contact at the post office, see what he knows about Mary. He found the text with the contact information Bean had sent. Like many things in the town of Winslow, population 10,000, the post office was convenient. They parked, went inside, and asked for the man Bean had mentioned, Arnold Sakiestewa.

"Arnie's in the back. May I help you?"

"No. I needa talk ta him." Leaphorn showed the woman his Apache County deputy credentials, presented to him on retirement. Their official look and the embossed gold badge on the card got her attention.

"I'll get him."

Sakiestewa, a well-muscled man of average height, came to the counter in a few minutes. Leaphorn spoke a few words of Hopi in greeting, surprised that they came to him, then introduced himself and Louisa.

Sakiestewa looked startled, too.

"You speak pretty good for a Navajo."

"Bean said you hepped Mary wid a box?"

"Who?"

Leaphorn turned to Louisa.

"Jim Bean, the postal inspector. A man with a booming voice."

"Oh, right. About Mary and her package." Saki-estewa was probably in his forties and wore his long dark hair in a single braid down his back. "I told the inspector that I helped her bring in her package, that I knew who she was because she's been coming here for years. Is it against the law to be nice to someone?" He addressed the question to them both.

Louisa answered. "Sir, the world needs all the kindness it can find. I'm here because my friend was the one who received that box, and she had a question about something that was on the inventory list."

"I don't know anything about that. Ask Mary." Sakiestewa turned away.

"We did." Leaphorn noticed the customers waiting at the counter watching them. He lowered his voice. "Dat's why we're here."

"You think I took it?"

Leaphorn left the question hanging, aware that the man knew the box had been tampered with.

"Did you?" Louisa asked.

"Are you a cop, too?"

"No, I'm a college professor."

Sakiestewa grinned. "You remind me of my high school English teacher. Let's go outside a minute."

They moved through the big doors to the building's front steps. Sakiestewa put his hands in his pockets. "Look, this was not a big deal. Mary told me that her boss put a worn-out old weaving in there and she thought nobody would want it and she didn't like the idea that he could get embarrassed by giving away trash. She texted me to help carry the box because her boss lady was in the car and she couldn't take the thing out with the missus seeing her. She knew we had tape here to reseal the package. I carried it in—it was heavy—and put it on that counter by the door. I turned it over, and she cut through the tape on the bottom. That old weaving was right there.

"Mary has a big purse, and she put the thing in it. I taped the box for her and took it to the counter to mail. That's it."

Louisa said, "What happened to the weaving?"

"Mary said she was going to take it home and put it back where her boss kept it." Sakiestewa shifted his weight from one foot to the other. "That's all I know. I've got to get back to work."

Leaphorn took his notebook from his pocket, jotted something down, and handed it to the man. He read it, shook his head, gave back the note, and went inside.

"What was that?"

Leaphorn showed her what he had written: "Mary didn't put it back. She is in big trouble."

Louisa led the way back to the truck. "Joe, after all this time, can you tell when someone is lying?"

He shrugged. "Usely. I tink he tol da true."

"It's been a long day." She gave him a tired smile. "I'm ready to get back to Flagstaff."

"Sure ting."

They shared the highway with large trucks, but the vacation traffic seemed lighter.

Louisa sighed.

"Waz wrong?"

She turned toward him. "I thought Mary was telling the truth when she denied knowing about the biil. What can I say to Daisy?"

"Nutting yet. I do it."

They passed the exit for Homolovi State Park, part of the Hopi homeland along with the mesas rising to the north. Louisa pointed out that she'd never stopped there.

"Me needer."

"You know, Joe, we should take a vacation. Look at some of the places here in the Southwest we haven't seen. Would you like that?"

Probably not, he thought. The older he grew, the more he appreciated the predictable routine of home punctuated with the occasional diversion of a well-selected assignment.

"Or we could fly somewhere. Somewhere with some water. A big lake? A beach?"

"Hafta tink abow tat." His last big plane trip had been a flight to China many years ago for a tour. From what he'd read, airports were less friendly now and flying more stressful.

He was thinking again about Mary and the biil. The person who received the box wouldn't have known Rafferty sent it, so the "save him from embarrassment" excuse didn't wash. Why would Mary endanger a relationship with a family she obviously cared for? Why would a Hopi risk one of the best jobs in town to help steal an old textile or a piece of Diné heritage? He chafed at not understanding the motivation that led to such a risk.

What if Mary's goal had been stealing the bracelet? he thought. She removed the weaving to get to it and, unaware of the inventory list, didn't bother putting it back. Sakiestewa hadn't mentioned the bracelet and Mary had worked at the gallery, where she could have stolen things. The fact that she was still with the Raffertys said they must consider her to be honest.

His phone buzzed. He handed it to Louisa. She answered. "Hello."

"Oh, sorry. I must have the wrong number. I was calling Joe Leaphorn."

"This is his phone. May I help you?"

"Let me speak to the Lieutenant. It's Councilor Walker. Tell him it's urgent."

Louisa put the phone on speaker. Leaphorn said yá'át'ééh and then something else in Navajo and the councilor responded. The conversation lasted about five minutes. The woman clicked off and Louisa pushed the button to end the call.

"What was that about? I heard the word *Tiffany*. That's Daisy's assistant, right?"

He nodded. Thought about it. "Har to splain. Type it layer."

"You don't look happy."

"Doan worry bout me."

They passed the Twin Arrows Navajo Casino Resort without much conversation, and he took the exit for the college. Louisa's phone rang with a tone that reminded him of a doorbell. Her side of the conversation consisted mostly of listening. Then she said, "I'll ask him.

"Marsha wants to know if you'd like to stay for dinner. She's inviting some of the new teaching assistants she'll be working with. She wants me to meet them."

"No tanks. You go."

When she put the phone back in her purse, he saw her take something out. Mary's sunglasses.

"I should have left these at El Falcon. Why don't you take them back there for her on your way home?" Louisa put the glasses on the passenger seat when she climbed out of the truck.

Leaphorn watched as she unlocked her car. She rolled down the driver's side window. "Be careful on the road. Pull over if you get sleepy."

He nodded twice, feeling both touched and irritated by her mothering attitude. Then he drove out, following her car. When she turned, he continued straight toward I-40. But before heading east for the second time that day, he pulled onto the shoulder and called Councilor Walker.

"I'm glad you called back. You sounded so distracted before, I wasn't sure you understood me."

"I was driving, and Louisa had the volume low. Tell me again about the woman."

"A woman Tiffany never mentioned, a woman named Mary Nestor, was listed in the obituary in the newspaper as a surviving sister. I thought that was interesting." Walker's voice sounded full of static, as though she were standing in the wind.

"Are you sure about that name?"

The councilor laughed. "Lieutenant, give me some credit. Hold on." He heard some shuffling and then she was back. "I'll read it to you from the *Navajo Times*: 'In addition to her father, Lee Benally, Tiffany is survived by her sisters Collette Yellowman of Gallup and Mary Nestor of Winslow, nephew Andrews Yellowman, and many other relatives and friends.'"

"Thanks for your help with this."

"There's one more thing I found out about Tiffany. She was planning to quit that museum job."

Leaphorn thought about it. "How do you know?"

"A reliable source."

"Why would she leave?" He remembered Mrs. Pinto saying how much Tiffany liked her job.

"She was dating a marine stationed in San Diego. They planned to get married in the fall if she felt better."

He wondered about Tiffany's timing. Had she planned to leave so she wouldn't have to accommodate a new boss? Had she wanted to be the boss herself? Had she turned to thievery to pay for the wedding?

"I haven't come across anything else of interest about Tiffany. Her friends worried about her breathing troubles, but she said it was no big deal. She had no enemies I could find. A couple of friends said she joked about her sister Collette being so bossy. You know, there's usually some truth behind whatever we joke about."

Leaphorn was about to end the call when he remembered something. "I won't see you for breakfast. I've got some more work on the case."

"We will do it another time. But now you're buying."

After that, he called Mary Nestor. He opened the conversation with her sunglasses. What he thought was Louisa's mistake turned out to be a benefit.

"Just bring them to the house if you want."

"I'll come by now, on my way back to Window Rock."

"Good. Mr. Rafferty said you and Louisa stopped by and I told him the truth. I said we talked about the box, but I hadn't given you his name or address. He's trying to figure out how you knew about him. He wasn't mad at me for talking to you guys when I explained how you sort of tricked me. He said the professor did the same to him."

When Leaphorn arrived, Mary met him at the door.

"Where's your lady friend?"

"She had to get back to Flagstaff."

"Tell her thanks for picking up my glasses."

He handed them to her. "Before I go, I need you to answer a question for me. When we mentioned the father who was mourning his daughter, why didn't you tell us that we were talking about your own father and sister back in New Mexico?"

He thought the question would surprise her, but it didn't.

"My sister and I weren't close. And it was none of your business." Mary opened the door a bit wider. "Please come in. Mrs. Rafferty wants to meet you. She's waiting in the living room."

Barbara Rafferty looked emaciated, with the almost translucent skin elderly bilagáanas sometimes have. Her hair, a blinding white, was her most vibrant feature. She motioned Leaphorn to a seat on the sofa across from her wheelchair. "Join us, Mary." The strength of her voice surprised him. It was as though it held what remained of her power.

Mary sat.

"I understand you asked my husband and Mary

some questions about our box of donations for the museum. I was the buyer for the business for years. Perhaps I can help you. Proceed."

He started to speak to her in Navajo. He was half done with the sentence when he realized his mistake.

Mrs. Rafferty responded in Navajo. "Continue. I learned a bit of Navajo when I taught on the reservation. I enjoy the challenge of it."

"What can you tell me about a textile that they say was created by Juanita, the wife of Manuelito?"

"The biil was one of our treasures. I am happy the museum has it now."

"No, ma'am."

Mrs. Rafferty narrowed her eyes. "Don't joke about that. I went to the post office with Mary and saw her take in the box."

"The box arrived, and the biil was on the inventory Mr. Rafferty prepared, but the dress was not with the shipment."

The elderly woman spoke English now. "I'm ___ Lloyd put that in the container. Textiles are always the first things he packs because they are fragile. Did you ask him?"

Leaphorn nodded. "He packed it. Mr. Sakiestewa at the post office said Mary asked him to help her remove it."

"No. You must be mistaken." Mrs. Rafferty looked at Mary.

Mary studied the carpet at her feet. Leaphorn continued.

"The woman at the museum who received the box asked me to find the missing piece. She is concerned that her assistant, Mary's sister, may have been involved in the disappearance." He didn't say Tiffany's name out of respect. "Mary's sister is dead, but I'd like to make sure that she isn't blamed for something she didn't do."

"Dead?" Mrs. Rafferty turned to Mary. "Collie is dead?"

"No, ma'am. Tiffany." Mary put a hand on the woman's shoulder. "Our baby sister."

Leaphorn had not imagined that Mrs. Rafferty could grow any whiter, but she did.

"I'll get you some water." Mary rose and walked away.

Leaphorn leaned toward the wheelchair. "I'm sorry to have shocked you. Did you know Tiffany well?"

"I never met her, but I heard Mary speak of her. Our Mary had just gone to visit her last month. They were trying to repair their relationship. I hoped . . ." Mrs. Rafferty's voice trailed off. "Why would that post office man steal the dress?"

Leaphorn left the question and asked his own. "Do you know Collette?"

"Yes. Collie is the eldest of the three. She came to help us years ago, but it didn't work out. She has a different personality than dear Mary. Mary always dreamed of getting along better with her sisters." Mrs. Rafferty looked at him. "I wonder why she didn't mention Tiffany's death? I sensed that something was bothering her, but when I asked, she didn't want to talk about it."

They heard a car engine starting.

"Mary?" Mrs. Rafferty began to roll herself toward the front door, pushing with arms as thin as willow twigs. Leaphorn raced ahead of her.

The door stood open, and the white Mercedes he'd seen in the driveway was gone.

"Lloyd? Lloyd!"

"What's wrong?" He was in the room a moment later.

"Something's upset Mary and she just drove away." She looked at Leaphorn and frowned.

Lloyd Rafferty's face contorted. "What did you say to her?"

Leaphorn had his truck keys in hand. "Do you know her friend Sakiestewa?"

"Yes." Rafferty pursed his lips. "He's a good man. If that's where she went, he'll calm her down."

"Where does he live?"

Rafferty gave him the address and directions.

Mrs. Rafferty rolled to the entryway. Her voice sounded shaky. "I keep my gun in that drawer in the table by the front door. It's open and the gun is gone."

Leaphorn double-checked his weapon before he left the house.

Rafferty's information led him to an apartment building on the south side of town. The Mercedes stood out among the well-used vans, pickups, and aged sedans. Lights shone in the windows of about half the units. Evening quiet blanketed the complex except for the wail of an infant and blaring rap music from a lower apartment. He climbed the stairs to the second floor and heard a woman shouting before he reached the door.

He tried the knob, and it moved in his hand, unlocked. The room's air-conditioning reached him milliseconds after the angry voice. ". . . trust you and look at what happened, you worthless piece of . . ." The woman stood with her back to the door, the gun pointed at the Hopi's chest.

"Baby, calm down." Sakiestewa spoke slowly. "Tell me what's up. Why are you here?"

"Mary?" Leaphorn said her name with all the calm he could muster. She turned, and when she did, the weapon pointed toward the floor. As Sakiestewa lurched toward the door, she swung around and leveled the gun at his heart. "Back up, idiot."

The Hopi complied, and Leaphorn noticed that the man's pants had a dark stain in the crotch and partly down one leg. Mary moved so she could see both men. "This has nothing to do with you, Lieutenant, except that your meddling led to it. Get out. This is between me and my boyfriend."

Leaphorn took a breath, remembering similar situations and the same cold fear. He spoke in Navajo. "Mary, what's going on here? Put the gun down. Talk to me." He wondered if Sakiestewa understood. Even if he couldn't follow the words, Leaphorn hoped his tone of voice would get the message across.

She spoke fast, her English fueled by anger. She kept the gun leveled at Sakiestewa's chest. "He betrayed me. He's a scumbag."

"I'm sorry that happened. Put the gun down, and tell me about it."

"He said you and the professor came to talk to him, and he told you about that dress."

Sakiestewa clenched his hands in front of him. "Baby, I gave him the truth. You wanted to come clean, you told me as much. I only helped so you and your sister could embarrass Tiffany, remember? And then make peace with her. You're my girl, but I can't lie for you."

"That's not what Collie told me. She said you were calling Tif behind my back, trying to set up something with her. You don't deserve to live. Neither do I."

Leaphorn moved closer. "Put the gun down. Let's talk about all this."

She shook her head. "This lying jackass deserves . . ."

Sakiestewa raised his palms as in prayer or surrender. "Mary, Collette is the one who caused this. I'll help you make things right. It's not too late, baby."

"You're wrong. Tiffany died before I could explain, and now I'll never have a chance to ask her to forgive me. It *is* too late."

Leaphorn took another step toward Mary. "Andrews needs you. Think of the boy. He's already lost one of his Little Mothers." Her shoulders drooped, and Leaphorn knew she was listening. "The Raffertys are worried about you."

He could see her thinking.

"They only want the car back and their gun. And me, their sweet Mary who helps with everything without complaining."

Sakiestewa said, "Think of your father."

"Azhé'é?" When she said the word in Navajo, her heartbreak came through. "I abandoned him."

"No, babe, you told me he was happy for you to go. To spread your wings."

Leaphorn noticed that Mary's hand holding the pistol had begun to shake.

"I left him. I'm a thief and a liar, and I will only bring shame to him now." She moved the gun, shifting the aim away from Sakiestewa toward her right temple.

Leaphorn lunged, pushing Mary to the floor. The gun clattered away as they both fell. Mary struggled against his weight for a moment, and then he felt heaving sobs flood her body. He rolled onto the floor to catch his breath, then stood and secured the gun.

Sakiestewa was gone, the staccato beat of his boots reverberating on the metal stairs. Mary lay where she had fallen, weeping. He called 911.

19

Chee and Bernie both awoke early. Bernie hadn't gone for her regular run since she'd found the body. It was time, and she knew where she needed to be.

"Come with me this morning. I understand that jogging isn't your thing, but I'd really like some company."

"Sure, if you make some coffee first."

She said her morning prayers with white cornmeal, and by the time the coffee was ready, so was Chee. They sat on the deck and drank a cup and then headed off. Bernie jogged toward the trail where she'd found the body now known as Nicky and Michael.

The day was still cool, the air seductive with a hint of moisture.

"This is lovely." Chee matched her pace. "Why don't I do this more often?"

"Good question." Bernie began to run faster. It didn't take long to reach the jogging path.

"See that black Honda?" Bernie raised her arm to point it out to him.

"What about it?"

"It was here after I found the body. I think it belongs to Summersly, a guy who gave me a hard time."

"Interesting."

She felt a tingle down her spine as they ran close to where she had encountered the dog. She left the trail and headed toward the river. The place the body had lain looked like other spots now, and Bernie took a moment to be sure of the location. "I found Nicky there, partly hidden in the weeds. I would have missed the body if not for the dog."

Chee looked toward the place and back at her. "I can help you arrange a ceremony."

"Let's talk when we get back to the house."

They jogged back to the trail and to the fallen tree at the turnaround point. That's where they found Ed Summersly drinking from a water bottle, his foot on a tree stump. He recognized Bernie.

"Hey, you're the one who talked to me about that crime scene out here, right?"

"Right. Thanks for helping with that."

"A man called me from the FBI. Very formal and efficient. I guess I saw something they found interesting."

"Like what?"

"They kept asking about a guy I hadn't seen out here before, a man wearing jeans and a white shirt, heavyset, perspiring hard. He looked kind of green." Summersly glanced at Bernie. "I think you ran by then, about the time he started, well, losing his lunch. I fiddled around tying my shoes so I could watch him, make sure he was OK. After a few minutes, a car drove up and the man climbed in the back seat and they drove off. The car had California plates and a strange dent in the back bumper, like it had backed into a big pole or something."

"Did you see who was driving?" Chee pulled out his cell phone as he asked the question.

"No, even if I'd tried, I don't think I could have seen through the tinted windows."

Summersly ran on.

Bernie noticed Chee dialing a number. He spoke to her while he waited for Agent Johnson to answer. "The car Summersly identified? It matches the description of the one I saw when Mr. Natachi got shot."

The run home, always quicker than the trip out, went faster than usual. Chee pushed himself harder and she kept up, enjoying the challenge.

By the time Bernie emerged from a quick shower, Chee said he had spoken to Lieutenant Black about the new developments with Nicky's murder, and Agent Johnson had called and talked to him about the car used in Mr. Natachi's shooting.

"She wouldn't confirm anything, but from her questions, I assume she's moving pretty quick on this. She wants you to call her at work in about an hour. She wouldn't say why."

"My money's on Ryana."

Chee fixed eggs with onions, green peppers, and Spam, and they had a quick breakfast together. Then Chee drove his police unit to the station, and

Bernie followed in her Tercel. Largo was waiting to talk to her and ushered her into his office.

"Sage Johnson called me this morning, bright and early. Guess what she wanted to talk about?"

"Well, since you pulled me in here, I'm guessing it was me."

"Agent Berke complained about you yesterday. He claims you interfered with his questioning of a suspect and impeded his investigation."

Largo sat back in his chair. She studied the floor, getting her anger under control.

"Manuelito, this is the part where you tell me what happened."

"Sir, Berke kept badgering a young Navajo woman, Ryana Florez, who had spent most of the day with her grandfather in the hospital. Not only that, she had just learned that her boyfriend was dead and that he had been living under an assumed identity. Berke continued to push her even when I could tell she honestly couldn't answer his questions. The guy acted like a jerk, so I called him out on it." She looked at Largo. "I'd do it again."

"Write up the details and give it to me."

"Yes, sir." Bernie hated paperwork. "Do you have time to talk about something else?"

"Go ahead."

"I'm looking for a link between the Chinle burglaries and what happened at our flea market. If the parking lot of the store where Stevens says the guy sold him the bolo has a camera, maybe I'll get lucky. Do you have any other ideas?"

"No. Get that rolling before you talk to Johnson." She stood to leave.

"Manuelito, take the rest of the day off after you talk to Johnson."

"Why, sir? Is this because of Berke?"

"No."

"A budget thing?"

Largo smiled. "You've been working nonstop since you found that body. Chill this afternoon. And don't worry about Berke. He has a chip on his shoulder as big as Agathla Peak."

She phoned the store. They did have a few outdoor cameras positioned here and there in the parking lot. The head of security would review the footage and email a digital file to the station if they saw anyone selling anything to anybody on the morning in question.

"I need it as soon as possible."

"Of course you do." The voice on the phone sounded tired. "If you don't see it in a couple of days, call me back." She made a note of the man's name and phone number. A couple of days! She'd call back and build a fire under him in a few hours if the file didn't show.

As it turned out, typing notes for Largo about her time with Ryana was a good exercise. She remembered things that Johnson might find of interest. Bernie was almost done when Sandra buzzed her.

"Baby news?"

"I wish. Agent Johnson on the line."

A woman who always got right to business, Johnson lived up to her reputation. "Manuelito, I thought you were going to call me."

"I was, as soon as I finished a report for Largo. What do you need?"

"I've got an interview with the woman who was living with Michael Debois. She said she'd only talk if you are in the room, too."

"What's the focus of the interview?"

"We think she can identify some of Michael's recent associates in Chinle. We see her as a valuable witness. Between us, except for the fact that she had his car with the loot in the trunk, we don't have much on her."

"The Navajo Police are looking into the burglaries that might involve the items in that car."

"It sounds like you can fill me in." Johnson paused. "Let's grab an early lunch, and you explain why Berke is so grumpy today, too. Then we'll talk to Ryana."

Bernie hesitated. "I'm waiting for some information to arrive here—"

"I'll talk to Largo. Don't sweat it. Just a quick bite. An extra half hour." Johnson named the place and time.

"I'll see you there."

They met at Farmington's Three Rivers Restaurant and Brew Pub and talked about the menu and the weather until Bernie ordered a burger and a Coke and Johnson requested the Cobb salad and iced tea.

The agent waited until the waitress left. "I called Chinle, but Black was out and Chee's cell went right to message. Just give me the headlines."

"OK, but first, tell me about Michael. Why was his body there, and what did it have to do with you?"

"That's a long story. You're looking at stupidity on Michael's part, a deep-seated desire for vengeance from the gang he betrayed, and a gotcha attitude toward me."

Hearing the agent say it could have been personal grabbed Bernie's attention.

Johnson read her reaction. "I felt sorry for the man, got a little closer to him emotionally than I should have, even though I knew better. He was a master at manipulation. When he tried to get me to help him with something fishy, I severed all connections. Then Michael called to tell me he had left the program. He went back to what he'd always loved—internet cons."

"And that decision got him killed."

Johnson nodded. "If he'd stayed in California with the identity we provided, he'd still be alive. But he wasn't one for following the rules. And the internet is everywhere, of course, so he could do his computer work from wherever. He had worked at Canyon de Chelly out of college on an Ameri-Corps program. He knew the area and I guess he figured he'd be safe out here. Bad move."

The waitress brought their drinks.

"When we tracked Michael's car, I expected to find his computers in the trunk but not the other electronics and the jewelry. Tell me about that."

Bernie gave her the edited version, then sipped her Coke and waited for questions.

"That Coke looks good. I used to live on soda, especially colas. Then I went to the dentist and got some bad news, so I cut back."

Bernie studied the glass, the carbonation bubbles popping on the surface like little celebrations. She had a spare straw. "You want a sip?"

"No, I'm mostly on the wagon now." Johnson's smile showcased her perfect teeth. "Talk to me about Ryana. Convince me that a woman driving her dead boyfriend's car with his laptops and stolen property in the trunk is not a party to his cons or his murder."

"Ryana's story is complicated."

Johnson chuckled. "That could be said of everything out here."

Bernie mentioned Ryana's time in Phoenix. "Did you search for Roxanne Dee?"

"Not yet."

"In a nutshell, Ryana worked in adult films. It looks like she has been paying someone to keep it a secret from her grandfather."

"Go on." She could tell by the way Johnson raised her eyebrows that this was news.

"At first, I assumed Ryana was involved with the burglaries for two reasons. She needed money to pay the blackmailers, and Chee told me she had arranged for Nicky to make a safety presentation at the senior center. He tricked the old folks into talking about where they hid their valuables, and after that, those folks were targeted." Bernie stopped for a sip of Coke. "Now I believe that the only thing she took was her grandfather's bolo. Her regret over that led her to try to end the extortion. That's when the blackmailer got violent."

"And you've come up with this theory because . . ."

"Except for Mr. Natachi's bolo, the rash of burglaries in Chinle all fit the same pattern, and they all seem to be tied to Nicky, I mean Michael."

The arrival of lunch interrupted the conversation. Bernie gave Johnson time to think about what she'd said and went to work on her burger. Good, but not as good as the ones Chee made. Or, perhaps, the company made the difference.

Johnson sipped her drink and then resumed the conversation. "I'm thinking about the burglaries. I'll talk to the guy in charge in Chinle. Michael probably wore gloves, but we have his prints on file. And DNA."

"Chee mentioned some blood at Ryana's house."

"We'll look into it."

Johnson picked up the bill when the waitress offered it and handed her a credit card.

Bernie thanked her. "What about the Berke business?"

Johnson shook her head. "Did you interfere with his interviewing?"

"No." Bernie unzipped her backpack and pulled out an envelope. "Here's a longer answer. Largo asked me about the incident, so I did this report for him. I made you a copy. He acted like a heartless jerk."

Johnson left it in Bernie's hand. "'No' is good enough for me. Let's deal with Ryana. I'll take the lead on the interview. But if you want to squeeze in a question or two, go for it."

Bernie thought Ryana seemed tired yesterday. Today the black, puffy half-circles under her eyes had developed their own circles. Her shoulders slumped at the table. The young woman reminded her so much of Darleen in her dark days that Bernie wanted to give her a hug.

Johnson opened with questions about the car and returned to the topics Berke had covered: why Ryana was driving Michael's car, what she knew about the items in the trunk, and where she was heading with the loot. The interview moved quickly to new territory with questions about her relationship with Nicky. Ryana's answers were clear and brief.

Where and how had they met? At a party of a mutual friend. Johnson asked for the name and made a note.

What had he told her about his prior life? He was an only child, and his parents were dead. He grew tired of California, had fond memories of Arizona, and decided to move to Chinle. He'd never been married, and his last girlfriend left when he'd hit some rough spots with drugs and alcohol. He'd been sober for three years. And no, she'd never seen him high or drunk.

How did he support himself? Nicky told her he worked on the computer, helping people with websites and other projects. Ryana talked about seeing him at the table with his laptop open, absorbed in whatever he was doing.

"I never asked for details. Computers aren't my thing."

"Who were his friends and associates in Chinle?"

For the first time, Ryana looked surprised. "I . . . I don't know. I never thought about that.

Nicky kept to himself or went out with me and my pals. Once in a while someone would call him in the evening or on weekends. He told me that it was business."

Johnson closed her notebook.

Bernie gave Ryana a smile. "I've been thinking about what you told me about getting blackmailed. What are your ideas about who would do this?"

"None. I don't know. No idea."

"Did you mention it to Nicky?"

"No. We'd only been living together a few months. I was afraid—"

Johnson interrupted. "You were afraid of him?"

"No. I loved him. I was afraid he'd reject me if he knew what I'd done." Ryana's tone of voice changed. "You know, I didn't do anything illegal. I made a bad choice when I took that adult video job, but I liked the idea of making money. I made a worse choice when I decided to pay the blackmailer rather than talking to my grandfather about what I'd done."

Johnson said, "Did you consider the idea that Nicky, with his computer skills, could have known about the movies and could have been the blackmailer?"

"It's not him. It started before we met, a few weeks after I moved back to Chinle from Phoenix."

"How did the blackmailer contact you?" Bernie said.

"By mail. I received a letter with a screen shot of me from one of the videos. He wrote if I didn't give him a hundred dollars cash, he would mail my grandfather that photo. He included the names of all my movies." She tugged a strand of hair behind her ear. "Every month he wanted more money."

"How much did you pay?"

"It started at a hundred, then two hundred, then more."

"How did you get the money?"

Ryana sighed. "I sold the car I bought in Phoenix. I sold other stuff I moved back with. I worked all the overtime I could get. Finally, I took my grandfather's bolo and I put it in the envelope instead of money with a note that said I was done and if he tried to get any more money from me I would tell my grandfather myself about the movies. I decided that I should tell my shicheii about it anyway, and I was going to talk to him when he came for coffee with me, like he did every morning. But instead someone grabbed him. My grandfather might die because of me."

"Let's brainstorm this." Bernie knew what she needed to say. "Who knew about the dirty movies?"

"Nobody."

"Someone. Obviously." She let the silence sit.

"Well, when I first got back to Chinle, people asked me what I did in Phoenix. Once or twice I bragged that I had some acting jobs. But if they asked, like, what kind of acting, I stopped talking about it really fast. I never said what kinda videos I was in."

"I'd like the names of those friends." Bernie noted that Johnson had reopened her notebook.

Ryana came up with a short list of girlfriends and a friend's sister who tagged along on a hike.

"Think about this awhile, Ryana. Anyone else?"

Ryana looked at the table for a moment. "Elsie asked me about Phoenix, and I told her I was there learning how to act and working as a waitress. I hate discussing that part of my life. Elsie wouldn't hurt me, but maybe she mentioned it to someone else there at the center."

Bernie waited, glad that Johnson hadn't stepped in to change the subject.

"You know, when I first got back, my friend Mark and I went to a bar in Farmington and I had a few beers, and he kept asking about Phoenix and acting and teasing me that I was a wannabe and how come he'd never seen me on-screen. He thought I was lying and that it was funny, and I finally told him to look up Roxanne Dee. Somebody there might have overheard."

"What's Mark's last name?"

"Adakai. Nicky reminded me a little of him because they're both smart with computers, but Nicky is more mature. Was. Nicky. I can't believe he's dead." Ryana rested her forehead on the palms of her hands.

Johnson said, "Would you like a break?"

The young woman shook her head.

"Officer Manuelito, any more questions?"

"Just one." Bernie waited until Ryana had regained her composure. "You indicated that you gave the blackmailer a letter along with the bolo. What did it say?"

"I wrote that I would tell Grandfather about

the movies, and if the blackmailer tried to contact me again, I was going to the police. I let him know that I saved his first letter."

"Did you?"

"Yes. I have it."

Johnson made a note. "Manuelito, anything more?"

"Just one other topic. Ryana, tell me more about your relationship with Mark."

The young woman's eyes opened wider at the question. "Relationship? If you mean boyfriend and girlfriend, we never were that. He asked me out a few times and it was OK, but he wasn't my type. I told him I liked him as a buddy."

"How did he react?"

Ryana's eyes opened wider. "Mark! He knew about the videos and he was angry with me. How could I have been so dense?"

Johnson reopened her notebook and looked at Bernie. "Any more questions?"

"Not right now."

"Ryana, I want to talk to you about the man you knew as Nicky Jones, Michael Debois. Since you called him Nicky, I will use that name. Did Nicky's behavior change recently?"

"Yes." Ryana repeated what she'd told Berke, doing a good job of including the high points. "He acted nervous and withdrawn. Like there was something on his mind."

"What did he mean in that note, that you would know what to do with the items in the trunk?"

"Agent Berke told me he had a bunch of jewelry and other stuff in there. Bernie thinks he was involved in our Chinle crime wave. If any of the items belonged to my clients at the senior center, Nicky knew I would make sure they got their possessions back."

Johnson gave Ryana a stern look. "Really? Didn't he mean that you could take over the business of selling the stolen items on the internet?"

"No. I didn't know about that. I'm really not good at computers."

Johnson made a note. "Tell me more about Nicky's recent behavior."

"Well, he got quiet. He didn't sleep. I asked him if he was depressed. He said work wasn't going well. Then he left without saying good-bye. He took his dog and his laptops. I can't understand why he's dead."

Back at the substation, the surveillance footage from the parking lot, if it existed, hadn't yet arrived. Bernie called the security chief, and he apologized. "I got busy. I'll look to see if we have anything as soon as I'm done with my break."

"Do it now." Incompetence got under her skin. "I'll call you in fifteen minutes."

When she called back, no one answered.

Chee, who was in charge while Largo attended a meeting in Farmington, reminded her that she had the rest of the day off, and encouraged her to go home.

"I'll keep an eye out for it, and I'll take a look as soon as it gets here."

"I don't like being ignored."

"I know the store manager and I'll call him if we don't hear back soon. Did you learn anything interesting from Ryana?"

"Yes. She thinks the guy who blackmailed her might be a man named Mark Adakai. But she says he would never try to kill her grandfather."

Chee laughed. "Did I tell you that at first she blamed Arthur Green Yazzie? You know, the guy with that sister who keeps calling for Leaphorn? Turns out he's in prison. Mark Adakai works at the Chinle station. That young woman has a flair for telling tall tales. There's no way Adakai could have shot the old man. He was on the job. I saw him there at the station myself."

Bernie sighed. "She really sounded believable. Any news on Mr. Natachi?"

"I called the hospital. The nurse said he's about the same. If I could persuade him to talk, I know that would ease his mind and help him get better."

She changed the subject. "Maybe I will go home, but let me know when you get that tape and I'll come in to look at it. I keep thinking that the bolo and Nicky's death must be connected. Maybe getting away from here will give me an idea. What's on your schedule?"

"I'm doing my first mentor session with the rookie, unless he rejects me like he did the Lieutenant."

"Good luck with that. Could you ask Black what he knows about a relationship between Mark Adakai and Ryana?"

"Sure. I'll let you know."

Although she couldn't get Ryana and Nicky off her mind, Bernie looked forward to an afternoon away from the station. She had changed out of her uniform and was checking to see if there was a Coke in the refrigerator when her cell phone rang.

"Hi." She recognized Darleen's voice. "Are you working hard as a crime solver?"

"Believe it or not, I have an afternoon off."

"Is the Cheeseburger still in Chinle?"

"No. He drove home last night. He had a meeting with a new officer, a mentoring session to help the man handle his job better."

"That's good. I could use someone like that." Darleen said it in an offhanded way, but it rang true. "I'm in a jam, Sister."

Bernie's heart sank. "What's going on?"

"It's nothing life-threatening, don't worry."

*Don't worry.* The words that foreshadow news of disaster. "What happened, girl?"

"Well, Ryana asked if I would drive her to see her grandfather. We started toward Chinle, but my car broke down and now we're stranded. Could you pick us up?"

"Your insurance has emergency road service. They could help."

"I sort of forgot to pay the bill. Stoop Man can tow me back home with his truck when he gets off work, but that's not until tonight. Can you please come and get us?"

"Where are you, Sister?"

"Near Roof Butte." Darleen laughed. "I'm surprised my phone works."

Bernie sighed. "OK. I'm leaving now. Text me the closest mile marker."

"Thanks. You are the best."

She and Chee had talked about Darleen and agreed that they needed to let her solve her own problems. This time, apart from driving without insurance, it sounded like her sister had done her best.

It took forty-five hot minutes of driving along Indian Route 64 to find Darleen's stranded car. Her sister had parked on the shoulder, and Bernie pulled in behind her. The two young women looked hot, bored, and discouraged.

Bernie leaned out the lowered window. "Get in back, you two. The seat up here is full of stuff."

They silently complied.

"There's some water there. Help yourselves." Now that she'd found Darleen, Bernie noticed the tension in her shoulders relax.

"Thank you for coming. I'm sorry I've caused you two so much trouble." Ryana's voice sounded high and tight. "I have another favor to ask you."

"Go ahead."

"Can you take me to the hospital so I can see my grandfather?"

Bernie thought about the mysterious bolo salesman who, she hoped, would be on the footage Chee was acquiring. She needed to go back to Shiprock to follow up.

"I can't right now."

Ryana's soft voice floated over the back seat. "I did some thinking after we talked. I need to explain about the bolo, to apologize to my grand-father, to tell him I was foolish and that I love him. What if the blackmailer sends him that picture of me while he's in the hospital? What if the worst happens and I miss that chance to explain? Please, Bernie." She said it again. "What if he dies before I have the chance to set things right? I called the hospital and they said he was too weak to talk on the phone."

Bernie took a breath. Chee had promised to look at the footage. She called the Shiprock station and talked to Sandra.

"Do you know if that parking lot footage came in?"

Sandra made a snorting sound. "No. Sergeant Chee stomped out of here, on his way to talk to the security guys over there. He's seriously an-noyed."

"Tell him I went to Chinle and to call me on my cell, OK?"

"Chinle? I will. By the way . . . no baby yet."

Darleen said, "Ryana and I were talking about something. She will have to have help with her grandfather once he gets out of the hospital, but she also needs to get back to the senior center. I could stay with him. You know my work-at-home job? I can take that with me. I can do those enve-lopes anywhere."

Ryana said, "Darleen, that's chump work. You're good with elderlies—I've seen how sweet you are to your mother. You can stay at my house until my grandfather is better, and then you should try to get a job at the senior center here in Chinle."

Bernie passed the turnoff for Lukachukai and saw a mileage sign for Chinle. "How far is your house from here, Ryana?"

"It's about fifteen minutes."

"You mentioned that you had saved that first blackmail letter."

"Yeah. I thought it might be important."

"Is it in a safe place at the house?"

"Yeah. Well, I guess." She told Bernie the location.

"I want to stop there. You can get a change of clothes, a toothbrush, whatever else you need, and you can give me the letter. I will make sure it's safe. After that, we'll go to the hospital."

"Uhm. I . . . I . . . I don't want to see the place where my grandfather almost died. I just want to go to the hospital. I hid the letter really well. It's safe." Bernie heard the panic in her voice.

"Hold on. I'm going to make some calls." She pulled onto the shoulder.

Agent Johnson answered on the second ring, and Bernie explained the situation with the blackmail letter. Johnson didn't hesitate. "The letter is important, but not as crucial as the other things we're working on. I'll have Berke or someone get it tomorrow. Thanks for letting me know."

Bernie pulled back onto the highway. "I'm dropping you both at the hospital. Then I'll go out to your house, Ryana, get what you need, and come back to see how Mr. Natachi is doing. Then, Darleen, you and I will deal with your car."

She heard relief in Ryana's voice. "I have a black travel bag on the floor in my closet. Just put in some T-shirts, jeans, some underwear, whatever's easy. And get my stuff from the bathroom."

Darleen spoke up. "I could go with you to Ryana's house. I mean, if you'd like some company."

"No, you need to spend some time with Mr. Natachi and make sure that you're comfortable with him if you are going to help later." And, Bernie thought, I don't know what I'll be walking into at Ryana's house. No need to put her sister at risk.

Since Ryana's driveway was a crime scene, she called for Lieutenant Black. Black was out, so she identified herself as a police officer to the man at dispatch. "I know about the shooting at Ryana Florez's house. I'm going over there to get some things for her. Thought I ought to let you let them know."

"How far away from there are you, Officer?"

She thought the question odd. "I'm not sure. I plan to make a quick stop at the hospital first."

"Is Ryana with you?"

"Yes."

"Thanks for letting us know."

She left the young women at the hospital entrance and found the house with no trouble using Ryana's excellent directions. Bernie parked next to an old truck that looked like it hadn't been driven or otherwise tinkered with in quite some time. She spotted the second, smaller house, Mr. Natachi's place, but no other vehicles. She walked to the main house, noticing that the front door stood open.

The house had been ransacked—the couch

cushions slit, rugs flipped, pictures ripped from the walls. Bernie drew her gun. "Hello. Navajo Police. Anyone here?"

A voice echoed from the bathroom. "Is that you, Manuelito? Chinle police back here. Looks like another burglary."

"You're the dispatcher I talked to, aren't you?"

He paused. "Yeah. A neighbor called and said he heard a noise here and, well, someone sure made a mess. I didn't have time to see if they hit the grandfather's house."

"Wow you got here fast. I didn't see your vehicle."

"I parked behind the house. Could you check the granddad's place?"

"I'll do it."

"Be careful."

She replaced her gun and jogged to Mr. Natachi's house. Again, the door stood open.

"Police. Come out now. I have a gun."

Silence answered her.

She could see that the living room and kitchen looked like a whirlwind had passed through. She noticed the same methodical destruction she'd seen at Ryana's.

She radioed the Chinle station and a woman answered. Bernie identified herself. "The officer who responded to the burglary at Ryana Florez's home asked me to check her grandfather's place next door. Sign of an intruder here, too."

"What? A burglary?"

"The officer who was working dispatch said he

got the call from a neighbor and responded. He's in the other building."

"I don't know what you're trying to pull. Mark is the other dispatcher. He's a civilian like me, and he went home with a migraine an hour ago."

"Mark who?"

"Adakai."

"Can you hold on?"

She remembered what Chee had said about the rodeo buckle and went to the bedroom. Someone had ransacked it, too, but the buckle and the precious bolo sat right where Chee said they'd be. Whatever had happened, she realized, was not a burglary.

Bernie reached for the phone again. "Let me speak to Lieutenant Black or whoever is in charge."

"Who are you, again, ma'am?"

"Officer Manuelito. ASAP. It's urgent."

She left the old man's house and ran back to Ryana's. She almost tripped over the red plastic gasoline can in the front hallway. She heard a noise coming from the next room and moved inside toward the sound. "Hello? Mark?" She had her hand on her gun in the holster. "Stop what you're doing and come out here. Now."

A few more steps gave her a view of the kitchen. She saw the man rummaging through the freezer. He pushed the freezer door closed with his left elbow and gave her a look she'd seen before, the demeanor of a person confident to the point of arrogance.

"Mark, don't . . ." As she went for her weapon,

he threw something. She dodged, missing the brunt of the blow, but the box hit her right shoulder hard. In the split second it would have taken her to regain her equilibrium, he gave her a hard push to the floor. She saw his gun. Then she noticed the bags of vegetables and frozen dinners defrosting. The impact of their fall from the freezer had broken some of the boxes. That gave her an idea.

20

"Where's Ryana?"

"What?"

"Re-ah-na?" He spoke more slowly. "On the phone, you said she was with you."

"Mark, put the gun down before you get yourself in trouble." Bernie kept her voice level. "Why are you asking about her?"

"You know. Chee told me about the letter, about the blackmail. He must have told you, too. I need it back. I know it's here somewhere."

That explained his rummaging in the freezer. "Ryana isn't with me. Why would she give it to you after all the heartache you've caused her?"

"Two reasons. She saw what those guys did to Mr. Natachi. Him getting shot was her fault. They gave me more than I paid for, that's how it goes."

"I can't hear you very well. What's the second?"

He laughed and spoke louder. "She really wants to be with me. She plays hard to get because I've seen her in those movies. Everyone else thinks she's a good girl, but I understand what a woman like that needs."

Bernie noticed that the gun was pointed to the floor, not her chest, as he continued.

"All I ever asked was for her to be my girlfriend. I'd give her the money back; it wasn't about that. Where is that beautiful devil?"

"What?" Bernie lowered her voice. "My head's spinning from that box you hit me with. I can barely hear you. Come closer."

"You lied about Ryana being with you." He took another step toward her.

"Huh?"

"Did she tell you where the letter is?"

Bernie groaned. "My head hurts. I can't hear you. Move closer."

"Do you know where it is, Cupcake?" He was yelling now.

"What?"

"Stop it." He kicked at her, missed, and when he tried again, Bernie clawed for his leg. Her grasp and her strength threw him off balance. He fell hard, dropping the gun. She rolled away and pulled her own weapon as she stood, pointing it at him as he tried to rise. She yelled, "Stay on the floor. Facedown."

"Let's talk this over." He raised his head. "You don't know the whole story. You've got it all wrong."

She kept the gun aimed at his spine. "Down. Face on the floor. Now."

Instead, he lurched for her. She kicked as he tried to rise, connecting firmly with his groin.

He yowled in pain and slumped back.

"So, Mark, what's with the gasoline? If you didn't find the letter, were you going to burn the place?"

"What else could I do?" he whimpered.

"Where did you come up with those over-achievers to do your dirty work?"

"Why should I tell you? What's in it for me?"

Bernie smiled, but kept the gun pointed at him. "I'm going to see Ryana next. I can let her know that you didn't mean to hurt her grandfather. Or I can keep quiet."

"I didn't want that old guy shot."

"Then tell me what happened."

"One of those thugs came to the station. He had a cool tattoo, a thin snake around his wrist, and I asked him about it. We talked, and then he mentioned that he was looking for a guy named Nicky. He told me they were friends from California, but I knew there was more to it than that. I gave him the address. Tattoo Man said he owed me a favor, so when Ryana wasn't paying anymore, I called him. I just wanted to scare her. I respect Mr. Natachi."

"You're lying. If you respected him, why did you send those men to hurt him? Why did you ex-tort money from the granddaughter he loved? You can think about how to make all this right while you're in jail, Cupcake." She called for backup and, this time, talked to Lieutenant Black himself.

Black arrived quicker than she'd hoped. After they'd asked a million questions and learned the name of Tattoo Man, Lieutenant Black hauled Adakai away in the patrol car.

Bernie met Ryana and her sister in Mr. Natachi's room. The old man slept while she told the girls what had happened.

"I don't have to worry anymore." Ryana's relief showed in her smile. "But I'm not leaving here until my grandfather can come home, too."

She and Darleen walked back to her car and, while they drove, Bernie explained the mess at Ryana's and Mr. Natachi's house.

Darleen said, "No problem. I can help with that. And Ryana called her boss at the senior center and talked to her about me. The lady offered me a little job while Ryana is with her grandfather at the hospital. Because Mama's better now, it all worked out."

Darleen's luck held. Stoop Man showed up with the promised tow and a ride home for Darleen in the cab of his truck.

Bernie called Chee and filled him in before he asked. "I'm going to contact Agent Johnson next and tell her about Tattoo Man and the connection between Adakai and Nicky's murder."

"And I thought you'd still be obsessing about that security tape."

"Oh, right. It slipped my mind."

"Well, Ryana was right. Adakai showed up on the surveillance video as the man with her grandfather's bolo. When I talked to Black about him earlier, he said he hadn't had any trouble with the guy, but Mark went through a bad period after a girl he was dating dumped him. Black didn't know who she was. Someone he'd had a crush on in high school."

"Thanks for checking that. I'm on my way home."

"Guess what?"

"The Bigman baby is here?"

"No. Burgers on the grill await."

21

Joe Leaphorn pulled into the truck stop just west of Gallup, New Mexico, around sunrise for fuel and a cup of coffee to go. He had only slept an hour or two, and that in the cab of the truck, but he felt energized and eager to put the case of the missing dress to rest. For the last half hour, he had admired the beautiful glow that transformed the dove gray of early morning into a dusty pink, and then to red-orange and gold. By the time the gas tank filled, the blue that made the Four Corners sky famous among photographers stretched from horizon to horizon.

He remembered his grandmother welcoming the day with song and white cornmeal. He thought about her as a young captive at Hwéeldi and of her suffering there. He imagined how her voice must have joined with those of more than a thousand joyful Diné on the journey back to their home-land when they caught the first sight of Tsoodzil.

Then he started the engine, and the dreaded grinding sound set his teeth on edge.

He knew Bernie was up at dawn. He called her cell phone in case Chee was still asleep. She answered on the second ring.

"Lieutenant, what a great surprise to start the day with a call from you. I hope everything is going well."

"Yes. It came to me that I never followed up with you and Chee on that Green Yazzie business. The case I'm on has grown more complicated, but I didn't mean to ignore you."

"That's fine. I talked to the woman when she called the station for Chee and explained how busy you were, and she said she'd catch you later. She wouldn't tell me what any of it was about."

"Well, fine then. I'll put that on the back burner. What have you two been up to?"

"It started as a burglary, became a rash of burglaries that were linked to an unsolved murder, blackmail, an attack on an old man, and an FBI informant. And, oh yeah, that dog you gave a ride to." The energy in her voice reminded him of why he loved police work.

He asked about her mother and Darleen and was moving on to Chee when Bernie changed the subject.

"Tell me about your case. I heard that woman's body went to Albuquerque for an autopsy. I wonder how she died."

"I think I've got the how under control. The why is gnawing at me. I'm driving out to talk to her father again now. It looks like the young woman might have been in the middle of a family squabble."

"That's terrible." Bernie said it again for emphasis.

"Her father blames witchcraft, and I'd agree that evil played a role. Not the supernatural kind but heartbreaking things people do to each other." He felt his spirits sag as he thought about it. Time to move on. "Anyway, I am driving east into the dawn now, surrounded in beauty."

"I remember a few years ago, when Chee and I just got back from our honeymoon, you asked us to help with an investigation that concerned a Hwééldi weaving. Do you think cases tied to that sad time have more than the usual set of, well, problems?"

Leaphorn remembered again the old case of a Tale Teller, a rug supposedly destroyed in a mysterious trading post fire. It reappeared later and led to a very bad man. The case was the closest he'd come to abandoning the law for a deeper sort of justice. The incident still disturbed him.

"That rug served as a reminder of the bad times. I see Juanita's dress, and the woman herself, as a symbol of courage, bravery, and resilience, the rich heritage that helped our ancestors survive." He thought about how to explain the difference. "The rug was a manifestation of loss and sorrow. Juanita's dress reminds us of the strength that led our people to where we are today."

Bernie didn't respond immediately, and when she spoke, her voice was softer. "Mama never talks specifically about what our relatives went through out there, but she says they wouldn't have survived without knowing that the Holy People wanted them to live on the land they gave us. Be safe, my uncle. I'll tell Chee hello for you."

After Bernie hung up, he pushed a button that read the text message in a mechanical voice. It was from Louisa: Joe, please make sure Kitty has food and water. And remember you need to eat, too.

It was still early when Leaphorn arrived at Mr. Benally's place. The windows stood open to let in as much cool air as possible before the day turned hot. Benally came outside when he heard the truck. The impact of losing his daughter had aged the man considerably.

Leaphorn eased out of the vehicle, his stiff back and hips lecturing him about the wisdom of stopping more often on road trips. His wrestling match with Mary Nestor hadn't helped either.

Mr. Benally greeted Leaphorn like a relative. "Have some coffee with me, my friend. Help yourself. I was glad to hear from you. Someone else is coming, just as you asked."

Leaphorn went inside and saw two clean cups sitting by the coffeepot. Andrews stretched on the sofa watching television and fiddling with his phone. They chatted a bit, and then Leaphorn asked the boy for a favor.

Back outside, Mr. Benally began the conversation.

"The one you want to meet, my daughter Collette, comes every Saturday. She doesn't have to work until later. She and I are raising my grandson. She helps around here when she can."

"Where does she work?"

"Bashas' in Window Rock."

Leaphorn tucked away the information. "Can she speak with us in Navajo?"

Mr. Benally smiled. "It's easier for me, too, Hosteen. What do you want to talk to her about?"

"As you know, I am helping the woman at the museum with a project. Your daughter who died was involved with it, too. I have some questions for Collette about her sister."

They sipped their coffee, Leaphorn's in a mug that said "Diné College." Mr. Benally sighed. "My baby daughter had been sick, you know. She was born with a lung condition, but the bilagáana doctors figured out what medicine helped her." The days immediately after death, when it is especially important not to speak of the dead, had passed. "I know her troubles came from the woman at the museum. I wanted to pay a hand trembler to tell my girl what was wrong and then for a ceremony to cure it. She said no, I was old-fashioned."

"So, are you the one who left the note about her boss on my truck?"

"The note and then the rabbit for that woman." Mr. Benally shook his head. "I couldn't understand why after so many years, my sweet girl got sick again. The thought of witchcraft visited my mind and stayed there. My daughter said she worried that her boss would blame her when she found out that some things were missing from the shipment. My baby liked that job, and she wanted to keep it when the new boss came, then she would get married."

"Why did you think the boss caused her to get sick?" Although Mr. Benally had not said that, exactly, Leaphorn made a logical assumption.

"That box." Mr. Benally puffed out his cheeks and exhaled. "My daughter said that they had packages like that arrive before, you know, where they don't know who sent it or what's inside. The medicine people open those first, in case they contain bones or sacred objects that shouldn't be seen.

"But the boss lady is retiring, so she wanted to get things set before she left. It can take a long time for the medicine people to do their work. Maybe she told Tiffany to go ahead and see what was in there. I think her boss was jealous. My girl was young and pretty and happy about getting married."

Mr. Benally sipped his coffee. "The woman didn't want Tiffany to get married. When she told her boss, she said wait to see if it was real love or, you know, physical attraction. Her sister Mary married a marine, Jason Nestor, and then he got killed in Afghanistan."

The comment gave Leaphorn the entrée he was waiting for. "I met Mary in Winslow. She's the one who mailed the box to the museum. She told me that the dress that caused the trouble wasn't inside."

Mr. Benally brushed the thought away. "It doesn't matter now."

"It does to me. That is why I want to talk to Collette. What can you tell me about her?"

"Collette came to live with Tiffany to help them both with finances. Her boy moved in with me.

He had stayed with us, his grandmother and me and then just me, many times before when his mother didn't have a job. It was good that Collette came when she did, because Tiffany started to get worse right after that. Tiffany had to take a special medicine. Collette made sure her sister had enough pills."

Leaphorn didn't interrupt, but his expression spoke for him.

"Collette helps in the pharmacy at Bashas'." Benally picked up his cup and drained the last of the coffee. "I called her the icing between the two cookies, the frosting in the Oreo. She looks the most like her mother. She complained that we loved her sisters more than we loved her, no matter what her mother and I did."

Before the man turned away, Leaphorn noticed the tears welling in his dark eyes.

A gray car turned onto the road that led to the Benally house and came straight in to park behind Leaphorn's truck. The woman wore jeans and cowboy boots and a long-sleeved white blouse. Her hair was pulled in a ponytail through the back of a yellow ball cap. She had Mr. Benally's lean build.

In Navajo, Benally introduced Leaphorn as a retired police lieutenant.

"Is there coffee, Dad?"

"Inside. A clean cup for you. Your boy is in there, too."

Leaphorn listened but heard no conversation. Collette joined them on the porch.

She switched to English and asked her father for advice on her car—the steering was off, and it needed an alignment and maybe new tires. Leap-horn noticed that the woman was twitchy, as though she wished she were somewhere else, or as if some chemical in her blood had left her un-settled. Drug use could lead to this, but so could guilt and anger.

When Mr. Benally offered advice but not fi-nancing for the repairs, she spoke to Leaphorn. Her Navajo was passable.

"Andrews likes his granddad better than me. Do you turn your grandchildren against their parents?"

"I don't have grandchildren. No little ones around. No sisters either who could have produced some babies."

"You're lucky you don't have sisters. They are highly overrated. So, what do you do with your-self, Mr. Retired Policeman?"

Leaphorn put his phone on the table next to Collette's car keys. A small light blinked. "Oh, I'm not totally retired. I work now and then, helping the police or private clients investigate puzzling cases. Like the missing dress at the museum and your sister's possible involvement in a theft." He watched for her reaction.

Collette stopped fiddling with her bangs. "You know, I think that dress was the reason she got so sick and died. I think she felt bad about steal-ing it."

Leaphorn looked directly at Collette. "But Tif-fany didn't steal it. It was Mary. And you were the mastermind."

"That's quite a thing to say."

"I don't say it lightly."

The woman laughed. "What's in that coffee? You're fantasizing. I don't know anything about art or collecting old stuff. I work at Bashas'. Why would you think I had any connection to the dress?"

"Why? Oh, the classic reasons. Greed. Revenge. Jealousy. My colleagues at the police department should be at Tiffany's house right about now with a warrant, searching for the dress and a bracelet that was also stolen, and confiscating the pills that you gave your sister, looking for evidence of how you tampered with her medications."

"They won't find anything. And how dare they invade my home!" Collette stood, keys in hand.

"It will be easier for the police to arrest you if you're there. That's why I asked your father to make sure you'd come by this morning. I wanted to talk to you about all this before you get arrested. I want to ask how we can help Mary, while there's still time."

Collette put her hands on her hips and turned to her father. "So this is about Mary? You always favored her over me, and Tiffany over both of us."

"No, no. I loved you all. My beautiful girls."

"Stop it. You gave Tiffany everything because she was sickly. You never put our sister in her place."

Leaphorn said, "You were very clever to set this up the way you did."

"Father never gives me credit."

"How did it start?"

"Mary told me about Mr. Rafferty planning the donation and how carefully he worked on it bit by bit. She told me that she hoped he would let her take the box to Window Rock and she could visit us, surprise father. But then she called back and said no, the man was mailing it and it was going to be an anonymous donation." Collette sipped her coffee. Now that all attention was on her, the twitchiness disappeared. "I had the idea to remove something to tarnish that golden girl, to put her in her place. A lot of people knew she was upset at her boss for not wanting her to get married. Who could blame her for a little revenge? For making Pinto's life difficult right before the old lady retired."

"How did you get Mary to go along?"

"Oh, I persuaded her. I'm a hard one to say no to. Rafferty had some old dress he'd always been crazy about that he planned to put in the box. Mary thought it was embarrassing to give away a ratty thing like that. I agreed and told her even though he was doing it anonymously, people would find out."

"How?"

"I was going to tell everyone that the Raffertys were behind the donation. Those two fired me for nothing. Payback time."

Leaphorn listened, disturbed to hear so much hate. "What happened next?"

"I told Mary she had to remove something else, too, something more valuable so we'd get Tiffany in real trouble. I told her jewelry was good, so she took that bracelet because Rafferty had packed it next to the old dress. It turned out that Mrs. Pinto wanted the dress more than anything."

Collette looked at the clear blue sky and smiled. "As soon as Tif started to panic, I'd told Mary I would explain that we'd done it just to stop her from acting like she was better than us. Then Tiffany could give back the stuff."

"But Tiffany didn't have a chance to give it back."

When Collette stared at him, Leaphorn knew he was looking evil in the eyes. "That girl was so full of herself, I couldn't stand it. I couldn't stand her. That the old dress had more value than dumb Mary realized. The joke was even better than I hoped."

"Joke? Joke!" Mr. Benally's voice rose with rage. "Your baby sister is dead. I thought the museum woman was the evil one, but no. I realize it is my own child." His voice fell to a whisper. "Did you kill your sister?"

Collette left the question unanswered and faced Leaphorn. "Earlier you said something about helping Mary. What did you mean, 'while there's still time'?"

"She wanted to kill herself. She's at the hospital now."

Collette laughed. "So she went to blow her brains out and missed. How dumb is that? I'm the only sister left standing." She turned to her father. "It's not my fault Mary went crazy. You let her move out after Mom died. Last year, she met that Hopi guy and started going woo-woo, getting into all that mending-relationship garbage. He's the reason Mary drove over here to give the dress and the bracelet to Tiffany so she could sneak them back into the museum. So Mrs. Pinto would find them and everything would be wonderful again."

Leaphorn heard the derision. Maybe Bernie was right, he thought. Maybe the spirit of Hwéeldi did still bring out the worst in people. "Collette, where is the old dress? And where's the bracelet?"

Mr. Benally's voice had fire. "That's not important. Why did you kill your sister?"

"Poor little Tiffany got sick and sicker and never got well. And Daddy always loved her best."

Mr. Benally held his head in his hands, and his voice was just a whisper. "I have lost one daughter already. I don't want to lose you . . ."

"Shut up. You've already lost me." Collette's rage poured out like molten lava. "Don't pretend you care about me. It's too late, you old fool."

Mr. Benally stared at her, a look Leaphorn had seen before on parents who were brokenhearted. He moved back in his chair, away from Collette's anger, and when he spoke, his voice shook with emotion. "Daughter, you make me ashamed."

She mimicked him. "I make you ashamed? You ruined my life, old man. You never loved me. You—"

Her father raised his voice to drown out her vitriol. "All this goes back to that time of sorrows. My parents taught us not to talk about Hwéeldi. When Tiffany told me what worried her, I knew something bad would come. The old ones were wise when they said we should think of the days ahead, not the sad times."

Collette groaned. "You're an idiot. Tiffany was weak. That's why she died."

"No." Leaphorn injected himself. "She died because of your greed and jealousy."

"So what if I killed her? She deserved it. Where's the proof? I'm not afraid."

Leaphorn heard a siren in the distance. He noticed the boy standing in the doorway. "You have time to say good-bye to your son."

"I'm not going anywhere, you jackass. You think you're brilliant, but you're just a poor Navajo living in the middle of nowhere."

Leaphorn picked up Collette's car keys and his phone from the table. The screen was dark, but a small light blinked until he touched a button to turn it off. "I recorded everything you said, and you've said more than enough."

Collette stood. "Give me my keys, or when the police get here, I'm telling them you tried to steal my car."

He shook his head and ignored her as she ranted. Leaphorn realized he was tired. Exhausted, in fact. Ready to go home, feed the cat, and catch up on his sleep. Ready to be done with this broken family and this sad case.

She turned toward Andrews, addressing him for the first time. "What are you doing here?"

The boy cowered at his mother's stare. "The policeman asked me to show him how to use the recorder. I loved my Little Mother, and I wanted her to get well. I miss her and . . ." Andrews stumbled for words.

"You stinking little piece of slime. I wish you'd—"

Leaphorn raised his voice. "Stop. Don't talk like that to this fine boy."

Mr. Benally put his arm around Andrews and pulled him into a tight embrace. The child buried his face in his grandfather's shirt.

The wail of the siren grew closer. Mr. Benally took Andrews into the house.

Leaphorn was pleased to see Officer Manygoats step out of the police car, and happy that the station had sent backup, an unusual occurrence for the Navajo force, who were always spread thin. Collette acted genuinely surprised when they ignored her story. She slapped and kicked at the officers as they put her in handcuffs. When they did, Leaphorn noticed the silver bracelet on her wrist. He was too far away to tell for sure, but it reminded him of Louisa's. He asked Manygoats to log it in as evidence.

"We will. I confiscated the pills and the dead woman's checkbook. It looks like someone had been forging checks on her account. But that's all we found at the house."

"Did the warrant cover Collette's car?"

"No, sir."

Leaphorn made sure that the car was locked and handed the keys to Manygoats. "When you get a warrant, take a look inside. I think you'll find the evidence you need to tie her to the murder of her sister."

When the police left, Leaphorn went inside to thank the boy for his help.

Andrews stared at his shoes. "What will happen to my mother?"

"I'm not sure, but I know she'll be OK. She's a tough one." Leaphorn never speculated about how the wheels of mainstream justice and the Navajo code of what was fair and appropriate might mesh.

"Just ask me if you forget how to play that recording."

"I will. I would be happy to do you a favor."

Then the boy spoke in Navajo. Not perfect, but understandable. "Could you tell my grandfather that we need a dog? I promise to take care of it every day."

"I will."

Mr. Benally's face looked like a mirror of his own. "After you get some rest, you and your grandson could visit Mary. She will be in the hospital for a few days."

Mr. Benally nodded. "Come back and see us."

Leaphorn followed the route the police cars had taken away from Big Rocks to the capital city of the sprawling Navajo Nation, happy to turn toward home instead of toward the jail. He found Giddi pacing by the kitchen door, her food bowl full and plenty of water in the other dish. The cat followed him into the bedroom. He sat on the bed and took off his boots. He texted Cat OK! to Louisa and then, before he lay down for a nap, sent her another message: I miss you. I want to tell you about Mrs. Pinto's case. Please come home soon.

22

It seemed as though he had just drifted off to sleep when something woke him. The phone in the kitchen, he realized. He scrambled up to answer.

"Sir, it's Manygoats. Thanks again for your help with this."

"Of course. Did that woman calm down?"

"Not a bit. She denies everything. She claims the bracelet is hers." He stopped and then started talking again, this time more serious. "Collette gave us permission to search the car, and we found the old Navajo dress you mentioned. We booked her on possession of stolen property as well as murder."

"Could you take a picture of the bracelet and the dress for me?"

"Of course, sir. How shall I send them?"

"Texting will be fine."

"Do you want the packaging for the dress, too?"

"What do you mean?"

"It looks like she had already sold it to a museum in Europe. I'll send you all that information. She was ready to ship it out."

"What about the bracelet?"

Manygoats paused. "I think she planned to keep it. She told me she'd see to it I was fired if it disappeared in the evidence room."

Before she heard the news through the Navajo grapevine, Leaphorn called Mrs. Pinto. The woman listened without interrupting. To his surprise, she had only two questions.

"When do we get the biil and the bracelet?"

"I don't know, but they are safely in police custody. I'll send you a photo as soon as I get one."

"Do you know why Tiffany died?"

"It had something to do with her medicine and suffocation, something to do with jealousy and serious evil."

"So it was murder. Collette."

He let his silence speak for him. Then he changed the subject.

"I talked to a couple people at Northern Arizona University, and they have some good information on Juanita and her weavings. They can help whoever comes to take your place authenticate the dress and its history."

"Thank you. I'm retiring next week and I . . ." She laughed. "How many times have I told you that?"

"I never asked, but why are you so eager to leave? You seem to really enjoy your job, and you do it well." He pictured her running for Tribal Council, serving on committees, volunteering at the local schools. Or maybe taking a more financially lucrative position.

"My daughter wants to finish college, and she has three little ones at home. School starts for them in a few weeks. I want to get there so we can have some fun this summer." There was noise in the background. "I have to go. Bring me a bill for your time, and tell Louisa hello."

Energized by that conversation, he called the Raffertys. Mrs. Rafferty answered. He asked about Mary, learned that she was doing better and had agreed to work with a therapist. "She might be able to come home to us soon."

"I'm glad. I have some news about your husband's missing items."

"Hold on. Let me get Lloyd. I'm putting us on speakerphone."

He heard muffled voices, and then Mr. Rafferty was on, too. Leaphorn switched to English. "Mary took dem. Her sisser was behin it."

"Tiffany?"

"Collette." He summarized the story.

"My husband and I tried to help Collie when she was a girl, but nothing we did was ever enough. We gave her another chance when we caught her stealing from us. Then she killed our cat, and we had to send her home."

Rafferty said, "We were dealing with your cancer then, remember. We hoped going back to her family might change things."

Leaphorn didn't mention Collette's implication in Tiffany's death. They would find out soon enough.

Rafferty cleared his throat. "I'm glad you and the professor found us."

"One mo kestin for you," Leaphorn said. "Do you member buyin da Peshlakai bracelet?"

Before Mr. Rafferty could answer, his wife responded. "I do. We were living in Gallup. I was a VISTA program worker at the high school. Neither of us had been to Santa Fe, and the weekend we decided to go turned out to be the Indian Market. We walked all over the place and found this young man selling carved animals and some jewelry. Lloyd bought it for me with a necklace and earrings to match. The seller said his friend made them. I remember the name, Peshlakai, because it sounded so musical. I loved it, but it's too heavy for me to wear now." Leaphorn remembered her slim wrists.

After that, Leaphorn made himself some instant coffee and sat at the dining room table, creating a list of what he had to do:

Call Mona Willeto
Call Jessica and thank her for her help
Collect fee from Mrs. Pinto
Fix truck

He paused and then added:

Schedule more sessions with Jake

He called Willeto first, assuming it would be one of the easier of the tasks. She got to the point quickly.

"One of those documentary crews is making a movie about my brother. They want to talk to you about how you figured out he was the one to arrest. I told them I would try to find you."

Leaphorn's skepticism kicked in. "Why me? Why your brother, for that matter?"

The woman chuckled. "This is kinda funny. The only thing my brother has done right is being in prison. He learned to read, got his GED. He started a prayer group. The anniversary of his sentencing is coming up."

"I have to think about it. I'm not one who enjoys the spotlight."

"They'd like to know by the end of the month. For me? The whole idea makes me nervous. I was saying no, but my brother encouraged me. He said I could put in some Navajo words if my English failed me."

Ah, he thought. His trouble with English would offer him the perfect excuse.

"Here's the number you need to call." She rattled it off. Then Mona's tone of voice changed. "My brother says you saved his life, that he would have just drunk himself to death if he hadn't gone to prison. He's doing some good now, especially with young guys who think they're tough. So, thank you. That's what I needed to say."

After that, he called his friend Jessica Taylor and asked her another favor. She phoned back with good news. The dog Bernie had discovered, the dog with the clear eyes he had taken to the Fort Defiance shelter, could be adopted.

When Leaphorn called Mr. Benally, the man

asked for the animal shelter number and then had some news.

"I called the woman my daughter worked for to say I was sorry about that rabbit. She said that she loved the one who died as if she were her own daughter."

He sipped his coffee, trying to decide if he should make bacon and eggs for a late lunch or head over to the Navajo Inn. His phone beeped with a text.

Louisa had written: Coming to WR today.

He responded: After meeting?

Bowed out of meeting. Leaving soon. Coming home.

"Coming home." Not "Coming to Window Rock." She had typed "Coming home"!

He texted back, Wonderful. He looked at the word and typed it in again and then one more time, adding an exclamation point.

Her message reminded him of something he wanted to do. He finished his coffee and picked up his keys.

As was their habit, the Lieutenant, Louisa, Chee, and Bernie had dinner once a month. The elders came to Shiprock this time, lured by Bernie's promise of fresh peach pie.

Chee shared some stories about his work with the rookie. "I took someone's advice and called Agent Johnson. She spent an afternoon with him."

"And?" Leaphorn asked.

Bernie shook her head. "I haven't noticed much difference."

Louisa, who had told Chee she wasn't much of

a meat eater, had nearly finished her steak. He noticed a striking brooch with a greenish stone on her shirt. "That's a nice pin. Is it new?"

Louisa put her hand on the jewelry, which was over her heart. "Yes. I admired it at the Hubbell Trading Post. Joe bought it for me as a gift when I got back from NAU. He shouldn't have, when he needed the money to fix his truck. But I'm glad he did. I love it."

As was usual, after-dinner talk turned to recent cases. Chee summarized the high points of the missing bolo case. "You know, if Ryana had told her grandfather about the movies in the first place, she never would have been blackmailed."

"But would she have broken the old man's heart?" Bernie had been thinking about that.

"No." Leaphorn smiled at her and said something in Navajo.

She translated for Louisa: "'We old guys are tougher than you'd think.'"

Bernie stood to clear the table. "I hope you're all in the mood for pie for dessert. I found the summer's last peaches yesterday at the market."

Louisa picked up her plate and Leaphorn's and headed inside. "Sit down. I'll clear the table and bring the pie. I know you guys wanna talk shop."

Bernie said, "Lieutenant, what happened with your case? Did the autopsy show what happened to that woman who died? She had some rare disease, right?"

"That's what killed her, but indirectly. Her sister Collette stocked Tiffany's pill box and picked up her medicine. I suspected she'd poisoned Tiffany, but the first toxicology screen came back negative. When we asked for a special tox screening, it showed extremely low levels of a drug, Hinditunayzine chloride, that had been prescribed to keep her lungs functioning. She did die of the disease, but only because her sister had been withholding the correct dose of the medicine intended to keep her alive. She should have taken one little blue tablet three times a day. Instead, the report showed levels consistent with one pill every three days. That's why there was so much medicine in the prescription bottles in Collette's car. The autopsy also found evidence that she was suffocated toward the end. Mrs. Pinto said Tiffany was alive when Collette asked her to go outside to wait for the ambulance. She would have died anyway with that low dose of medicine, but not quick enough for Collette."

Louisa came back with the pie. The crust, the color of golden sandstone, made Bernie remember the night Bigman had politely declined to take the burned version home to his expectant wife. Their baby boy was thriving.

Bernie served everyone. "I thought of one more question. Lieutenant, what happened to the dog I found on the trail, the one who alerted us to the dead man?"

"Da dog has a new home. Wid a boy who needed him."

Louisa smiled. "You said that well. I'm glad you went back to working with Jake. I think those sessions have helped you."

The therapist had urged him to practice his English as much as he could, especially with friends who would offer encouragement. Leaphorn smiled to himself. Peach pie therapy made a sweet ending to a fine evening.

# Acknowledgments

*The Tale Teller* drew its inspiration in part from a real-life tragedy. The Long Walk took the Navajo under armed guard from their sacred homeland to Fort Sumner, New Mexico, to a concentration camp known as Bosque Redondo. Hwéeldi, as the Navajos call it, left its impact on every Navajo family, including those who escaped the soldiers seeking to capture them.

The year 2018 marked the 150th anniversary of the signing of the treaty that established what is now the Navajo Nation and enabled the ragged, starving Navajo families to return to their land between the four sacred mountains. The Southwest's version of the Trail of Tears lives in infamy, and the story deserves to be recognized as a true and shameful part of United States history. I extend special thanks to Thelma Domenici, Mary Ann Cortese, and the hardworking Friends of Bosque Redondo—the site of the imprisonment—

for inviting me to revisit the monument which respectfully commemorates this sad event. I was humbled and honored to speak to your group.

Jennifer Nez Denetdale's remarkable book, *Reclaiming Navajo History* (University of Arizona Press, 2007), offered another source of inspiration as I considered the Long Walk. Thanks to Joyce Begay Foss for her efforts to bring Ms. Denetdale, the author and historian, to the Museum of Indian Arts and Culture. I am also grateful to her and to museum director Della Warrior for arranging the public display of an amazing rug that dates to the time immediately after the treaty signing and was influenced by the weaver's memory of the years at Bosque Redondo.

The cover of Denetdale's book has an iconic photo of Navajo leaders Manuelito and Juanita, his wife. Manuelito, one of the signers of the 1868 treaty, wore a black top hat along with traditional Navajo clothing. The photo shows Juanita in a traditional woven Navajo dress, a biil. That very dress, which dates to the time of the Long Walk, was displayed at the Navajo Nation Museum on loan from its home in the collection of the Autry Museum of the American West. The Navajo museum also displayed an original copy of the treaty that allowed the Navajo to return to their homeland. Heartfelt thanks to Clarenda Begay, curator at the Navajo Nation Museum, for helping me understand the museum's process for accessioning gifts and for her work to bring Juanita's dress and the treaty to the Navajo Nation.

Although I could find no records to support my

idea that another dress woven by Juanita still exists, part of the joy of writing novels is the freedom an author has to elaborate on the known universe. And as we know, the world is rich in the unexpected.

Luckily for me, I did not have to invent the Hubbell Trading Post in Ganado, Arizona, or the Navajo Nation's library and law enforcement headquarters in Window Rock, or the towns of Oak Springs, Chinle, Winslow, Fort Defiance, Crystal, Shiprock, Flagstaff, and most other places in the book. However, the community of Big Rocks is a product of my imagination. My sincere appreciation to Edison Eskeets, the trader at the Hubbell Trading Post National Historic Site, for his wonderful explanation of Navajo weaving.

Retired Navajo Police Captain Steve Nelson drove out of his way to share some law enforcement stories with me. Lt. Michelle Williams of the Santa Fe Police Department gave me insight into the process whereby an officer moves from patrol to detective. Lt. Chad Pierce, New Mexico State Police, helped me understand the fate of vehicles involved in fatal accidents. Speech therapist Jeanne Jebb-Tracey passed along information about the challenges people face as they recover from a brain injury and learn to speak again. *I Choose Life: Contemporary Medical and Religious Practices in the Navajo World* by Maureen Trudelle Schwarz (University of Oklahoma Press, 2008) guided me in dealing with other medical issues. Dorothy Fitch, this book's official godmother, opened her guest house to me as a writing studio. I sat surrounded by her marvelous collection of books and, often, with a plate of her special cookies for inspiration. I am forever grateful.

Authors sometimes are asked to offer naming rights to a character as a way to help a non-profit group raise money. In Santa Fe, ARTsmart provides children in northern New Mexico with educational opportunities in the arts that promote confidence, self-discovery, and creative problem-solving skills. At their annual fund-raising event, I met Jim and Wanda Bean, the high bidders for a dinner with me and a name in this book. Jim died unexpectedly after the event. I am grateful that Wanda followed through, inviting me to share a meal with family and friends and giving me wonderful insight into who Jim Bean was. The world needs more people with his love for the arts and tremendous generosity. He was not a postal inspector in real life, but I'm sure he would have handled the job with passion and been a great friend to Joe Leaphorn.

Without Rebecca Carrier's devoted and fierce attention to Bernie, this book would not be half as good. I mean it. Thank you. David and Gail Greenberg, I appreciate your insights on the inner workings of law enforcement and the intricacies of grammar, and your ongoing tolerance for my mistakes. Your help means more than I can say. Jim Wagner of Daddy Wags Editing saved me from some embarrassing errors, including a river that flowed the wrong way. Lucy Moore's tremendous wisdom and generosity encouraged and buoyed me and Bernie as we confronted the bad guy.

A shout-out to my agent, Elizabeth Trupin-Pulli, and my editor, Carolyn Marino, for not flinching when I told them it was time to bring Lt. Joe Leaphorn back as a crime solver, and for their wise assistance in making him true to the character Tony Hillerman created thirty-some years ago. Thanks to copy editor Mary Beth Constant for her skilled work and to Rachel Elinsky, Hannah Robinson, and Tom Hoppe at HarperCollins for their assistance in bringing *The Tale Teller* into print.

And a warm thank you to John Harris Trestrail, III, for his sage advice on microdosing as an interesting tool for murderous villainy. His book, *Criminal Poisoning*, and his generosity with his time and ideas were tremendously helpful. I am delighted that the New Mexico chapter of Sisters in Crime, Croak and Dagger, invited Trestrail and me to speak at the same writing conference. Trestrail also worked with the man to whom I owe the deepest debt of gratitude, my father, Tony Hillerman.

Bookstores and libraries have millions of titles to choose from and I appreciate all of you for stocking my books. Special thanks also go to the librarians and bookstore owners who have welcomed me into their community rooms to talk about what it's like to be a writer. From Datil's Baldwin Cabin to Murder by the Book in Houston, with a special shout-out to Collected Works in Santa Fe, Maria's in Durango, and, of course, Poisoned Pen in Scottsdale. Thank you and your colleagues for all you do for us authors.

Finally, there would be no need for books if

there weren't readers out there to enjoy them. A standing ovation to all the readers and book clubs who helped me continue the legacies of Bernadette Manuelito, Jim Chee, and Joe Leaphorn. Stories are made to be shared, and I am honored and humbled to share them with you.